The Nightmare Merchant

CODE OF MISCONDUCT II

C.A. Griffith

Doris,
Thank you for your wonderful support

[signature]

BRIGHTON PUBLISHING LLC
435 N. HARRIS DRIVE
MESA, AZ 85203

THE NIGHTMARE MERCHANT

CODE OF MISCONDUCT II

C.A. GRIFFITH

BRIGHTON PUBLISHING LLC
435 N. HARRIS DRIVE
MESA, AZ 85203
WWW.BRIGHTONPUBLISHING.COM

COPYRIGHT © 2015
PRINTED IN THE UNITED STATES OF AMERICA

ISBN 13: 978-1-62183-264-5
ISBN 10: 1-62183-264-3

First Edition

COVER DESIGN: TOM RODRIGUEZ

ACKNOWLEDGEMENTS

Thank you to my wonderful wife, Beverly, for her continued support of my writing.

Thank You to my independent editors...and friends:

Joanie George

Stephanie Bistline

Denise Heath

And Thank You to Dr. Karen Ruskin, not only for her hard work on the afterword, but for her enthusiastic support of the effort to keep our children drug free and our society free from the scourge of addiction.

"Without boundaries there are no goals, no fouls, no penalties, and no rewards. If unopposed, the continuous efforts to remove one boundary after another in our society can only lead to its ultimate destruction."

CHAPTER ONE

Joshua Bartlett stared at the four-inch plastic syringe loaded with heroin lying on the bathroom sink. His hand trembled with anticipation as he cinched the belt around his scrawny bicep. At eighteen years of age he could already insert a needle through the skin into his vein so skillfully he no longer felt the pinprick. He caught a glimpse of the pale thin face, scraggly mustache, and scabbed-over sores on his neck in the mirror above the sink and quickly looked away.

Joshua had been using drugs since he was twelve years old. At first, it was alcohol and marijuana with friends who came to his house. By the time he was fifteen, he was snorting cocaine and selling pot to middle school kids to support his addiction. The coke began irritating his nose and making his throat raw, so he started injecting. At seventeen he was arrested and charged as an adult for selling cocaine. After serving a year in the county jail, he was released on parole and, with the help of a cellmate who turned him on to heroin to "mellow him out," he graduated to full-blown heroin addiction.

Joshua had scored this gram of smack only ten minutes earlier from the new dealer behind the coffee shop on Candler Road. He ran the half mile back to his fleabag motel room, set the deadbolt, put the safety chain in place, and locked himself in the filthy bathroom. He quickly cooked up the heroin in the same tablespoon he'd used the day before and loaded the syringe. His mouth watered, and he almost doubled over from the stomach cramps as waves of craving washed over him. He grabbed the syringe and inserted the needle into the vein at the bend of his left arm. As he pulled back on the plunger to boot up, a trickle of blood entered the syringe and mixed with the heroin. He pushed the plunger and shot the entire contents of the syringe into his vein.

"No doubt about it," he whispered to himself. "I'm a booting, shooting addict."

Joshua felt the electrical jolt as the liquid rushed through his blood. He waited for the heroin to fill his brain with the familiar warmth and sweep his thoughts away, but something was wrong... horribly wrong. The warm dizziness he was expecting did not come. Instead, a blinding flash of light exploded behind his eyes, twisting his brain into throbbing spasms of pain. The agonizing ache raced from his head to his chest, scorching his nervous system with needles of fire. The pain slammed into his chest with enough force to pin his bony back to the wall. Then Joshua felt a sledgehammer blow to his lower back. Uncontrollable panic seized his mind, and he thought, *I'm going to die!*

It felt as if he had been stabbed with a heavy molten knife that was now being twisted within the wound. He held onto the sink as his vision blurred. He could feel the drug ripping its way through his entire body, burning like acid in his bones. His blood seemed to have crystallized into thousands of razor blades tearing through the skin. He tried to open his eyes but quickly squeezed them shut as another wave of pain shook his skinny frame. His body flushed with a suffocating heat that stopped his breathing. His lungs were on fire and collapsing within his body. He fell to his knees, bit his tongue, and tasted blood as he crumpled to the floor against the door. His pupils fixed and dilated in the gaze of death. A terrible darkness enveloped him. His final earthly sensation evaporated as black claws reached up from the stained tile floor to pull him down to oblivion.

Within ten minutes of Joshua Bartlett's death, his assassin slowly opened the motel room door. Picking the lock was child's play, and using a chain jiggler from outside the door left no damage or clue of forced entry. He quickly crossed to the bathroom, inserted an ice pick in the center hole of the cheap doorknob, and released the locking mechanism. Joshua's fallen body prevented the assassin from opening the door fully, so he adjusted the amyl nitrate-coated glove on his left hand, reached through the gap, and felt the boy's throat for a pulse. Feeling nothing, the assassin smiled and allowed the weight of Joshua's body to push the door closed and locked again. He walked over to the air-conditioning unit under the window, turned the dial to sixty degrees, and quietly left the room.

The Butcher had been killing professionally for twelve years. Despite a much less than optimal upbringing, he had received a decent education thanks to the state of Alabama's lottery-funded education system. In addition to a B.S. in biology, he was self-educated in arts and science: the art of weapons, the martial arts, and the science of poisons. He was proud of his abilities and the career he had chosen. Being a man of many sought-after talents, he regarded himself as the consummate professional. But as intelligent as he was, he still had to live, travel, and interact in the very real world of human beings. He also required information to do his job well, and at times depended on others to acquire it for him. Reclusive individuals have a way of drawing the attention of nosy people. It was natural for people to be nosy, no matter how much he despised them for it, so he hid where he wouldn't draw their undue attention: in plain sight, among the throngs of people who worked meaningless jobs to keep their wives happy with three-bedroom, two-car-garage houses and children supplied with band instruments, cheerleading outfits, and baseball uniforms. One day he would leave it all behind. When there was enough money in his offshore accounts to vanish, he would leave them all to their petty lives. *Good riddance.*

His client list included government officials, corporate CEOs, criminal organizations, politicians, and private citizens. In addition to orchestrating a high-level assassination in a foreign country, his resume boasted the elimination of two political rivals, the silencing of three federal witnesses, the execution of a state court judge, and the murders of four cheating spouses. So talented was he in avoiding detection that all but two of his contracted hits had been ruled suicides. He never met a client face-to-face and never would.

The Butcher had grown up in the slums just outside of Mobile, where he was raped by his alcoholic stepfather at age nine, killed his first house cat at age eleven, and didn't stop wetting the bed until age fourteen. From his psych courses at Winston Community College, he learned these childhood events were known as the *Terrible Triad*, used to predict the development of a serial killer. One thing he did not know, nor would he ever begin to realize, was that a part of his humanity was missing. He would never cease committing inhuman acts.

He had discovered at an early age that he enjoyed killing. By the time he reached his teens he had developed into a certified cold-blooded killer. As an adult, he decided the next logical step was to get paid for his passion. Since that revelation, he had always found good reasons to kill—hundreds of them in fact—always supplied by those who hired him. He accepted his lot in life: a single-minded man without sentiment who, for the right price, would commit any act or perform any abomination.

By the definition of some, he was certifiably insane, but he proclaimed himself a professional rather than a psychotic killer because he killed for money, not at random or for personal reasons. He often smirked at the thought of being caught. If that improbability ever occurred, he would play the game of a society grown soft, guilt-driven, and liberal-minded: he would simply plead insanity and let the psychologists dig into his brain. His attorney would then play the heartstrings of the jurors like a violin when a childhood filled with neglect and molestation was revealed. They would embrace him as they had done countless others and sentence him to an all-expense-paid hospital stay until he could slip away, leaving a dead psychologist or security guard in his wake.

Now that this job was done, he would have to change his name again, but it wouldn't be the first time in his career. In his line of work, frequent changes of identity were standard operating procedure. If the cops got lucky and somehow tied him to the dead junkie, the name he used would lead them nowhere. He knew cops; they weren't that intelligent. Otherwise they wouldn't be cops. With certain connections, he would know in advance if they tripped over some miniscule piece of evidence or information pointing to him. His escape plan was constantly updated for any such inconvenience, and if necessary he would instantly vanish to his tropical retreat on Lakka Beach in Freetown, Sierra Leone, which has no extradition treaty with the United States.

The irony of the name, Freetown, was one of the only things that made him smile. The only other time he occasionally smiled was upon thinking of the name he had assigned himself. Of course it was known only to him. He had fancied himself by the name ever since he could remember. Every killer has a unique name, either assigned to him by the press or adopted on his own. He thought how striking it would be in huge font across the top of a national newspaper, but that would mean either he had been caught or the police were hot on his trail. He occasionally daydreamed of such a headline, but it was in his best interest never to allow it to become a reality.

Today he silently took pleasure in congratulating himself for yet another job well done. The Butcher had prevailed to kill another day.

This contract had been one of the easiest yet. Killing a junkie and making it look like an overdose was as easy as picking that lock. It was almost too easy to get the kid to buy the heroin from him. All he had to do was lower the price. And with the numerous old track mark scars on the victim's arms and feet, the arrest record, and the body having been found in the room of a hotel in a known drug area, there would be no reason for an already overworked medical examiner to be suspicious enough to order an autopsy. But even so, the extremely high levels of heroin in the body should mask the remaining trace amount of the poison called abrin.

Only an expert in forensics could confirm a person's exposure to abrin, but if poison was suspected as the cause of death, chances were they wouldn't go to the trouble for what was obviously another overdose. He grinned, thinking of how the junkie kid had done him the favor of converting the heroin and powdered abrin into a liquid before injecting it into his bloodstream. *It's always nice when the mark does the job for you,* he thought.

The Butcher sat behind the wheel of a five-year-old gray Honda in a Kmart parking lot. He had stolen the vehicle from Louisiana the day before his drive to Atlanta. He always chose nondescript cars to blend in with four or five other cars of similar make and color in sight at any given time. He had liberated a current Georgia tag from another Honda of the same make, model, and color earlier in the day. If the police fed his tag number into the computer for any reason, it would return as "active" and "valid," registered to a

2005 Honda Civic just as they would expect. He had watched the owner of the Georgia tag exit his Honda after parking in the long-term parking section at Hartsfield-Jackson airport. It would be at least a week before he discovered it was stolen and reported it, if he even noticed the tag was missing.

He bent his head and carefully removed his brown-tinted contact lenses, revealing deadly gray irises as cold as storm-tossed seas. He would remove his fake beard and mustache when he returned to his hotel room and get his hair cut shorter the following day. The Butcher threw the tinted contacts out the car window, pulled a disposable cell phone from his briefcase, and dialed a ten-digit number. The call was answered on the second ring by an automated tone. He punched in 3663—the code for DONE—knowing it would be recorded on the other end. The second half of his payment would now be deposited into his Grand Caymans account; the electronic transfer of funds would be confirmed by email. With deposit and investment arrangements in several foreign countries, receipt of payment had never been a problem, especially with this particular client. Everything was smooth and simple. They mutually understood there was no need to complicate the process unnecessarily.

Several minutes later, as he was pulling out of the parking lot onto Roswell Road, his phone vibrated. He glanced at the sender's name on the screen and immediately pulled over into a shopping center lot. He decoded and read the email, exited the Honda, and retrieved a black duffel bag from the trunk. He got back in the driver's seat and drove around to the back of the shopping center, where he unzipped the duffel bag on the passenger seat and pulled out two handguns. One was a small .380 automatic, the other a larger 10mm pistol. He removed the magazines from both weapons, thumbed the shells out, and restacked them. He carefully screwed a black silencer onto the barrel of the larger gun, laid both weapons back in the bag, and drove to his next assignment.

Clara was seven years old. She wore a bright blue, one-piece bathing suit, and her short blonde hair was wet and matted to her head. She trotted cautiously on the bright orange tile in the exterior hallway of the condominium complex, clutching wet dollar bills in her right hand. Dad had given her the money to buy a soft drink from the vending machine. She had taken the same route yesterday, but bumped her knee when her wet feet slipped out from under her. She was eager to get back to the pool, but experience had taught her to be more careful today. She rounded the corner of the hallway and stopped short. Even at a slower pace, she still slid across the tile and had to throw out her hands against the wall to keep from hitting the rough stucco or the large man standing in her path.

Even though he stood at the edge of the concrete, the man was large enough to block the entire narrow walkway. His head was bent forward, and a long string of black juice shot from his mouth, disappearing in the grass surrounding a tropical shrub. Clara's eyes were drawn to a tattoo at the base of his neck that looked like three connecting T's. Clara scowled and squinted. "That's nasty," she said before realizing the words had escaped her mouth.

The large man turned to face her. He wore a white wife-beater undershirt, black parachute-type pants, and white tennis shoes. Clara couldn't see his eyes through the dark, wraparound sunglasses. She peered up at the menacing figure as he turned toward her. Her eyes grew wide. The man looked like a life-sized version of one of the plastic wrestling figures her little brother played with. His shoulders were broad and his muscles were massive, stretching his tank top to its limit.

She was frozen in place, waiting for a strong retort or demeaning insult from the man. But he just looked at her. No grin, no frown, no comment. He turned away in silence and walked off the curb and into the parking lot. Clara watched him for a beat, dismissed the encounter from her mind, and continued about her task.

The man in the white undershirt stepped into the shaded guest parking area on the north side of the Sundowner Condominiums. It was 10:30 a.m., and the sun had yet to climb high enough in the sky to begin baking the asphalt on this side of the building. He rounded the front corner of the building where the office and clubhouse were located and walked past the front office entrance, pausing briefly to glance at the mid-morning traffic on A1A. He spit on another low shrub and then continued to the south corner of the structure. He looked to the rear of the parking area, where an open drive-through permitted vehicles to pass under the building and into the visitors' beachfront parking lot.

Movement on the fifth floor of the building caught the man's eye. The door to condo 510 was standing open. A shirtless man in black swim trunks stepped out onto the exterior walkway holding a white plastic bag. He appeared to flip the door-lock bar and rest the door against it before making his way down the hall and out of sight.

This was the opportunity the large man in the parking lot had been waiting for. He allowed himself a final spit on the shrub and jogged across the parking lot to the stairwell. He pulled open the heavy steel door at the foot of the stairwell and took the steps two at a time until he arrived at the fifth-floor landing. He peered through the narrow vertical glass in the stairwell door where he could see condo 510. Leaving the door propped open was a sure sign the occupant would be returning soon.

The quick ascent had left him slightly out of breath—he was in very good physical condition, but climbing five flights of stairs in less than fifteen seconds would make almost anyone need to stop and catch their breath. The man took three deep breaths to regulate his breathing, spit a stream of tobacco juice in the stairwell corner, and waited.

Grey Colson read the last page of the file in his hand and flipped the cover closed with a nod of approval. "Good job," he said aloud. He dropped the file on the side table next to his lounge chair.

The file was quite thin. The papers were two-hole punched at the top and held in place by a two-pronged metal clamp between two sturdy black covers. A white label stuck to the front of the file read, "Ocean Front Sea Foods," and a clear sleeve containing a DVD was stuck to the inside front cover, labeled with identical wording. Colson had insisted on the use of this type of file set-up for years during his tenure as commander of the Clay County Sheriff's Office Internal Affairs Unit. No matter how thick or thin the file, the one-size-fits-all expandable folders were far more practical than using various sizes of three-ring binders that were a pain to file in a cabinet.

Colson had been retired for over a year and a half now. He couldn't believe how time had flown. He slipped on his sunglasses and admired the Atlantic Ocean from his fifth-floor balcony while thinking of the circumstances that brought him to this point in his life, but mostly about a recent addition to his life he had failed to anticipate; his handsome new grandson, Jack. He smiled at the thought of the simple, masculine name. It had been his father's nickname, but he never knew why, since his father's given name was Charles Eugene.

Young Jack made Colson's decision to accept his new interim job a no-brainer. Retirement felt great after his first six-week adventure in Daytona Beach. He had spent the rest of the summer enjoying the ocean breezes and admiring the beach, boats, and babes through his old surveillance binoculars. There were a few bikini-clad females he wished his binoculars hadn't captured. Colson almost considered running for county commissioner to propose a city ordinance prohibiting certain women from wearing two-piece bathing suits and all men from wearing Speedos.

Colson had no desire to become involved in politics, but the need to stay active and maybe even a little relevant grew stronger as the fall season approached. The trip to Atlanta following Jack's birth was Colson's first time back since moving to the Daytona Beach condo. The drive from Hartsfield airport to Clay County felt strange. Almost surreal. The same thought repeated itself in his head as he drove through old, familiar territory. What had changed? Colson had driven the rental car past the high school where Nichole graduated years ago and stopped at the traffic light on Highway 61, just a quarter mile from the home he had lived in for almost twenty years. For some unknown reason, that's when the answer came. What had changed? He had. People moved on. Sometimes after a tragedy, sometimes after finding new love, but most times it was simply because they had to. It was built into humans—just as time heals old wounds, time changes us. In Colson's case, time was coupled with distance, throwing an additional weight on the scale. That explained why he felt so off-balance in this familiar yet alien place.

The visit with Nichole, Bobby, and baby Jack in late spring had restored Colson's balance. He had chalked up the previous struggle with his feelings as a moment of temporary insanity and self-pity, after which he had properly scolded himself and enjoyed the visit. His only regret when he left was the realization he would be seeing Jack only once or twice per year. He had hugged Jack's tiny body gently, kissed the top of his head, and promised he would do better than twice a year.

Colson rested his head against the cushion of his lounge chair and took a sip of his drink. A lot had happened. He had taken an hour's detour on his way back to the airport to see a few buddies at the Clay County Sheriff's Office. He had pulled the rental car into the public parking deck and walked one block to the Public Safety Complex: three buildings connected by a two-story atrium years ago to keep jurors and judges dry and warm. As Colson expected, time had reeled backward when he rounded the corner and the complex came into view. Nothing had changed except the people on the sidewalks, making their way to court or their county government jobs. The men in suits would be either attorneys or their clients. Those in comfortable clothes were either witnesses or jurors. The jurors were easy to identify, with their clip-on tags and bored-out-of-their-minds facial expressions. A young woman carrying a white plastic box piled high with interdepartmental mail had scurried around him on the sidewalk and mumbled something under her breath, causing Colson to suspect that he wasn't walking fast enough for her. He had given her backside a grin—it was nice being retired and no longer captive to the clock.

He felt as though he could read people well, and thirty years in police work had taught him a simple fact of life: every single one of the hundred or so people walking these hectic sidewalks believed they were special—that they were the reason the judicial system worked, or the tax assessors' office collected revenue, or the county budget didn't collapse. There was a time when even Colson thought he was special. Young and new to law enforcement, he was convinced the agency couldn't survive without his special talents and loyalty. But it didn't take many years for him to realize a person is only really special to God and his family. When you resign from your job in protest, you retire, or you take the proverbial dirt nap, there is always someone right behind you to take your place. No matter how many mountains you move, lives you save, or bad guys you lock up, once you're gone, it's as if you never existed.

That day Colson had stopped, slid his sunglasses off, and wiped sweat from his brow. He glanced at the newly refurbished Theater in the Square marquee alternately flashing the time and temperature—2:35 p.m., 89 degrees. He had checked his watch to verify the time. The flight from Hartsfield didn't depart until 6 p.m., but he would need to arrive no later than 4 p.m. to make it through security. He slid his glasses back on and turned toward the public safety building entrance, looking forward to the air-conditioned atrium. The temperature in Daytona Beach probably exceeded 89 degrees that day, but the constant ocean breeze would have offset the stifling heat and humidity. There was no relief from the heat and humidity on a Clay County summer day unless you were inside. With no breeze, the only sounds Colson heard were the dress shoes and high heels scratching the concrete and the low, unintelligible mumblings of attorneys advising worried clients.

A man's voice came from behind him. "Well, look who's back."

Colson turned to see the last person he'd hoped to run into. He tried to be polite. "Hello, Sutton. Are you coming back from a sensitivity training class or from your lunch with the sheriff?"

Sutton forced a smile. "That would be Major Sutton to you. Thanks to you cutting and running to your little beach house, the sheriff promoted me to your position."

"I'm sure the troops love that," Colson said sarcastically.

Sutton crossed his arms. "Damn straight they do. They deserve firm supervision. Not the same old smart-mouth, speak-softly-and-carry-an-expandable-metal-baton mentality."

"It's called an ASP," Colson said with a smirk. "Things really must have changed since I left. I mean, majors used to have to put in fifty hours a week at minimum, not just show up when there's an opportunity to cut a lower-ranking deputy down to size and gloat about it later."

"I'm a busy man, Colson. In fact, too busy to talk to a civilian like you."

"Major Colson, hang on a minute," came a second familiar voice as Sutton turned his back on Colson and marched toward the atrium.

Colson spun on his heel and saw someone waving at him from the sidewalk across the street. He hadn't seen Larry Morgan since he retired eighteen months ago. Morgan looked the same, except maybe a few pounds heavier.

When Colson left Georgia, Morgan was just one of many assistant district attorneys. Since the last election, he was now the Clay County D.A. Colson had always liked Morgan and knew he was a sincere man, but also knew that he was a full-blown politician and equally full of crap. Colson figured that went for anyone who ended every conversation with, "If there's anything I can ever do for you, just let me know." When Colson heard Morgan had been elected to his now-lofty position, he wasn't surprised. The man was a born politician.

Morgan jogged across the narrow street and weaved through the knot of people, stopping in front of Colson a little out of breath. He extended his hand. "I haven't seen you in forever, Grey. I thought you moved south after retirement."

Colson removed his sunglasses and grinned as he shook Morgan's hand. "I did. I'm just stopping in to see if anyone I know still works here. You know, just to say hello and catch up." Colson's smile was replaced with a disgusted squint as he looked over Morgan's shoulder at Sutton disappearing through the glass doors.

Morgan followed Colson's gaze. "Something I should know?

"If you only knew," Colson said.

"Seems like a nice enough guy to me."

"The only reason he's still here is because he owns half of Clay County and is a big campaign contributor. He doesn't deserve the rank. This is just a hobby for him."

"I don't think he tries to hide that," Morgan said. "Seems he just wants to serve the community and give back a little."

"Huh!" Colson blurted with a sarcastic cough. "Right."

Morgan eyed Colson. "So I can assume you don't approve of him because of some history between you two."

"You could say that. A lot of history and no, I don't like him. I don't like anybody who can go from zero to asshole in two-point-two seconds. But enough about ancient history. Congratulations on the election, Mister District Attorney."

Morgan flipped his hand in a dismissive wave. "I'll always be Larry to you, Grey. So what are you doing these days?"

Colson shrugged. "I'm keeping myself just busy enough not to go crazy. A little investigative work—nothing special."

"Those divorce cases can get a little hairy if you don't watch it," Morgan said. "My ex-wife had a guy tail me for two weeks, and I almost—"

Colson raised his hand to interrupt. "It's not like that. I mainly accept jobs for small business owners whose employees are ripping them off."

Morgan nodded understanding and replaced his smile with a more serious, down-to-business look. "I won't keep you long, but I was talking about you just last week with a friend and almost called the sheriff to see if anyone still had your cell number."

"Really?" Colson said with a grin. "Was it about an old case, or did I smack a perp so hard it took him eighteen months to shake off the headache and sue the county?"

"No, no, nothing like that," Morgan said. "Did you know I'm on the board of directors at DBHDD?" Colson squinted, not recognizing the acronym, and Morgan continued. "The Georgia Department of Behavioral Health and Developmental Disabilities."

Colson shook his head. "I can't say I've heard of it."

"You've heard of the Drugs Don't Work program though, right?"

"Sure," Colson replied. "Wasn't there a retired Smyrna officer doing your programs?"

"Yes, but he retired again, and you were the first person who came to mind as a replacement."

13

"It's very flattering," Colson said, "but that's impossible. I've moved and am retired myself. Besides, I haven't been involved in public speaking or the narcotics division in years."

Morgan crossed his arms and leaned toward Colson. "Don't try to pull the wool over my eyes. Your drug presentations to the newly seated grand jurors were excellent, Grey."

"Again, I appreciate the offer, but I was reassigned from narcotics in 1992. A lot has changed in the drug culture since then."

"Not as much as you may think," Morgan explained. "People still become addicted; the mentality is still the same. People are still the same, but the problem isn't going away. People still need to be educated. You wouldn't even have to move. You would set your own schedule and practically be your own boss."

Colson tilted his head back and looked at the sky, then down at the ground. He had seen more than his share of addiction, crime, death, broken lives, and devastated families over the years. Darwin had it all wrong. People weren't evolving for the better; if anything, people and society were devolving into something worse. Something evil. Drugs and substance abuse had always been the main catalyst, the trigger that fired the gun. Colson had worried about his daughter for years, seeing firsthand how the world was being altered by drugs, crime, and the resulting mental health issues. But Nichole was grown now and married. He had successfully shielded her and taught her the inherent dangers of the world around her. She had turned out even better than Colson could have prayed for.

But now there was little Jack. What kind of world would he face when Colson was long gone? Colson wouldn't always be around to shield and warn him. And what about his promise to Jack? This could be a way for him to keep his word. Colson leveled his gaze at Morgan.

"I understand how important the program is, and I've always supported it, but clearly there are others more qualified than me. I could name a dozen retired DEA agents still living in the Atlanta area."

"Look," Morgan said, "I know you, Grey. I've heard you speak and have seen how you relate to people. That's why you were the first person I thought of. If nothing else, consider it on an interim basis. A favor for an old friend."

Colson cocked his head and grinned at Morgan's polished political speak. He crossed his arms waiting for part two of the sales pitch.

"And besides," Morgan said with a broad smile, "I'm sure you could use the extra money."

"Truth is, I don't need the money," Colson said.

Morgan's eyebrows rose. "Oh?"

Colson paused a beat, allowing Morgan to dangle in curiosity, and then smiled. "But the people I owe want it real bad."

Morgan slapped Colson on the shoulder as they walked through the double glass doors and into the cool, conditioned-air of the Public Safety Building.

Colson's reverie was interrupted by "Twinkle, Twinkle, Little Star" being played by a light blue ice cream truck rolling down the beach. It looked like an old bread truck with a drive-through window cut in the side. It halted its five-mile-per-hour progress when two children in bathing suits ran up to the side window.

It was turning out to be a gorgeous day. He glanced over his shoulder at the digital clock on the DVD player inside—10:45 a.m. His meeting with the owner of Ocean Front Sea Foods was set for 1:00, so setting up camp on the beach was out for the day. Colson's condo was his two-bedroom, two-and-a-half-bath refuge, a space not even half the size of the Georgia home where he and his beloved Ann had lived for almost twenty years until her death two years ago this Christmas. Colson looked down at the wedding band on his finger and shook his head. "Almost two years," he whispered. He looked to his right at the empty balcony chair. It was nothing but a crude frame formed from PVC, with a dark blue moisture-resistant cushion and backrest tied to the structure at the corners. Like everything else in the condo, it was clean and unremarkable. Sand-colored tile, beige wall paint, and clean white cabinets and counter tops. Two large sliding glass doors opened onto the long, narrow balcony; one allowed access from the kitchen and the other, from the master bedroom. Thick vertical blinds hung inside the doors to hold off the searing light and heat from the Atlantic sunrise, but he typically left the bedroom blinds open a foot or two, allowing the sun to be his alarm clock if the one on his nightstand failed him.

Colson sighed, let his feet drop from their rest on the white aluminum railing, stood up, and walked inside. He grabbed the garbage bag from the kitchen and promised himself a full day on the beach tomorrow as he walked to the door. He pulled the heavy steel door open and felt a wash of sea air rush past him and through the opening. He had neglected to slide the balcony door closed, causing a strong vacuum effect of air granted access from the sea side of the building to the street side. He flipped the bar lock, allowing the door to rest against it, and made his way to the trash chute a hundred feet down the exterior hallway.

In the fifth-floor stairwell, the man in the white tank top moved to the right side of the narrow door window to look as far down the exterior hallway as possible, but it wasn't much help. He would prefer to get inside the condo and catch Colson by surprise, but he had no way of knowing if he would be seen stepping out of the stairwell. The door would open inward, from his left, which meant he would have to pull the door fully open to get a view of the long hallway. He opened it silently and took a quick peek around the frame. The hallway was vacant, and condo 510 was no more than a dozen feet away. The door still rested against the lock bar, meaning Colson hadn't returned during his quick sprint up the stairs. The man stepped into the hallway, froze, stepped back, and eased the door almost closed.

Colson appeared from around the corner by the elevator the instant he stepped out the door. Had he been seen? He would know soon enough. He pulled off his sunglasses, wiped his forehead with the back of his hand and slid them back on, and waited. Hearing his own breathing in the hollow stairwell, he could only imagine the temperature in the humid concrete structure at 4 p.m. And what was taking Colson so long to walk a hundred feet? He gripped the steel door handle tight and prepared to move.

He hadn't been seen. Colson stepped to the condo door and pushed it open. The man in the stairwell jerked the stairwell door open and covered the twelve feet in three long strides. Colson had his back to him as he stepped over the threshold of the condo. He moved in behind Colson silently and shot his right arm around Colson's neck. He secured the headlock by locking his right hand in the crook of his left elbow and planting his left hand around the base of Colson's skull. He used his forward momentum to push Colson against an interior wall just inside the doorway. The collision of the two men against the wall made a dull thud and knocked the plastic cover from a thermostat two feet from the point of impact. The man had a two-inch height advantage on Colson, and the headlock was firm.

Colson raised his right foot and shoved it into the wall in front of him, propelling the two men back against the opposite wall. The man's thin tank top provided little cushion when the corner of the wall dug into his back. Colson lifted his right leg and drove his heel down on top of his attacker's foot. The man released a loud grunt, sounding more of aggravation than pain, but his grip on Colson's head remained firm. Colson must have realized the man wasn't trying to suffocate him, but choke him out. If his attacker could find his carotid artery and maintain pressure for just a few seconds, Colson would black out—and be defenseless.

ᶜ᠕ᵖCHAPTER TWO᠕ᵒ

Keith Bartlett was brought up in a blue-collar, working-class family. Even as a child, he knew the lack of money was a constant concern for his parents. In order to provide for his family, his father worked two jobs for more than half his life, sending him to an early grave. He dropped dead of a heart attack at the age of fifty-three while driving from his day shift job at Lockheed to his evening shift at the box factory. The police told Keith's mother she was lucky no one else was injured in the accident. *Lucky?* Keith had thought at the time. *Some luck.* Shortly after his father's death, his mother began abusing what she referred to as "nerve pills" and remained addicted until her death several years and two assisted living homes later.

Keith promised himself he wouldn't end up like his father. He refused to spend his entire life working for someone else with nothing to show for it. He worked his way through college and earned an MBA before he was twenty-two, but accepted the fact that a degree alone didn't guarantee success. His goal was to own a respectable business and work hard to develop the leadership skills needed to inspire a successful team of employees. Bartlett Security currently served more than eleven hundred commercial, government, and residential customers, providing turnkey electronic systems for many of the Fortune 500 companies throughout the Southeast. Several of Keith's smaller clients went belly-up in the great recession, and inflation was rising faster than the blood pressure of most other business owners. But Keith diversified his business sufficiently and, as a result, his company was not only surviving, but thriving. In a world seemingly headed toward socialism and stagnation, only a few private businesses remained relatively stable—undertakers and security companies.

Keith and his wife Teresa bought a large, beautiful brick house in an upscale neighborhood in Gwinnett County and lived comfortably among their fine art and antique collections. Each of their sons received the benefit of a private school education, but that luxury didn't prevent Joshua from experimenting with drugs. Their hearts broke when Joshua was arrested for selling cocaine. It hurt Teresa the most. Keith tried to comfort her, attributing his son's rebelliousness to a passing phase he would eventually grow out of. He figured most children went through a rebellious phase—just not all of them get caught.

Keith achieved success where others had failed. At forty-five years of age, he stayed in excellent physical condition for a man who dedicated a minimum of seventy hours per week to work. His 5'11" frame supported naturally muscular shoulders and a well-defined chest. His narrow waist and hips gave him the classic V shape and symmetry many women were attracted to. His brown hair showed only a touch of gray, and his boyish features and an unruly cowlick erased ten years from his true age.

As usual for a weekday afternoon, Keith was in his high-rise office on Peachtree Street in downtown Atlanta. His was one of the few small businesses in Atlanta that hadn't been forced to move to less expensive office accommodations in the suburbs. He enjoyed having his office in the middle of the largest metropolis in the Southeast. On a clear day he could admire the Sun Dial restaurant from his desk, its slow rotation at the top of the high-rise hotel giving its patrons a panoramic view of the city. A photo of Keith, Teresa, and their sons sat proudly in a bright silver frame on his desk. They were much younger in the photograph. Next to the family photo was a more recent picture of Keith and Teresa on the deck of the cabin cruiser they had purchased last year—a forty-two-foot Catalina Cruiser they could sail anywhere in the world on a whim. Keith often daydreamed of a retirement in the Florida Keys, spending his days fishing, getting sunburned and fat in his declining years. But daydreaming wasn't on the schedule today.

He finished reading the last page of the CFO's monthly report and slipped off his reading glasses just as a knock came at the door. His receptionist stuck her head inside.

"There are a couple of detectives here to see you, Mr. Bartlett," she said. Katrina was usually up beat and bubbly, but not this morning. He never received so much as a visit from the building security guard, let alone real police detectives. Keith returned her announcement with a look of confusion and dread.

"Detectives?"

"Yes sir, should I send them in?"

Keith flipped the file closed and laid it on his desk. "Yes, ask them to come in, please."

He stood when the detectives entered the office and stepped around his desk to greet them. The first man to enter wore a serious look. He was tall and thin, wearing a blue wool suit and a white shirt with what appeared to be a rayon tie. The second detective was short and thin, dressed all in gray and black. They both had close-cropped hair that reminded him of TV detectives. For a moment he wondered if their visit was some kind of joke. Keith noticed the shorter cop had a gun on his belt as he reached for a wallet in his back pocket. He opened his badge case, displaying a gold shield.

"Mr. Bartlett, we're here about your son."

Keith's heart sank, and he froze in place. "Is it Josh?" he asked, his parental intuition answering his own question.

"Yes, sir. I'm afraid we have some very bad news," the shorter detective said.

For a moment, Keith felt as if his heart had constricted and blood no longer flowed through his veins. His mouth went dry. "Tell me," he said.

"I'm afraid your son is dead," the larger of the two answered, taking a step toward him.

The words echoed in Keith's head. He couldn't catch his breath. It felt as if all the air had been sucked out of the room. He shook his head in disbelief. Looking from one cop to the other, he tried to swallow the enormous lump lodged in his throat. "No," he said, quietly. "Please—it can't be true."

"He was found in a motel room on Candler Road a few miles from here," the shorter detective said. "It looks like a drug overdose."

For a moment Keith had the sensation of floating. All sound stopped. Then, with a jolt, he felt an electric-like current punch through his chest. He clutched at his tie and stumbled backward against the desk. The detectives moved quickly to steady him.

"Get us a glass of water," one of the detectives called toward the door.

"I'll call it in," the other said, reaching for the radio clipped to his belt.

Keith struggled to regain his balance. He took several quick breaths and tried to exhale the reality of the situation from his body. The cops eased him down into his chair as the receptionist came in with the water.

"Mr. Bartlett," she said, with a worried look, "are you okay? What's happened?"

"Ma'am, please wait in the other room for the ambulance." The tall cop took the water glass and handed it to Keith, who grasped it with a trembling hand and lifted it to his lips.

"Are you going to be okay, Mr. Bartlett?" the tall detective asked.

"The ambulance is on the way," the other said.

"No—no ambulance please," Keith said, still looking pale. "I'll be ok. Just give me a minute."

The shorter detective looked at his partner. "Should I cancel?"

"Yeah. I think he's okay."

"Three-eleven, cancel the signal four," the cop said into his radio.

"Where is he?" Keith asked, looking from one detective to the other. "Where's my son?"

"He's at the morgue downtown. We can give you a ride, or you can follow us if you wish," the tall cop said.

"I'm sorry," his partner said softly, "but we need you to officially identify the body."

Colson shot his right elbow back into his attacker's stomach, striking hard muscle. The hold around his neck relaxed enough to encourage Colson to strike again with his left elbow. The attacker's breath was forced from his diaphragm. Colson felt hot air rush past his ear. It stank of stale tobacco. A strong gust of air from the balcony washed past the struggling men and down the hall, forcing the steel door closed with a loud slam and obliterating the bar-lock as it raced to find an outlet. Colson felt his body being pulled slightly to the left when his attacker was momentarily distracted by the noise. He felt his only chance was to take the man to the ground, but he had a height disadvantage and the hall was too confining.

Colson dug his heels into the tile and pedaled backward. The pair moved slowly at first. The man behind him was strong, but Colson had been a regular at the gym for the past twenty years and even more frequently during these first eighteen months of retirement. His calves bulged as he used the floor to leverage the large man and gain momentum. Once in the open space of the living room, Colson worked his legs harder and grabbed the arm around his neck with both hands, preparing to land on top and pull from the man's grasp when they slammed on the floor.

But the man wasn't going down easy. For a moment, Colson began to notice a dark fog developing in his peripheral vision. Until then he had been able to struggle enough to prevent the man from finding his main artery, but now he was getting too close. Colson shot his left hand back over his shoulder and struck the bridge of the man's nose with his palm. He felt the man's head jerk back and heard plastic breaking, followed by the sound of choking. Two halves of a pair of sunglasses clacked on the tile floor on either side of Colson. The man behind him coughed violently and involuntarily loosened his hold on Colson's neck, but not enough for him to break free. Colson transferred his remaining strength to his legs and pedaled backward again. The two men stumbled back over the balcony threshold, their momentum abruptly halted by the balcony railing. Colson felt his back bury into the attacker's stomach as the man continued his violent coughing. What he didn't hear was the popping sound as the three bolts securing the top balcony rail were being sheared off and flung to the parking lot five stories below, bouncing off two parked SUVs.

Colson broke free and spun, ready to confront the man face to face. He raised and cocked his fist, but then froze.

"Are you insane, Taylor?" Colson shouted. The one-eyed former UFC fighter was bent slightly with one hand resting against the concrete wall and the other on the PVC deck chair. He coughed for another ten seconds before he replied, "You made me swallow my dip."

Colson just stared at Taylor while catching his breath and rubbing the side of his neck. He could count on three fingers how many times he had seen Taylor without his dark glasses. The first time was in the daylight basement of Martin Cash's enormous beach house when Taylor had a Glock leveled on Colson and his daughter. The second time was in the hospital where they wouldn't let him wear them, and the third time was today. Seriously self-conscious Colson guessed. Taylor's good eye was tearing up from his coughing frenzy, but his dead eye was just that—motionless and a hazy representation of its former self.

Taylor regained his composure and glared at Colson with his good eye. "And you broke my Ray-Bans," he protested. Colson's jaw dropped.

"You've got to be kidding me. You see that rail? You almost got us killed." Colson pointed at the loose aluminum railing and three holes where bolts had once held it secure. "What in hell is wrong with you?" he said, still breathing hard. "I'm not Inspector Clouseau, and you're not Cato. I don't need surprise attacks to keep me on my game."

Taylor slumped down in the PVC chair and motioned for Colson to sit. Jay "The Terrible" Taylor, as he was known in the mixed martial arts world, was a rising star until an incompetent eye doctor misdiagnosed an infection, causing him to lose one eye and one very lucrative career. But that was old news. The life Taylor expected to lead in no way resembled the life he was currently living—employed as a private investigator for a retired cop. The chain of events leading to him sitting on Grey Colson's fifth-floor balcony couldn't have been predicted by the world's greatest psychic. Even if it had, Taylor never would have believed it. But in the end, it was as real as it got. He had saved Colson and his daughter's life and was shot in the process. In return, Colson had given him a new lease on life. It worked out, but Taylor often wondered if Colson was just paying off a debt. Maybe at first. Other than the Gideons who came to the hospital for fifteen minutes to hand him a Bible and pray for him, Colson was the only one who visited, twice a week for the entire two months while Taylor's liver mended itself. They had become friends. Friends from two different worlds, but friends just the same. Their bond was built upon mutual convictions. Hard work, integrity, justice, and a determination to do the right thing. But the main thing they had in common was the most obvious. They were both—alone.

Taylor stared straight ahead at the Atlantic Ocean over the unstable balcony rail. "It's not smart to leave the front door propped. What if I was really a bad guy?"

Colson walked around Taylor to the second chair and plopped in the seat. "I could have taken you," he said flatly.

"Huh," Taylor grunted sarcastically and followed up with a chuckle under his breath. "How did you ever arrest a guy my size without getting the brakes beat off you?"

"We had a tool box to select from. Cops walk around with guns, Tasers, pepper spray, and expandable batons," Colson said.

"That hardly sounds fair."

Colson laughed. "Fair? Cops don't play fair. They play to win. It's not like the UFC, Jay. You're not guaranteed to be matched up with a bad guy according to weight and ability. It's not a game."

Taylor sat silent, still looking at the ocean. Colson paused for moment to scratch his nose and continued. "And the most important tool we used was our brain. You had to learn to talk your way out of bad situations. Cops who have to fight everyone they arrest forget to engage their brain before running their mouth." He picked up the case file from the side table and held it up. "I was going to say good job on this case before you decided to draft me into the Ultimate Fighting Championship."

Taylor turned to Colson, his one eye squinting from the glaring Daytona sun reflecting off the white stucco exterior walls. Colson continued. "Of course I had to fix all the typos. You should spend more time reading the report-writing lesson plan I gave you instead of practicing your chokehold techniques on me and trashing the condo. That's why they have fitness centers."

Taylor pointed to his own face. "I'm not going to the gym with this eye."

"Why not? It doesn't make you any uglier."

"Thanks a lot," Taylor said. "Hey, I have to admit you were right about the delivery driver in the Ocean Front complaint. They thought their product was being walked out the back door."

"But their warehouse cameras never caught anything, did they?" Colson said, confirming a prediction rather than asking a question.

Taylor nodded. "Right, but their inventory kept coming up short. They didn't think about one of their guys selling a box or two of frozen fish to their customers under the table—or should I say, out of the back of their truck for half price."

Colson slipped on his sunglasses and looked out over the ocean. "The owner didn't want to think his customers would take advantage of him. He said he had been doing business with these restaurants for nearly ten years."

Taylor shook his head. "Then the managers who paid half price are just as guilty as the Ocean Front delivery guy. What are they going to do about that?"

"Whatever they want, as far as I'm concerned," Colson said. "Of course they fired their delivery guy, and they'll have a copy of this file and the video to turn over to the sheriff's office investigators—that is, unless they go soft and begin feeling sorry for the man's wife and kids. Then they might just be glad to be rid of him. Either way, we did the job we were paid to do."

"You mean I did the job."

"Yes," Colson said, rolling his eyes, "you did the job."

"What about the restaurant managers? Do they get a free pass?"

"Look, Jay," Colson said, "you can't be taking this stuff personally. You did a good job collecting the evidence and making a solid case. Most likely the owner will back charge the restaurants for their loss. If I had worried about what kind of sentence the slugs I arrested got in court, I would have been miserable because ninety-nine percent never got what they deserved. The only thing you can afford to be is satisfied you did a good job on your end and not worry about things you can't control."

"Isn't that like your new job?" Taylor said. "Why spend so much time and effort to go on a crusade against drugs when it's a losing battle? Didn't you already do your duty for king and country over the past thirty years?"

"It's an interim job," Colson said, "only until they find a permanent replacement. Truthfully, I felt the same way before doing all the research. Sure I worked as a narc years ago, but this is not an enforcement position, and the approach is from an entirely different angle. It's about education and prevention, not cleaning up after the mess has already been made."

Colson paused, looking down at a woman walking from her car to the breezeway, holding hands with an excited toddler. A little girl with short curly hair and a bright yellow dress. She was skipping, but the ocean breeze masked the clickity-clack of her sandals on the pavement. His tone turned more serious.

"Until recently I was satisfied I had done all I could do. What was left undone was the world's problem, and someone else could worry about it because I would probably be gone before it completely went to hell in a hand basket. But now I have a grandson. A lot of people think it's even more of a losing battle than it was twenty years ago, but you don't give up a fight because it's inconvenient, costs too much, or the tide of public opinion has changed."

"So when do you fly back to Atlanta?" Taylor asked.

"I'm driving this time and taking a break from that madhouse they call airport security. That place is already in the hand basket."

"So, I'm going solo again with the next Colson Confidential case?" Taylor said with snappy sarcasm.

Colson sneered at him. "Don't be so smug. You're the one who came up with that name." He closed his eyes in thought for five seconds. "Just do a little background and write up a plan for me to review. I want to see what you come up with."

"Okay," Taylor stood, and Colson raised his hand to stop him.

"Just write it up. Don't let anyone see it unless you want them to think a third grader wrote it. Where are you going anyway?"

Taylor walked toward the sliding door and mumbled, "Where do you think? To get new sunglasses." Colson turned to the door and raised his voice through the opening. "Then you need to go by the hardware store and get something to fix this railing, you one-eyed psycho."

CHAPTER THREE

Keith stared straight ahead through the windshield as he followed the detective's car through downtown traffic. He drove past cyclists and runners in Piedmont Park on the right side of the street without seeing them. The autumn sun reflected off the high-rise buildings on his left, but he was driving in a dreadful darkness. Beginning to feel sick to his stomach, he took a deep breath as he removed one hand from the steering wheel and pinched the bridge of his nose. He thought of calling Teresa to tell her what was happening, but he needed to wait and make sure it was really Joshua. A moment of hope flashed in his mind, but just as quickly vanished. Surely the police would be certain before delivering the worst news a parent ever wants to hear. He wouldn't tell Teresa over the phone either way. He caught a glimpse of himself in the rear view mirror. It occurred to him that he didn't look old as much as he looked beaten.

The drive seemed to take hours, but in reality it took less than twenty minutes. When they arrived at the morgue, the detectives apologized again for having to put him through the trauma of identifying Joshua's body almost immediately after the shock of learning of his death. Keith raised his hand briefly in a gesture of understanding. It had to be done.

The Fulton County morgue was a white-tiled, windowless box with built-in stainless steel cabinets and a stainless steel hydraulic operating table bolted to the center of the floor. The acoustics in the room created an eerie, hollow sound, and it stank of sterile death. Keith stood, staring at the channels on each side of an empty metal operating table where he suspected bodily fluids were captured. Just beyond the table, a large cast iron drain plate lay in the center of the floor. Nausea replaced his normal bodily functions. A subzero chill flooded his bloodstream and a cold line of sweat ran down his back.

The morgue technician walked toward them, snapping off a pair of blue latex gloves. She was strikingly attractive. Keith saw a name stitched on her shirt as she walked closer: "B. Walls." She slid the mask down, revealing a lovely face, but solemn expression. She briefly glanced at Keith and offered a short nod before stepping up to the taller of the two detectives and pulling him by his coat sleeve, but not so far away that Keith couldn't overhear the conversation. It suddenly occurred to him that he couldn't remember the detective's name or whether he had even been told what it was.

"Any idea on the approximate time of death?" the detective asked.

"Well, as you know, it's not like on TV," she answered. "We can't pinpoint the time without pathology and toxicology reports, which won't be back for several weeks."

"Yeah, I understand that," the cop whispered impatiently, "but you can ballpark it, right? The family is going to want to know." He motioned with his head in Keith's direction.

Eavesdropping might not be polite, but Keith was straining to hear every word.

The tech looked to Keith apologetically, and then back to the detective. "Rigor and lividity aren't fixed yet. Based on the postmortem changes and algor mortis, I would estimate four to six hours ago."

"Okay, thanks." the detective said, making a note on his pad. "So you are going to do an autopsy then?"

"Yes, we always do an autopsy when the victim is this young."

The detective seemed embarrassed he hadn't known that. "We need for the father to ID the body now," he said gruffly.

B. Walls nodded to a younger man standing off to one side in a white smock with his hands clasped at his waist. Keith had yet to notice he was in the room. The young man spun slowly, walked to a metal table in the corner of the room, and reached for the corner of a drab hospital blanket covering the lifeless form beneath. He paused a beat while turning to Walls and gently folded the corner of the blanket back, revealing Josh's lifeless face. Keith shivered as a cold draft, real or imagined, swept over him. His heart beat against his ribcage, and all the air rushed out of his lungs. He sensed Walls stepping to his side as she whispered the question he would remember for the rest of his life. He anticipated the question but wasn't prepared for it to hit him like a body blow.

"Can you identify the body?" she asked.

Keith's mouth was dry. There was a slight taste of vomit from deep in his throat. He had a strange, vacant feeling, as if he were lying on the cold table instead of his son. He closed his eyes and slowly nodded his head. "Yes, that's my son."

Before leaving the morgue, the shorter of the two detectives gave him a plastic bag containing Joshua's personal effects. Tears welled in Keith's eyes as he looked at the items in the bag. Josh's clothes, a wallet, a cell phone, and fifty-three cents in change. He couldn't control his quivering hand as he signed the property release form.

Jonathan Raines drove his wife's black Lexus toward his appointment with his mind on anything but driving. His mind was on business—how he had built Raines Pharmaceuticals from the ground up. An Atlanta-based concern with satellite distribution centers in Jacksonville and Chicago, it appeared in the Fortune 500 list for two consecutive years in 2006 and 2007. The first three start-up years were a challenge, but they were followed by the best ten years of his financial life. His wife was more than happy to become a stay-at-home mom in their half-million-dollar house, and his children had been extremely well provided for, but the long hours were making him feel old. Then came the great recession, and the sinking tide lowered all the boats—including his. He had considered the possibility of difficult financial times when he embarked in the pharmaceutical business, but he was comforted in the fact that the need for prescription medication was as secure as the need for funeral homes. That would have been the case if the politically correct attacks from the government hadn't begun to eat into his profits.

His working hours lengthened after he'd had to lay off a good portion of his staff last year, and the lack of operating funds forced him to steal from Peter to pay Paul on a constant basis. Although he was the hands-on type of manager, being away from his family to this extent wasn't worth it.

He tried to put it all out of his mind and concentrate on the task at hand—driving in heavy traffic—when his cell phone rang. It was his only remaining executive assistant, Rick. He pressed the Bluetooth icon on the dashboard screen.

"Hey, boss," Rick said, "I've got a quick question for you about one of our accounts, ah—" he paused and then continued, "Athletics RX."

Jonathan turned right on Cedarcrest Drive and spoke to the dash. "Yeah, Rick, I'm familiar. I just renewed their distribution agreement a week ago. Is there a problem?"

"Well, that's an awful big order."

Jonathan chuckled. "That's what we do, Rick. Fill a lot of big orders."

"Yeah, right. It's just that they've doubled their quantities from last year."

Jonathan paused, distracted with driving in unknown territory and listening to his subordinate. His cell phone was interrupting the conversation with GPS coordinates. "Ah—well—that's good for business. Look, I'm a little busy right now. Let me review the file when I get in. Could be an oversight." He reached over, disconnected the call in the middle of Rick's "Okay, talk to—" and backed the Lexus into a parking space near the side of the small church on Cedarcrest Drive and out of view from the roadway. He checked the digital display on the dash: 2:55 p.m. Confident he couldn't be seen from the road, he opened a notebook and wrote the date and time at the top of the second page.

He looked through his binoculars at the driveway entrance to the house across the street and brought the numbers 415 on the mailbox into focus. Within five minutes, a blue Prius approached from the south and turned left into the driveway. He could only read the last three numbers of the tag—3-8-8—before the car flashed out of view. He'd be sure to get the first three letters when they left. He noted the make and model of the vehicle, along with the time of arrival in the notebook.

This was the second consecutive day he had spied on the dealer's house. He earlier had identified the house as his daughter's most likely drug source using GPS tracking software on her mobile phone. It required several heated arguments between Jonathan and his wife to settle their differences regarding where a daughter's right to privacy ended and where a parent's responsibility began. At first Sheila had insisted Jonathan shouldn't be tracking Emily's whereabouts, but he finally convinced her that Emily's health and safety far outweighed any perceived privacy issues.

The computer store tech geek had explained to him that the mobile phone tracking software used GPS and GMS technology based on repeater triangulation—whatever that was. He had added that the terrorist attacks of 9/11 and the increased demand for 9-1-1 emergency call tracking capabilities resulted in GPS tracking being made available to the general public for cell phones.

Jonathan didn't care why the technology was available, how it worked, or even how much it cost. He only wanted to help his daughter.

He watched as the Prius backed out of the driveway less than ten minutes later. He wrote down the first three letters of the tag when it made a left on Cedarcrest. The police could now identify the owner of the car and crosscheck the name against known drug offenders. Now if they would only do it—that part was an unknown. He had nine total vehicle descriptions and tag numbers to give the police from his two-day unsanctioned surveillance. What he had learned from Grey Colson at the seminar made sense. One of the identifiers of a low- to mid-level drug dealer was the number of vehicles coming and going and the length of time each remained at the house or apartment. It was just one indicator, but an indicator nonetheless.

Raines had met Colson just weeks ago while attending a drug-free workplace seminar at the Fulton County Chamber of Commerce. As the owner of a small pharmaceutical company,

Jonathan had been active in the local chamber for years. The seminar was titled, "The Solution to America's Drug Problem" and featured a retired police officer who provided assistance to the businesses of Fulton County in the implementation of a drug-free workplace program.

Certified drug-free workplaces in Georgia received a state-mandated discount on workers compensation insurance that would result in thousands of dollars of savings for his company annually. He needed every dime he could save in this struggling economy. Saving money was his top priority. There were a few financial decisions he wasn't proud of, but nothing could undo them now. His tax attorney had also given him some advice he strongly suspected was shady, but didn't everyone cheat a little? It was all about him, his company, and his family. Or was it? If he were honest with himself, it was only about him. But after Colson's presentation, he realized having a drug-free workplace was about more than just saving money. He had approached Colson when his presentation was over about obtaining state certification status for his company. Over the course of several lunch meetings with Colson, he'd learned about the world of police narcotics investigations.

Colson was passionate about the subject and took a light-hearted approach that Raines appreciated and admired. Yet there were a few telltale references Colson sprinkled in their conversations that convinced Jonathan he would never want to be on Colson's black list. He wondered how Colson would react if he knew he was using some of his war-story tactics to play cop on his own.

Jonathan's cell phone rang from its dash-mounted bracket, and a photo icon of his smiling wife appeared on the screen above her name.

In the upscale neighborhood of Buckhead, Sheila Raines stood in the middle of her Emily's bedroom and turned in circles to take it all in. It was like looking through the eyes of a stranger. The cheerleading trophies her daughter had so proudly displayed a year ago were now dusty relics crowded in the corner, and her highly prized purse collection was shoved under the bed. The stuffed animals she imbued with her own personality now sat piled lifeless and forlorn on the floor beyond the open door. She looked with sadness at the familiar objects, each with its own place in her memories of Emily growing up. She sat on the bed, looking at the throw rug on the floor—the same rug she had laid on night after night, until Emily became comfortable enough to sleep in her own room. She closed her eyes. That was fifteen years ago. Sheila bit her lip, holding back tears.

Looking up, Sheila counted the banners hanging on the walls. Emily's team had won every regional cheerleading competition in the southeast for three years in a row and went on to win the world championship just two years ago. The World Cheerleading Competition in Orlando was the highlight of Emily's cheerleading career. She smiled at the memory of the standing ovation Emily had received when she hit her double at the end of the performance.

But there was no more cheerleading. No more applause from excited parents and no more championship banners. Emily was no longer interested in cheerleading or bouncing out of bed early to see her friends at practice. She had moved on. At seventeen, she had lost interest in everything that had once been important in her world. Emily still lived with her parents physically, but mentally and emotionally she had checked out.

Sheila had caught Emily drinking when she was fourteen. It was her first year in high school, and she had developed curves earlier than other girls her age. With her father's deep blue eyes and Sheila's blonde hair, Emily was a gorgeous young lady. As expected, the boys noticed and were instantly slain. She frequently had sleepover parties with her girlfriends on weekends, mainly to talk about boys. Sheila found empty wine cooler bottles hidden at the bottom of Emily's trashcan one Sunday morning, but she didn't confront Emily at the time, writing it off as typical teenage experimentation. Had turning a blind eye then led to a drinking problem that ultimately grew into drug use? Sheila always considered herself Emily's best friend. She wished now she had assumed the role of parent then and taken the episode seriously. She hit Jonathan's speed dial icon on the wireless phone. He answered immediately.

"Is anything happening?" she asked.

"I've only been here fifteen minutes, but already one car has come and gone," Jonathan answered.

"Are you sure this is the best way to handle this?" Sheila said. "Shouldn't we just call the police?"

"I already told you, honey, we don't have enough information yet. The police won't do anything unless we give them specifics to go on."

"But how will having a list of tag numbers make any difference?" Sheila said. "What if the people who live in that house are just selling Tupperware or something innocent like that?"

She heard him sigh. "Come on, Sheila, you know better than that."

"But Jonathan, it seems dangerous for you to be the one conducting surveillance, as you put it. You're not really trained for this you know. You're a small business owner for God's sake, not Sonny Crockett."

"How can it be dangerous if they're just selling Tupperware?" he said.

"This is not funny, Jon. I'm already worried enough about Emily without having to wonder if you're going to do something stupid and end up getting shot by some drug dealer."

"Hold on a minute," Jonathan said. "Someone just came out of the house with a big bag. It's a white male with a ponytail. He's walking to the end of the driveway with a large plastic bag in his hand."

"Jon, don't you dare do anything crazy." She bit her lip, worried about him.

"I'm not, just hold on—the guy with the ponytail set the bag down on the curb beside the mailbox and walked back toward the house. It was just garbage. But wait a minute; that gives me an idea."

"Great. What now?" Sheila asked.

"Colson mentioned doing trash pulls when he worked narcotics. He said once someone puts their trash on the curb it becomes abandoned property. The police don't need a search warrant to seize abandoned trash, so they wait for a suspected drug dealer to take out his garbage. They watch the house and grab it before the sanitation department picks it up."

Sheila rolled her eyes, even though Jon wasn't there to see the dreaded eye roll. "Why on earth would the police want someone's garbage?"

"They go through it looking for evidence. Things like plastic sandwich bags with powdered drug residue, or sticks, stems, and seeds from where they cleaned their marijuana, or maybe a phone bill with a list of long distance calls to their supplier. They can use that stuff as probable cause to get a search warrant for the home and to identify people the dealer is doing business with."

"Jon, don't tell me you're going to steal someone's smelly garbage and put it in my Lexus," Sheila said. "Why don't you just ask that Colson guy for help? I'm sure he still has law enforcement friends who can do something with it."

"I don't want Colson to know about Emily's problems yet. We're not that close, and it's embarrassing to have to admit I failed as a parent. I just want to get enough information to get her supplier busted, then get her into counseling and cleaned up."

"Okay, if you say so—but I still think it would be better to let the professionals handle it from the beginning."

"Listen, honey, I promise I'll turn everything over to the cops within the next couple of days. And don't worry; I'm not going to put a sack of garbage in the Lexus. I'll come by in one of the pharmaceutical company vans early in the morning before the sun comes up and just toss the bag in the back."

"Fine," Sheila said with an exasperated sigh. "Will you come home now?"

"I'm on the way."

Sheila was too distracted by her thoughts to notice the gray Honda passing slowly by the house and parking in the cul-de-sac up the street.

ᘓ⌀CHAPTER FOUR⌀ᘐ

olson's cell phone alarm began playing Steely Dan's "Deacon Blues" at 4:30 a.m. Faint moonlight seeped through the open vertical blinds of the sliding doors to his left. A faint blue glow illuminated the tile floor from under the bedroom door, varying in intensity, blinking off and on sporadically. Colson rubbed his eyes. Taylor must have left the television on again. He dropped his feet to the floor, stretched, and walked to the kitchen to make coffee.

He found Taylor sitting on the couch, riveted to the plasma TV hanging above the entertainment center. Taylor turned his head for an instant to Colson, then snapped it back to the program he was watching. Colson couldn't see what Taylor was so interested in, but he recognized it was Fox News by the anchorwoman's voice. He poured water in the machine, slipped in a filter, dumped in four heaping lumps of coffee grounds, and toggled it on.

"You're up awful early. I guess you wanted to make me breakfast before I left," Colson said with a hint of sarcasm. Taylor didn't turn to Colson, but instead leaned forward to hear the low volume report. Colson shrugged. "You can turn it up now that I'm—"

"Hang on." Taylor held up his hand. "I need to see this"

Colson picked up the remote and raised the volume. The anchorwoman was saying, "And we'll be right back with the controversial issue before the Georgia house in a moment," just before an ambulance-chasing attorney began shouting a disingenuous sales pitch. Colson toggled the volume back down to spare them from the obnoxious ad and set the remote on the table.

37

"It's 4:30, Jay. What got you up so early?"

Taylor finally faced Colson. "I was watching the news last night, and about an hour later, it was watching me."

"So you fell asleep on the couch again. What, the bed in the guest room too soft for you? You might find the concrete balcony more comfortable," Colson said with a grin, gesturing to the sliding doors.

"No," Taylor said, shaking his head, "I caught the tail end of a report last night and hoped they'd replay it. That's what I'm waiting for."

"Since when have you been interested—?"

"Here it is," Taylor cried, interrupting Colson for the second time in two minutes. Taylor grabbed the remote and punched the volume button. The anchorwoman was mid-sentence, captured in split-screen with a man standing on long concrete steps. Reporters were shoving microphones in the man's face. He was talking, but the sound was muted, allowing the anchorwoman to describe the scene.

"Strawn told reporters he was encouraged by his meeting with the governor," she said evenly.

The half screen showing the anchorwoman was shoved aside as the man filled the screen. The man wore a gray suit jacket, white shirt, and black tie. A large, bald man stood behind him wearing an almost identical suit. He wore dark, expensive sunglasses and was scanning the crowd as if he were a Secret Service agent. It only took Colson a few seconds to recognize the building in the background as the Georgia State Capitol, but he recognized the man standing on the steps immediately. Jack Strawn. Colson couldn't have picked him out of a line-up just a year ago, but in the course of his research for his new job he had become quite familiar with the billionaire. And Colson didn't like him or his haughty attitude.

On the TV, a faint ribbon of smoke rose between Strawn and his bodyguard and disappeared above their heads. Strawn was apparently holding an expensive cigar to his side. Colson couldn't make out the reporter's question, but Strawn finally spoke in his typically condescending manner.

"The governor understands the logic of my position. Not just my position, but clearly the position of a majority of not only Georgians, but all Americans. This is a popular and overdue bill that will receive bi-partisan support in the Georgia House. This state is behind the curve when it comes to making recreational substances legal, and the governor agrees that the cost of arresting, housing, and prosecuting nonviolent people for victimless crimes is not only crippling the state in this recession, but is depriving its citizens the freedom to do as they please in their own homes and businesses. It's naive to incarcerate people when what they really need is treatment."

Colson squinted at the man's practiced delivery. The reporter blurted a follow-up question as Strawn seemed to pause. "Mr. Strawn, you previously said you were heading up a nation-wide campaign to legalize drugs."

Strawn held up his hand to stop the reporter. His cigar was now visible, stuck between his index and middle fingers. "Let's not get carried away and generalize by labeling all substances as drugs. Most substances are grown naturally, but that's an argument for another day. I met with the governor here and plan to meet with many more governors in the coming weeks and months. It's a grassroots effort to make recreational substances legal in all fifty states, but it has to begin here at home. Why not let Georgia lead the way and be a model for the nation to follow?"

Colson and Taylor watched Strawn and his large companion shoulder through the lump of reporters and climb into a black limousine parked at the curb. The screen split once again with the car pulling away, and then the anchorwoman reclaimed the full screen, speaking with a suspicious tone.

"Georgia's governor, Richard Peal, hasn't made a public statement regarding his meeting with Strawn or the proposed legislation. In a short written statement, the governor said he was leaving the representatives to their debate and subsequent up or down vote. Polls indicate Americans are split when it comes to the legalization of marijuana. The margin is slightly higher in favor of making medicinal marijuana legal, but much lower when asked if all recreational drugs should be legalized. We will be watching and reporting the progress of this proposed legislation and Strawn's state-

THE NIGHTMARE MERCHANT ~ C. A. GRIFFITH

by-state crusade when the house returns from recess. When we return—"

Colson took the remote, muted the sound, and turned to Taylor, who sat on the edge of the cushion, nodding his head. Colson cocked his head slightly. "You're not going to tell me you agree with Strawn, are you?"

Taylor shot Colson a confused look. "What?"

"You think he's right, don't you?"

"No," Taylor said, pointing to the screen. "I didn't even pay attention to what he was saying."

It was Colson's turn to display a confused face. "So what was the big deal about waiting for the report if you weren't—?"

"No, no, no," Taylor said, "his bodyguard. I just caught them getting into the limo last night with their backs to the camera, but I knew just from watching him walk who it was. Now I know for certain. Clay Haggart."

"Who's Clay Haggart?"

Taylor looked genuinely shocked and replied as if Colson were a naive child. "Clay 'The Mad Man' Haggart. I would have fought him in the championship if I hadn't lost the eye. And I would have beaten his ass."

Colson's confusion vanished. "How could I forget? You've told me about it a thousand times. Why would he be working for a slug like Strawn?"

"I heard he retired after getting the belt," Taylor said. "He took thousands of head punches over the years, and I guess he decided to retire before it got to the point he couldn't count to three or black out every time he farted. It looks like that guy probably pays more anyway."

"That guy, as you call him," Colson said and pointed to the flat screen on the wall, "has more money than Carter has liver pills."

Taylor looked at the TV and back to Colson. "Who's Carter?"

Colson rolled his eyes and dismissed Taylor with a wave. "Forget it."

Jonathan considered his next move on the drive home. He would pick up the trash from the house on Cedarcrest tomorrow morning, go through it for any evidence, and turn everything along with the tag numbers over to the police. Hopefully, that would be enough information to get them to open an investigation. If he could get Emily's supplier arrested and his daughter into counseling, maybe he could keep her off drugs.

As he exited the interstate, his cell phone buzzed again. Jonathan answered the phone and heard Sheila's panicked voice. "Jon, Emily's missing."

Jonathan's heart sank as fear gripped him. "What do you mean, missing?"

"She didn't come home from Sara's house at three-thirty like she promised. I just called there, and Sara's mom said she hasn't seen Emily."

"Did you talk to Sara?"

"Yes, Sara said Emily wasn't in school today. She said she didn't even know Emily was going to come over after school. Jon, something awful must have happened. I can feel it."

"Did you call Emily's cell phone?"

"Yes, of course," Sheila said. "It just goes to voice mail."

"I'm ten minutes from the house," Jonathan told her. "I'll be right there."

When he arrived home, Sheila met him at the door, clearly wild with worry. All the color had drained from her face, making it as white as the dress shirt he was wearing. Overcome by rising panic, and blinking back tears, she said none of Emily's friends had seen or heard from her. She said in a voice full of fear, "Where could she be?"

Jonathan's worst fears were his children being kidnapped or killed, but that always seemed to happen to other people, not to them. His mind raced, and he felt nauseous as he wondered, *has Emily been abducted?* He quickly tried to push the thought aside and fought to

41

remain calm for Sheila's sake. Her panicked state of mind wouldn't help them find their daughter.

He held her tight and said into her ear, "Maybe she's still angry about us not allowing her to go to the concert last week, and she's with a friend we don't know about."

"Maybe," Sheila said, and when she looked up at him, there was a glimmer of hope in her eyes.

Jonathan suddenly remembered something. He snapped his fingers and said, "We can track her through the GPS on her phone."

"No, we can't." Sheila held up their daughter's phone. "I found it in her dresser drawer. I kept calling it and finally heard it vibrating."

"Why wouldn't she take her phone with her?"

"You know she's always forgetting it. Or maybe she figured out we had the GPS tracking on it and doesn't want us to know where she went. I told you we shouldn't have put that stupid thing on her phone."

"Honey, let's please not argue about that again right now. Did you check the call lists in the phone?" Jonathan asked. "Maybe we can figure out where she is by the last numbers she called, or by who called her."

"Yes, I checked. She cleared all of the call lists."

Jonathan shook his head in frustration. "Have you called the police?"

"Yes, and they're sending an officer out to take a report. He should be here in a few minutes."

A loud knock on the front door startled Jonathan, suddenly making him worry about their seven-year-old son. "Where's Austin?" he asked, looking toward the stairs.

"He's taking a nap," Sheila said. "He was worn out from his friend's birthday party after school."

Jonathan opened the door to an Atlanta P.D. uniformed officer. He invited the officer in, and the three of them stood in the center of the living room. Bold white letters on the patrolman's black nametag identified him as S. Cohen. He wore no emotion on his face, as if he responded to these types of calls a dozen times per day. Jonathan suspected as much and figured in most cases the teenagers were runaways or the parents were overreacting.

"You called about a missing child," Officer Cohen said as a statement more than a question.

"Yes," Sheila answered, "our daughter Emily is missing."

The officer's radio blared, "APD 311 signal 29 corner of Peachtree and Harris, 315 code seven." Jonathan glanced to the stairs, worried the radio would wake Austin. Why was the volume so loud? It would compound their worry if Austin came downstairs with a million questions about why the police were in the house. He considered asking the officer to turn it down, but he didn't want to offend. If this was more than Emily getting mad and pouting at a friend's house, they would need all the help they could get from the police. Thankfully the officer reached to his shoulder and lowered the volume.

"How old is the missing child?" Officer Cohen said.

"She'll be eighteen in two weeks," Sheila replied.

The officer took out a notepad and prepared to write. "What is her full name and date of birth?" Sheila rattled it off so fast the officer asked her to slow down. "And what was she last seen wearing?"

Sheila closed her eyes to pull up a virtual photo of Emily in her mind. "Black Levi's, a black leather belt with double rivets, black ankle boots, and a black cropped sweater."

While Sheila was giving the description, it occurred to Jonathan how Emily's wardrobe had recently changed from bright pinks to goth black almost overnight.

"Any distinguishing marks?" the officer asked.

"No."

"Does she wear glasses, does she have braces, any piercings?"

"She wears contact lenses," Sheila said, "and her ears are pierced. That's all."

"Has she ever run away before?"

43

Jonathan wondered why he said "before." Sheila and Jonathan looked at each other. "Yes," Sheila said. "Three months ago. She disappeared for half a day. We tracked her down at a friend's house."

The cop glanced up from his notepad. "Did you file a report?"

"No," Sheila said, "because it was during the summer and school was out. She was mad at us, and we were pretty sure she was staying with a friend. We found her quickly by calling around, so we didn't see a need to involve the police." She watched as the officer jotted a note on the pad and then quickly added, "I've called all her friends this time though, and no one has seen her."

Officer Cohen nodded his head without looking up. "Did she go to school this morning?"

"Yes—well, she left for school," Sheila said. "But she didn't show up there. I checked with the school."

"Are any of her clothes missing?"

Sheila looked down at her hands. "I can't be sure," she said. "She has so many clothes, she could have taken some with her this morning in her backpack."

He nodded again and made another note. "Does she have a car?"

"Yes." Jonathan gave a description of Emily's Toyota along with the tag number.

"How have things been here at home lately?" Officer Cohen asked. "Any problems with her?"

Sheila glanced at her husband, silently asking him to answer. "Yes," Jonathan said. "We've suspected there may be some drug use going on."

"What kind of drugs?" Cohen said, leveling his gaze at Jonathan.

"Just some pot," Jonathan lied.

"Do you suspect there may be drugs in the home at this time?"

"No," Sheila answered, in a stronger tone. "I've searched her room." Jonathan looked at Sheila with surprise. This was the same woman who threw a fit about the GPS tracking on her daughter's phone. Sheila glared at Jonathan, but spoke to the officer. "I was looking for anything that could tell us where she might be."

"Do you have a recent photo of her?"

"Yes, her yearbook picture. I'll get it." Sheila left the room and returned a moment later with a photo of Emily staring sullenly at the camera. The cop took the picture and put it in his shirt pocket.

"We'll put a lookout on her and the vehicle to all units. We'll enter her name, date of birth, vehicle description, and tag number on NCIC. I'll create a BOLO using her picture, and it will be distributed to all APD officers at shift change. We will also put her picture and information on the missing children's website."

"Is that all?" Sheila said worriedly. "Isn't there more that can be done? What if she's been abducted?"

Officer Cohen looked at Sheila for a moment, as if struggling to be diplomatic with his reply. "Ma'am, do you have any reason to believe she has been abducted?"

"No," Sheila's agitation was surfacing. "But she's a child, a female child. Can't you issue one of those Amber alerts or something?"

"She's almost eighteen," he said. "Amber alerts cannot be issued on a seventeen year old. Plus, with the possible drug use and the fact that she's run away before—" He shrugged his shoulders. "The case will be turned over to the detective division as a missing person, and a detective will follow up with you in the next couple of days. That's all we can do." He turned and walked out the door without another word, leaving the parents staring at each other.

"I don't think they're going to try to find her," Sheila said.

Jonathan looked at the open door, down to the floor for a moment, then back to Sheila. "I'm afraid you may be right."

CHAPTER FIVE

The Butcher popped out his wireless earpiece and pulled the surface microphone contact element from the exterior glass of the living room window when the police car backed out of the driveway and drove away. He crouched in the thick shrubbery against the house, wearing a dark jacket with "Meter Reader" stenciled in white on the back. He had searched the junkie's room thoroughly, but what he was looking for wasn't there.

The only logical answer was the girl, but he had clearly overheard the parents' conversation with the cop: she was gone. She probably didn't even know what she had, but that was her problem. It wouldn't be a problem for him unless he couldn't find her. It might take a few more days, but he hadn't failed an assignment yet, and he had no intention of failing this time. He would find the girl, whether her parents did or not. But either way, they would never see their daughter alive again. They might as well get used to it now. He zipped the eavesdropping device into a leather pouch and casually walked back to his car.

Colson sipped his coffee and swung the Corvette eastbound on International Speedway Blvd. He'd wanted to be on the road no later than 5:00 a.m., but Taylor had delayed him with a hundred questions about their best approach for the next theft investigation and blabbering about the newscast. It was already 5:35 a.m., so he wouldn't be able to avoid the morning traffic in Jacksonville.

With the temperature reading a comfortable seventy-seven degrees, he powered the windows down to enjoy the fresh sea air. The sky was beginning to show the glow of a new day, and so far traffic was light for a Monday morning. But the traffic would only get worse from here. He reached the Jacksonville I-295 by-pass at 7:45 a.m. and turned east on I-10 toward Lake City. Another hour and Colson was northbound on I-75 for the longest leg of his journey to Atlanta.

He stopped just south of Macon to stretch his legs and get a coffee refill. The middle Georgia sun was doing its job on the glass panel roof. He set the air-conditioner to sixty degrees and rolled down the ramp, accelerating to match the northbound traffic. The two tractor-trailers moving northbound in the right lane gleamed like mirrors. Colson had to decide whether to floor it and merge in ahead of them or slow down and drop in behind. He chose the latter and shifted down to third gear. Any other time the monstrous vehicles would ride your tail because you weren't moving fast enough for them. These two seemed to be hugging the speed limit as if a parade of state troopers were behind them. As Colson coasted down the on-ramp, he caught the company name written in a large, elegant black font on the side of both trailers. It simply read "STRAWN" in all capital letters. Apparently when you are a billionaire tycoon known the world over, you no longer require long, descriptive business names or snappy slogans for people to recognize your product or worth.

Colson couldn't help admiring the two identical Peterbuilt trucks. The cabs were solid black with the exception of their perfectly polished chrome bumpers and exhaust stacks. The trailers were bright aluminum and nearly as reflective as the bumpers. Massive chrome wheels with lug nuts the size of silver dollars and dual black propane tanks mounted behind the cab finished off the package. And they were spotless. Colson gave a light whistle and shook his head while estimating the price of the rigs. Strawn obviously wanted to project a clean, professional image, so why on earth would he want to screw up the country more than it was already by leading a crusade to legalize drugs? How "clean" and "professional" would that be? It didn't make sense.

Colson slid in behind the big rigs and waited for a row of cars to pass in the fast lane. He glanced at his speedometer. These guys were on a downgrade, doing almost ten miles per hour under the limit. The cars speeding up behind him were shifting into the fast lane, not giving him a chance to jump over. He decided to drop back and wait for an opening. The grade of the highway leveled and almost immediately began to ascend. Colson rolled his eyes, waiting for an opening. He fully expected the rigs to soon be slowing to forty miles per hour, but they finally kicked it in and began their climb. Dark exhaust bellowed from their stacks as Colson found an opening and jerked the 'Vette into the left lane. He hated the smell of propane. The Clay County Sheriff's Office flirted with propane-powered patrol cars for about a year until the constant leaks and mechanical problems cost the county more money to service than they hoped to save. Not to mention the stench of the obnoxious gas made most of the deputies nauseous. But he didn't smell the propane exhaust he expected. These guys were running on tried and true diesel.

Something caught Colson's eye as he overtook the first truck—the driver's side propane tank mounted behind the sleeper cab. He lifted his foot from the accelerator, allowing the big rig to move past him until he was even with what he wanted to see. The tank resembled the fifty-gallon water heater that used to stand in his garage, except it was painted gloss black and lying on its side, cradled and bolted to U-shaped brackets on the front and back. A pressure gauge sat on top of the tank with its dial facing out. Colson glanced at his rear view mirror for any cars breathing down his neck, but the road was clear behind him. He looked back to the gauge and tried to focus on the dial. The needle was buried to the right, indicating FULL. But that's not what originally caught Colson's eye. What had caught his attention was on the end of the tank, around the weld seam. A perfect score in the metal along the edge of the weld where it had been cut open. Nothing outlandish about it if the pressure gauge didn't indicate FULL. Colson was no scientist, but a science degree is not required to understand gas, pressure, and containment. There was no way that tank was full of propane under any amount of pressure.

A crazy thought flew through Colson's mind, but he dismissed it. *That would be ridiculous,* he said to himself. He was dangerously close to the big rig, with his passenger side tires encroaching into the right lane, so he drifted back into the left lane and caught a glimpse of the truck driver glaring at him through dark sunglasses from the cab. He drove forward and slowed as he approached the tank on the lead truck. He didn't want to risk getting too close, but he didn't have to this time. He knew what he was looking for—and there it was. Same as the other tank. Compared to the height of the Peterbuilt, the Corvette was extremely low to the ground. The driver of a truck that size could easily open his door and use his car as a step stool. Colson glanced up through the glass roof panel and saw the driver of the lead truck now glaring at him. He dropped the gear to third, shot around the small convoy, and cruised at a comfortable seventy-five miles per hour until the trucks disappeared behind him.

The driver of the lead truck held his lane and his speed. He was forty years old and clean-shaven. His partner was younger by ten years and sported a neatly trimmed goatee. The pair wore sunglasses, jeans, and light gray polo shirts with STRAWN logos embroidered above the left breast. The interior of the Peterbuilt where they sat was as new and clean as its exterior. A cell phone rested in a cradle on the massive dashboard in front of the driver's partner, who sat typing furiously on his open laptop. A man's serious voice on the cell's speaker broke the relative silence over the deep-throated rumbling of the massive Cummins ISX 445 horsepower diesel engine.

"You get the tag number on that 'Vette?"

"Yep," the man with the goatee replied, closing the laptop. "Just sent it."

Keith drove his Volvo from the morgue toward Duluth in a daze. He drove slowly, ignoring the horns of the angry drivers behind him. Memories of Joshua paraded through his mind. Slide show images cascaded across the windshield—the day of his birth, his first birthday party, the times he'd helped Keith rake leaves in the yard, and his first hit in T-ball. The images sharpened, blurred, and sharpened again. He couldn't remember the last time he had cried before today. Now the wetness of his tears smeared and distorted the snapshots in his memory.

When did it all go so wrong? he wondered. *How did I lose him to drugs?*

He realized the memories stopped at about the time Josh turned six years old, when he launched his business. Was that the mistake he made? Had concentrating on becoming a successful businessman and spending so many hours at the office caused him to neglect the most important thing in his life—being a good father to his sons? Building a business seemed like an admirable endeavor, but it was damaging to his marriage. Sixty-hour weeks with no vacations. Too many missed holidays and birthdays. Too many excuses for why he had to miss another baseball game or karate tournament. *I was too busy making money to be there for my son,* he mused.

He drove past the exit to the gym where he exercised after work religiously four days a week without giving it a thought. He considered driving the Volvo into an upcoming bridge support on I-85 and ending the painful thoughts of Josh, but immediately he recognized how selfish that would be. His family would be experiencing just as much grief and would need his support and strength. What strength?

Nausea suddenly overwhelmed him. He swerved across two lanes of traffic to the emergency lane, threw open the door, and dry heaved violently. He stumbled from the car and sat on the edge of the concrete, dropping his head in his hands. His son was dead, and he could have done something to prevent it. He would have done anything. His silk necktie was choking him. He angrily jerked it from his collar, wadded it, and threw it into the grass at his feet before remembering it was a Father's Day gift from Josh two years ago. He scrambled to his feet and snatched the tie from the grass. He looked down at the tie and closed his eyes, lifting it to his cheek in a caress. The whoosh of tires on the scorching Georgia asphalt behind him made him feel isolated. People were moving on with their lives just as he had been a few hours ago, without the slightest thought of tragedy waiting around the next corner. The world continued as it had yesterday and as it would tomorrow. That was the only option available to him and Teresa. She had to be told.

He returned to his car and resumed his sad journey, dreading what was ahead. He drove through the gate at their home and parked next to Teresa's BMW. He took an unusually long time to go inside, and by the time he was walking to the door, Teresa had stepped outside. She wore jeans and a sweatshirt and her hair was pulled back, but she was still stunning at forty-two. Keith's heart constricted when he saw her.

"What are you doing home?" she asked as he walked slowly toward her with his briefcase in hand. She wasn't used to him coming home before dark. The look on his face must have said everything to her, because her hands instinctively went to her mouth. "Keith, what is it?"

Keith felt the crushing dread of having to break the news to his wife. How do you tell a mother she's lost her son? He remembered her once saying she was worried Josh would end up either dead or in jail by the time he was twenty-one. Her motherly intuition and grim prediction were right on both counts.

Teresa chewed on her bottom lip and stared at him. Keith stopped in front of her, reached for her.

"How bad is it?" she asked, taking his outstretched hand.

"It's bad," Keith answered. "It's Josh." Her hands flew to her face and she backed away, shaking her head. "He's gone, baby." On the word *gone*, a sob escaped him. He dropped the briefcase and caught her as she collapsed, and carried her to the sofa. He brushed the hair from her face and looked into her eyes. She was conscious, but her eyes were glazed. He held and rocked her like a child while she cried. They sat and cried together for what seemed like an hour before she finally spoke.

"What happened?" she asked. "What happened to my baby? Where is he?"

Keith was used to being in control, making the decisions, and having all the answers. But now he was the father of a dead child. He felt fragile and out of control. He took Teresa's face into his hands. "It was a drug overdose," he said. "He's at the morgue. I had to go identify—the body—" His voice broke again, and he retrieved his briefcase from the floor, toggled the lock and held up the plastic bag containing Joshua's belongings. "They gave me these."

Teresa looked sadly past the bag, unable to focus. "I—I can't even seem to think—" Her voice trembled. "Where did they find him?"

"In a motel room. The cleaning crew found him in the bathroom this morning."

"How will we tell Danny?" Teresa sobbed.

Keith shook his head slowly and closed his eyes. There wasn't an easy answer to her question. How do explain to a four-year-old boy that he'll never see his big brother again? "We'll need to make the funeral arrangements—call the rest of the family..." His words trailed off. They sat together in silence, watching the clock, until Danny came down the stairs rubbing sleep from his eyes. Teresa went to Danny and hugged him to her.

"What's wrong?" he said in small voice.

Keith placed a gentle hand on his head. "We have some very bad news, son."

Jonathan drove Emily's route to school and back half a dozen times, looking on both sides of the road and in parking lots for her car. No luck. Sheila called both hospitals in their area and gave them Emily's name and description, but no unidentified females had been brought into the emergency room during the time she had been missing. Sheila used a publishing program on her computer to create missing person posters with Emily's picture and called everyone she knew to help put them up the next day. By midnight both Jonathan and Emily were emotionally distraught and mentally exhausted.

Jonathan walked into Emily's room while Sheila showered. He sat on her bed and dropped his head in his hands. He remembered hearing her tossing in her sleep when she was much younger, and he saw himself peeking into her room, then going to her bed and watching her move around restlessly under the covers. On those nights, he had lifted his daughter in his arms and rocked her gently. Protecting her had been so easy back then.

He heard movement at the door and looked up to see Sheila standing there in her robe. He started to tell her what he was thinking, but his voice caught in his throat. She came to him, and he took her in his arms. "Don't worry, honey, we'll find her," he whispered. Sheila met his eyes and reached up to wipe a single tear from his cheek. It seemed like they sat there for hours, but it was only minutes before they released each other and automatically checked their cell phones and emails, hoping to see a message from Emily. There was nothing. They set their phones on their nightstands, hoping to hear something. Anything.

There was no sleep for Keith or Teresa Bartlett. At least, not what one would call real sleep. Keith heard his wife whimper and occasionally doze, but the tossing and turning meant she wasn't resting at all. He couldn't blame her tossing and turning on his lack of sleep. His thoughts and grief took all the credit.

Every twelve or fifteen minutes, he snapped from his thoughts and glanced at the clock and his cell phone lying on the nightstand. It occurred to him suddenly. He quietly eased himself out of bed and went downstairs. Joshua's cell phone lay dark inside the plastic bag with the clothes and wallet. He slipped it out, powered it up, and selected the icon for recent calls. He slid the list upward to see the last number dialed. A local number, but not one he recognized. He pushed the CALL icon and held it to his ear.

Jonathan Raines was startled awake from an exhausted and dreamless sleep by the vibration of Emily's mobile phone. He snatched the phone from the nightstand and squinted at the screen's glaring display. Sheila sat bolt upright in bed beside him. "Who is it?" she asked anxiously.

The name "Josh" was displayed in the middle of the screen. "I don't know," he said, simultaneously pressing the green answer button.

"Hello?"

"Who is this?" Keith Bartlett asked.

"Who is *this?*" Jonathan said in a suspicious tone. "You called me."

"This is Keith Bartlett."

"Keith? Keith Bartlett?" Jonathan paused and rubbed his eyes, trying to clear his thoughts and conjure up the faint recognition of the man's name. Had he been thinking clearly, he would have recognized it immediately, but recent events distorted everything. He wouldn't have recognized his own secretary's name or voice on the phone that night. Especially his daughter's phone. Jonathan and Keith lived in different cities but had been serving together on the Fulton County Chamber of Commerce board of directors for nearly a year.

"Why are you calling my daughter's cell phone at—" Jonathan turned to the clock on the nightstand. "At midnight?"

"Your daughter's cell phone? I didn't know who I was calling. I'm very sorry to disturb your family so late, but something terrible happened today," Keith said, and Jonathan heard him take a deep breath. "Our son was found dead from an overdose, and I'm grasping at straws. This was the last call Josh made. I thought whoever it was might give me some answers."

Jonathan sat up straight on the side of the bed and ran his hand through his hair. "Dear God, I'm so sorry to hear about your son. Is there anything we can do for your family?"

"No, but thanks. We are going to make the—the arrangements tomorrow," Keith said.

"Please let us know when and where the service will be held."

"I will," Keith said. "Do you have any idea how your daughter and my son know each other?"

"I didn't know they did, but they must have since his name came up on the cell." Jonathan turned to Sheila. "Did you know that Emily knew Joshua Bartlett?" She shook her head.

Jonathan reached for Sheila's hand. "We had no idea they knew each other."

The line was silent for a moment before Keith spoke again. "Again, I'm sorry to disturb you. If you don't mind asking Emily about it later, I'd appreciate it."

"I wish we could," Jonathan said, "but Emily is missing."

"Missing? What in God's name is going on? How long has she been gone?"

"I'm thinking the same thing you are, and it worries the hell out of me," Jonathan said. "You mentioned your son's death was an overdose? We believe Emily has been using drugs, too. That may have been how they knew each other."

"It could be," Keith said sadly.

"I know this isn't the time, but we are desperate to find Emily. Could my wife and I please meet with you if we don't find her soon? I don't mean tomorrow, but at some point after your son's services. It may help us find her, and that means more than you can imagine."

"Of course." Keith sounded as exhausted as Jonathan felt. "I want to know that myself. I'll call you with the details. It will probably be on Wednesday."

Keith considered calling the remaining six numbers in Josh's phone after speaking with Jonathan, but decided to just jot the numbers down and do a reverse look-up on the Internet the next day. Waking up another half dozen people tonight wouldn't bring his son back, and he had to get some sleep.

CHAPTER SIX

S trawn Tower stood out among the other high-rises in Midtown Atlanta. At eighty stories it dwarfed all other structures in sight, making them appear squat and insignificant. The Westin Peachtree Plaza, recognizable from its role in the movie *Sharky's Machine* and its rotating Sundial restaurant, paled in comparison.

Strawn had been determined to build the tallest high-rise in Atlanta and summarily dismissed the first two architects who submitted plans below his lofty standards. Floors two through fifty-two were leased to various corporations who could afford the staggering cost of a five-year lease. Strawn's corporation occupied the first floor and floors seventy-one through eighty, leaving eighteen floors hauntingly vacant.

It went without saying that the Strawn name would be the first thing a visitor would see when stepping from the polished glass and stainless steel revolving doors into the two-story lobby. A twenty-five-foot diameter sunken water fountain sat in the middle of the lobby, adorned in terra cotta tile. Beyond, a lavish semi-circular reception desk draped in mahogany judge's paneling sat against the far wall, manned with no less than three receptionists at any given time during business hours. Six-foot-high letters spelling out "Strawn" hung on the wall above the reception desk in bold relief, in the same elegant font that appeared on every piece of stationery, business card, polo shirt, corporate jet, and tractor-trailer he owned.

Six elevators serviced the tower. One on either side of the reception area and twin banks of elevators on the north and south walls were utilized by lowly executives and their minions who leased office space. The two closest to the reception area were express elevators reserved exclusively for employees of Strawn Industries. Two hidden elevators remained, and only one of those was known to exist—that being the service elevator used to lift large items such as furniture and inventory from the underground parking garage to the upper floors. Knowledge of the last elevator was entrusted to only a handful of select people. It serviced only two locations with no stops in between. Strawn's private garage, located on the ground level on the south side of the building, accessible only through an electric gate and an automatic, corrugated steel rolling door, and his office suite in the executive penthouse.

The proper-looking man seated across from Strawn had been ushered to the eightieth floor in Strawn's private express elevator after the limo pulled through the security gate and into the private garage. The driver had remained behind the wheel, watching the rolling door close completely before stepping out and opening the rear door for the man to exit. They had walked across a mirror-finished concrete floor to the elevator and were propelled upward like a missile before stepping out directly into Strawn's office. The driver had stood silent while the doors closed and dropped him back to the garage.

The visitor's admiration of Strawn's Midtown empire, James-Bond elevator, and massive corner office had vaporized in an instant. He now sat quietly, waiting, looking at the top of his hands resting on the soft chocolate leather arm rests. The large chair seemed to be swallowing him.

Strawn leaned back in his chair with a fat cigar stuck deep in one side of his mouth. He touched what appeared to be an inset piece of glass on his desktop and gestured to the opposite wall. The man had to crane his neck to see the computer monitor. Had the photo on the screen not raised his blood pressure a hundred points, he might be jealous of the massive monitor. He raised his eyes to Strawn just long enough to see him leaning forward with both palms on the desk, a satisfied smirk on his face. Strawn gently removed his cigar and laid it in an ashtray to his right. He didn't speak before making a circle with his mouth and popping out three perfect smoke rings that floated lazily skyward and dissipated above his head.

Just beyond Strawn the man caught a glimpse of the Richard Russell Building far below. Only the top three floors were visible from this height, but just enough of the structure was exposed for him to recognize the far left corner window. His office. But for how long?

Strawn touched the glass panel on his desk a second time and glanced over the man's thin, gray hair to the monitor. He cut his eyes back down and shook his head. "Truly disgusting, Judge Carter, but this next one really takes the cake." Strawn touched his desk again and pointed at the huge monitor. "I'll bet you never saw that one in four-by-six-feet high definition before, have you? What, you don't want to look?"

"Enough," Carter whispered.

"I'm sorry?" Strawn said, leaning farther over his desk.

"I said, enough!" Carter shouted. "I can't believe you broke into my home."

Strawn chuckled and his eyebrows shot upward. "Your home? These are from the hard drive in your office." Strawn plucked the cigar from the ashtray and settled back in his chair. "I'll tell you what. You go ahead and tell the police I had someone break into your computer, and I'll share these pictures with the world. We can go down in flames together. I can see it writ large in every newspaper in the country: 'Federal judge indicted for possession of child pornography.'"

They sat silent as Strawn enjoyed his cigar, the aroma filling the room. Carter looked back at his hands. "Why are you doing this? How did you do this?"

Strawn pulled the cigar away from his face and waved it around. "I don't employ idiots, Carter. I have some very talented people working for me. People who don't have to break into someone's office to access their secrets—and oh," Strawn said, interrupting his own line of thought, "don't think you can trot back to your office and delete everything, believing you'll get out of it. As I mentioned, I employee very talented people, including a variety of FBI agents." Strawn reached down to his right and held up a tiny flash drive, turning it over and over in his fingers. "Technology is amazing, isn't it? You can literally hold someone's life in your hands."

The judge watched Strawn's taunting gesture for a moment and then shook his head. "But again, why?"

Strawn eyed the flash drive for a moment before setting it next to the ashtray. A thin vein of smoke rose from the cigar beside it. "You are familiar with legislation I'm supporting, correct?"

Carter squinted. It wasn't a question he had expected. He was certain there was a federal case Strawn wanted dismissed or special treatment for some friend in trouble. "It was on the news. You're supporting legislation to legalize drugs."

Strawn smiled. "Very good, your honor."

Carter shrugged. "What does that have to do with me?"

Strawn stood, rounded his desk, and leaned against it, facing Carter. "The bill will pass and the governor will sign it. But then," Strawn held up a finger to emphasize his point, "the legal challenges will come, and it will inevitably end up in federal court. Is the light coming on in your head now, judge?"

Carter shrugged again. "I see where you're going with this, but I can't control who hears the case."

"You let me worry about that," Strawn said evenly.

Carter continued as if Strawn hadn't spoken. "And you must already know that any decision I make, for or against you, can be appealed all the way to the supreme court. I can't control that, either."

Strawn walked back to his chair and eased himself into it. "Again, you let me worry about that." Strawn reached for the flash drive and held it up for a second time. "You have to see the bigger picture, judge. The other side of the coin, if you will. You see, I can reward just as much as I can take away. For instance, have you not aspired to sit on the high court yourself?"

Carter raised his eyebrows. "First I'm being blackmailed, now I'm being bribed?"

Strawn chuckled. "Which chair at the bench do you want? The one currently occupied by the judge addicted to Oxycontin, the one who has two illegal alien housekeepers, or the one who has been keeping his mistress up in a million-dollar condo with their illegitimate child for the past ten years?"

Josh's funeral was held two days before what would have been his nineteenth birthday. Jonathan and Sheila Raines stood next to Keith, Teresa, and Danny during the graveside service. The grounds in Rosewood Cemetery were shady and peaceful, but that was impossible to appreciate on such a grim afternoon.

The group of five mourners remained at the gravesite after the small knot of extended family and friends quietly dispersed. Teresa sat in one of the folding chairs, rocking back and forth, one hand pressed against her mouth. She was dressed in a black knee-length skirt, white blouse, and black heels. Her makeup was perfect, but beneath lay the face of a stricken and drained mother. To Keith, she appeared to have aged ten years in the past three days. He wanted to take her hand and magically whisk them both to the past and make things right again.

With as much dignity as she could muster, Sheila tried to console the grieving mother, but the dark circles under her eyes and ashen face couldn't mask her own personal grief as the mother of a missing child. Jonathan stood with his head down, hands in his pockets, staring at the freshly turned earth.

The emotions running through Keith were difficult for him to contain. His mind would not let him forget how terrified Joshua must have been in his last moments. He felt overwhelming guilt and remorse over his son's death, and powerless to comfort Teresa. She looked up at him with puffy, tear-filled eyes. He wished he could reach down into the cold earth and return Josh to her. He had failed miserably as a husband and father, and guilt crushed his soul. He instinctively covered his face with his hands as tears ran freely down his cheeks.

Jonathan rested his hand on Keith's shoulder and squeezed gently. "I'm so sorry," he whispered.

"I don't understand how this could happen," Keith said, fighting to keep his voice from breaking. "He was too young. He shouldn't be dead."

Jonathan looked down at his shoes, and then back up to the staggered line of grave markers, ending at a thick wall of hardwood and pine trees in the distance. "This is how the unforeseen happens," he said hauntingly. "Just like you read about in the newspapers or see on television, but never think it will happen to you or those you love. Then one day, everything goes from normal to horrible in the twinkling of an eye, and you've lost a loved one—or your child goes missing." Tears began to well in Jonathan's eyes as he visualized Emily chatting and laughing at her sweet sixteen-birthday party.

Keith didn't say anything. He didn't know what to say. He shook his head and shrugged as if he had forgotten how to speak. Neither broke the silence for several minutes while starring at the grave. Jonathan finally turned his attention from the distant tree line and focused on Keith. "I can't even imagine the pain you and Teresa must be feeling."

A crease appeared between Keith's eyes. "I keep seeing his face. It's as if someone is constantly holding up a picture of Josh in front of me and moving with my every move. Sometimes, I... I imagine I hear him calling out to me."

Jonathan shook his head. "I think I can understand. I wish there was something I could do or say..." His voice trailed off.

Keith took a deep breath and exhaled hard, as if he were blowing as much grief from his diaphragm as possible. He turned to Jonathan, his grieving face replaced with a determined stare. "I want to help you find Emily."

Jonathan nodded. One corner of his mouth raised slightly in a reluctant smile. "If our kids knew the same people, maybe we can find Emily and find out more about your son's accident."

"I think so too, but where do we start? How do we start?"

"I have a friend who's a former undercover police officer," Jonathan said. "I think he may be able to help us. You may have heard about him. He conducts a drug-free workplace program, affiliated with the Chamber of Commerce."

Keith closed his eyes, searching his memory. "What's his name?"

"Grey Colson. His office is in the same building as the chamber. I can call him and get us an appointment if you're up to it."

Keith looked over at Teresa and saw she had been listening to the conversation. She was nodding her head. "Yes," Keith said, keeping his eyes on his wife. "Please set it up."

Grey Colson's office in the suite above the Fulton County Chamber of Commerce was small and simply furnished. The walls were bare except for a retirement plaque from the Clay County Sheriff's Office, an Appreciation of Service plaque from the narcotics squad, a commemorative badge from the DEA, and a photo of Colson with the former governor.

Two photos sat on the desk, facing his chair: one of his daughter Nichole and late wife, Ann, taken after Nichole's graduation from high school. Nichole smiled proudly, sporting her cap and gown. Ann stood proudly next to her with watery eyes and a forced but proud smile. The other photo was a five-by-seven of little Jack wearing a soft blue gown and lying on a fuzzy white blanket. His large, bright eyes revealed an innocent naivety about the cold world he was born into. They were Colson's favorite photographs.

There was enough room in his office for a small conference table and couch sitting against the far wall. Colson occasionally slept on the couch when he didn't feel like fighting the afternoon traffic to the hotel. About once or twice a month he would drive over to Clay County and stay overnight with Nichole, Bobby, and little Jack. He made a point not to intrude too often, but he was more than happy to babysit little Jack and give Nichole and Bobby the chance to enjoy a date night.

He was looking at the photo of Ann and Nichole and thinking about that graduation day when his cell phone startled him, suddenly playing Steely Dan. He reminded himself for the fourth time in two years to change it to something new, and then he answered it.

"Good morning, Larry. How's everything in Clay County?"

Morgan's voice was jovial. "We're doing everything we can to keep the jail full and the courts empty."

Colson chuckled. "Like we used to say around the holidays, Christmas in jail, no bond, no bail."

"You got that right," Morgan said agreeably. "Hey, I've been getting great feedback about your work, Grey. People really like your presentation. They can tell you're the genuine article. You really are making a good impression and a difference."

"Thanks, Larry. I've learned a lot of things from this perspective that I never thought about before."

"I knew you were the man for the job."

"Whoa there," Colson said. "I've enjoyed these past months and have no problem sticking with it for a while, but you still need to keep someone in mind, because I don't have another thirty years to invest in a second career."

"I know, I know," Morgan said dismissively, "but you can't blame me for trying. Hey, did you happen to see the new public service announcement against the pro-drug lobby yet?"

Colson nodded as if Morgan could see him. "Yeah, last night. The campaign slogan 'Will this be the new normal?' is a good strategy. I thought it was well made and very compelling, especially that scene of a school bus full of kids and their driver having an LSD hallucination, thinking the steering wheel had disappeared."

"We had to pull out all the stops. Strawn's influence is growing, and the number of people in his pocket multiplies by the day."

Colson sighed. "As a buddy of mine used to say, all we can do is all we can do."

The line was silent for a long moment, then Morgan said, "You still drive that 'Vette?"

"What?" Colson said at the unexpected change in the subject.

"I just bought a C7," Morgan said proudly. "We're having a charity car show this weekend at church if you'd like to clean yours up and show it off."

"Sorry, man. I'll be spending time with little Jack and giving the kids a well-deserved weekend away."

Morgan wouldn't let it go. "Well, if you're free the next Saturday, you should come down to Road Atlanta. My club is having another charity get-together, a breast cancer event. I can teach you how to drive like a real man."

"Right," Colson said with a chuckle, "we'll see about that. I'll be around you so fast, you'll step out of that C7 at ninety miles per hour, thinking your engine died. I can come by for an hour or so, then I'll need to head back south."

ᴄ◈ᴄʜᴀᴘᴛᴇʀ SEVEN◈

W hen Keith and Jonathan arrived at his office promptly at 10 a.m., Colson invited the two men to join him at the small conference table in the corner. He pulled two bottles of water from a small refrigerator against the wall and handed one to each man.

Colson was dressed in a black suit, a white starched shirt, and a black tie. His shoes were the shiniest Keith had seen since leaving the Navy. The fact that Colson's suit was tailored didn't escape Keith's attention. He couldn't have purchased a suit jacket off the rack to accommodate his broad shoulders and thick chest so well. Keith had no doubt if he and Jonathan were strapped to opposite ends of a weight bar, Colson could bench-press them a dozen times without the need of a spotter. He looked at the perfect Windsor knot in Colson's tie and couldn't help but feel it was a display of respect for Joshua. Keith still felt numb from the funeral and had managed only two hours of sleep, which were interrupted by nightmares and tossing. He told Colson about the circumstances surrounding his son's death, and Colson silently shook his head.

"I'm so sorry," Colson said. His attention turned to Jonathan as he explained the situation with Emily, including his surveillance and trash pull at the house on Cedarcrest Road, and how they had discovered one of the phone numbers in Joshua's cell phone was associated with the same house.

"They knew each other," Jonathan said in a matter-of-fact tone. "There has to be a connection to help lead us to Emily. There has to be. What can we do from here?"

Colson set empathy aside and got down to business, admonishing Jonathan for playing cop. "You're dealing with something very dangerous, Jon. May I call you Jon?" Jonathan nodded as Colson continued. "You two really need to let the police handle this."

Jonathan cut his eyes briefly to the floor in mild embarrassment. Watching him, Colson recalled his own actions when his daughter was being held captive by a lunatic. It was only by the grace of God they both hadn't been killed. He understood what Jonathan was feeling this very second, but it wouldn't be right to encourage him to act on his own. Colson was being a hypocrite, but it couldn't be helped.

Jonathan raised his eyes. The frustration in his voice was clear. "Do you really think the police are going to actively look for Emily?"

Colson met Jonathan's serious gaze and took a deep breath. "Probably not," he admitted. "I'm afraid it's a numbers game, really. The APD gets hundreds of missing person reports every week. A seventeen-year-old who's only a couple of weeks from her eighteenth birthday, with a history of drug use and threats of running away, is not a high priority for them."

Jonathan's expression was sullen. He sadly shook his head and rolled the bottle of water between his hands. Keith took the opportunity to break the silence.

"Do you think the cops will try to find Joshua's dealer? Can't he be charged with Joshua's death?"

"Theoretically," Colson said. He leaned back and made a steeple with his fingers. "If he could be identified, and if it could be proven the heroin Joshua shot up had came from that particular dealer, then the D.A. might be able to get a conviction for voluntary manslaughter because Joshua died as the result of a felony committed by the dealer. But I really don't see it happening."

Keith held out his hands, palms up, and spoke more sharply than he intended. "Then what can we do? Someone should be held responsible for my son's death, and we have to try to find Emily."

"I understand," Colson said.

"Well, I don't," Keith blurted and sank back into his chair, staring at Colson. He looked around the small office as they sat silent for several moments. "I'm sorry," he said finally, "I'm just having serious doubts about our criminal justice system right now."

Colson looked up at the ceiling and closed his eyes as he spoke. "There's an obvious connection with your children and the Cedarcrest house. We need the police to look into it and find out what's going on there." He rolled his fingers on the table and leveled his gaze on Jonathan. "Give me the list of tag numbers you wrote down, and I'll get them to someone I know in the narcotics division."

"What about the bag of garbage?" Jonathan asked.

"I'll meet you tomorrow and pick it up," Colson said. "I'll get it to the right people, but it probably won't result in a search warrant, even if something is found."

"Why not?" Jonathan said with a tone of frustration. "Why is everything so complicated?"

"It's a chain of custody issue, Jon," Colson explained, "but finding something may keep them looking."

Keith took a sip of water. "I hope so."

"Oh, I have something else in mind that will definitely get them interested." Colson grinned, relaxed now as the wheels in his head began turning. He hadn't formulated such plans in his mind for almost two decades. His undercover persona was rising to the surface, an identity he thought long dead and forgotten.

Keith and Jonathan glanced at each other, then leaned forward and rested their elbows on the small table, intrigued by Colson's tease.

"What is it?" Keith said.

"It involves a CI who used to work for me in narcotics," he answered. "I'll let you know how it works out when it's over."

"CI?" Keith said.

"Confidential informant."

"Oh, okay. Can I ask you a personal question?" Keith said, momentarily thankful to be distracted from his grief and anxious about the prospect of finding answers to help bring some amount of closure.

"Sure, go ahead."

"Why did you leave law enforcement? Did you burn out?"

"No, I enjoyed my career with the exception of a few co-workers who had no business being in police work. I intended to stay a full thirty years, but my wife passed away, and that's when I realized I needed a change. A fresh start."

"I'm sorry," Keith said. "I shouldn't have been so nosy. I didn't realize—"

"It's okay. I just don't bring the subject up often." He stood, stepped to his desk, and gently lifted little Jack's picture in his hands. He looked fondly at the photo. "It was a difficult time, but God has a way of healing us. In my case," he said, turning the photo toward Jonathan and Keith, "he blessed me with a grandson named Jack."

Both men smiled. "Handsome boy," Jonathan said. Keith's smile was genuine but forced, as the photo refreshed his memory of Joshua as an infant.

Colson set the photo back on down, crossed his arms, and leaned back against the desk. "When I worked undercover years ago, we worked the supply side of the drug problem. That's what we were trained to do, and it's the only thing we knew how to do. It was only recently I realized attacking the supply side alone can't eradicate the entire problem."

Keith looked puzzled. "What do you mean?" he said, finding a sudden interested in drug enforcement.

"Do you know that since 1980 the U.S. government has spent more than two hundred and ninety billion dollars of taxpayer money trying to stop drugs from coming into this country?" Colson said. His visitors shook their heads. "That's more money than we've spent on all biomedical research combined. We've spent more money trying to stop drugs from coming into America than we've spent on finding a cure for cancer and heart disease combined." He looked directly at Keith. "And what do you think has been the result of this enormous expenditure of our tax dollars?"

"Not much," Keith answered.

"That's right. Not much. In fact, in the last ten years, cocaine and heroin production in source countries has doubled. Cocaine and heroin are cheaper today on the streets of America than they've ever been." He paused, looking from Keith to Jonathan. "I finally realized that in order to really have an impact on America's drug problem, we need to attack the demand side through drug prevention, drug treatment, and drug education. Through research to determine the demand for drugs in America, we have learned that seventy-seven percent of the people who use illegal drugs in this country are employed. That means the largest concentration of demand for drugs in America is one place—the American workplace."

"So that's why you decided to work in the drug-free workplace program," Jonathan said.

"Yes, but only after doing my own research. I wasn't a believer until a few months ago, but now I'm convinced if we could get every single business in this state drug-free, we could potentially reduce the drug and crime problem by seventy-seven percent. Drugs and crime are intertwined. They are one and the same."

"But I don't understand," Keith said. "How can drug-free workplace programs attack the demand side of the problem?"

"In several ways," Colson answered. "First, it has been proven that drug testing at work is a deterrent to drug use. Second, in order to qualify for state-mandated discounts on workers comp insurance, the employer must provide drug education to every employee, every year. That's drug education delivered to a captive audience that parents can take home and share with their children to help keep them drug-free. That's prevention, and that really is the only way we can get drug education to parents by the way. They won't attend a free seminar to get the information. Believe me, we've tried. And third, the employer makes drug treatment available to employees who test positive. That's drug treatment the employee otherwise might not be able to afford."

Keith nodded, and Jonathan said, "Makes sense to me."

Colson smiled. "That seven-point-five percent discount on your workers comp premiums probably helped out some too, didn't it?"

"Well, yes, of course," Jonathan said.

"Did you enjoy undercover work?" Keith asked, changing the subject.

Colson shook his head. "Yes, I enjoyed putting the bad guys away. But it's not as glamorous as TV makes it out to be. The drug world is full of tragedy and human beings at their worst. Sometimes I felt I was in a position where good and evil were traveling too close together, and that made me uncomfortable."

"What do you mean?" Jonathan said.

"To do some of the things necessary to be a good undercover cop, to protect the innocent, you have to do things you'd rather not do."

"Like use drugs?" Keith asked.

"No, absolutely not," Colson said adamantly. "I've never used an illegal drug in my life and I never will. I'm talking about the way you have to use people. The way you have to use informants, the way you have to let some of the smaller drug dealers go in order to move up the ladder to get the higher-level dealers—things like that."

Keith shook his head. "I never really gave it any thought. But isn't drug use always going to be around? Isn't it so deeply embedded in our culture that America will always have a drug problem?"

Colson's voice was measured and relaxed. "Drug use may be a way of life right now, but it doesn't have to stay that way. And we don't have to passively accept it."

"So you think we really can do something to stop America's drug problem?" Keith said.

"Probably not while guys like this are around." Colson walked around the desk and pulled a brown accordion folder from the bottom drawer. He sat and drew out a two-inch-thick stack of papers and dropped them with a dull thud in front of the two men. "Those papers document a billionaire named Jack Strawn and his cohorts in their ongoing crusade to legalize drugs in America."

Jonathan's jaw dropped as he stared at the thick folder. "A billionaire is trying to legalize drugs?"

"Not just one billionaire; there are three," Colson said, holding up three fingers. "Do you realize that forty years ago there were only five billionaires in the entire country? Today there are more than four hundred. And these three are all working together to legalize drugs. They have flooded the Internet with pro-drug propaganda, and the sheeple are eating it up."

Jonathan leafed through the stack for several minutes before handing the papers to Keith. Keith took his time, reading topic headings and summary statements, trying to digest as much information as possible. He found himself becoming irate. He took a deep breath and sharply exhaled when he had read enough, then he looked at Colson while holding up the stack of papers.

"My son just died because of a drug these guys want to legalize," Keith emphasized by pointing at the papers. "This is outrageous. Legalization of drugs is repulsive to me. What's being done to stop them?"

Colson shook his head. "Not much, I'm afraid. We've tried to take a stand against them, along with a few other nonprofit drug prevention groups and some law enforcement agencies. You may have seen Larry Morgan's public service announcement recently, but there isn't enough money in the operating funds to support a large campaign. It's the billionaires who have all the money."

"Doesn't it make you angry?" Keith asked.

Colson shrugged. "Can't be mad every minute of the day,"

"I want to stand up against these guys as the father of a dead, drug-addicted child," Keith said. "What can I do? I don't even care how much of an impact it will make, but I have to do something."

Colson considered Keith from across the desk for a moment. He turned to his laptop, flipped it open, and waited for it to come to life. He clicked his calendar and looked back to Keith. "I'm scheduled to talk about the drug-free workplace program at the chamber's breakfast networking event next Monday. Would you want to take a few minutes of my presentation time to talk to the group about what happened to your son? There will be more than four hundred business owners there."

"Absolutely," Keith said without hesitation.

Colson gave both men his cell phone numbers at his office door. "I'll have my mobile phone with me day and night, and I don't expect to be anywhere out of range. Call me the minute you find out anything new about Emily's disappearance, regardless of the time of day, okay?" Jonathan nodded, and both men shook Colson's hand.

Keith and Jonathan walked in silence to the sidewalk, each digesting information he hadn't anticipated hearing. Before parting ways on the sidewalk, Keith put a hand on Jonathan's shoulder. "What did you think of that meeting?"

"Colson is hard to read," Jonathan said. "I think it's because he operates behind some protective emotional barriers. But don't get me wrong, I really believe he wants to help. I admire people who know who they are and stand firm on their beliefs. He obviously believes in the work he's doing."

Keith checked the time. "To his credit, he never looked at his watch even once during the meeting. He gave us all that time without seeming at all concerned about his schedule."

Jonathan nodded. "Yeah, I think meeting with us was more than just professional courtesy. He's a little rough around the edges and sarcastic at times, but I believe he's sincere about the drug problem and doesn't seem afraid to stick his neck out to be lopped off by a bunch of powerful people. He told me his grandson's future is driving him."

Keith slid his right hand into his pants pocket and fidgeted with loose change, trying to convince himself that the actions he intended to take were to protect other children and not to soothe his own battered conscience. He wanted to ask Colson, but he had been too timid at the time. He needed to strike while the iron was hot.

"If I can get an appointment with this Strawn character, do you think Colson would go with me to talk to him?"

Jonathan raised an eyebrow. "What are you going to say to a billionaire? And don't you think Colson would have talked to him already if he thought there was a snowball's chance of making him reconsider?"

"You could go with us," Keith added. "There's strength in numbers."

Jonathan shook his head. "I'm afraid I'm not cut out for a confrontation—sorry."

Keith shrugged. "I don't want that either. I'm going to try to reason with him. I find it absurd that such successful businessmen would involve themselves in a crusade to make drugs legal. It doesn't make sense. Even billionaires have employees—thousands of them. Surely they wouldn't want a bunch of dope-head addicts working for them and screwing up their dynasties. It's insanity. Maybe he's just surrounded by yes-men who don't have the guts to make him realize how harmful drug legalization will be."

"Okay, okay," Jonathan said, holding up a hand to slow Keith's emotional tirade. "You know what power does to these people. They're used to having their way and squashing their enemies like a steamroller. Let's just say, hypothetically that is, you request an appointment and Strawn actually agrees to give you five minutes. Then when you make your emotional yet reasonable plea, he tells you to go to hell. Who's to say one of his goons won't toss you off the top of Strawn Tower when you lose it and get in his face?"

Keith eyed Jonathan and grinned. "Why do you think I want Colson with me?"

CHAPTER EIGHT

Jack Strawn closed his eyes, crossed his arms, and rocked back and forth in his executive leather office chair. Bright reflections of early afternoon sunlight blazed through the floor-to-ceiling windows behind him from the steel and glass office buildings across the street.

Clay Haggart squinted at the somewhat eerie silhouette of Strawn across the desk and tapped on his tablet, minimizing the media player icon when the recording came to an end. Strawn continued his slow motion rocking. Haggart couldn't tell if he was listening to the recording of Morgan and Colson's conversation or taking a nap. Nearly ninety seconds after the recording ended, Strawn finally spoke without opening his eyes.

"When was that recorded?"

Haggart quickly tapped his tablet, recalling the recording to make certain he provided Strawn with the precise information. "Nine fifty-five a.m. today, sir."

Strawn finally ceased rocking, opened his eyes, and swiveled his chair to face the former UFC fighter. "Public service announcement, my ass," he said, forcing a disgusted exhale from his diaphragm. "The only thing they do for the public is pick their pockets to pay their ridiculous salaries." Strawn pointed a finger at Haggart as if he were to blame. "And they have the nerve to call it a service? Morgan is trying to make a name for himself because he wants to be the state attorney general."

Strawn flipped open a mahogany box on his desk, pulled out a fat cigar, and snapped the lid closed. Although Haggart towered over Strawn and everyone else in the multi-billion-dollar corporation at six feet, four inches—and easily outweighed them by seventy pounds—his eye twitched involuntarily when Strawn slapped the box shut. He had a difficult time accepting his reaction to this short, dumpy, overweight weakling boss. The fact that Strawn made him flinch infuriated him. The combination of money and power was the only possible explanation. He sat silent, watching his boss light a cigar with a monogrammed Zippo lighter.

Strawn continued his lecture between puffs. "What Morgan doesn't realize..." He paused and glanced at the cigar's tip to satisfy himself it was well lit before continuing. "Is that I couldn't care less about his personal ambition, until his ambitions get in the way of mine."

Haggart sat straight. Stoic. Strawn carefully placed his cigar on the edge of his ashtray and pointed to the tablet. "Morgan and his new flunky, Colson, are really starting to piss me off."

Haggart permitted himself a slight grin as he swiped a document to life on his tablet, filling the screen with a confidential report on Strawn letterhead. His research was thorough. He hoped Strawn took note of his diligent work. He would prove he was far more valuable than just a brain-damaged bodyguard and washed-up fighter. He began reciting the information as if reading an obituary from the paper: "Grey Colson, former major with the Clay County Sheriff's Office. Widowed. One female child, Nichole. The daughter is married and resides with her husband, Robert Roper, in Clay County with Colson's grandchild, Jack. Robert is employed as an assistant D.A. in Clay County."

"Jack?" Strawn mouthed and raised his eyebrows in approval of the child's name as Haggart continued. "Colson currently lives in a Daytona Beach condo and commutes to Atlanta twice per month to conduct drug-free workplace programs for the state. He—"

Strawn held up his hand, stopping Haggart's laundry list of information. "He," Strawn emphasized, "is not important. A little fish you don't need to be wasting my time and money to investigate unless and until I direct you to do it."

Haggart's grin vaporized. He sat silent as Strawn narrowed his gaze. "You understand?" the boss barked.

75

Haggart nodded quickly, but his eye twitched for a second time at the outburst. He silently fantasized about what type of noise Strawn would make if he used his 270-pound frame to launch Strawn and his leather chair through the window to the street below. His grin returned, but his affirmative nod made it appear respectful.

Strawn held his gaze for another five seconds, lifted his cigar, and eased back in his chair. He drew a long puff and blew three perfect smoke rings at the ceiling. "My resources are used wisely, young man. We deal with a problem only when necessary—and right now my problem is with Morgan, not some part-time, run-and-fetch retiree he employs."

Haggart resumed his nod of understanding. "Yes, sir," he said.

"How many people does Morgan have working for him in his ridiculous 'Drugs Don't Work' program?" Strawn asked mockingly while forming air quotes at the mention of the title.

Haggart swiped another file on his tablet and studied his notes. "Actually, just one. Colson."

Strawn nodded and cut his eyes upward in thought. "Here's what you're going to do," he said in the tone of a teacher assigning homework. "You're going to make the call and—"

"Actually, sir," Haggart said, "he doesn't talk on the phone. I have to use a—"

"Don't interrupt me!" Strawn shouted. "You know what I mean. Send your code or whatever the hell you do, but Morgan's campaign against me is going to stop, and I want it stopped yesterday. Are we clear?"

Haggart nodded once again. He knew Strawn expected to be called "sir," but he had used those all up for today. Strawn was extremely lucky he hadn't reached across the desk and popped his head like a zit. There was nothing he could do to impress or please such a hateful human being. Three years of loyalty. Three years of coming to work even when he was sick and spewing from both ends. Three years of taking notes, driving Strawn all over the city, picking up his dry cleaning and stinking black-market cigars. And three years of being belittled and spoken to like a child. He deserved better than

76

this. He would send the code all right; he just wished he could double the price and have the assassin whack Strawn instead. He lowered his head in mock humility to shield his sneer. He didn't dare meet Strawn's gaze until he could force a straight face.

Strawn's stern expression returned to its normal state of haughty condescension as he enjoyed another long puff from his fat cigar. "My bill will pass and the governor will sign it into law by the first of the year. There will no longer be a need for social programs, drugs-don't-work speeches, or public service announcements. Nothing left for Morgan's little sidekick cop to do, so he'll just tuck his tail between his legs and go back to his little apartment on the beach to recycle aluminum cans for a living."

Haggart swiped another page on his tablet. "Colson does private investigations when he's not working for Morgan," he said cautiously. Strawn didn't blow up this time. The man was totally and completely unpredictable, but that's how he wanted to be perceived. That was his tactic—to keep everyone off balance.

Strawn stood, turned to the city skyline, and spoke to the glass. "You've obviously done a lot of research on Colson. There must be something you think I should know about him or you wouldn't have gone to so much trouble." Strawn faced Haggart again with cigar in hand. "Go on, I'm all ears."

It was the opportunity Haggart had been waiting for. Among all the petty assignments and crappy chores he had been ordered to do over the past three years, he had learned this man. As unpredictable as he may seem, there was a pattern to his behavior. It was as if he looked forward to dressing down everyone who worked for him. Once he blew his top and re-established his alpha-male status, he was open to more reasonable conversations. And there was one thing he couldn't hide: a hunger for information.

"Over a year ago," Haggart began, "Colson became involved in a case being worked by the FBI and the Volusia County Sheriff's Office. It was focused on a dirty cop and a prominent businessman in the Daytona Beach area."

Strawn shrugged. "And why should I have an interest in that?"

"The case report indicates the dirty cop and businessman kidnapped Colson's daughter," Haggart said.

Strawn exaggerated a shrug and held out his hands. "Again, why should that concern me? I sure as hell didn't kidnap his kid."

"It's what Colson did I thought you should know about."

"What might that be?"

Haggart scrolled the page down to the last paragraph and read aloud. "FBI Agent McCann's investigative case summary concluded that Mr. Grey Colson should not be held criminally liable for his actions on 20 July 2013 regarding Mr. Martin Cash and/or Sergeant Franklin Pickett. The subsequent Federal Grand Jury returned a No Bill of Indictment regarding same on 17 August 2013." He glanced from his notes to Strawn. "Colson is a vigilante. He killed them— both."

Strawn's face remained solid rock, waiting. Haggart took it as a prompt to continue. Strawn obviously was waiting on the connection, but he wouldn't wait long.

"We also red-flagged him just days ago," Haggart said, raising his eyes to meet Strawn's, "on Interstate 75, just north of Macon."

Strawn nodded slowly. "Why?"

"He was being nosy around a couple of our transport vehicles coming from our East Coast warehouse."

"So that explains your extensive research," Strawn said.

Haggart adjusted his large frame in the small chair and wondered how harshly he would be verbally disemboweled after his next statement. "I have to admit I took some personal interest in Colson's activities."

"Oh," Strawn said with raised eyebrows. "Should I dock your pay for the wasting company time for personal matters?" he added sarcastically.

Haggart didn't directly answer Strawn's question. "Colson does employ another man in his investigation business. Jay Taylor."

Strawn bellowed laughter and slapped the top of his desk with his palm. "You mean Jay 'The Once Terrible' Taylor?"

"The very same."

"Well, damn," Strawn said, shaking his head as his hysterical outburst subsided. "Small world, ain't it?"

Haggart didn't echo his boss's laughter or nod in agreement. His face remained a solid block of stone. "Yes, sir. It certainly is."

Haggart touched the power icon on his tablet as Strawn slipped into his chair and took another draw from his cigar. There was no more information on Colson to offer, nor would there be unless or until he was directed to expend resources to do so by Strawn himself. "Will that be all?" Haggart asked, breaking several moments of silence.

Strawn answered only by nodding and tapping his index finger on the inlaid glass on his desk.

Haggart slipped his tablet in a satchel next to his chair and stood. He watched Strawn for beat. His boss appeared deep in thought, still tapping on the glass. Haggart crossed the oak floor to the door without being dismissed. Strawn stopped him as he reached for the handle.

"When you place your order…"

Haggart spun on his heel at Strawn's voice. "Yes."

Strawn had already settled back in his chair amid a light fog of cigar smoke. Although a man of quick decisions, Strawn was not one for knee-jerk reactions. It wasn't unusual for him to briefly ponder important issues, but that went without saying since there were no inconsequential matters surrounding a man of such wealth and influence. He leveled an even stare at Haggart.

"Make it a double."

The Corolla's engine died, and the car chugged to a stop. The driver managed to miss the mailbox as she coasted partially into a driveway, leaving the left back portion of the bumper sticking out into the road. Thirty-seven-year-old Erica Lance, former Miss Crawford County and winner of three regional beauty contests, checked her makeup in the rear-view mirror. She never used her real last name while doing this type of work. It was something Grey Colson had taught her, and she could hear him as clearly as the day he said it:

No matter where you are or where you go, it's inevitable someone you know will see you and call you by name. If you're working with a target, you'll get burned if you've used a fake first name. You can always get around the last name by saying you are divorced or adopted by a stepfather.

Colson was her first controlling agent, but that was almost eighteen years ago when she worked at Barley's Billiards, serving drinks and handing out pool cues. Barley's wasn't the normal dive one might expect, but rather a high-class billiards establishment with eight- and nine-foot Schmidt tables with leather pockets, a large rectangular mahogany bar situated dead center among the sea of green felt, a single snooker table with a private score keeper, and floor-to-ceiling windows providing a breathtaking view of the downtown skyline from its fourth-floor perch on Powers Ferry Road. The clientele were the properly dressed and groomed businessmen and women of the northern Atlanta suburbs.

Colson and his partner came in almost every night. And almost every night they entertained different friends. Most of the customers were stuffed-shirt business types who tried to act cooler than they were in real life while flirting with the waitresses and bragging about business deals. Colson and his partner were different. They never flirted, drank too much, or caused any problems. They dressed a little more casually than the businessmen with their untucked shirts and sneakers, but they were always well dressed and within the club's standards.

Erica knew Colson as Grey Travis for the first six months. That was until Colson and his partner invited her for a drink in another bar on the first floor. She had felt comfortable enough since it was the middle of the day and one floor below her work. Colson had ordered coffees for all three as she slid across the table and into the booth. Colson had grinned at the waitress after placing the order and turned his attention to her.

Erica didn't know what to expect from Colson, or Travis, at that time. Some get-rich-quick scheme came to mind, but several of her friends had already tried to sucker her into those, and she wasn't interested. She hoped Grey and his partner were modeling agents or, better yet, movie producers who wanted to discover her and make her famous.

What Colson proposed was the last thing she considered. It wasn't even on the list.

"You're a cop?" Erica had said in bewilderment as she studied the badge Colson laid on the table in front of her. Her eyes traveled from the table to Colson as he closed the wallet and slid it back off the table.

Colson had nodded. "My real last name is Colson, and this is my partner, Mike Whitaker."

"Am I in some kind of trouble?" Erica had asked, her voice revealing a hint of fear.

Colson had laid both hands palms-down on the table and smiled. "Of course not. I think you could be a huge help to us, and you stand to make pretty decent money on the side. That is, if you are interested."

Erica had listened to Colson through two cups of coffee and was intrigued to say the least. Her once-boring job handing out pool cues and racks of billiard balls instantly became a game of cat and mouse, *Miami Vice,* and *The Spy Who Loved Me* all rolled into one. She looked forward to coming in to work, knowing a secret no one else knew, alerting Colson to new players who tried to impress her, bragging about their connections and access to designer drugs. Things they would never reveal to other men. And Colson paid handsomely for an introduction.

The adrenalin rush had become so addictive that, for Erica, the money became a non-issue. It lasted three years with Colson before he transferred out. There hadn't been anyone like him since. Erica kept in contact with him off and on for a couple of years, but he moved up in rank and they lost touch. She had heard he finally retired and moved away after the death of his wife. Then, like a voice from the grave, Colson had called her last week. She considered not answering the unknown number that popped up on her cell phone, but was glad she did.

They had spent an hour catching up, laughing about old dopers and agents who had retired and how things had changed—before he asked for this favor. She had hesitated. It had been a long time since she had enjoyed the game, but after all, it was a favor for Colson.

Erica checked herself in the rear-view mirror once again. Even at thirty-seven, her natural skin color, long lashes, and full lips made for a stunning sight to be admired by men of every age. In fact, she was even more attractive than she had been in her twenties. She pulled the keys from the ignition, opened the driver's door, and swung out her long, tanned legs and feet adorned with five-inch heels. As she walked toward the house, she hiked her already too-short skirt an inch higher and unbuttoned the third button of her tight-fitting cropped sweater.

The door was opened after the third ring by a tall, thin hippie reject wearing a decades-old Grateful Dead t-shirt under a tan leather vest. His eyes were half-closed, and a cigarette hung casually from his lips. Erica looked at his pale skin, gaunt look, and track marks. He might as well have the word "junkie" written in magic marker across his forehead. She and her friends referred to these hippies without a cause as "rippies" because they were ripping off the hippie culture to justify their copious drug use.

"Yeah?" the guy said, looking first at Erica's "come-do-me" shoes then up the twenty miles of legs to her Lycra miniskirt, before finally coming to rest on the faint freckles in the cleavage between her perfect, natural breasts.

"Hey sweetie," Erica said in her best Southern belle accent, "my piece-of-crap car just broke down again. I'm such an airhead," she added with her signature eye roll, "I forgot to charge my cell phone, and I was wondering if I could use your phone to call my brother? He's the only one who knows how to fix it."

The would-be hippie hesitated for ten seconds while the long-dormant interest in his groin area stirred to life and overrode the paranoia from his drug-addled brain. He looked past Erica to the eight-year-old Toyota blocking the entrance to his driveway and made a decision that could later cost him the next ten years of his life.

"Yeah, come on in," he said, the cigarette jiggling with his words.

Erica brushed her breasts against the man's chest as she squeezed past him through the doorway and into a dark living room. She walked to the middle of the room, did her best center stage pirouette, and looked at him sweetly. "Phone?" she asked.

"Uh, it's in the bedroom. I'll get it." He shuffled past Erica, almost bumping into the wall as he focused on her flawlessly sculpted assets.

"Crap on a cracker," Erica whispered to herself, surveying the filthy sofa, worn carpet, broken and threadbare recliner, and food left out on the coffee table. Breathing through her mouth to avoid the odor of houseatosis to the *nth* degree, she brushed imaginary cockroaches from her arms. The hippie returned with a cordless phone handset.

"What's wrong?" he said.

"Oh, nothing, I'm just a little chilly," Erica lied. She took the phone and dialed Rick's cell. It answered on the fifth ring.

"You've reached Rick, please leave the name of your first pet and your mom's favorite color, and I'll call you back."

"Very funny, bro," Erica said. "Now be serious a minute; I need your help. My car broke down again." No answer. "Yeah, yeah, I know," Erica said, nodding her head. "But you know I don't have the money to get another one right now." Silence. "I don't know, hold on a minute." She looked innocently at the hippie. "Hey sweetie, what's the address here?"

The man closed his eyes tight, as if working long math in his head. "It's, uh, 415 Cedarcrest Road," he finally said, opening his eyes and grinning at his accomplishment.

She smiled and gave him a wink, thinking, *that must have hurt.*

"It's 415 Cedarcrest Road," she said to the still-silent phone. "Yeah, yeah, I figured you would be getting ready to go out, but can't you please come and get this thing started?"

Continued silence.

Erica had played this game for years and was as good as anyone at it. Maybe the best. Unfortunately, there are no national "best of" categories or academy awards for best performance by a confidential informant. Of course, being named on such a list or receiving such an award would totally defeat the purpose. If anything, it could get her killed. The least that could happen would be for one or more of the dope heads she set up to stalk and rape her raw. Her one-sided conversation with Rick was frustrating at best. He thinks he's cute and funny, but he could be a jerk at times. Why make her little act more difficult than it already was? She continued without him.

"Okay, if you come and help me out, I promise I'll try to find something to party with."

"Ten minutes," Rick said. His unexpected voice almost startled her. "Get to work."

"Thank you bro, you're the best," Erica said with a hint of sarcasm. She hit the OFF button and handed the phone back to her host. "He'll be here in ten minutes. He only lives about five miles away." They stood staring at each other until Erica reached out and patted his scrawny arm. "You were so sweet to let me use the phone. Do you mind if I wait here for my brother?"

"Yeah, I guess that's okay." He looked nervously at the clock.

Erica held out her hand. "Thanks, what's your name?"

"I'm Derrick."

She looked at his dirty fingernails and resisted the impulse to recoil while shaking hands with her new friend. "I'm Erica. Do you mind if we sit down?" she said, secretly preferring to do anything but be in physical contact with the disgusting furniture.

Derrick pointed to the sofa as he lowered himself into a recliner. "Sure, go ahead."

Erica eased her graceful frame onto the couch and crossed her million-dollar legs. She waited politely for her host to offer tea and crumpets, but that was never going to happen. At the risk of being rude and violating the first rule in Ms. Pettigrew's Guide for Nice

Refined Young Ladies, she asked, "Do you have anything to drink— beer or some wine, maybe?"

Derrick's eyebrows scrolled upward toward his receding hairline while he groomed his goatee with his index finger and thumb. "You want a drink?" he said.

"Yeah, that would be very nice," she said in her best Scarlett O'Hara imitation.

"I think we have some Jack Black."

She produced the same smile that earned her $400 a night as an exotic dancer. "Got any Coke? You know, the kind you drink—to mix with the Jack." He stood and took two steps before Erica's next comment stopped him in his tracks.

"But I'll take the other kind if you have that too."

Derrick eyed her for a long moment, and she guessed what was running through his mind. She was gorgeous, but that was the problem. She might be genuinely grateful he let her use the phone, but he also knew if she hadn't needed help, she wouldn't stop to check his pulse if she had run over him in the street with that piece-of-crap Toyota. The little paranoia devil on his shoulder stirred. No question he would like to wear her like a feedbag, but he had to be careful.

"I'll get the drink," he said evenly and walked from the room.

She glanced at her watch once he was out of sight—10:45 p.m. Rick would be here in about five minutes, so she had to work fast, maintaining a delicate balance between aggressiveness and subtlety, sprinkled with a dash of potential erotic fantasy. The hippie appeared through the door a minute later and handed her a plastic cup.

"I'm out of Jack," he said, "but there was some vodka and orange juice left."

"Thank you, sugar," Erica said, taking the cup and raising it to her lips. The odor of alcohol was so strong she stared down into the cup, surprised the clear 100-proof liquor was discolored at all by the miniscule amount of juice added. She took a tiny sip and almost winced.

"You're not gonna have a drink with me?"

"Nah, I'm not much of a drinker."

Erica surmised Derrick was most likely strung out on heroin at the moment and didn't want to damage his liver. She suppressed a laugh from the irony and smiled instead.

"Well, you know what they say: everything in moderation." She raised the cup in salute and took another dainty sip. The drink brought back memories of Grey Colson, who had always cautioned her to be careful when drinking anything given to her by guys like Derrick. He told her to take fake sips, but she figured if Derrick had put anything like roofies in the drink, the strong liquor would dissolve all chemical properties of the drug down to a harmless sugar base. She shrugged it off, knowing Rick would arrive in a few minutes. Maybe the liquor would stifle the sweaty stench from the room that currently lodged in the back of her throat. She leaned forward and looked around the room, as if checking for invisible eavesdroppers. Her eyes eventually landed on Derrick.

"Hey listen, sweetie, my brother was getting ready to go out partying when I called. Once he gets my car running again, I'll probably follow him to the club. You wanna go along?"

Derrick's eyebrows shot up. "You want me to go out with you?"

"Sure. It'd be loads of fun. My brother always insists on paying for everything, and I know he'll want to thank y'all for helping me out. Consider it my way of thanking you for being so nice and letting me use your phone."

"Nah, thanks anyway." Derrick shook his head. "I'm not much for dancing in the clubs."

A line from the old Adam and the Ants song popped into Erica's head. *"Don't drink, don't smoke, what do you do?"* She drummed her fingers on the flimsy plastic cup and thought, *this one doesn't even like dancing. He's a tough nut to crack.* At first glance, she had thought this would be easy, but Derrick was either smarter than he looked or stayed so jacked-up, nothing else mattered to him. She'd had to play lesbian on the last target and was relieved when Rick told her this one was a spaced-out doper dude. It was time to take the only angle left. Erica cocked her head slightly and pouted.

86

"Awww. Are you sure?"

"Yeah, I'm sure. I can't leave anyway. I'm waiting for someone."

"Okay, then, if you're sure. But you're gonna miss the party."

"Maybe some other time," he said.

Erica surrendered Plan A and her look of disappointment was genuine, but not for the reason Derrick suspected. "Sure. Why don't you give me your phone number, and I'll check back with you in a few days." She knew Rick already had Derrick's home number, but he had told her to try getting the hippie's cell number.

Derrick tore the corner off a newspaper from the pile next to his lounge chair, jotted a number down, and handed it to her. Erica smiled and dropped it in her clutch purse.

"Thanks. Could I ask you for one more teeny-tiny little favor?"

Derrick sighed. "Yeah, what is it?"

"Do you know where I could get something for me and my brother to party with?"

He paused, but not as long as he had with the "Coke" comment Erica had made earlier. The little paranoia devil didn't seem as excited as he had been ten minutes earlier. "What are you looking for?"

Erica immediately brightened. Even in the grocery store they don't ask you what you're looking for unless they know where it is. Plan B was going to work, and she wouldn't have to entertain this doper all night to get what she wanted. "Just some pot if you got it," she said. "Or some coke would be really nice."

"You ever tried heroin?"

"No, I'm afraid of needles," she said, telling the truth for the first time since she had walked into his rat-hole of a house.

"Oh, you don't have to shoot it, you can snort it," Derrick offered helpfully.

Erica shrugged and gave him an innocent smile. "Really? Well... okay, I guess I'll try it."

Derrick left the room again and was back in less than a minute with a small zip-lock bag containing a tan powder. When he held it out to Erica, she jumped to her feet and stepped to the window instead of taking the bag. Not touching the dope and staying out the chain of custody was always the hardest part. Derrick laid the bag on the coffee table and walked to her side, following her gaze outside.

"What is it?" he asked, and she heard anxiety in his voice.

"My brother should be here any minute now," she said, and then pointed at the red Porsche pulling into the driveway next to the Toyota. "Oh, good, there he is now." Erica slid past Derrick and opened the door before Rick had a chance to knock. She wrapped herself around him when he stepped into the dreary living room. "Hi bro, thanks for coming." She completed her full-body hug with Rick and gestured to Derrick. "This is Derrick—look what he's got for us." She pulled Rick to the coffee table and pointed at the small bag.

Rick eyed the bag, picked it up with two fingers, and shook it gently, examining the contents. He opened the baggie, licked his index finger, surreptitiously switched fingers and put his dry middle finger into the bag, then licked his index finger again. He looked at Derrick. "How much?" he asked.

"Uh, it's a gram," Derrick said.

"Yeah, I figured that," Rick said. "How much cash do you want for it?"

"Its $500 per gram."

Rick looked at Erica. "Damn," he said, "what are we gonna do with a whole gram of smack?"

Erica put her right index finger to her temple and twisted it as if trying to solve a puzzle in her head. "I dunno, maybe party our butts off with some of it, and sell the rest at the club?"

Rick responded to her snide tone with a smirk and a shrug. "Okay, but it better be good." He reached for his wallet and counted out five $100 bills on the coffee table. Derrick grabbed the bills and stuffed them into his jeans pocket. Rick bent over, slid the heroin into his sock, and looked up at Erica. "Let's get your crappy car running and head downtown."

Erica turned to Derrick and held her breath while kissing him on the cheek. "I'll call you next week to see if you want to party." She took a deep breath through her nose and exhaled through her mouth while following Rick to his car. Once the door had closed behind them, she hissed in his ear, "That place stank like a cross between a grow house and an outhouse."

"Not so loud," Rick scolded under his breath, glancing back at the front door. "Did you get his cell number?"

"Of course," she said, handing him the scrap of paper.

Rick raised the hood of Erica's Toyota, and they both leaned in under the hood. "He uses a cordless phone when he's at home," she said.

Rick cocked his head and grinned. "Good. That'll make it easy to monitor."

"I know. Colson used to do that when—"

Rick cut her off mid-sentence. "There you go about Colson again. That was almost fifteen years ago, and you're still hung up on that has-been."

Erica bit her tongue. She wanted to remind Rick that Colson had been like a big brother to her and never tried to get in her pants like he had the first time they worked together. That's why she quit working with him and made it clear to him this was a one-time gig because Colson had asked for the favor. Rick would never be the agent Colson was, no matter how high-tech his gadgets were or how smart he thought he was. Erica knew monitoring and recording the calls from a cordless phone didn't require a wiretap court order—not because she had learned it from Rick the Jerk, but from Colson. She knew she likely had forgotten more about undercover operations than Rick had learned in the past two years of being an agent.

Rick made a show of working on the engine for two minutes, and then slammed the hood as Erica slid behind the wheel and started the car. She smiled and clapped when the engine came to life. Rick leaned into the open driver's side window and whispered, "Meet me around the corner in back of the Target, and I'll pay you."

Erica drove to the shopping center and around the rear corner, where she was greeted by four of the narcotics undercover cars and the takedown van parked in a little group. She pulled alongside the Porsche and glared at Rick. "Why is the van here? Were you guys gonna take him down with me in there? Colson would never risk burning me as an informant."

Rick rolled his eyes in disgust. "Would you just lighten up and shut up about Colson. No, we weren't going to bust him. We were using the van to monitor the bug."

"You were wired?" Erica scolded. "Now my voice is on the tape and I can be subpoenaed to court. That's just as bad as taking him down with me there."

"Stop being so paranoid. We weren't recording, just monitoring in case anything went wrong."

"I'll bet," Erica mumbled. She snatched the $100 bills and CI receipt from Rick's outstretched hand, pulled a pen from the center console, held the receipt against the steering wheel, and signed her name. "What happens next?" she said.

"As if you've forgotten the drill," Rick answered. "Wait a couple of days and call him. Order up another gram, and I'll show up without you to buy it. A few days later, I'll order up a half-ounce and cut in another UC agent. You will be cut out of the deal entirely. After we work our way up to his supplier, we'll take everybody down, and we won't charge Derrick with the first buy. That way, he'll think I'm the CI, and you're safe."

Erica stared at him a beat, pondering his credibility. "You promise that's the way it'll go?"

"Scouts honor," Rick said, giving her a middle finger salute.

Erica returned the gesture and shot around the Porsche to the opposite rear corner of the building and out of sight. "Now you owe me a favor, Colson," she mumbled while pulling into traffic. She paid no attention to the man watching from the dark blue stolen Taurus in the middle row of a dozen other parked cars in the Target lot.

ᒚ⁀CHAPTER NINE☜

K eith and Colson met for breakfast at Ria's Bluebird Café on Memorial Drive two days after their first meeting. An imposing waitress who outweighed Keith by about a hundred pounds greeted Colson and steered them to a table by the window. She brought them both coffee, and Keith ordered a Coke. Colson ordered orange juice and looked at Keith quizzically.

"Coffee and a Coke?"

"I like a lot of caffeine."

Keith fidgeted while the waitress took their breakfast order, poured coffee in their cups, and then waddled away from the table. Impatiently discarding pleasantries and small talk, he turned his attention to Colson. "Have you found out anything about the Cedarcrest house?"

"Yeah, one of my old informants pulled a stop-and-cop there last night."

"Stop and cop?" Keith asked with a squint.

"That's when an informant or an undercover agent stops at a suspected dealer's house and cops some drugs. It means they made an undercover buy."

Keith's look of confusion dissolved. "Really? That was fast."

"She's a good informant and plays the part well."

"What did they buy?"

Colson took a sip of coffee and looked over the brim of his cup. "Heroin."

Keith shook his head. "Heroin being sold in a quiet little neighborhood. I expected marijuana, maybe cocaine."

Colson nodded, set his cup on the table, and crossed his arms. He gazed out the window at the thick Atlanta traffic moving along Memorial Drive—people going to their day jobs, thinking about where they were going for vacation, or maybe their favorite team's play-off chances, but oblivious of the extremely tumultuous world around them.

"There's another entire world out there most people know nothing about," Colson said to the window. "People in this country are so prosperous and so distracted by their big screen TVs and electronic gadgets that they don't want their fun diminished by having to admit anything dangerous exists. It's just like that movie *The Matrix*. They don't know what's going on—and they don't want to know."

"So what happens now?" Keith poured more cream in his coffee, seeming to forget he'd already done so.

"The dope's been sent to the lab for analysis. When the report comes back, it'll tell the cops how pure it is."

"What if it turns out to be too pure? I mean if it's toxic or whatever you call it, can the dealer be charged with Joshua's death?"

Colson shook his head. "As I said before, not unless it can be proven he sold him that particular lethal dose."

"Is that possible?"

"Short of the dealer confessing to it, no. I'm sorry, Keith."

Keith tightened his lips and rapped his fist on the table. A couple of customers gave him a glance, but they quickly turned their attention back to their breakfasts and newspapers. Keith lifted the coffee to his lips for a short sip before setting the cup back on the table, slowly turning it around and around in the saucer. They sat silent for a long moment while Keith looked down at his cup. When his eyes met Colson's, he said, "So, they arrested him, right?"

"Not yet. They'll make several more buys from him first, trying to work their way up to his supplier and to also prove he's a genuine dealer, in case his attorney tries to argue it was a one-time, isolated sale to a good-looking woman he wanted to spend the night with."

Keith nodded understanding. "So—"

Colson held up a finger when the waitress walked up to the table and set two plates in front of them. "Would you two like something else?" she asked. They both smiled and shook their heads. "No, thanks," said Colson.

"So," Keith continued when she walked away, "how long do you think the case will take? I mean, for them to work their way up to his supplier?"

Colson shrugged. "It's really hard to say. Could take a couple of weeks, could take a couple of months."

"Have you found out anything about Emily's missing person case?" Keith asked.

"I talked to a friend at APD and asked him to give the case priority. He said he would, but nothing's turned up yet. She'll be eighteen in about a week, and I'm afraid his supervisor will make him ex-clear—or I should say, close the case."

Keith turned his palms up on the table. "Do you have any theories about the connection between Joshua and Emily?"

"I usually try to deal in facts, not theories," Colson said evenly.

Keith looked down at his food. "Is there anything else that can be done?"

Colson took another sip of coffee and glanced over the brim of the cup. "I'm working on it."

Keith offered a hopeful nod. "Emily's parents are at their wits' end."

"I'm sure they are. I wish there was more that could be done." Colson said. "The truth is, there isn't a lot that law enforcement can do, and our program focuses on prevention. In my current capacity, I don't usually get involved after the fact. I'm supposed to be preventing problems like this from occurring in the first place."

Keith nodded as if he understood. It seemed to Colson as though he didn't understand it at all but didn't want to appear totally naive. He waited for the waitress to freshen their coffee before asking his next question.

"How are you supposed to prevent it? I mean, other than just telling your kids to say no to drugs?"

"The program is designed to teach parents how to make sure their kids never use drugs to begin with, by implementing a five-step drug-free family plan." Colson took a bite of toast and washed it down with coffee. "Step one," he said, counting them off on his fingers, "a written family policy against drug use that makes the parents' position on the issue very clear to the kids. No ambiguity. No gray areas. It gets signed by all family members and posted on the refrigerator, along with 'drug-free home' magnets and stickers throughout the house to remind the kids and their friends. Step two, random oral fluid—that's saliva, not urine—drug testing of kids in the home between the ages of twelve and eighteen."

Keith raised his eyebrows at that one. Colson took notice, accustomed to the reaction, and then continued. "Step three, a parent-child contract that spells out the specific privileges each kid will lose if he or she tests positive for drugs or alcohol.

"Step four, monthly parent training newsletters that teach parents how to talk to their kids about the dangers of drug and alcohol use in age-specific and culturally competent language.

And step five, counseling and treatment already arranged for and in place, in case a kid tests positive for drugs."

Keith sat silent for a moment, trying to process the information. Colson cocked his head and looked at him. "What's wrong?" he said.

Keith squinted slightly and shook his head. Colson had noticed a similar reaction from parents who attended his presentations. He couldn't blame Keith. He had given Morgan the same look. "Drug testing kids?" Keith said in a loud whisper. "Is that really a good idea?"

"Absolutely not," Colson said. "Not if it's urine testing. Research shows urine testing is invasive and could hurt a parent-child relationship. And any fifth-grader with Internet access can beat a urine test anyway. That's why only saliva testing is recommended. It's non-invasive, can't be adulterated, diluted, or substituted. How are you going to beat a saliva test? Hold someone else's spit in your mouth?"

Keith stared at Colson, unaware his mouth was hanging open. "I've heard of employers testing their employees and people on probation being tested, but drug testing your children? Really? Parents really drug test their own kids?"

Colson shrugged. "Only those parents who want to make sure their kids don't use drugs. By the time a parent begins to suspect a kid is using drugs, the child has been using for at least two years and is already in third-stage addiction. Random, monthly drug testing prevents that. And more importantly, it takes the peer pressure to use drugs off the kid. If a kid can say, 'My parents test me,' it removes the peer pressure to experiment."

Keith looked down at his plate. "Teresa and I have always been very liberal in our thinking. We would never consider drug testing our kids."

"How has that worked out for you?" Colson said gently.

Keith met Colson's eyes with a dead stare. Colson knew it was a cold statement and probably made Keith a little mad at him, but probably more so at himself. "Not very well," he admitted, raising his hands in mock surrender. "Do you test your kids?"

"My daughter was an only child and is an adult now. I certainly would have if I knew then what I know now. She grew up in a cop's house—an undercover cop's house—and knew I would never tolerate her using drugs. But that was also when I thought the only way to combat drugs was through enforcement. It seemed almost glamorous at the time."

Colson glanced out the window at the passing traffic as if suddenly recalling ancient memories. "The days of *Miami Vice*, preppy dress shirts, and skinny ties," he said to the window before turning back to Keith. "My daughter has already agreed to follow the program with my grandson, but she wasn't sold on the idea either, until she heard another mother give an account of what her fourteen-year-old son experienced in middle school last year. He was offered pot twice by two different groups of boys. All he had to do was say, 'I'm cool, but I can't. My parents drug test me.' After giving him a shocked look, similar to what you're giving me now, they left him alone."

"Maybe we should drug test Danny," Keith said, thinking aloud.

"Only if you want to be a hundred percent sure he'll stay drug-free," Colson said. "But you also might have to make some very difficult lifestyle changes."

"Like what?"

"Do either you or Teresa drink alcoholic beverages—beer, wine, or liquor?"

"Yes, of course," Keith said. "You're not going to tell me we have to stop drinking are you?"

"No, of course not. But do you drink in front of Danny?"

"Yes," Keith said. "A man should be able to have a drink in his own home, shouldn't he?"

"Sure, but there are some adult things that shouldn't be done in front of kids. You and Teresa don't have sex in front of Danny, do you?"

Keith's previous look of shock was replaced by one of horror. "Of course not."

Colson held up his hands to assure Keith. "I'm certain you don't, but drinking is an activity for adults over the age of twenty-one, so why should kids be subjected to watching adults engage in an activity that is only for adults? That could only encourage kids who think being an adult is cool to mimic their parents."

Keith cut his eyes away. "What about a few glasses of wine with dinner out, or a few beers with pizza at a restaurant while Danny is there? What's wrong with that?"

Colson's eyes widened slightly. "Are you telling me that you drink and drive with your son in the car?"

Keith's face flushed. "Yeah," he stuttered, "I've had a few too many Margaritas at the Mexican restaurant, and then driven home with Danny in the car."

"What kind of message does that send to Danny?"

"Okay, you made your point," Keith said. "What else have I been doing wrong all these years?"

"Do you or Teresa smoke?"

"Cigarettes? No. I used to smoke years ago when Kevin and Joshua were young, but I quit a few years ago. But why is that a problem?"

"Research has shown that children of parents who smoke are sixty percent more likely to use marijuana, and if you think about it, it makes sense. You know why?"

"Why?"

"If a kid grows up in a home where parents walk around with something on fire hanging out of their mouths all the time, it becomes commonplace for them. Later, when that kid's friends ask them to try pot, it's not an alien idea for them to light a joint on fire and inhale the smoke. Kids these days claim pot is harmless because of all the pro-drug propaganda they read on the Internet. But any time a human being sets anything on fire and inhales the smoke, it is going to be harmful. The poor little sheeple aren't even thinking logically."

Tears began to well in Keith's eyes. "Are you saying I caused Joshua's drug use?"

"No, of course not," Colson said, figuratively tamping down Keith's building guilt with his hand. "Family members don't cause their loved ones' addictions. And once addiction takes hold, family members can't control or cure it. What I am saying is that there are some things that can be done to help prevent it."

Keith pushed his plate away, leaned back, and heaved a sigh. "Sorry, I think I've lost my appetite. Even though Joshua's addiction was his own doing, I downplayed his drug use, and that is my fault." The waitress brought the check and both men reached for their wallets. "I've got this one," Keith said. "It's on my company."

"Am I a legitimate business expense?" Colson said.

"Well, I do want to talk to you about how my company can help your program. I mean, after all this is over."

"Are you ready to do the speaking engagement at the chamber on Monday?"

Keith hesitated. "I was," he said. "But after hearing about your five-step drug-free plan, I may change what I was going to say."

Colson raised an eyebrow. "I thought you were going to counter the billionaire's arguments for legalizing drugs."

"I was—still am," Keith said. "But now I'm also thinking I want to tell the group how much I wish I had known about the importance of drug testing kids while Josh was growing up. It would have probably saved his life."

"That's cool," Colson said. "But don't expect too much to come of it."

"Why not?"

"Parents are in deep denial. No parent ever thinks their child will become a drug addict or alcoholic. They all have the "not my child" attitude. But millions of kids do become drug addicts and alcoholics every year, don't they?"

"Yeah, why is that?" Keith said. "I drank when I was young, even smoked a little pot for a while. I didn't have a problem. Why do so many people become addicted?"

"You were one of the lucky ones. You obviously weren't predisposed to addiction."

"Predisposed?'

"Some people are either genetically predisposed or biochemically predisposed to the disease of addiction."

Keith shook his head. "Hang on, Colson. I have to differ with you on the disease part. You can't convince me that someone is born already addicted to some substance that they've never used, unless it's a child born from an addicted mother with drugs in her system. My wife wasn't using drugs, drinking, or anything of the kind when she was pregnant. I just don't—"

"Hang on, Keith," Colson said. "I agree, and that's not what I'm talking about. Not that kind of disease. I'm talking about an addictive gene that also could be called a defect. You've probably known of or have come in contact with people over the years that seem to have what you might refer to as a lack of self-control. For instance, was there any addiction in your or Teresa's family?"

"Yes," he said. "Both of us have a parent with addiction issues—her dad had a drinking problem, and my mother uses a lot of painkillers. But neither of us is an addict or alcoholic."

"No? That's because the addictive gene skipped a generation. It happens like that sometimes. Do you think Josh may have inherited the addictive gene from his grandparents?"

Keith sat with a blank look.

"Addiction is a disease in that respect," Colson continued. "It's a chronic, progressive disease, attributed to a defective gene. Many people don't believe that, but take a good look at a drug addict. You can almost see the virus swimming through their veins and eating them from the inside. In many cases, it runs in families. Are people still responsible for their actions? You're dang right they are, but you know as well as I do that some can control their actions better than others—and in a lot of those cases, there is a physiological reason for it."

Keith nodded. "I'm trying to process all of this. I always believed a person chose who they wanted to be—to be decent or not, to be an addict or not. That's why Joshua's lifestyle was so tough for me to accept. Don't parents need to know about this kind of stuff? I never knew any of this." Keith shook his head and looked down at his hands. "I wish I had."

"Me too," Colson agreed. "I think every parent on the planet needs to know about it, but the question is how to get the information to them. Like I said in our first meeting, they won't attend a free seminar to learn about it. We can't get this information to them through school; they don't go to school any more. We can't get it to them through church. Even if they attend church, there are very few, if any, drug education programs available at churches."

Keith shrugged. "Then what are the other options?"

"Ah," Colson said, holding up a finger, "that's where the drug-free workplace program comes in. You remember we talked about how certified drug-free workplaces in Georgia receive a state-mandated discount on workers comp insurance?"

"Yes," Keith said. "And you said annual employee drug education is mandatory for a company to get that discount."

"That's right, my friend." Colson paused while the waitress refilled his coffee cup. He winked and smiled at her. When she walked away, he said, "The program will deliver mandatory drug education every year to a captive audience of parents in these certified drug-free workplaces."

"I follow you now," Keith said. "That's how you prevent drug use through the workplace."

"Exactly. That's why drug-free workplace programs are so important. They help attack the demand side of America's drug problem. Do you have any employees who are parents at your company?"

"Of course," he said. "Several."

"Think they would benefit from drug education at work?"

"Of course they would."

Colson took a last sip of coffee and stood up. Keith reached out his hand and Colson shook it. "Thanks for what you've done with trying to find Emily," Keith said, "and getting the cops to investigate that scum who sold to Josh. And thank you for what you are doing for the community."

Colson nodded. "You're more than welcome, Keith. I hope I wasn't too rough on you. Believe me when I say I wasn't parent of the year—any year. I was caught off guard just as much as you were when I began research for this job."

"No, not at all," Keith said. "It was hard to hear, but I needed to hear it for Danny's sake."

With a final handshake, Colson turned to walk away. Then he heard Keith clear his throat.

"Hey, Colson—I mean, Grey."

Colson turned. "Yeah?"

Keith rubbed down the wrinkles from his pant legs that had developed during their conversation. "What you said earlier, when I asked if there was anything else that could be done—you know, about Josh? You said you were working on something?"

100

Colson nodded. "Other than what you've learned about me during our short, professional relationship, I have a few modest abilities not limited to conducting drug-free workplace programs. Trust me."

"I'll take your word for it," Keith said with a smile.

"Are you ready for your speech to the chamber?"

Keith took a deep breath. "I think so."

Colson gave Keith a lazy salute and turned away. Keith stood motionless, watching as Colson pushed through the door of the café and disappeared down the sidewalk.

CHAPTER TEN

Aftertwo days of research, writing, memorizing, and rehearsing his speech, Keith felt half confident and half nervous. Before he took the stage, Colson clapped him on the back and told him he knew the feeling, but he would do fine once he began. After Colson finished speaking, he gave the audience a brief history of his and Keith's relationship and welcomed him to the podium. Colson shook his hand and whispered, "Go fight the good fight."

For a moment Keith completely forgot the opening statement of his presentation. Then, suddenly, he was turning to the podium and facing four hundred of Fulton County's top business people. He thought of Josh as he began, and the nervousness started to fade. He needed to do this in honor of his son. He didn't want Josh's death to go unnoticed. He wanted these people, especially the parents in the audience, to learn from the tragedy of such a young life cut short, to hear the story of a boy who was denied the chance to grow into a man. He wanted them to realize the danger of legalizing drugs. Wanted them to understand the importance of keeping these poisons out of the hands of kids, and to learn the things they could do to keep their own children drug-free.

He began by talking about Joshua's childhood and what a wonderful boy he had been. He explained how his son began using drugs and how everything changed after that. He described how Joshua's innocence vanished because of drug use and explained how he now believed Josh suffered from the disease of addiction.

"As we meet here today," Keith said to the audience, "there are people spending a fortune to promote the legalization of drugs. If they succeed, the problem of addiction will become too large for scientists to ever find a cure."

Colson sat off to the side, nodding in approval of the grief-stricken father's comment. The audience sat riveted to every word Keith said. With growing confidence, he continued as if he had been involved in public speaking his entire life. He spread his arms to make his point.

"And if drugs are indeed legalized and their use becomes commonplace, who would be left to pursue a cure? More and more people will be neglecting their families, their jobs, and their responsibilities." His voice rose with genuine emotion. "Hundreds of millions of lives will become slaves to the disease of addiction."

Keith's eloquent and moving words were from the heart. His speech was filled with emotion, but also included scientific data. "Statistics prove that when drugs become cheaper, their use and addiction skyrocket. Legalization and taxation won't help the American economy. It will do the exact opposite through higher insurance costs, more drug-related accidents, hospitals and morgues flooded with OD patients, and thousands more crack-addicted babies. The pro-drug assertion that legalization would reduce crime is a fallacy. It's a fact that the majority of addicts engaged in criminal behavior long before they became addicted, and even those who receive treatment and become drug-free are very likely to continue to commit criminal acts."

Keith paused and looked around the room, making eye contact with as many in the crowd as possible. His voice softened. "You see, committing crime is a problem of character. If drugs are legalized, users will simply spend whatever money they have to buy more drugs and continue committing crime to get money for food, clothing, and rent." Keith pulled a stack of documents from his briefcase and held them above his head. "This is real research, folks, proving that crimes such as assault and child abuse will increase if drugs are made legal. I can provide anyone here with this data, and you can read it for yourselves."

Keith slid the documents back in his case and looked at Colson, who gave him another grin and a nod. He turned back to the audience. His delivery took an unintended, sarcastic tone.

"Then there's the argument about drug use being an individual right and a victimless crime." He shook his head and closed his eyes for a moment. "Look at me, folks," he implored them. "My wife and I have been devastated by Josh's death. Our other son lost his brother. We will never, ever have an opportunity to enjoy his children and bounce them on our knee. But it's not just our family that has been devastated by the drug use of family members. Drug users perpetrate violence on innocent people they don't even know.

"Consider it this way: the government does not hesitate to protect people from themselves by implementing seat belt laws, social security laws, and child labor laws. But even for those of the libertarian mindset who insist on little or no government interference, the moral cost of legalizing drugs is too high. This is a potential catastrophe for our families, and I implore each of you to stand against anyone who advocates the legalization of drugs. Educate not only your kids, but your friends who may be persuaded by the idea that legalized drugs would never affect their personal lives or ever take a loved one away from them."

Keith closed by reciting Colson's five-step drug-free family plan and thanked the audience for their time. The room was silent as he nodded to Colson and walked toward his seat. He felt more nervous now than before he began, but any doubts about his impassioned plea vanished with the sound of chairs moving against the floor and the rustle of freshly pressed business attire as the audience rose for a standing ovation. Keith turned and smiled to the crowd of nearly four hundred staunchly conservative business owners, hoping they appreciated and agreed with his message and weren't acting out of pity for a father who had lost his child.

His question was answered when they lined up in front of the podium. One after another shook his hand and expressed how he or she appreciated his passion and encouraged him to continue telling people his story. Several offered their assistance and support, but the majority simply wanted more information about the program.

Colson pulled Keith aside as the crowd disbursed. "You have a good opportunity here, you know."

"Yeah, that's what I figured." Keith couldn't help grinning.

"What are you going to do with it?"

"I was thinking I would see if I could get a meeting with Strawn and try to change his mind about legalization."

Colson silently shook his head. "You're never going to change his mind. Drug legalization is like abortion. Neither side is going to change their mind, no matter what you say."

"How about challenging him to a public debate? At least that way we could get everything out into the open so people who are on the fence can hear both sides of the issue."

"He might go for that, but for selfish reasons," Colson said. "His people have already introduced legislation in Georgia, and more bills are being drafted in several other states. He might see this as an opportunity to gain more public support."

"I don't want to be the reason he gets any free publicity," Keith said.

"I don't either," Colson agreed. "But he doesn't need free publicity. His money buys him plenty of airtime. On the other hand, an impassioned plea from the father of a dead child may make a lot of people think twice about Strawn's position—if they actually listen to both sides."

"If I can get him to agree to a meeting," Keith said, "will you go along with me?"

Colson squinted and rubbed his temples. "Look at it this way, Keith. Strawn has spent millions of dollars on his legalization campaign, not to mention attorney's fees, advertising, and hours of news show appearances promoting his agenda. What will a meeting with us accomplish? Will he go on television and admit he was wrong all these years? That he had been ill informed and misguided? That all the time and money he spent could have been used for the greater good of combating drug use or financing treatment programs?"

Keith stood silent for a long moment considering Colson's questions. He knew the answer was a resounding *no*, yet he couldn't reconcile in his mind why a man like Strawn would squander a fortune for a hippie fantasy. There had to be a motivation. Whatever was driving Strawn, there was more money, and even more power attached to it.

"Believe me," Colson continued, "It would be no different than meeting with Billy Graham and convincing him to join the church of Satan.

Keith turned his palms up as to plead his case. "But doing something was always better than do nothing."

Colson bent slightly and lifted his briefcase. He looked back to Keith with a half smile. "Actually, I'd like nothing more than to meet Strawn face to face. There are a few questions I'd like answered. Not that any good would come of it, but why watch the devil on TV when you might get the chance to meet him face to face."

A young man appeared before Keith as he slid his research papers into his briefcase. He introduced himself as a reporter and said, "Mr. Bartlett, would you give me a recorded statement for our radio program?"

"What?" Keith said, surprised. "You want to interview me?"

"Yes, sir. For the *Good Morning Atlanta* radio show. It'll be a taped interview that we'll play on tomorrow morning's broadcast."

"Why would your station be interested in this topic?"

"Drug legalization is a hot issue right now," the reporter said. "Especially marijuana legalization. I'm assigned to cover the chamber's First Monday Breakfasts in case a controversial business matter comes up, but one rarely does. This, on the other hand, is an extremely hot topic."

Keith nodded and answered questions for ten minutes, giving the young reporter plenty of tape for the following day's morning show. The next day, the station aired the interview immediately following a previously recorded pro-drug legalization statement made by billionaire Jack Strawn. The story was sufficiently controversial enough to be picked up by the Associated Press, and it quickly became national news.

Derrick Ramey felt the cold circle of steel from the muzzle of a gun barrel shoved against the base of his skull. Suddenly, his

106

perception was clearer than it had been in years. He wondered who the hell this guy was. From the corner of his eye he could see the man smiling; his gray eyes stared at him with amusement. "Here's the deal," the intruder said. "I need some information from you. I don't want to hurt you, but I will if you act any more stupid than you really are."

Derrick stuttered, "I—I—I don't know anything."

"That's the understatement of the year," the man said, "but you better hope you know this."

"What?" Derrick said pitifully.

"There was a junkie kid named Joshua, goes by the street name JayBee. Let's start by finding out if you're going to tell the truth. Do you know him?"

"Yes," Derrick said. "I heard he OD'd in a hotel room a week or so ago."

"Very good," the man said, still pressing the gun into the back of Derrick's head. "Good truthful start. Now, next question. He was here with a girl last month. They were leaving as your supplier arrived to deliver you four ounces of heroin. Do you remember that?"

Derrick racked his brain to remember. "Yeah," he said, "I remember. Cute little blonde with a cheerleader body, right?"

"Very good," the man said again. "You may get out of this thing alive after all. Now, as they were leaving, the boy took something very valuable out of your supplier's car. We need it back, and we think the girl has it. Where is the girl?"

Derrick's heart sank. He had no idea where the girl was, or even her name. He began sweating profusely and his hands shook. "They told me about the computer, but I didn't see anyone take anything. I told Josh they damn well better return it if they took it, but I don't know where the girl is," he said pleadingly. "But I can find her for you."

"Wrong answer," the man said. "You couldn't find your flat butt with both hands in the dark. In fact, you don't even have the good sense not to sell drugs to an undercover cop."

"What?" Derrick said. "I ain't sold no dope to no cop."

"Red Porsche," the man said, ignoring the double negative. "Good-looking sister?"

"Oh, crap," Derrick said. Then, not wanting that to be his last words, he asked, "Are you going to kill me?"

"What do you think genius?" the man said.

Derrick tensed and started to speak, no doubt to plead for mercy, but he didn't have time to form the words. The bullet slammed into the back of his head, launching him forward as his world exploded in searing pain. His head snapped back, and he collapsed onto the stained carpet, his blood quickly turning it a darker shade of brown.

The Butcher toed the limp body with his boot, then knelt down and used the tail of Derrick's shirt to wipe away the blowback from his pistol and hand. He had originally planned to force the dealer to inject enough heroin to cause his own death, making the murder look like another overdose, but decided at the last minute he wasn't worth the trouble. Besides, the police weren't going to care about the murder of another drug dealer.

He calmly walked from the room. In keeping with his normal mode of operation, he stopped to lower the thermostat in the hall to sixty degrees. The stench of marijuana combined with sweat and mold enveloped him. He realized the smell of a dead body might actually improve the aroma of this dump. A mischievous thought turned him back to the thermostat. The Butcher flipped the side control to the maximum heat setting and chuckled. "I love my job."

Keith called Strawn Industries late in the afternoon following his speech and asked to speak with Jack Strawn. He was instantly transferred after a short hold by the female who answered.

"This is Jeff Evans," a male voice said. "How may I help you?"

"I would like to speak to Mr. Strawn."

"Who's calling please?"

"Tell him Keith Bartlett is on the phone."

"Does Mr. Strawn know you, sir?"

"He is going to get to know me quite soon."

"What is this about?"

"I'll explain it to Mr. Strawn."

The assistant raised his voice an octave. "He's not available; leave your number, and I'll see that he gets it."

"My call concerns the death of a young man," Keith said, consciously working to remain calm. "He needs to be made aware of the circumstances because the media has become involved. This is not information he would want shared with an employee. I suggest you get him on the phone immediately."

The assistant hesitated. "I'm sorry, but—"

"Fine," Keith interrupted. "I'm on the way there with a reporter and photographer from the Atlanta Journal-Constitution. Camera crews from 11 Alive News will be on the way to Strawn's home and your corporate office within the hour. You can explain to Mr. Strawn why all of this is happening without a heads-up. Good day."

"Wait," the assistant blurted. "Hold the line a minute, sir."

After thirty seconds of being on hold and listening to elevator music, Keith heard, "He'll be right with you, Mr. Bartlett." A few moments of silence were followed by the raspy voice of a stern and clearly aggravated Jack Strawn.

"Who the hell is this?" he barked.

Keith identified himself and asked Strawn if he had seen the national news story about Joshua's death and Keith's anti-drug legalization speech. Strawn said he had not, but Keith didn't believe him.

"I'd like to request a meeting. I'm a professional businessman, Mr. Strawn, not some out-of-control kook looking for media attention. I'm asking only for a civil conversation with you about the issue. Maybe we will both come to understand our concerns better."

Strawn paused a moment, as if giving Keith's request serious consideration. "I'm sorry," he said. "I'm sorry for your loss, but I honestly don't have time in my schedule—"

"Let me be clear," Keith said. "I didn't seek out the media; they approached me. They already know I'm requesting a meeting with you. The reporter informed me they are extremely interested in the outcome of the meeting and are chomping at the bit to do a follow-up story."

Strawn asked Keith to hold, and the elevator music kept him company for several minutes. He suspected Strawn was consulting with his attorney, public relations people, or both. Strawn's voice and demeanor seemed to brighten somewhat when he returned to the line.

"It seems I can work you in at ten in the morning, Mr. Bartlett, but only for thirty minutes."

CHAPTER ELEVEN

Strawn Tower sat in the middle of Midtown Atlanta, among several other lucrative corporations and government buildings. At exactly 10:00, Keith and Colson walked up to the receptionist's desk in the lobby of the tower. A woman wearing deep blue business attire and a white blouse forced a smile, asked for their names, and directed them to wait on a plush sofa in a corner of the atrium.

At 10:15 they were escorted to the top floor by two security guards dressed in gray slacks and matching blue blazers with the Strawn company logo embroidered on their breast pockets. The guards led them to an elegant waiting room outside Strawn's office. They sat in silence, surrounded by floor-to-ceiling mahogany judges paneling, occasionally glancing at a huge aquarium inset in the far wall.

A whoosh of air alerted them to the opening of the solid mahogany door to their right, followed by the appearance of a large man wearing a dark gray and tailored V-shaped suit jacket and black tie. Colson immediately recognized him as Jay Taylor's nemesis, Clay Haggart. He looked taller and thicker in the chest than in the Fox News report. Colson had always heard that television cameras add ten pounds to a person's weight. Whoever started that rumor obviously had never encountered this man.

Haggart motioned with his head for Colson and Keith to follow him, and they fell in behind. The huge man gave Keith a moment of pause and he briefly wondered what he was getting them into and hoped Colson was packing a gun or something. Just in case.

Strawn's office was the largest Colson had ever seen and was decorated more lavishly than the Biltmore estate. The Vanderbilts would have been envious. A beautifully polished table with a chair on each side sat in the corner. The chairs were upholstered in first-class, top-quality Italian leather. Colson doubted such furnishings were available in any of Strawn's retail outlets, unless an Arab sheik had taken up residence in small-town America and had recently become his customer. The atmosphere of the cavernous office reeked of a fortune, and its design conveyed the image of a man who had enjoyed a long and prosperous business career.

Colson whispered to Keith, "The furniture business, huh?"

Keith glanced back at Colson wide-eyed, shaking his head. Haggart shot Colson a look.

"You need something?"

Colson chuckled under his breath. "Not unless Strawn is having a ninety-nine percent off sale."

Haggart motioned for them to sit in two chairs facing the large desk. The black chair behind the desk had its back to them, facing the floor-to-ceiling windows. Colson patted the leather armrest of his chair and looked up at Haggart, who now stood to one side with his hands clasped behind his back, looking on. Colson wondered how uncomfortable it must be for the former UFC fighter to stand at parade rest, wrapped up like a pig in a blanket. Taylor had mentioned on several occasions how he wanted to strangle his previous employer for demanding the same dress code.

"So," Colson said lightheartedly to break the tension of the room, "how many furniture tycoons need bodyguards?"

Haggart glared at Colson. "I'm Mr. Strawn's executive assistant," he said, and cut his eyes forward, looking into space.

Colson pursed his lips and nodded. Keith turned to Colson, his eyes even wider than before. Colson raised his hand briefly and let it drop back to the armrest. He peered at Haggart and surmised he didn't have a neck, just skin stretched over a short stump connecting his earlobes to his shoulder blades. "My bad," he said apologetically and glanced from side to side, surveying the cavernous office. "He must have you rearrange this gargantuan furniture a lot—or maybe he likes someone to bench press his desk while the maid vacuums underneath."

Keith reached over and grasped Colson's wrist, squeezing hard and shaking his head again. Haggart dropped his arms to the side and focused his full attention on Colson, who noted that Haggart was trying to control his breathing and had a vein bulging above his right eye. They stared each other down for a long moment.

Colson felt Keith release the death grip on his wrist, and he glanced over at his companion, who was sitting with his eyes closed. Keith jerked his eyes open at the sound of a metal click and sighed as Strawn stepped through a side door and marched to his desk. Keith glanced around the room, paying little attention to Strawn's desk but seeming to be fascinated by a theater-sized computer monitor that almost smothered one entire wall.

Haggart stepped to a side table and removed a wooden box, holding it out to Strawn and raising the lid. Strawn eased into the chair behind his massive desk and lifted out a cigar. Haggart immediately stepped back and slid the box back into the table. A green banker's lamp sat on a corner of the immaculately clean and paperwork-free desktop; a bottle of Jack Daniels sat beside a bourbon glass on the side table. Colson craned his head slightly and peered over the desk, half suspecting the billionaire to be holding a cat in his lap and stroking it like an evil genius from the movies. Instead, he snipped one end of the cigar, expertly lit the other end, and leaned back in the chair with his hands folded over his ample midsection. Strawn wasn't hideously overweight, but he was barrel-chested. His pants were worn a little too high but appeared to have been pressed just seconds before he walked in. He wore a brilliant white button-down shirt and red power tie. Colson couldn't help but notice the huge gold cuff links that glinted as Strawn crossed his arms. His hair was as white as it appeared on television, but seemed thinner in person, combed flat with hair gel.

A non-aloof businessman would have extended a micron of courtesy and stepped around the desk to shake their hands, but Colson wasn't surprised that Strawn did not. Strawn was a self-absorbed prick whose only motivation was to pretend to listen, and then get him and Keith out of his office as quickly as possible. Colson always sat with his visitors at the small table in his office. It was rude to keep a desk between oneself and one's guests.

At last Strawn leaned forward and placed his elbows on the desk. "So," he began, examining Keith with penetrating brown eyes, "how can I help you, Mr. Bartlett?"

Keith sat in silence for a long moment, causing Colson to look and see if he had slipped into a trance. Perhaps this was too much and too fast for the grieving parent. The small trickle of sweat running from Keith's forehead down his right cheek made Colson angry at himself for agreeing to this insanity.

"Mr. Bartlett?" Strawn said with a hint of frustration.

Keith licked his lips nervously. "As I mentioned on the phone, it's vital that we talk."

Strawn nodded. He hadn't even acknowledged Colson's presence. He glanced at his Rolex for effect and drew on the cigar before continuing. "Gentlemen, I'm a very busy man. Let's get to it."

Keith gestured to his left. "This is Grey Colson, he—"

"I know who he is," Strawn said, not taking his eyes off Keith.

Colson smiled. "It's nice to be famous."

Keith threw Colson the glare of an embarrassed wife whose husband was making a fool of himself in front of everyone at her class reunion. Then he turned his attention back to Strawn. "Mr. Strawn, I want to encourage you to reverse your position on the legalization of drugs."

Strawn chuckled. He looked to Haggart as if Keith had just told a stupid joke. "Why would I do that?" Strawn said, still chuckling under his breath. "This country has lost the so-called war on drugs. The black market for drugs is killing thousands of people every year, and hundreds of thousands more are being jailed. Not to mention we are losing billions of dollars in tax revenue that could be realized if drugs were made legal."

Keith looked to Colson, not knowing the proper retort to Strawn's practiced argument. Colson spoke evenly, counting off his points with his fingers. "One, America has not lost the war on drugs," he said. "We may not have won it yet, but that doesn't mean we've lost. We just need to fight the war a little differently, not throw in the towel. Two, it's true that a black market for drugs creates violence, but legalized drugs would result in countless more deaths, not to mention all the lives ruined. And three, any tax revenue generated by legalized drugs would not come close to covering the increased costs of substance abuse."

Strawn looked at Colson for the first time. He grunted and shook his head. "Prohibiting drug use hasn't worked any better than prohibition of alcohol," he said. "End of discussion."

Colson smiled and eyed Strawn. "People have been clamoring about legalizing drugs since the sixties. The old 'prohibition didn't work' argument was tried then and fell on its face, and it won't hold up now. The truth is, the use of alcohol dropped dramatically during Prohibition, and so did alcohol-related medical problems. After Prohibition was repealed, use of alcohol went up three hundred and fifty percent. That's exactly what will happen if drugs are legalized. Drug use will drastically increase, along with all the medical, social, and economic problems that go along with it."

Strawn turned back and forth in his swivel chair, looking from Colson to Keith. "Look," he said, "everybody knows Prohibition didn't work. It was repealed fourteen years after it was constitutionalized. It didn't stop people from drinking; it just created a black market that resulted in a lot of violence."

"That's because the law didn't go into effect until a year after it was passed," Colson said. "That gave people time to store up a lot of booze and then sell it on the black market. And," he continued, "the law didn't prohibit the possession or use of alcohol, just the commercial manufacturing and distribution. That's one reason there was such a black market problem. But the fact is, organized crime already existed before Prohibition; it just coincidentally became more visible during Prohibition, and that made people think the increased crime was a result of the law. Actually, Prohibition did work. Even though it was a weak law with lots of problems, it still reduced alcohol use by one third."

Strawn and Colson stared at each other silently for a moment, and then Strawn turned his palms up on the table and said, "Don't you think people should have a right to do whatever they want, as long as it doesn't harm others? The government shouldn't be allowed to interfere in a person's private life. After all, drug use is a victimless crime."

Colson kept his reply soft and respectful, because he knew that a person's opinion was rarely swayed by arguing. "A victimless crime? Are you really saying it doesn't harm anyone? The death rate of drug addicts is twenty-eight times higher than for non-users. And what about crack babies addicted in the womb? What about the spouses and kids of drug addicts? Ask them if it harms others. What about increased health care costs and automobile accidents? Ask family members of people killed by drivers high on drugs if it's a victimless crime. What about lost productivity in the workplace? Ask business owners if drug use hurts their company. It most definitely is not a victimless crime. And the U.S. government has a right and a duty to protect its citizens, even if it means protecting them from themselves. The American government is actually mandated to provide public health services that protect American citizens—especially children."

Strawn shook his head, obviously annoyed. "That's another reason we should legalize drugs, then," he said in a barely controlled tone. "Taxes on drugs would pay for treatment for addiction, and drug education to keep kids off drugs. The government could use that tax money to protect its citizens." He paused, looking at Colson. "Whose side are you on, anyway?"

"The facts," Colson answered. "I'm on the side of the facts, and the fact is, drug education won't work if drugs are legalized. The absolute best drug education message we can send our kids is to keep drugs illegal. If we legalize drugs, it will send kids the message that we don't believe drugs are harmful. It is very difficult to dissuade a child from doing something legal. And the 'taxes on drugs to pay for treatment' argument won't fly either. Drug addicts don't voluntarily go into treatment. But they do go into treatment when they are charged with the crime of using illegal drugs and the court orders them to go. If you take away the illegality, you take away the compulsion to get treatment. We will end up with a nation full of junkies."

Colson and Strawn's eyes remained locked, and Strawn's voice rose as he spoke. "So we restrict drug use to adults only then, and if the adults want to use drugs, we let them do so until they kill themselves."

Colson looked to Keith and nodded. He had noticed him fidgeting in his peripheral vision, a sign he was growing angry. It was time to let him vent.

"Let them kill themselves?" Keith blurted. "What if it was your child?"

Strawn ignored Keith's outburst and kept his eyes on Colson. "One of the main reasons kids use drugs is because drugs are illegal. It's the forbidden fruit syndrome. Make drugs legal, and kids won't want them anymore."

Colson was no stranger to a good debate. Whether it was a suspect he was interrogating or a point he was trying to make with a politically driven command staff, he knew when to push buttons and when to drive the argument in the direction he needed it to go. His cop brain was working out the logical progression of this heated discussion. He smiled at Strawn. "Do young people only want the things they can't have?" he asked. "Every boy I know wants an Xbox, and they are not off limits to kids. Kids don't want things just because they're forbidden."

Strawn looked at Colson with a glare of pure hate. Colson could see his wheels turning: Strawn had lost that point, but no one ever got the better of him in an argument. How dare this smart-ass retired hick lecture him? Strawn's only choice was to repeat himself since there was no other response available. He had been neglecting his cigar while focusing on Colson, and the small red glow at the tip had gone out. He made a fist with his left hand and pounded the glass inlay on his desk with each word for emphasis.

"Then we simply. Restrict. Drug. Use. To. Adults."

"That won't work, either," Colson answered. "Alcohol and tobacco are supposed to be reserved for adults, but kids do have a way of getting beer and cigarettes, don't they?"

Strawn's stare became poisonous. His face turned a dark shade of red not unlike the color of lava spewing from a volcano. He took a deep breath in an attempt to compose himself. "I'll speak slowly so even you can understand. If we legalize drugs, we take away the profit potential for the dealers, and they won't push the drugs on kids anymore. That will help keep kids from ever starting to use."

"That's not how it works," Colson said. "Very few people, if any, start using drugs because some drug dealer pushed it on them. Dealers don't want to sell to new people because they're afraid they might be selling to an undercover cop. Trust me, I know. People start using drugs because a friend introduced them to it, not because some dealer forced it on them."

The three men sat in a deadlocked silence for a few seconds before Strawn decided to make his closing argument. "Here's the bottom line, Colson," he said, jabbing his finger in Colson's direction. "The people of this country want drugs legalized, and that is exactly what is going to happen."

"That's funny," Colson said, "because when I was in law enforcement, the people in the crack neighborhoods weren't asking us to legalize drugs, but to get rid of the dealers. You couldn't be more wrong about what the people of this country want. Is drug legalization what the people of America want, Mr. Strawn? Or is it what you want? Why the crusade to infect the people of this nation with the scourge of legalized dope? If what you want is a nation infested with dopers, you'll get it, because that's what it will become."

Colson could see from the corner of eye that Keith was watching Strawn intently, waiting for his response. Strawn snatched his lighter from the desk and re-lit his cigar, taking three deep puffs. The tip glowed bright red as he drew the smoke into his lungs and exhaled through his nose, the desktop deflecting a cloud of haze in their direction. Strawn spread his hands as if declaring ownership of the entire world, and his mouth rose in a lopsided grin. "What I want is what the people want," he said, "because I tell them what they want."

Colson raised his eyebrows at Keith, not believing what Strawn had just proclaimed. The man was a raving egomaniac. Keith seemed to be fighting to keep his emotions in check. "What you want is not what I want," Keith said. "Drugs killed my son. I do not want them legalized."

Strawn responded in a low, condescending growl. "Then you're a total idiot. Your son killed himself; it wasn't the drugs that did it."

Colson had known it from the start, but he was here to support Keith even if this meeting would change nothing about this man. You couldn't change a man's mind unless you could change his heart, and Colson knew this man didn't have one to change. Colson maintained a little composure for Keith's sake. "Mr. Strawn," he said gesturing to the room, "you must be an intelligent man; otherwise we wouldn't be sitting in such a fine office. Surely you can have a passionate debate without resorting to insults and name-calling."

Strawn jumped to his feet leaned forward over his desk. "It's impossible to have an intelligent debate with a couple of imbeciles," he shouted.

Colson stood slowly, ready to take it up a notch. "Sit down, Strawn," he said in a controlled command, as if directing a suspect to put their hands behind their back. Strawn immediately dropped into his chair. As quickly as it appeared, his expression of total contempt and hate fled from his face. Colson's reaction had caught him by surprise. It was clear to everyone in the room he wasn't accustomed to being challenged or called out for his behavior.

Haggart instantly materialized to Colson's left, ready to pounce like a tiger. Strawn shook his head at Haggart. "It's fine," he said to the former fighter. He spread his hands and smiled. "Okay, Mr. Bartlett—I didn't mean to speak unkindly of the dead." His chuckle sounded like two dry pieces of wood rubbing together. "Look, I just want to see drugs legalized so we can reduce crime and use taxes on the drugs to pay for education and treatment. What's wrong with that?"

Strawn's bipolar personality didn't surprise Colson. He had gone over this territory with Mr. Hyde already, so he must be speaking with Doctor Jekyll now. Colson walked behind his chair and rested his hands on the back. "We just went over that. Reduced crime is great, but an increase in the number of addicts is bad. I don't know any simpler way to say it. And once again, legalizing drugs wouldn't do away with drug-related crime. Strangely, drug addicts don't make good employees. And if they can't hold a job, they will steal to eat, to buy clothes, to pay their rent and their car payments. Or are you suggesting that we support them on welfare? And as far as the black market goes, unless you give away drugs for free, there will always be a black market and there will always be black market crime. The drug cartels aren't going to give up their turf to legal retailers or the government. They'll undercut the retailers and the government's price and sell untaxed drugs, and we'll be right back where we started, but with even more drug addicts." Colson sat down again, quietly looking at Strawn. He had testified in enough trials to know that you shut up when you've won.

A blank look crossed Strawn's face, and he turned his attention from Colson to Keith. "Was your son living at home before his death?"

Thrown by the sudden change of topic, Keith faltered, "Uh— yeah. He still had his room there, of course, but we hadn't seen him in a couple of months."

"Not even for a few minutes?" Strawn said. "He didn't even stop by his room for a short visit?"

Keith appeared puzzled by Strawn's question. "Yeah, come to think of it, my wife said he stopped by and moved some things around in his room one day a week or so before his death, but neither one of us were home at the time, so we didn't get to see him. Why do you ask?"

"No reason, really," Strawn said waving his hand. "Just wondering if you and the wife got to see him before he passed." He looked at his watch and stood. "As I said, I'm a very busy man. This meeting is over." And with that, he abruptly walked out of the office, leaving Keith and Colson sitting in front of his desk staring at each other. Haggart returned to parade rest across the room.

"I didn't even get a chance to ask him about a public debate," Keith said.

Haggart escorted Keith and Colson to the lobby in silence. They stepped into the concrete courtyard, with Haggart's large frame standing behind the plate glass, watching. Colson could feel his eyes pushing them away from the building until they were out of sight.

It was a beautiful Atlanta day, with a warm breeze rustling the leaves of a line of trees planted between the sidewalk and the busy downtown street. Sunlight glinted off the chrome, glass, steel, and concrete buildings. Colson reached into his suit coat pocket, removed a pair of sunglasses, and slid them on, thinking of how he preferred the sunlight reflecting off the waves of the Atlantic from his fifth-floor balcony on the beach.

They walked to the entrance of the parking deck. The air was fifteen degrees cooler inside, but Colson noticed that Keith's face was dripping perspiration. "That was like emerging from the rabbit hole in *Alice in Wonderland*," Keith said. "What did you think of that guy?"

"He's a kook," Colson said.

"That's obvious, but how did a lunatic like that become a billionaire?"

"Beats me," Colson said. "Maybe he inherited it, but I tend to think he turned into a lunatic after he became a billionaire. Power and money can do that to people. Everyone starts acting like your friend because of the money. The employees kiss his butt, and no one crosses him or argues a point. He can make or break thousands of people and their families on a whim. Many people like Strawn develop a god syndrome, and it drives them insane—or makes them a tyrant." Colson stopped and turned to Keith. "Did you see that lock on his office door?"

"Yeah, so what?" Keith said. "I have a lock on my office door."

"I do too. So do a lot of people. But his had a keyed lock, a computerized lock with a keypad, and a card reader."

"Maybe he loses his keys a lot."

"Maybe," Colson said. "That would make sense if the lock could be opened with either the key, the card, or the code, but I think that lock requires all three in sequence to be opened. C'mon Keith. You're the security guru."

Keith squinted at him. "I did notice the motion detectors and window and door alarms in there. I'm always checking out the competition's security equipment out of habit. I didn't think about it at the time, but now it seems redundant. Why would a furniture company CEO's office require that much security?"

"Exactly," Colson answered. "Same reason I asked his gorilla why he needed a bodyguard

"Yeah, I guess that is kind of weird," Keith said. "I was meaning to ask you about your little banter with his bodyguard. What was that all about? There was Strawn in his three-thousand-dollar suit and condescending attitude, and you're sitting there in khakis, open-collared shirt, hundred-dollar off-the-rack blazer, and devil-may-care attitude. I've never seen that side of you. I thought you were going to get us thrown out or sent to the hospital before we even had a chance to get started."

Colson chuckled. "Sorry about catching you off-guard, but I had good reason."

"I'm afraid to ask." Keith's tone was openly sarcastic.

Colson took a deep breath. "It's about identifying the good guys from the bad guys, or in short, poking the tiger."

"You were poking, all right." Keith said, rolling his eyes. "You were getting under my skin with that sarcasm, and you weren't even talking to me."

"Sorry, I didn't think to warn you," Colson said with a grin. "The test is to see how a person responds, and that separates normal people from thugs. You get a stick and poke a cow and it will moo a complaint, but you poke a tiger and see what happens."

"So, normal people are cows, now?"

"You miss my point. With humans it's a matter of self-control and civility. Haggart would have had a good reason to ask me to leave. That is, if it had been his office. You saw the look on his face and the bulging veins—he wanted to beat me like a drum."

Keith nodded. "You knew the bodyguard's name? Strawn didn't introduce him."

"I'm familiar with him by name only, but I wanted to test him."

"We didn't have to test Strawn to know he's a bad guy, but what is the verdict with Haggart?"

Colson shook his head. "The jury is still out, but I'm thinking they come back with a verdict of guilty for the charge of being a scum without a clue."

"Do you know what else seemed odd?"

"What?"

"He was extremely interested in Joshua's movements before his death," Keith said. "Why would he want to know about that?"

Colson pondered for a few seconds. "That's a good question."

Keith squinted. "You don't think he could have had something to do with my son's death, do you?"

Colson shrugged. "That's seems a stretch, but I have a better opinion about him. When I was in law enforcement, we always had our own completely inadmissible, off-the-record, not even in our personal notes, gut feelings about a suspect or a case. Is that what you're asking me for?"

"Yeah, I guess I am."

"He may be a billionaire," Colson said, "but he's just a thug, as far as I'm concerned. And I can't imagine why a CEO of a billion-dollar corporation would care about the actions of an eighteen-year-old kid he doesn't even know." Colson scratched his head; this one had him troubled more than usual. "He's got more up his sleeve than his stinking armpits. Maybe it's time we found out what that is."

ᴄ⁀᷿CHAPTER TWELVE᷿⁀

The Butcher studied the face of the third girl in the photo and flipped back to the individual senior photos in the middle of the yearbook. It was a time-consuming task. And frustrating. He had never experienced such difficulty locating anyone before. Then again, he'd never before been paid to find a juvenile, someone with no—or extremely little—documented past. No credit or work history. No marriage certificate, criminal history, or previous residence history to track. If a juvenile ran away from home or was abducted, they were a virtual ghost unless they ran only as far as a friend's house or were found dead on the side of the road.

He was confident she hadn't been abducted, so identifying who her friends were and where they lived was the next logical step.

Obtaining school records wasn't an easy task. Without his unwitting source, it would be almost impossible unless he wanted to risk breaking into the school's administrative office after hours. No, that wasn't an option. Juvenile and medical records were sacred and sealed from public eyes. You had to have an inside source, and the Butcher would exhaust every cautious means available before risking an unnecessary burglary and possibly leaving a fingerprint or a hair to identify him. The source he had conned into loaning him the yearbook would think nothing about giving him the information he needed to locate Emily's friends. He had a talent for being persuasive.

His vibrating cell phone distracted him for an instant, causing the image of one of the girls in the photo with Emily to fade from his memory. He gave the number on the screen an irritated glance and touched the answer icon.

"What?" he blurted.

"Uh," the female voice said hesitantly, "I have the registration information you needed on the Raines' vehicles."

"Go," was the Butcher's one-word reply while he jerked a pen from his jacket pocket.

"First is a 2010 Lexus, black in color, tag number—"

"No, no," he interrupted. "Go with the next."

"Second one is a 2004 Porsche 911 Cabriolet, red—"

"No, no, no damn it. Any others?"

"One more," the female replied with a hint of annoyance. "A 2006 Toyota, blue." The voice hesitated, awaiting the next barrage of ungrateful retorts. The Butcher's eyes widened with a moment of minor satisfaction. That's what the girl would be driving. The Lexus would be the wife's car, and no doubt the Porsche belonged to the husband. Both were in the driveway during his last visit.

"Give me the tag number on the Toyota," the Butcher said. There was a brief pause and the sound of papers being shuffled, followed by the recitation of a short series of numbers and letters. He scribbled the tag letters and numbers on a pad, disconnected, and laid his phone on the table without another word. He turned his attention back to the yearbook photos, cursing under his breath.

He flipped back to the photo of three teenage girls. A caption above read simply, "Best Friends Forever." Growing more frustrated with the task of flipping the pages back and forth, he snatched at the page, tore it from the binding, and laid it next to the book. The three smiling young ladies were pictured from the waist up, standing with their backs to a bank of lime green lockers, clutching books to their chest and posing for the photographer. He knew the girl on the right was Emily Raines, but with no names listed below, he was forced to match the other two faces with their individual formal class photos in the back of the book.

Another ten minutes of scanning the remaining hundred or so photos, and he had the girls' names. He scribbled the names under the Toyota tag number and slapped the yearbook closed. His disposable cell began to vibrate again and began sliding like an air-hockey puck across the table. He snatched it up, saw the text notification on top of the screen, and touched the icon. The Butcher already knew who the message was from before it opened on his screen. Only one other person besides his insider had the number.

"What is it now?" he said to the phone. "You better not be pestering me again about the girl, or I'll—" His comment trailed off when the message opened and he read the code. "You've got to be kidding me. I know I'm good, but I can't be in three places at once." He looked at the code for a second time after transposing it. "67337464-2-368253" was displayed above three web links. He concluded he was not mistaken as he held the small slip of paper showing the corresponding letters next to the numbers in the text.

"ORDERING A DOUBLE" was the message.

He shook his head and touched the top link. A blank Internet screen popped up with a little circle rotating in the middle, silently instructing him to wait for the page to load. A photo of a balding man appeared, wearing a shirt and tie and smiling for the camera. The Butcher's eyes widened as he touched the screen and slid the photo upward, revealing the writing beneath. "Larry Morgan—Clay County District Attorney" was written boldly under the photo.

"Tall order," the Butcher mumbled. The photo was displayed in the staff section of the Clay County district attorney's web page.

He backed out of the screen to the next link and touched it. He waited for the page to load and took a long look at his second target—or third, counting the girl. "Hmm," the Butcher hummed under his breath. The photo sat in the middle of an announcement with text above and below. The man pictured was smiling and wearing a Class A sheriff's dress uniform with gold major oak leaves embroidered on black shoulder epaulets. The wording above the photo spelled out, in an elegant font, "Come Celebrate Major Grey Colson's Retirement." Below it read, "January 30th—7:00 p.m.—Clay County Senior Center Banquet Room."

The Butcher had never been assigned three hits within a span of a month. Four if you add the junkie kid. He shook his head at the task. It was entirely too risky to expose himself to his employers, but he wished he could in this case and tell the man how blatantly stupid he was for ordering so many hits so close together. They really needed to get their priorities straight and not panic. The girl had to be the first priority because she held the smoking gun. These other two would have to wait if he agreed to accept the contracts at all. The money was tempting, but at the same time, greed could be deadly.

The Butcher touched the final link and waited. Media software appeared on the screen, followed by a phone ringing. It was an audio file. He suffered through the boring conversation between Morgan and Colson without interest until he heard the last portion. His contact would or should know he had no need to hear the call, with the exception of the mention of where both Morgan and Colson would be a week from Saturday.

He considered refusing, due to the added risk of taking them both out at the same time. He would have to examine all possibilities before attempting anything so blatant. It would cost them.

He touched the reply icon, typed, "368253$," and waited.

Detective Mike Meador studied the man's face. He had been shot in the back of the head. His long, dirty hair was matted and stuck to the carpet in a dark brown pool of rock-hard blood, surrounding the head and shoulders. His head was turned to the side, and his nose and mouth had dissolved into a bloody pulp. Either the bullet had exited just below his nose or someone had beaten him before issuing the killing shot.

Meador shook his head at what was left of the face before turning away to make notes on his 007 pad. *'Slaying in the Suburbs,'* he thought. *Not a bad title for a murder mystery.* He figured he would see how this case shaped up and maybe use the facts to at least knock out a short story for *Murder Mystery Magazine*. Nothing wrong with making a few extra bucks.

He looked around the filthy room for a moment and then began carefully drawing a sketch of the crime scene. "Typical rat-hole doper's house," he said to himself as he worked.

The small, cracker-box style house was almost identical to every other home in this neighborhood—with the exception of its contents, of course. One dead drug dealer and the pound of heroin. A neighbor walking her dog had called in a bad smell coming from the living room window, and the experienced first responder who arrived recognized the stench the moment he stepped onto the porch.

Beginning to sweat through his shirt, Meador pulled off his suit jacket and draped it across his arm. He considered laying it across the back of the couch, but the fear of fleas or other nasty creatures hitching a ride on it made him think twice. "It's hotter in here than two bunnies making babies in a sock. You see a thermostat?" Meador said to the CSI technician standing just inside the front doorway.

The young technician couldn't be more than thirty years old. It was difficult for Meador to estimate with the boy wearing a ball cap pulled tight over his head and a paper mask covering most of his face. He stood silent, peering at Meador over the mask and holding an expensive digital camera to his side with a large flash extension sticking from the top. Without a word, he gestured to the hallway. Meador stepped around the body and found the small box on the wall.

"Hell, no wonder," he said when he noticed the heat was set to 80. "Another day or two and we would have had to scrape this guy up with a spatula." Meador turned back to the technician and saw his mid-section flinch. The wave of nausea started a chain reaction up through his chest and throat, but he shut it down like a real trooper. *Must be a new guy,* he thought. He decided not to torture the young man further with colorful descriptions of the rotting corpse and tried to divert his attention away from the obvious. "Ah, you can go ahead with the photos, but don't touch anything." Meador held up his index finger for emphasis.

The technician nodded, spun his cap around, and began snapping photos of the scene while Meador walked cautiously through the rest of the house. In addition to the pound of heroin in the back bedroom, he located a box in the closet filled with several ounces of powdered cocaine, and a shoebox stuffed with cookies of crack.

He paused in the kitchen, looking at residue-coated pots and pans strewn on the counter and in the sink. He had seen these hundreds, maybe thousands of times and immediately recognized they were being used for cooking crack. It was a very simple process. The "cook" would add baking soda to cocaine causing it to rise, then bake out the water. The coke would then crystallize into crack. The cooking process removed any impurities, such as sugars and resulted in a much purer and more potent form of the drug. Dealers loved crack because it sold for twice the price of pure cocaine and was easy to conceal and sell. And crack being instantly psychologically and physiologically addictive guaranteed return customers.

He estimated the house contained at least a couple hundred thousand dollars worth of drugs at the moment. He flipped open his pad to make a note. *"The killer left all the dope in the house."*

He walked to the front porch as another crime scene guy walked up the driveway. "Don't touch the dope," he said, as the second tech stepped around him.

"Which one?" the tech said, looking through the open doorway and seeing the man's body on the floor.

"Very funny," Meador said while rolling his eyes. "I may use that line in my short story. There's a pound of heroin in the back bedroom, so the narcotics guys are on the way." The tech nodded and walked inside. "Hey," Meador said, and the man paused and faced him. "Your partner said he wants spaghetti for lunch." The tech threw Meador a confused glance, but he had already turned and bounced down the front porch steps.

Meador nodded to a young uniform cop who lifted the crime scene tape and jotted a note in his own 007 pad when Meador walked underneath. He drew in deep breaths while walking across the neglected, weed-infested lawn. The aroma of hot asphalt and vehicle exhaust smelled of honeysuckle in contrast to the stench inside the doper's house. His cell chirped about the same time he reached the forensics van at the bottom of the driveway. He pulled it off his belt.

"Meador."

A male voice responded, "This is Agent Willard. I'm the on-call agent for narcotics. Please tell me you have more than an eight-ball, because I was having dinner with my wife's parents. It's the mother-in-law's birthday, and I'm not going to hear the end of it." His frustration was plain to hear.

"Triple D," Meador said, "Dead Drug Dealer. Pound or so of smack in his bedroom, along with a few ounces of coke and crack.

Whoever did this guy left over a hundred thousand in street value in the house. Looks like it might be a contract hit."

"You ID the victim yet?"

Meador flipped open his notepad. "Yeah, white male, thirty years old. Derrick Ramey."

Willard's frustrated tone changed to interest. "I know that guy," he said. "Sells heroin and a little coke to the street dealers, small-scale pushers and addicts on the south side. One of his customers OD'd in a motel room on Candler last week. Eighteen-year-old kid went by the street name JayBee."

"Sweet justice, I guess."

"What do you mean?"

"Dealer sells a kid a hot dose; kid dies, dealer ends up dead."

"Yeah, I guess so," Willard said. "I'm on the way to process the dope. Be there in ten minutes."

Fifteen minutes later, Meador was leaning in the doorway, watching Willard work. He waited while Willard weighed and packaged the dope in evidence bags, marking each for identification and lab testing. The medical examiner's investigator bagged and tagged Ramey for his trip to the morgue, and the CSI guys finished their gig, both exiting the house drenched with sweat.

Meador considered what Willard had told him on the phone about the kid who overdosed and considered the fact that the killer left the drugs untouched. He opened his pad and wrote two words for follow-up later: "Retaliation" and "Revenge."

Agent Willard walked to his car with the last paper bags of evidence and dropped them in the trunk. He stepped up to Meador and extended his hand. "Okay, man. All done. I'm outta here."

Meador shook Willard's hand. "Sorry about your dinner plans."

Willard shook his head. "No problem. To be honest, I was delighted to get away."

"I'll make it up to you," Meador said with a mischievous smile. "Next year I won't interrupt your dinner with the in-laws. Hell, you can even have dinner with mine if you like."

Willard cocked his head. "You're a real pal, Meador, thanks." He gave Meador a dismissive wave on his way to the car.

"He wants double the money," Haggart said, sitting across from Strawn at his desk. Strawn didn't appear to be listening; his attention was focused on the giant monitor on the opposite wall. A reporter spouted a short blurb about Strawn's proposed legislation and Morgan's efforts to squash it, and then a clip of a distraught Keith Bartlett came on the screen, preaching against drug legalization. Strawn held up one finger to momentarily silence Haggart. By the time Haggart turned to catch the report, it was over and a commercial began blaring. Strawn slapped the glass inlay on his desk, turning the monitor off.

"Damned Morgan running his mouth to the press again," Strawn shouted. The office was so well insulated with soundproof acoustical material that a marching band could be playing at full tilt and not a sound could be heard in the lobby. Strawn was specific in that little detail so he could throw a tantrum like a spoiled child, and no one would ever be the wiser. He rolled his fingers on the glass and eyed Haggart.

"He still hasn't found the girl or our property yet, and he wants double?"

Haggart shrugged. "I can tell him no if you'd like."

Strawn kept his stare on Haggart for what seemed like five minutes and continued to roll his fingers. It was as if he were in a trance. Haggart never knew if he was expected to speak again or just sit there like a bowl of fruit until Strawn snapped back to reality. The man had serious issues, but Haggart couldn't care less as long as his paychecks cleared the bank. He relaxed in his chair and waited for Strawn's decision.

He didn't have to wait much longer; soon Strawn leaned forward and rested his elbows on the desk. "Capone had the same problem," Strawn said. "The treasury boys were after him, but they weren't smart enough. They had to settle for a snitch accountant to do their job for them."

Haggart scratched his head, bewildered. Did Strawn actually fancy himself another Al Capone? Strawn read Haggart's confused expression and continued his analysis.

"Morgan is trying to stop me for political reasons, and Colson is still just his flunky, but he's a smart-ass, dangerous one. The girl is like the accountant and is just as dangerous in that regard. All three problems have to be eliminated. I don't care how, in what order, or how dirty it might be—you tell him to get it done. And I want it done now."

"And the money?"

Strawn pointed at Haggart. "He can have double, but I want my money's worth. You tell him he has fourteen days to get it done. All of it."

☙CHAPTER THIRTEEN❧

T he corrugated steel garage door inside the secured gates of Strawn Tower rose in silence from Colson's position a hundred yards away. He lifted his binoculars and zoomed in on the rear of a black Cadillac stretch limo. Colson punched the tag number in a text message and waited for the registered owner's information. As he suspected, it came back to Strawn Industries of Atlanta.

The Midtown Atlanta traffic was just beginning to make its transition from mildly annoying to extremely frustrating at 5:00 p.m. Keith sat next to Colson in the low-slung passenger seat of his 1994 Corvette. They had been parked in the lot of a two-story business office across the street for forty-five minutes. Keith adjusted his feet and kicked a fast-food paper bag from under the seat. Grabbing the bag and the door handle, he said, "You want me to throw this out?"

Colson held up his hand. "Not yet—just drop it behind your seat. We may need it later."

Keith shrugged and laid the bag behind him on the deck of the hatchback. "Do you always keep binoculars in your car?"

"They're not the only tool I keep in the car."

Colson focused on the corner of the tower as employees began to exit the building. He shifted the binoculars to the limo and saw Haggart leaning against the car. The bodyguard wore dark sunglasses, and his huge arms were folded across his chest. He was massive and strangely larger against the car than in person. His head was shaved and he wore a black suit coat, probably tailored by the Atlanta Tent and Awning Company. Haggart stepped into the open parking area and scanned in both directions as Strawn came into view near the rear door.

"Did you see Haggart?" Keith said.

"As I expected, they're attached like Siamese twins," Colson said.

"That's what I was thinking."

"Did you notice the limo's tires?" Colson said. "Heavy duty to support the weight of a reinforced frame. That also means it's armor-plated and has bulletproof windows. No reason to armor plate a limo and leave windows you can penetrate with a pellet gun. I'd have to sell an organ every day just to fill that thing up with gas."

Keith raised his eyebrows. "Armor-plated and bullet-proof? The furniture business must be pretty dangerous."

"You never know," Colson said, "Could be his ancestor was Ethan Allen and the British are still pissed about losing Fort Ticonderoga."

"What?"

"You know, the Revolutionary War? Never mind, don't worry about it."

"They're leaving," Keith said.

The limo backed slowly and pulled to the exit. The long chain link gate rolled to one side, and the limo made a right turn, away from their position. Colson allowed two additional cars to fall in behind the limo so he could follow at a discreet distance. The limo reached its destination twelve minutes later, pulling up to the gate of an industrial park with warehouses of various sizes constructed of corrugated steel. A uniformed guard standing in a glass booth operated the slow-rolling chain link gate for the limo to enter.

Colson parked at a fast food restaurant across the street and watched the limo maneuver to a position in front of one of the largest warehouses. Colson lifted the binoculars and focused on the top corner of the drab, flat-roofed warehouse. The building was no more than a nondescript metal box.

"There's a number on the building," Colson said, handing the binoculars to Keith. "Eleven. Otherwise, there's no signs or markings.

I'm not really surprised." Colson drummed his fingers on the steering wheel. "He doesn't want to draw any attention to the building. The only reason it has a number is because the city requires it for firefighters and police to respond during an emergency."

Keith looked over the binoculars at Colson. "These come in handy."

Colson nodded and grinned. "I'm glad you're getting into it. This type of work can become addictive—but in a good way."

A metal overhead door rose as the vehicle approached and the limo disappeared inside the dark opening. Only the brake lights were visible until the door closed behind it.

"So," Keith said, "what do you think?"

Colson shrugged. "You got me. Could be purely innocent. He might be checking on his furniture inventory for all we know." Colson pulled a 007 pad and pen from his console and held them out to Keith. "How about jotting down where he goes. Could mean something."

"Right," Keith said.

They waited patiently for ten minutes, until the rising overhead door caught their attention. The limo backed out and pulled out onto the street. Colson waited until the car was just out of sight and then fell in behind.

Colson was enjoying the game, and Keith seemed to notice. "It must feel good," he said. "You know, doing what you used to do."

Colson caught himself grinning and forced a straight face. He felt bad for Keith. They wouldn't be following Strawn if he hadn't lost his son. When his daughter was kidnapped, there was no time for smiles and loose surveillance. He looked back to Keith, who was concentrating on the limo like a bloodhound. "I'm sorry," Colson said. "I do take this very seriously. I hope you know that."

"Of course," Keith said, not taking his eyes off the limo in the distance. "I never doubted it."

They rode in silence, following the limo as it turned right on South Cobb Industrial Drive. The limo pulled to a stop in front of an office in another warehouse complex, and Strawn exited and waddled through the door, puffing on a cigar. Colson turned left and parked on a parallel street where they could see the limo between two buildings. A row of retail stores sat to their right, although all were vacant with the exception of two—a Dollar General with two cars parked out front at one end, and a barbershop on the other, with a lone car parked at the door. A barber chair was occupied just behind the plate glass, where a man in a white jacket clipped his customer's hair.

Five minutes passed, then ten. Colson noticed the barber's attention was drawn away from his customer's head and focused in his direction. It wasn't difficult to determine since his was the only car parked on the street. Overwhelming curiosity must have been more than the barber could bear. He stood up against the plate glass window with his hands on his hips, glaring at the green Corvette on the street.

Colson shook his head. "Here we go."

"What?" Keith said. "I didn't see him come out."

Colson reached behind the seat and placed the paper bag in his lap. The barber pushed open the shop door and strutted across the small lot and across the street. He made a slow arc behind the Corvette and stopped at Colson's window. Keith looked back and forth between Colson and the man standing outside with clippers in his hand. Colson hit a button on the console and the window rolled down.

"Can I help you?" the barber said in a tone suggesting the last thing he was offering was help.

"Sure, partner," Colson said cheerfully. He held the bag out the window. "Can you throw this away for me?"

The barber looked at the bag, then back to Colson. The man's face contorted, as if he had momentarily lost his train of thought due to Colson's ridiculous request. "No!" he said. "What the hell are you doing here?"

Colson maintained his cheerful tone. "Nunya."

"What?"

"Nunya business," Colson said less cheerfully and shot the window up.

The barber's voice was now muffled with the air-conditioner blowing in the closed cockpit of the car. "I'm calling the po-po," he announced as he stepped back on the street and walked away.

Colson powered Keith's window down and raised his voice to the barber. "Sir!"

The barber turned in the middle of the street without a word. Colson smiled. "Ask them to stop on the way and pick up a couple more burgers and donuts."

The barber stalked across the street, slung open his door, and grabbed a cordless phone, turning back to the window for Colson to see. Keith sat and gave Colson an expression of shock.

"What was that all about?"

Colson chuckled. "Us two crackers just got profiled. I can't think of a time doing surveillance when some citizen didn't give me crap about sitting in my car, minding my own business for longer than thirty seconds. Especially in this city. Some people are just stupid. If we had been bad guys up to whatever he thought we were up to, he'd already be bleeding out on the sidewalk."

"I guess people are just curious in general," Keith said.

"That may be," Colson agreed, nodding to the strip mall, "but not when it counts. You let a real crime occur in that parking lot and the police respond, asking questions and trying to identify witnesses, and that same guy will say he didn't see anything, even if he did. I've seen it and dealt with it too many times. Most people are just sniveling busybodies who should thank their lucky stars they haven't been shot in the face."

"But what about when the police get here?" Keith said. "Surely you don't know them all personally."

"Atlanta PD uniform?" Colson said with a laugh. "Even if he did call them and report two suspicious dudes, legally parked across from a strip mall at eleven a.m., I would estimate their response time to be around, oh… two p.m. tomorrow—if then."

The barber positioned his chair toward the window after his customer left and sat checking his own watch for the next eleven minutes. Colson had turned his attention to the warehouse in time to see Strawn reappear and get back into his limo.

"What do you think he was doing in that office?" Keith said.

"Probably whatever evil billionaires do before they take over the world," Colson said with a smirk. He dropped the gear into first and discreetly followed the limo as it pulled out of the industrial park, back onto South Cobb Industrial Drive heading westbound. They drove parallel for a few blocks and then swung in behind, keeping three cars between them. Colson shifted through the five-speed transmission as naturally as a seasoned street racer. He jerked the car right, took the next left, gunned the 'Vette down another parallel course, and turned back onto South Cobb Industrial Drive and dropped in front of the limo. He kept the limo in his rear-view mirror until the driver turned off, squealed through a U-turn, and fell in behind them on the I-285 on-ramp. The limo continued on the interstate to Douglas County and took the Thornton Road exit. They followed at a distance of about six car lengths, allowing other cars to merge between them.

Four miles later the vehicle turned off into yet another industrial park and stopped in front of one of the offices. Colson drove past, made another U-turn, steered the car back toward the warehouse, and pulled off the highway fifty yards past the gated entrance. They parked off the side of the road where they could just see the complex driveway. He turned off the engine, and they sat in silence for a few minutes.

"He visits a lot of different warehouses," Keith said finally

"Yeah, I noticed," Colson answered. "You writing these locations down? And the time?"

"Ah, yeah, sure," Keith said, scratching notes in the pad. "You think he's actually looking at furniture in these warehouses?"

"My gut tells me no." Colson picked up his cell phone and made a call. He identified himself and gave the address of each of the locations Strawn had just visited. He waited a few minutes and then nodded. "Thanks, Carol," he said into the phone. "I owe you one." He ended the call and looked at Keith. "Each building they've stopped at so far is owned by Strawn Industries. I'm sure you noticed the armed guard patrols at all three locations. Each has a high chain link fence surrounding the property and video cameras mounted in strategic locations throughout the area."

Keith squinted through the windshield. "I didn't notice the cameras."

"I did," Colson said.

"Why so much security?"

"Same question as his Fort Knox-style office. Something tells me it's not because Strawn's afraid someone will break in and steal a recliner." Colson started the car and drove slowly toward the entrance of the industrial park. "It would be extremely difficult to get a look inside those buildings. There are only three ways in. We could be invited in, which isn't going to happen, or we could drive a truck through the door in a frontal assault, which would get us both locked up or shot." Colson went silent, nearing the entrance.

"What's number three?"

"Stealth." Colson just got the word out of his mouth when the limo roared out of the industrial complex and turned right, tires barking as it fishtailed in the oncoming lane. The limo rocketed toward Colson's car, headed in the opposite direction. As the two vehicles passed each other, Colson caught a glimpse of Haggart through the dark windshield, giving him the finger. Colson slammed the accelerator to the floor, launching the Corvette forward with a cloud of burning rubber in its wake. "This is my game, Haggart," Colson said as if the bodyguard could hear. "And you don't even know how to play."

Keith snapped his head around to watch the limo. "Why are we going in the opposite—" His question was cut short when his shoulder belt cut into his chest as Colson pulled up on the emergency brake, locking the rear wheels. He spun the steering wheel sharply left, swinging the back of the car around a full 180 degrees in the opposite direction and floored the accelerator. Smoke enveloped the Corvette momentarily as the rear tires squealed for traction on the hot asphalt. The rear of the low sports car dropped slightly when the wide tires bit the road, and they were propelled forward as if they had been struck from behind by a Mack truck.

"Looks like you've done this before." Keith sounded nervous.

"A few times, but it seems like a long time ago." Colson chuckled. "Well, maybe last summer."

"I'm disappointed," Keith confessed. "No *Dukes of Hazzard* rebel yell?"

Colson grinned and kept the accelerator glued to the floorboard, speed shifting the stick through the gears with two fingers.

"I think you may be a little crazy," Keith said, as he moved his hands to brace against the dash.

"Pursuit driving was my favorite training course. Came in handy working in uniform and later doing undercover work." Colson downshifted and merged onto the interstate. "I'll admit if you do the job long enough, it'll make you a little crazy." He cocked his head in thought while shooting off the on-ramp, slipping between two tractor-trailers, and jumping into an open lane with a fresh boost of torque. "Come to think of it, I wasn't like this at all when I started, but you learn to get a little crazy just to survive."

"I'm surprised we're just doing ninety," Keith said. "I would've bet a month's pay that we were doing over a hundred and twenty."

"Sorry, these aren't built for comfort."

Colson expertly weaved in and out of the lanes of I-285, dodging traffic. Within thirty seconds the limo came into view. Both vehicles were now traveling eastbound toward the city at an extremely high rate of speed, but the highway was moderately clear of traffic since few people would be trying to get into the city at this hour.

Colson grabbed his mobile phone from the console and dialed 9-1-1, identified himself as a retired police officer, gave their location, description, and tag number of the limo, and told the dispatcher to notify the Georgia State Patrol of a vehicle driving erratically at a high rate of speed. He listened momentarily and then ended the call. "There's a state trooper two exits up," Colson said. "He'll stop the limo."

Colson maintained his speed on the limo until the blue lights of a Georgia State Patrol car came into view far ahead, and then he eased back on the pedal. Haggart apparently was experiencing his own case of tunnel vision, being so focused on losing Colson that he didn't touch his brakes until the GSP unit jumped in behind him. Colson dropped to fifty-five, giving the trooper enough time to approach the car and command Haggart to step out. The trooper was scribbling on his note pad as Colson eased the 'Vette by the limo at a crawl.

"You do know about the slow-down law don't you?" Colson said. "We certainly wouldn't want to put that fine trooper or his guest in danger by driving by too fast, would we?"

Haggart glared at Colson as they drove past the limo. Colson declined to return Haggart's finger offering, instead smiling and offering Haggart a lazy salute. He tuned the radio to an eighties satellite channel and thumbed the steering wheel to the beat of "Double Vision" by Foreigner. He drove the speed limit back into the city and appeared to be quite satisfied with what they had accomplished.

"Didn't we get—what did you call it—burnt?" Keith said.

Colson turned his concentration away from the music. "I'm sorry?"

"I mean, Strawn knows we were following him and is probably really pissed now."

Colson shrugged.

"And why would Haggart speed off like he did?"

"He made us for surveillance and was just being a jerk. It's not easy to conduct surveillance with one car. Almost impossible," Colson said. "He wanted to prove he could lose us, and I wanted Strawn to know we were following him."

"You wanted Strawn to know?"

Colson nodded his head slowly. Keith answered with a confused look and waved his hands around the confining interior of the car. "I don't get it. Then why all the laying back and running parallel and everything?"

"Well," Colson shrugged again. "We wouldn't want to be too obvious of course. If I was stuck doing solo surveillance, which I've had to for various reasons, I would rent a nondescript sedan that smelled like a baby puked a pine tree air freshener."

Keith shook his head. "I still don't know what good it did us."

Colson drove in silence and coasted down an off-ramp. He looked down the intersecting road in both directions, then made a right and looked over at Keith. "You wanna shake?"

"Huh?" Keith said. "Shake what?"

Colson swung into a Dairy Queen drive-through, ordered two small vanilla shakes, and found a parking space. He unwrapped his straw, stuck it through the lid, and took a long pull. "Remember what I said about poking the tiger?"

"Yeah."

Colson eyed Keith for moment, gathering his thoughts. "Let's say you're Jack Strawn and are a legitimate, world-renowned billionaire and one day you are being followed by a couple of guys to several of your highly protected business locations. What would you do?"

"I dunno," Keith admitted. "I guess I'd call the cops."

"Why would you do that?" Colson said.

"They might be trying to kidnap me for ransom or carjack me or steal my inventory. I dunno." Keith shrugged and took a sip of his shake.

"Right," Colson said. "A normal, law-abiding, and respectable businessman or woman would think the same thing. They'd be on their phone, screaming that a couple of jack-booted thugs were following them around and demanding the cops do something about it. Then they would probably go to the court for a temporary protective order to keep us away from him."

"But you don't think Strawn will do that?"

Colson gave Keith a dismissive wave. "Not in a million years. He has something to hide, and I'll bet you another milkshake it's in those warehouses."

Keith took another drink and smiled. "Sounds like we have more work to do."

"Yep." Colson started the engine and reached for the shifter.

"Hey—how 'bout I drive us back?" Keith said.

Colson reached just under his seat and pulled out a black rounded object, about seven inches long and an inch or so in diameter. He held it nose high and shook it slightly. It sounded as if it were full of coins rattling against each other.

"What's that?"

Colson gave him a stern look, one he'd used many times. "Another one of those tools I carry around. It's called an ASP. If you drove my car and put one scratch on it, I wouldn't be able to refrain from tenderizing you a little with this thing."

Keith held up his hands in surrender.

Colson smiled. "Just kidding."

⌒⌒CHAPTER FOURTEEN⌒⌒

A bank of a dozen fluorescent lights flickered to life overhead and the industrial steel garage door dropped behind the limousine. Haggart exited the driver's side and trotted to the rear door, opening it for Strawn. He felt embarrassed for being stopped by the state trooper, but he maintained his composure and patiently waited for the scolding that was certain to come. Strawn hadn't said a word since the trooper released them from the side of the road. Haggart stood at attention, holding the door until Strawn stepped out and dropped the nub of his cigar through the iron drainage grate at his feet.

"I apologize for the inconvenience, sir," Haggart said. With the preemptive comment, there was a chance Strawn would get it over with and curse him out here in the garage instead of letting his anger fester during the elevator ride and blowing his top in his soundproof office. Strawn turned to Haggart and said nothing. Haggart hated it when Strawn went into his trances. He decided to roll the dice and continue.

"I would have taken the ticket, sir."

"Damn right you would have," Strawn blurted out, "but I won't give Colson the satisfaction." Strawn gave a rare chuckle. "Did you see that boy's face when I told him he was making me late for a meeting with the governor and I was going to blame him for it?"

Haggart realized Strawn was almost giddy about their little movie-style chase and putting the trooper in his place, especially when Strawn pulled his cell phone and stuck it in the trooper's face. The trooper's staunch expression vanished when he saw a photo of the governor on the phone screen with his direct office number listed beneath it. "Better yet, I'll call your boss right now, and you can explain it to him," Strawn had told the trooper evenly. After a friendly warning, the trooper had extinguished his blue lights and merged into traffic with his tailpipe between his legs.

Strawn's face returned to its normal stony appearance. "Colson sure has a set of big ones if he thinks he can intimidate me." He pointed in Haggart's face. "Your contact had better handle it before I cancel the order and send you to do it yourself."

"And the other man in the car from the meeting, uh—"

"Bartlett," Strawn finished for Haggart. Strawn walked toward the elevator, but stopped before pressing the call button and turned back to Haggart. "He's nothing. Oh, he'll keep whining and pouting over his dead junkie kid, but the press will get tired of it soon and move on to something else. Colson's a different story. I could see it in his eyes, but putting an order on Bartlett isn't necessary."

Haggart nodded. "And if Bartlett doesn't go away?"

Strawn pulled another cigar from his jacket and stuck it in his mouth. "What are you up to, Haggart? You must be getting a commission from your so-called professional buddy. It's real easy for you to spend my money, isn't it?"

"No, sir, I was just—"

"I'll tell you what, Haggart," Strawn said, cutting him off. "You're so worried about Bartlett, you go have a talk with him yourself."

The Butcher slipped inside the heavy steel door, pulled it shut, and turned the lock. The motion detector switch on the wall to his right activated a bank of fluorescent office lights above his head. A cheap office clock hanging on the opposite wall read 2:12 a.m. He pressed a button beneath the detector to kill the lights and clicked on a mini-flashlight. There were two rooms to his right and left. Both doors stood open to dark offices. Straight ahead stood a vault door, closed tight in its steel frame. He walked on the concrete floor past the offices, glancing right and left to satisfy himself no one was burning the midnight oil. He faced the dull gray door and quickly spun the combination dial a full turn right, stopping at the first number he memorized earlier. He spun the dial left and right two more times, jerked the handle down, and was rewarded with a loud "clack" echoing against the walls of the vacant office.

The Butcher pulled on the heavy door, silently easing it open just enough to step inside the vault. A second motion detector switch illuminated the twelve-by-twelve room. The vault had no windows, so he didn't bother switching the light off manually. Floor-to-ceiling wire racks stood against the wall to his left, loaded with cardboard boxes. Labels written with a permanent marker indicated their contents. Some had coded lettering and numbers, and others were written in plain English. A flat-screen computer sat atop a worn wooden desk against the far wall; an emblem bounced across the screen in power-saving mode. On the right wall hung three steel cabinets, secured with padlocks dangling from hasps. Under the cabinets sat two six-foot-long folding tables with neatly stacked forms in their respective piles against the wall. He was almost impressed with the tidiness of the room as he began scanning the labeled boxes to his left.

A box caught his attention on an eye-level shelf near the end of the rack. He suspected it would be one of the smaller boxes, and he was correct. He pulled the box from the shelf and slid it onto one of the folding tables under the cabinets. The box had been opened previously, but it appeared none of its contents had been used. Two rows of small white boxes were stacked on top of a second row of identical boxes beneath. He removed three of the top boxes, pulled one from the bottom row, carefully flipped open the top, and slid the contents onto the table.

A small electronic device and booklet lay in front of him. He lifted the device and eyed it, turning it over in his hand. It was no larger than the old pagers everyone carried during the pre-cell phone days, except it was mostly rounded with one flat end. He shoved the device and booklet in his pocket and replaced the empty box in the vacant space he had taken it from, and then he neatly placed the three remaining boxes on the top row.

Twenty seconds later, the main box was back in its place on the shelf and the Butcher was back in his car. By the time anyone discovered the device was missing, if ever, he would be enjoying a cocktail in Sierra Leone.

Poplar Springs Baptist Church was located twenty minutes from Atlanta in the quaint town of Hiram, Georgia. The building was larger than it appeared from the street because much of its square footage stretched deep into the property. Although the charter of the church and membership rolls stretched back nearly one hundred and seventy-five years, the original building had been condemned to allow widening of the roadway, and a new facility had been erected a few short miles away, five years earlier.

The missions-minded congregation scheduled several events each year to support that specific purpose. In early spring, a car show and barbecue were the first of such events to draw attention and raise the much-needed funds for foreign missionaries. The newly elected Clay County district attorney, Larry Morgan, was pleased to be in charge of this year's car show, especially since he recently had purchased a new shiny show car of his own. He had spent the entire previous afternoon washing and waxing his red Corvette, sprucing up the interior leather seats, and buffing the chrome magnesium wheels.

At 10:00 on the day of the show, more than seventy-five gleaming cars graced the large church parking lot facing Hiram-Douglasville Highway. Hundreds of car enthusiasts and onlookers were already milling about between rows of antiques and muscle cars ranging in age from the 1950s to the latest models. Curious admirers strolled among the vehicles, examining spotless engines beneath raised hoods and immaculate interior appointments. One such admirer wore an Atlanta Braves baseball cap pulled low above his Ray-Ban sunglasses, a matching dark blue baseball jersey, and baggy tan Dockers. He had backed his stolen Honda into a space as near the exit as possible and blended into the crowd, lazily weaving through the lines of cars.

The Butcher feigned a smile and nodded his head in mock interest as he made his way closer to the red Corvette. He caught glimpses of Morgan waving his arms and laughing, presumably due to various comments being made by individuals as they passed by.

The snooty ones were probably whispering that Morgan should drop more money in the offering plate since he could afford such a nice car, and others would be lying through their teeth about being in the middle of a classic car restoration of their own.

The Butcher was two car lengths from Morgan when he turned to speak with two men at the rear of his car. The Butcher didn't have to force his grin. The timing couldn't be more perfect. He reached into his baggy right pocket and adjusted the small device in his hand. A thirty-second Internet search revealed the location of the vehicle's on-board diagnostic connection, or OBD port, for this specific model year. Morgan's back was to him, and no one else was paying attention to anything other than their bland conversations and barbecue sandwiches. He was just a blur, another on-looker wishing he could drive away in one of the sparkling sports cars. The Butcher stood at the driver's door. The windows were lowered and the targa top had been removed and now rested under the bubble-shaped back hatch.

Smooth, fast, and confident was the Butcher's move as he pulled the device from his pocket and bent forward as if examining the information screen above the console. In the same movement he reached under the dash beneath the steering column and plugged the device neatly into the OBD. He felt more than heard the device lock into the port.

The Butcher stood straight and smiled at his success. Morgan was still facing the opposite direction, chattering to the men and gesturing with his hands. He had been wrong about the conversation Morgan was having. He was rambling on about probable cause and domestic disputes. No one was interested in his car at all, but rather in how much free legal advice they could bleed from their fellow church member and D.A. The Butcher could have walked away in the opposite direction, but he decided to float a comment before making his exit. He walked to the rear of the car and brushed past Morgan. "Free-loading leaches," he mumbled under his breath. The three men watched the Butcher walk away, cutting in and out of the crowd. They turned and continued their discussion as if they hadn't been interrupted at all.

Keith wasn't exactly crazy about running, especially in mid-summer Georgia heat. Gnats and mosquitoes swarmed around him every time he stopped to cool down. He preferred the elliptical at the gym. Low-impact cardio was much easier on his forty-five-year-old knees, and there was a lot to be said for air conditioning. But this morning he would run and try to sweat out some of his anguish over Josh's death.

He thought about his adventure with Colson the day before. The last thing Colson had promised when he dropped him off at his car was to keep him informed of anything new he discovered about Strawn. It was hard to wait around, but he had run out of ideas. The best thing to do was keep busy until he heard from Colson.

Teresa and Danny had flown to visit her parents in Miami, just to get away from home for awhile. She had joined a support group of parents who also had lost children, and she had tried to persuade him to join her, but he wasn't interested in sharing with strangers right now. He believed people who spent too much time trying to analyze their feelings often ended up with none that were genuine. Maybe it was good for him and Teresa to spend some time apart before they began blaming each other for Josh's death. He had seen it before while watching boring Lifetime movies with Teresa, but he now believed there was a grain of truth in the fiction.

Keith was breathing hard and soaked in sweat after four miles on the Gwinnett Park asphalt track. He grabbed a towel from his gym bag in the truck and wiped sweat from his head and neck before dropping into the driver's seat and turning the air-conditioner to max. He had second thoughts on the drive home about not going with his wife and son. "Not the first bad decision you've made in your life, Champ," he muttered.

Arriving home, Keith unlocked the front door, tossed his keys on the foyer table, and went to the refrigerator for a bottle of water. He caught movement in his peripheral vision; before he could turn, something hard struck him across the left shoulder and knocked him to his knees. He tried to crawl forward and stand, but then another strike to his side knocked him back down, forcing the air from his lungs. He heard a shockingly loud pop when his rib cracked, and he tried to rise, wincing at the searing pain. He fell once again to the tiled kitchen floor and once again struggled to get up, but it felt as if a great weight were pressing him down. He could no longer move his arms or legs, and a dark fog began to envelope his vision. To think these may be his last moments horrified him. Images of Teresa and his sons flickered in the overwhelming fog of unconsciousness.

Then he heard a low voice, a whisper, but it wasn't Teresa or Danny. This one came from outside the fog. "Stay away from Jack Strawn—and shut up about your junkie kid," was the message before his world went black and silent.

Clay Haggart retraced his steps to the garage where he had entered Bartlett's house ninety minutes earlier and eased the side door open two inches to check for nosy onlookers or passersby. Most of the residents were already either at work or busy watching soap operas. He slid on his sunglasses and pulled a ball cap over his head before stepping outside. His motorcycle was hidden relatively well in the tree line behind a vacant foreclosure two houses down the street. He followed the tree line back to the bike and tossed the sawed-off baseball bat deep into the woods before straddling the bike and easing it back to the street. The humidity was almost unbearable for mid-morning, and the triple-X-sized windbreaker and baggy pants he wore didn't help matters at all, but they successfully concealed his bulging frame, making him difficult to identify.

Haggart swung the bike into the parking lot of a convenience store five miles from the subdivision, stuffed the windbreaker into a garbage can next to a gas pump, and shot back into traffic, allowing himself a smile. Strawn would be impressed and maybe give him a bonus. But then again, maybe not.

It would be impossible to describe the unmistakable scent of a morgue. The lingering smell and the look may be similar, but they vary in size. There would be a front office with a reception desk and waiting area; maybe two or three side offices for investigators, with the largest set aside for the coroner; and out of public view, for obvious reasons, would be the examination room. It would be drab, but intensely lit by the ceiling fixtures to ensure clear and accurate observations. Stainless steel tables on small black wheels would be scattered throughout the workroom, and a wall or maybe even two would hold nothing but oversized drawers to contain those who had lived, laughed, and loved at one point in their earthly existence. Recording devices and scales of various types and sizes would be displayed in the workroom, along with cutting, sawing, and stitching instruments.

But one thing was always the same, no matter what morgue you visited anywhere in the world. The smell could only be described as the aroma of cold, sterile death. There was no possible way to eradicate it. Colson had attended autopsies on many occasions but had never grown accustomed to the smell. Although the Clay County Morgue was the cleanest he had ever visited, no amount of scrubbing or painting would ever drive the scent from the building. Colson was convinced even burning the place down wouldn't do it.

He hoped the Fulton County Morgue was as clean as the one in Clay County. Detective Meador had invited him along this morning, so Colson met him at the office and rode along. He liked Meador as he did many other law enforcement types he had worked with over the years. Most cooperated with each other between agencies, sharing information and resources. That was the only way to stay ahead of the bad guys. The glory-hound cops who never wanted to share credit for anything were in the job for the wrong reasons and were eventually shunned by the law enforcement community.

Meador steered his unmarked Crown Vic left onto Pryor Street and hit the brakes behind a line of heavy mid-morning traffic. "What in the world are you doing back up here, Grey?" he asked. "I thought you liked being retired."

"I do."

Colson craned his neck, trying to see what was holding up the traffic. A raggedly dressed man was darting around the cars, holding a crumpled newspaper in one hand and a spray bottle in the other. He had a full beard, and his hair was matted with dreadlocks. The light changed to green, and the procession of cars moved slowly forward. The Crown Vic almost made the light, but was stopped just a car length short when it turned red again. Meador sighed in frustration as the man ran to the front of the car just ahead of him, squirting the windshield, and attacking it with the newspaper, smearing the liquid in a circle. He jogged to the driver's side window and held out his hand to the woman driver being held captive by the light, most likely horrified of what might happen if she didn't surrender her change to the vagabond.

Without a word or gesture of gratitude, the man turned the instant she dropped coins in his hand and ran to the front of the Crown Vic with his spray bottle at the ready. Meador had slipped his Glock from his side and sat with it in his lap. The man squirted water, either procured from a public drinking fountain or toilet, on the windshield and pushed it around with the paper for three seconds. He jogged to the driver's window, but instead of an intimidated woman digging in her purse for change, he saw Meador tapping the inside of the glass with the barrel of his Glock and jerking his other thumb to the left for the man to hit the sidewalk. The man's eyes widened for a moment before he flipped Meador off and scurried away.

Meador holstered the Glock and moved forward when the light turned green. Colson watched the man with mild amusement, standing on the sidewalk with his arms crossed and glaring in their direction through John Lennon-style sunglasses.

Meador pointed back at the man, "So, you miss this stuff, huh?"

Colson chuckled. "Not even a little."

"I don't get it then." Meador shook his head. "I figured you'd open a chain of tanning salons, kick back, and flirt with the customers."

Colson squinted and looked at Meador. "Tanning salons? I live in F-l-o-r-i-d-a." He drew out the word as if Meador were mentally slow. "If I lived in Alaska, I guess you would suggest I open a chain of snow-cone stands."

Meador shrugged and whipped the car into a parking lot. Colson was pleasantly surprised by the relatively new appearance of the complex. Fresh, black asphalt and new white parking lines surrounded a three-story, dull-red brick building. Colson estimated the square footage was at least three times that of Clay County's morgue. Fulton was a huge county and obviously needed the extra space. A four-foot-high wrought iron fence surrounded the entire parking lot. Meador backed into a parking space and killed the engine along with the struggling air-conditioner.

"I didn't call ahead," Meador said, lifting his coffee cup from the holder. "Doctor Walls may be busy. She may not even be in."

"Busy?" Colson said with a raised eyebrow. "I heard business was dead around here."

Meador spewed coffee on his steering wheel and coughed. "Don't do that when I'm drinking, Grey. These are supposed to be three-day pants, and this is just day one."

Colson laughed and slapped the dashboard. "I thought you said they called about the toxicology report being ready."

"They did," Meador said, brushing hot droplets from his lap. "I just didn't think to call ahead that we were coming to pick it up this morning."

Colson followed Meador to the front entrance, and Meador pulled the glass door open with a whoosh; Colson hesitated a moment when he stepped into the reception area. There it was. Cold, sterile, and dead, even from the front office. Some memories are aroused by music, some by locations, and others by smell. Colson just wished that particular sense wasn't working right now. Meador badged the receptionist and presumably told her what they were doing there. Meador's back was to Colson and his voice was low, as if he were in a funeral home.

The receptionist gestured to her right. Colson followed Meador down a short hall to the end where a door stood open. They stepped into a bright office with dark commercial-grade carpet. The walls and smooth ceiling were painted a soft teal and a large window admitted enough summer sunlight to make you forget it was a coroner's office. Almost.

"Detective Meador," Beverly Walls said as she stood and extended her hand.

"Doctor Walls," Meador shook her hand and pointed to Colson with his thumb, "this is Grey Colson. We worked together on a few cases when he was a major with Clay County S.O."

"Pleased to meet you," she said, shifting her hand to Colson. "Please call me Beverly."

Colson almost forgot to speak. She was a stunning forty-something-year-old beauty with shoulder-length brown hair and green eyes. She wore a white smock tied at the waist, revealing her slender figure. Colson guesstimated she was nearly six feet tall, depending on the shoes she was wearing behind the desk. A little tall for his taste, but definitely worth the climb.

"Glad I insisted on coming," Colson said with a smile, taking her hand in his. Meador looked at Colson and rolled his eyes.

Beverly sat in her swivel chair as Colson and Meador eased into their chairs across from her. Colson glanced around the neat office. A floor-to-ceiling bookcase stood against the wall to his left, by the office door. Dozens of books on human anatomy, forensics, and toxicology-related subjects stood tight against each other on the bottom two shelves. A mantle clock sat on the shelf above the books, flanked by two framed eight-by-ten photographs. The one to the right pictured a slightly younger, but no more stunning Beverly standing with a woman in her early thirties and a boy around eleven years old. They were pictured against the backdrop of the Magic Castle in Disney World. The photo on the left was of Beverly, about the same age as today, with her arms around the waist of an older man, probably in his late sixties. They were both in casual dress, and the man wore a yellow T-shirt with "Pedalfest 2011" in big red letters across his chest. On the top shelf were three expertly built model cars—a baby blue '57 Chevrolet Bel-Air, a '79 Camaro funny car with its entire body raised above the chassis from the front, and a Rail Drag Racer.

Meador spoke up, bringing Colson's attention back to the meeting. "Grey is currently working with the state's Drugs Don't Work program."

Beverly smiled and nodded. "Great."

"Interim," Colson said. "Actually, I'm retired."

"Anyway, Grey is close to the deceased boy's father," Meador said, flipping open his note pad. "Uh—Mr. Bartlett. He wanted Grey to update him on any findings."

"Well," Beverly said with a sigh, "not that there's any good news to pass along, but toxicology did reveal the cause of death, and it wasn't the heroin, although heroin did contribute to the pulmonary edema."

Meador's and Colson's eyebrows rose simultaneously. Colson kept silent since Meador was the official law enforcement agent at the meeting, and Meador said, "What was the main factor contributing to death?"

Beverly pointed to the report on her desk. "Ingestion of Abrin."

Meador and Colson looked at each other. "I've never heard of Abrin," Colson said.

"Not many people have," Beverly said, flipping through the report. "It's a toxalbumin."

"In English for us Cro-Magnon men please," Colson said.

Beverly smiled. "Sorry. It's a toxic plant protein that inhibits protein synthesis in the cells. There was only a trace, but it's more deadly than ricin."

"And it was injected with the heroin?" Meador asked.

"It's impossible to say for certain, but most likely. Abrin can be swallowed or even inhaled."

"There goes my case against the dealer," Meador said, flipping his note pad closed.

Colson gave Meador a dead stare. "The dealer is dead, remember?"

"Point taken, but why would anyone lace heroin with Abrin unless it was premeditated murder?"

"And why go to the trouble to poison a teenage junkie when you could just shoot him?" Colson said with a shrug. "It sounds very elaborate to me. Someone went to a lot of trouble to get their hands on that poison. It sounds like you have bigger investigation on your hands, Mike."

"Just my luck," Meador said, standing. "Thanks, Doc."

Beverly tapped her desktop with her fingernails. "I'm officially ruling the cause of death as a homicide. At least for now."

Colson stood with Beverly and the three shook hands. She picked up the file on her desk and handed it to Meador. "This is actually your copy of the M.E.'s report for the case file. And," she said, turning to Colson with a smile, "it was very nice meeting you, Major Colson."

Colson returned her smile. "My pleasure—and call me Grey." He gestured to the model cars on display. "Did your son build these? They're extremely detailed."

"My son?" Beverly said. She hesitated and glanced over at her bookshelf. "No, I don't have any children. The photo is my younger sister and her son." She held out her arms. "My entire extended family. As for the models, I built them myself."

Colson cocked his head in mild shock. "You built them?" Then he realized he sounded sexist and adjusted his tone. "I don't mean you couldn't—I mean that you shouldn't—"

Beverly laughed and waved her hand for Colson to stop. "I know what you mean. No offense taken. My dad used to take me to the drag races when I was a kid. I spent practically every Saturday there with him. I fell in love with the sport and while other girls were dressing dolls, I built model sports cars and drag racers."

"A woman after my own heart," Colson said with a grin. "What does your husband do, sew quilts with old ladies at the nursing home?"

Beverly raised her eyebrows. "He probably would if I were still married to him."

Colson looked into her deep green eyes and thought, *this just keeps getting better.* He crossed his arms, rocked on his heels for a beat, and made his decision. He hadn't come expecting this and hadn't even considered the possibility during their short meeting. Well, not the entire time anyway. Sometimes things just happened. Ann had been gone for nearly two years, and he still loved her dearly; no one could ever fill the vacuum left by her passing. He had kept busy with his part-time investigation jobs, and now this part-time state position consumed the majority of what remained of his free time. It was the most meaningful professional endeavor he had ever committed himself to, but the fact remained that he enjoyed retirement and sorely missed the company of a soul mate. Colson rocked back and forth until Meador touched his elbow.

"You ready to roll?" he said.

Colson ignored him, keeping eye contact with the lovely and gracious Beverly in her white coroner's coat. "You ever been to Road Atlanta?" he said.

Meador rolled his eyes and walked out of the office, leaving Colson and Beverly eye-locked. "Dear Lord in heaven," he muttered as he disappeared down the hallway.

☙CHAPTER FIFTEEN❧

When Keith finally regained consciousness, the pain hit him in pulsating waves. He tried to open one eye, but the light was too painful, so he kept both slammed shut. His whole body was a gigantic aching bruise. He raised himself gingerly to his elbows, surprised he was able to move at all. A wave of pain flooded the back of his skull, so he lowered his head to the floor, hoping the dull throbbing would end. After a few more minutes, he forced one eye open just enough to allow in a blurry sliver of light.

As his pupil adjusted, he was able to fully open his right eye. It required enormous effort to turn on his side and raise himself to one elbow. Nausea swelled from his stomach to his chest. He was either going to throw up or lose consciousness again, or both. He stayed still until the nausea somewhat subsided, and then he pushed himself up to a seated position.

He looked around the house and saw that it was totally ransacked and trashed. The living room was an utter shambles. He crawled to the phone, dialed 9-1-1, and waited for an ambulance and the police to arrive. It seemed like it took them an hour. He finally stood, wavered, and caught the back of a chair until he regained equilibrium. He made his way up the stairs, stopping multiple times to catch his breath and surveyed the chaos in the bedrooms. The master bedroom was destroyed. The bedclothes lay tumbled on the floor. Bureau drawers were overturned, their contents strewn in a wild jumble. A gaping wound split the mattress in Joshua's room. The closet door had been jerked from its hinges, and holes had been kicked or punched in the sheetrock walls. It made no sense. If beating him nearly to death wasn't enough encouragement to leave Strawn alone, would ransacking the house make any difference?

Keith experienced a moment of clarity amid his full-body headache. He stared at the long gash in the mattress and whispered to himself, "Josh had something they wanted."

Jay Taylor set his beer on the plastic side table, crossed his legs, and adjusted the iPad on his lap. At 3:00, the blazing Daytona sun was out of sight on the opposite side of the building, so the screen glare was tolerable. The temperature was in the high eighties, and the beach was lined with vehicles of every model and color. Hundreds of men, women, and children scurried along the shore, throwing Frisbees and footballs.

Two teams of teenagers jumped and slapped a volleyball at the foot of the seawall. Anyone else under the age of twelve who didn't have some type of ball in their hands was building sand castles or riding body boards in the shallow surf. The adults were baking in the sun or sitting under umbrellas.

Taylor was a lot like Colson in that he enjoyed the sun but preferred admiring its glory from the shade. It was almost like watching a silent movie. The sounds of hundreds of voices and car engines were completely muffled by the constant ocean breeze blowing in from the east and buffeting against the stucco facade of the five-story building.

He stared at the four-year-old YouTube video with his one good eye for a long second, touched the play button for the third time today, and grimaced at the shirtless man standing in front of a wall-sized UFC banner, flexing his pecs for the camera. The screen shot widened to include another man holding a microphone. Taylor pushed the volume to full for the small integrated speaker to combat the buffeting breeze.

A sports announcer stood holding a microphone to his lips to begin his interview. "This is Joe Goreman, and I'm back with Clay 'The Madman' Haggart for our fight night exclusive interview. You're nineteen and one," Goreman said, turning to Haggart, "and are just two months away from taking on the number one contender for the UFC belt, Jay 'The Terrible' Taylor. How do you prepare for a fight with someone as quick and aggressive as Taylor?" Goreman shoved the microphone at Haggart.

Easily a head taller than Goreman, Haggart glared down at him and pointed his finger at his chest. "You can't be serious. I don't know who's been deciding the rankings, but Taylor hasn't done anything to deserve the number one spot."

"But," Goreman interrupted, jerking the microphone back to his face, "Taylor is undefeated."

"I don't give a rat's ass!" Haggart shouted. "He's spent his short career matched up with pansies like Welco and Simmons. Hell, my sister could have beaten them."

Goreman raised his free hand in surrender. "Okay, okay, but you still need to prepare for the fight. Is there anything different you'll do over the next two months to ensure a victory?"

Haggart seemed to be in thought for a moment and smiled when Goreman shifted the microphone in his direction. Haggart grabbed the mic and took two long steps toward the camera. Millions of people had watched the live broadcast and no doubt millions more watched it on YouTube later, but Haggart wasn't speaking to the masses. His comment was aimed directly at Taylor, as if he had been the cameraman.

"I'll tell you what I'm going to do for two weeks, just to make it a fair fight. I'm gonna sit on my ass eating hamburgers, potato chips, and ice cream just so I won't hurt Taylor so bad he'll have to suck his dinner through a straw for the rest of his life."

Taylor stabbed at the 'x' on the top right of the web page, causing it to vanish from the screen. He slipped on his sunglasses and gazed out over the horizon. The Atlantic Ocean was a lazy curve where it met the sky, maybe ten or twenty miles in the distance. Taylor didn't care what the correct distance was, nor did he bother to guess. The thought of Haggart winning the UFC title just a couple of months after the taping of the interview consumed his thoughts once again.

Colson had warned him countless times to let it go, or he would never move on with his life. "Sure, that's easy for you to say,

Colson," would be his reply each time. Taylor didn't want to re-live his failure, but there was something driving him and keeping it forefront in his mind. He didn't know what direction it was driving him yet, but it was there, idling like a 500-horsepower engine, occasionally revving in anticipation of a red light turning green.

Taylor pulled the search engine back up, typing, "Haggart UFC Champion" in the search box and touching the little magnifying glass icon to "find." A long list of topics appeared down the page, including various videos of the fight. He had previously refused to watch the fight or the subsequent videos. The drive inside him changed his mind today, so he touched the first video on top of the list. It was the last thirty seconds of the third round. Haggart stood, bouncing in his black trunks in the corner and slapping his gloves together. The camera switched to his contender, Alfonzo Ramos, ranked third behind Taylor and Haggart. The sight of Ramos made Taylor cringe. His face was a bloody pulp from the first two rounds of abuse, yet he defiantly danced in his corner as if he had the point advantage. One of his eyes was swollen shut and looked as if someone had shoved an egg under the lid and sewed it closed.

Taylor shook his head and muttered, "Haggart would have been the one with the swollen eye if that had been my corner, but he would have never made it to round three." Taylor wasn't surprised the Las Vegas odds were adjusted from five to one in favor of Taylor against Haggart to three to one in favor of the heavier third place contender. No doubt someone—or a lot of someones—made a killing that day.

Taylor watched the men circle each other for ten seconds before Ramos dove for Haggart's waist in a takedown attempt, but Haggart sprawled and pushed the man away. The ground game wasn't Haggart's specialty and was exactly why he hadn't been favored to win. He preferred the standing game to take advantage of his longer reach against shorter contenders. Haggart took a long step toward Ramos and feigned a right haymaker to his jaw. Ramos instinctively raised his hands to block, but that was a bad mistake. Haggart drove his left fist deep into his stomach, causing Ramos to double over and stagger back against the octagonal cage. Haggart planted his feet and waited for him to bounce back in his direction. There was no room to execute his next move if he trapped Ramos against the cage.

His strategy paid off. As Ramos rebounded and raised his head, Haggart was in the middle of his spin. The last image Ramos saw until three minutes later when the ceiling of the Mirage arena came into focus was the left profile of Haggart's sweaty face as his back-fist strike impacted the side of his head.

Ramos's head rocked back and forth to the light slaps of his trainer, who knelt beside him. He had been knocked out cold. Haggart danced, bounced, and ran around the octagon. Blood trickled from the corner of Ramos' mouth while Haggart continued to celebrate by launching himself to a seated position on the cage and raising the huge championship belt as high as his long arms would allow.

Taylor watched the crowd's reaction with envy and shook his head in sharp motions. "That would have been me," he said aloud into the ocean breeze. The crowd looked like a sea of bobbing heads and waving arms, their cheering growing into a solid roar among a sprinkle of "boos" here and there from fans who were pulling for Ramos.

The camera swung in wide arcs across the crowd in the darkened arena. A hundred thousand or so camera flashes dotted each second of video as the roar continued to grow. The camera switched to close-ups of those wealthy and famous enough to secure seats in the first few rows. Taylor recognized several personalities from Hollywood movies, although he couldn't name them if a gun was held to his head. The same went for a couple of politicians in the first row. But then something caught his attention.

He touched the screen and slid the video bar at the bottom of the page back and pressed play, waiting for the moment that caught his eye. Taylor let his finger hover over the pause icon to stop the quickly panning camera at the right moment. There it was. He pressed pause and then the full screen icon at the top right. He had to tilt the screen somewhat to eliminate the glare. Even then, it was difficult to focus clearly with his one good eye. He stepped inside the sliding doors into the kitchen and sat at the breakfast bar with the iPad in front of him.

"Just, damn," Taylor whispered while staring at the still figure of a man in a tan suit, holding a smoldering cigar between the fingers of his left hand, his right fist pumping in celebration. Taylor had earlier assumed Haggart hooked up his job with Strawn after leaving the UFC, but they were obviously acquainted earlier than that. That would explain Haggart's extravagant personal training facility. Several present and former champions and contenders worked out in Haggart's gym, but Taylor was never invited because he was the only fighter who could potentially prevent Haggart from winning the title. Strawn must have sponsored Haggart from day one.

Taylor shook his head at the sight of the billionaire. Strawn obviously thought money could buy a world champion, but he was wrong. As much as Taylor couldn't stand the sight of Haggart, he still had to work his ass off to make it to the title fight. But there was no doubt in Taylor's mind he would have won if it hadn't been for his unbelievable bad luck when he was forced out of contention after losing an eye and his depth perception.

Taylor stepped back out on the balcony, promising himself to let the past be the past and follow Colson's advice. *Get on with your life,* he thought. He took one last look at Strawn and held his finger above the 'x' to close the screen, but something stopped him again. There was something else, but this time it wasn't a jolt of recognition, but of faint memory.

He backed into the kitchen and studied the still video one more time. There was something about the young female standing next to Strawn. She wore a low-cut, glittering evening dress, and her long blonde hair draped over both shoulders. The young woman was caught by the still video in mid-jump with her hands frozen in mid-clap. She looked familiar, but Taylor couldn't remember why.

He set the tablet on the counter and returned to his plastic balcony chair, deep in thought. He closed his eyes and inhaled salty air through his nose. He was born in Florida and had lived his entire life here, but never spent time on the coast. Not until this last year. Now he couldn't imagine living inland again. He stood and stepped to the rail, noting the sound of a lifeguard's warning whistle. A swimmer had strayed too far from shore. Movement from the parking lot caught his eye. Little Clara bounced across the pavement, holding hands with her mother. Taylor had made her acquaintance the second time he saw her trotting down the exterior hallway. He knew he had frightened her the first time when they had almost collided. The last time he had smiled and stepped aside to let her pass, but she had stopped anyway. "What's your name?" she had asked him. Although impolite, he dared not remove his sunglasses. The sight of the lifeless orb he used to call an eye would have horrified her. He had forced his best smile for her. "My name is Taylor. What's your name, sweetheart?"

"It's Clara."

"That's a very pretty name, Clara," Taylor had said.

Clara had clasped her hands in front of her and twisted from side to side, returning Taylor's smile. "It's my gee-gee's name."

"Really?" Taylor had said. "Who's gee-gee?"

"She's my great-gramma."

"Well, you be careful and don't get sunburned," Taylor had cautioned and patted the top of her head before walking away. Their little chat had taken place almost two weeks ago. Maybe her parents had rented the condo for the entire summer.

Taylor watched the pair until they stopped at a black SUV parked against the building. Clara looked up and waved to Taylor. "Hi, Taylor," she shouted over the breeze. Taylor smiled and returned the wave. "Hi, Clara. Aren't you going to the pool today?"

Clara's mother looked up and waved to Taylor. "Not today," she said. Clara peered up at Taylor and grasped her hair, pulling it back in a ponytail. "I'm going to get my hair done. I have an appointment," Clara said, as if only adults had appointments. Taylor laughed and waved again before plopping down in his chair.

Then it hit him. He hadn't recognized the woman with Strawn in the video because her hair was down and she was wearing a low cut evening dress. That was a far cry from a nurse's uniform and pulled-back hair, but it was her without a doubt. Taylor shot to his feet and paused, squeezing the balcony rail until his knuckles turned white.

None of it made sense. How on earth could such a coincidence occur? Him being just weeks away from a title fight with Haggart, being treated by a quack doctor who he blamed for lusting over his assistant nurse instead of giving him proper treatment, and then to see the nurse and Strawn and Haggart at the same event. An event stolen from him, because he was blinded by the incompetence of the eye doctor. The very doctor the woman standing next to Strawn worked for.

Taylor jumbled the pieces in his head, one on top of the other. Arranging the facts like a Rubik's cube until all the sides were the same color. Was the doctor incompetent? What other explanation was there?

"No!" Taylor shouted. He marched into the kitchen, nearly hyperventilating, uncontrollably blowing short bursts of air through his nose. All the pieces had fallen into place; he wanted to look at the girl one last time to satisfy his suspicion before secretly signing Jack Strawn's death warrant. He lifted the tablet, pressed the power button, and waited for the screen to light up. His breathing became more erratic as he studied the girl in the still frame. There was no doubt she and the nurse were one and the same. A seat for his old playboy eye doctor, Dr. Cooper, had probably been purchased by Strawn for the fight, but he would have been recovering in the hospital from a crushed eye socket, complements of Taylor. Most likely, Strawn got more than his money's worth with Cooper out of the picture, allowing him to fill the vacuum with his gold-digging assistant nurse. The rage once harbored in Taylor's soul for Cooper quadrupled at the thought he had been blinded not by incompetence, but for profit. Now he wished he had killed Cooper instead of blinding him.

"No!" Taylor shouted again, allowing his anger to transform the word into a haunting howl. He spun on his heel and threw the iPad like a Frisbee through the open sliding door and over the balcony rail with enough force to kill any man standing in its path.

C✒CHAPTER SIXTEEN✑

Keith had put the house back in order as best he could and tried to distract himself by working from home. It had been two days since the break-in, and he still felt beat-down and sore to the bone. "Home invasion," he said to himself, just to hear the words out loud. He had heard those words on the news a million times but never thought anything of the sort would happen to him.

His home office was set up with a computer, two monitors, cherry wood filing cabinets, an ornate wooden desk, and cherry wood bookcases. Normally it was a place of comfort to him, but today it felt small and confining.

This morning he had awakened at 7:00 as usual. The initial feeling of optimism he always had after a good night's sleep was immediately replaced by depression. It had been that way every morning since Josh's death. He dipped a corner of his toast in the yolk of his over-easy egg while he gave instructions to his employee over the phone for an alarm installation that afternoon, but his mind was on Teresa and Danny down in Miami. He nodded at the blank wall in front of him. He should join them, regardless of work demands or the police or strong-arm hooligans breaking into his house.

He slid the plate away and stood, trying to concentrate on his conversation with the young tech. Shadows moved in his peripheral vision, giving him a start when only three days ago he would have responded only with curious suspicion. It was from the frosted side windows at the front door. The outline of a man. "Hang on," he said to the tech and silently laid the phone on the kitchen table.

He fast walked to a utility closet in the hallway, pulled a driver from his golf bag, and trotted to the left side of the door. He adjusted his grip on the driver in his right hand and held it high while grasping the doorknob with his left. As if preparing himself for a high-dive, he counted to three, jerked open the door, and instantly grimaced from the pain in his ribcage.

A dark-suited man instantly stepped back and slid his hand quickly under his coat at the sight of Keith holding the driver. Keith's heart skipped a beat at the thought of being shot, and he instinctively shoved the door closed, but something stopped it short. A hand poked through the opening holding a police shield in a black wallet. "Police," the man said. "Detective Meador, APD."

Keith closed his eyes and sighed. He leaned the driver against the wall behind the door and pulled it back open. "I'm sorry, officer. I didn't know you were the police. Come in, please."

"Take it easy there, tiger," came a voice behind the first man.

"Colson?" Keith said, seeing him climbing the porch steps.

Meador stepped inside and glanced around the room and through every doorway, as if he were seeking any possible threat. "Keith Bartlett?" he said, extending his hand.

"Yes," Keith answered and shook Meador's hand. "We can talk in the kitchen if you don't mind."

They took a seat at the kitchen table, where Keith switched on the overhead lights and grabbed his phone. "I'll call you back," he said to the tech, and he disconnected without waiting for a response.

He saw Meador peering at him, searching his face. "Were you in an accident?" the detective asked.

Keith shook his head, looking between Meador and Colson. "Not exactly." He wanted to tell the truth, but what about Teresa and Danny? Could he risk some detective questioning Strawn about the assault and enraging him even more? The man was too big and obviously too well connected. He probably owned half of APD and maybe even the chief himself. If it wasn't for his family, Keith would run right back to the news reporter and tell her—and everyone else for that matter—but he had already lost one son and would go insane if anything happened to his wife or younger son.

"Well?" Colson said with his palms up. "What happened, Keith?"

"I—I interrupted a burglar two days ago. He ransacked the house and hit me from behind when I came in. I filed a police report. I thought you were here to follow up on that. Well, until I saw Colson."

"Where were your wife and son?" Colson said.

"Out of town in Florida."

"You should have called me," Colson scolded.

Keith rubbed the back of his neck and squinted in pain. "You've already done enough, Grey. I can't call you about everything like some spoiled child."

"I wasn't aware of the attack," Meador said. "Did you know your attacker?"

"No. He blindsided me and knocked me out. While I was unconscious he ransacked my home."

"Was anything taken?" Meador said.

Keith laid his head in his hands, slightly exasperated. "No, it's all in the report."

"Not even the cash on you?" Meador shook his head. "I'll pull the report. We came here this morning to talk to you about your son."

Pain shot through Keith's neck when he jerked his head up and sat straight. This was the second time he had heard that from a cop in the last two weeks. "Dear God, which one?" he practically shouted.

"Which one what?"

"Which son?"

"Oh, uh, I'm sorry. Your son Joshua."

"He's dead," Keith said flatly.

"Yes, I know," Meador said, flipping open the pad and scanning his notes. "Mr. Bartlett, is there anyone who would benefit from your son's death?"

Keith's eyes narrowed. "You think he was murdered?" he said. He gave Colson a surprised glance before Meador looked up from his note pad.

"I didn't say that. This is just standard procedure. We're looking at everything right now."

"But I thought it was a clear-cut case of overdose. Is there something that makes you think otherwise?'

"The heroin residue in the spoon he used to cook it up tested extremely pure. That's unusual for a user of your son's... level."

"Is that what killed him then—the high purity of the heroin?"

"Possibly. But the medical examiner found traces of another substance called Abrin that was possibly injected with the heroin."

"Are you saying Joshua was poisoned?"

"No, maybe not intentionally poisoned. We can't automatically jump to that conclusion. These dealers cut their product with all kinds of junk—quinine, caffeine, flour, milk, sugar, baby laxative, and who knows what else. If your son's supplier cut his dose with something new, he may not have known it was dangerous."

Keith suddenly felt dizzy and dropped his head back into his hands. "It just doesn't make sense. Why would want anyone poison Josh?"

"That's the part we don't know—even if it happened that way or not," Colson said. "But the medical examiner is ruling the cause of death as a homicide. That way Detective Meador can keep the case open until we find out for certain."

"Are you going to be okay, Mr. Bartlett?" Meador said.

Keith shook his head. "I don't think I'll ever be okay. Murder? Josh was only a kid." He opened his mouth to say something about Strawn—after all, the man had asked some unusual questions about Josh during their meeting—but he saw Colson give his head a quick, emphatic shake. He immediately understood. Meador would most likely chalk him up as a conspiracy lunatic if he even mentioned it. Keith acquiesced for now and held his tongue. "I don't know of anyone who would want to hurt my son. He didn't have any enemies that I know of."

"How long had he been using drugs?" Meador asked.

"At least a couple of years. He did some time in jail for selling cocaine and was just paroled a few months ago. But you probably already know that."

"Yes, I pulled his record. It's routine."

"I'm a little confused. What happened to the detectives who came to my office to tell me about Josh?"

"They closed the case as an overdose. I had it reopened and assigned to me at Colson's request," Meador said.

"Why did the first detectives rule it as an overdose so quickly?"

Meador counted the items off on his left hand. "First, there weren't any signs of forced entry into his hotel room. Second, the entry door and the door to the bathroom were locked from the inside when the cleaning lady found him. Third, nothing appeared to be missing from the room." Meador ceased counting, but continued. "There was no sign of foul play at all, but there was drug paraphernalia found—bags, needles, mixing spoon, the works."

Keith flinched. Meador's points were taken. No reason to mention the painfully obvious old and scarred track marks on the body, indicating his son was a long-time user. He leaned back in his chair, looking between Meador and Colson. "What else can be done at this point?"

"If you'll make me a list, I want to contact Josh's friends. I'm talking about anyone and everyone who was either a close friend or a passing acquaintance." Meador said.

Keith went to the kitchen counter and opened a cabinet. "Josh has been—was—very introverted over the past couple of years." He returned to the table with a cell phone and began scanning through the contact screen. "The only number I know is Emily Raines. The rest, I don't know. Half of them didn't answer when I tried to call, and the other half didn't return the messages I left." Keith stopped scribbling numbers and looked up at Meador. "I'm sure Colson told you about the missing Raines girl?"

Meador nodded.

"Anyway," Keith said, sliding a piece of paper across the table, "that's all I've got, unfortunately."

Meador responded by sliding his business card across the table. "My cell number is on the back. Please call me if you think of anything else, and I'll certainly call you if I learn anything significant."

Keith walked Meador and Colson to the door, where they shook hands. Keith used his limp to walk slowly and think of what to tell Colson about Strawn's threat. It was information he wanted to blurt out to Colson the moment he had walked in the door, but it was too late now. He had already lied to Meador and couldn't take it back without losing all credibility with him. But he trusted Colson and felt like a volcano ready to explode.

"Grey," Keith said as Colson bounded down the porch steps. Meador was already halfway to the car. Colson turned, but Keith still had not formulated anything in his mind to tell him. "Uh," Keith stammered.

"What is it?"

"Would you, uh, give me a call when you get back to your office?"

Colson cocked his head. "Something wrong?"

Keith shook his head, eyed Colson, and winked. "It's about the drug program. I know another parent who is interested in sponsoring a work meeting."

"Sure," Colson said. "I'll call around four."

Meador cranked up the radio while turning out of Keith's subdivision, then turned the volume back down to zero. Colson was looking at men riding huge mowers in the median, shooting grass blades out in the street, when Meador spoke. "He's hiding something."

Colson nodded. "He's totally distraught about his son."

"I understand that," Meador said, "but the fact still remains he's holding back."

Colson crossed his legs and patted his foot. "One thing about these Crown Vics—plenty of leg room."

"Colson?" Meador said with clenched teeth. "What was he afraid to tell us?" Colson looked back at the median and didn't respond. "Okay," Meador said with exaggerated sarcasm in his voice, and he cranked up the radio volume. Colson immediately reached over and turned it back down to zero.

"Tell me what you know about Jack Strawn and Strawn Industries," Colson said, as if it were Det. Meador who was keeping the secrets.

After Colson and the detective left, Keith went back into the kitchen and sat with his head in his hands. He hoped Colson had caught his urgent wink and would call soon. He raised his head and scanned the room in bewilderment. The attack by Strawn's thug, although absurdly criminal, initially made sense. Strawn was spending millions on a ridiculous campaign to legalize drugs, and he and Colson were being major thorns in his side. Keith's eyes widened in a moment of clarity.

"Colson," he snapped and slapped the table. He should have warned him before he left the house. Colson, an ex-cop, was more of a threat to Strawn than Keith was. If it was so important for Strawn's goon to beat him down, Colson obviously would be his next stop.

Keith snatched his phone from the table and urgently dialed Colson's number. The call went straight to voice mail. "Grey," Keith said, "you need to call me ASAP. Strawn sent his bodyguard to break in the house and attack me. He told me to stay out of Strawn's business, and he'll be after you next. I'm surprised you weren't his first stop. Don't go home or back to the office until you call me. Watch your back."

Keith ended the call, closed his eyes, and tapped the phone against his forehead, thinking. Maybe Colson couldn't answer because he was still with Meador. He sent Colson a text message, and then he tried Jonathan's number.

"Hello?" Jonathan said expectantly, his voice a mixture of hope and dread. Keith could only imagine what must be going through his head—would it be Emily calling to say she was safe? Or would it be the police requesting he meet them at the morgue to identify their daughter's body? Keith wasn't sure which situation was worse: already knowing your child was dead, or suffering through each day and each sleepless night not knowing.

"It's Keith. Any news on Emily?"

"I'm afraid not," Jonathan said, his voice full of worry. "We have fliers up all over the area, and we've offered a reward online for any information about her disappearance, but no word yet. I'm thinking of hiring a private investigator to search for her."

"I'm sorry, Jon," Keith said. "I just don't understand why the police aren't doing more to find her."

Jonathan released an exasperated sigh. "It's because of her age and because she fits the profile of a runaway. We've done everything we can think of. I'm worried about Sheila, Keith. She isn't getting any sleep. Not that I'm getting much sleep either, but knowing there's nothing more I can do for Emily or Sheila is driving me crazy. I just wish I could take it all on myself."

"I'll be talking to Colson later," Keith said, "and I'll ask him to follow up. Maybe he'll be able to encourage the police to look harder. He and an APD detective just left. This is getting complicated, and I thought you should know—"

"What is it, Keith? What did they tell you?"

Keith took a deep breath before answering. "There was poison in the heroin Josh injected. It's likely he was murdered."

"Dear God in heaven."

ᙍᗩCHAPTER SEVENTEENᗡᙎ

"**J**ack Strawn?" Meador said with a chuckle as he spun the steering wheel and jerked the Crown Vic onto the exit ramp. "What would Jack Strawn have to do with anything?"

Colson shrugged. "Keith Bartlett has challenged his agenda on nationwide television; other than that, I can't imagine."

Meador merged the car in an incredibly small space between a church van and the trailer of an eighteen-wheeler on I-20 and punched the accelerator to match their speed. "C'mon, Colson," he said, waving his hand in feigned thanks to the church van driver, "a lot of people have come out publicly against Strawn over the years. Surely you don't think he had anything to do with the death of the Bartlett kid, do you? His death happened before Bartlett got involved in his crusade against Strawn, remember."

Colson kept his eyes forward and shook his head. "Stranger things have happened. Are you telling me no one in your department has even looked at him or what he may be doing? Not even your intelligence people?"

"I didn't say that," Meador said. "They probably have, just like they've looked at anyone and everyone who has his kind of money."

Colson glared at Meador. "Of course they have. You know it and I know it. You always look at people with millions and billions of dollars, because even if the target farts too loud, it could be embellished to the point of a crime and give the government a reason to seize millions of dollars in assets. I haven't been out of the game so long that I've forgotten the basics of how government works, Mike. So who's working a case on him?"

Meador drove in silence, occasionally glancing in his rear-view and side-view mirrors. Colson watched him maneuver the bulky, unmarked detective sedan into the far left lane and accelerate to eighty miles per hour. He adjusted his frame in the driver's seat and relaxed, steadying the wheel with his wrist.

"You mean, who *was* working the case," Meador said.

Colson nodded, knowing Meador would see his response. Meador sighed. "What difference would it make anyway? They were just looking at him because of his fortune. You said that much yourself."

"I know what I said..." Colson's voice trailed off when he felt his phone vibrate. He pulled it from his belt and saw the missed call, voice mail, and text.

Watch your back. Strawn's bodyguard attacked me, Keith's message read.

Colson re-read the text before putting the phone back on his belt. He sat silent in thought.

"Everything all right?" Meador said.

"I want to know who was working the case."

Meador hit the blinker and began changing lanes to the right as the Spring Street exit came into view. "What good will it do? He doesn't know you like I know you. You're not a cop anymore, and he won't feel obligated to go into the case with you, if there was even a case to begin with."

"What's his name? Don't make me beat your eyeballs out."

The Crown Vic came to rest at the bottom of the exit ramp under a red traffic light. Meador looked to the left for a sedan-sized hole in the traffic zooming through the busy intersection. Apparently resigned to the fact there was no hope of moving until the light turned green, he turned to his old acquaintance.

"His name is Hugh Floyd. He works in the F5 task force."

The drive to Marietta wasn't bad, but then again it was 8:30 a.m. on Saturday. Colson had been upbeat all week about his first date in over thirty years, but this morning the multitude of butterflies fluttering in his stomach could rival the birds in the classic Alfred Hitchcock movie.

He spoke to Ann frequently in his private moments. He often told her he was doing fine, working hard, and being a good boy. He bragged about their grandson and told her how he wished she could see and play with him. Even though he believed with all his heart that in her heavenly form she knew and loved little Jack as much as he did, it just wasn't the same without her being physically there.

Today the conversation was different. Colson had put it off all week and even this morning until he exited off of I-75 onto Windy Hill Rd. He turned down the radio volume and glanced to the empty passenger seat where Ann had ridden countless times. He could see her in his mind's eye, chattering and occasionally laughing at his silly remarks. Colson realized he had been rehearsing what he would eventually say in his mind, but he knew they were only arguments to justify his behavior. He looked down the wide, four-lane road and shook his head. "You're just stupid, Colson," he said aloud and sighed. He glanced over at the empty seat and took a deep breath. "You know I love you, darling, and always will. I pray you understand."

Colson almost missed his turn into the townhouse community and probably would have if the female voice on his GPS had not cheerfully announced, "Arriving at destination." He downshifted and turned right next to a large brick sign that welcomed him to the Southern Oaks Townhomes. Small lettering underneath read A Gated Community. He stopped at a small metal box protruding from a post in the ground, punched in the four numbers Beverly had email him, and watched the black gate ahead of him swing silently open.

The townhomes appeared to be of either brand new construction or simply maintained superbly by a crew of neighborhood maintenance men. Colson had suspected there would be rows and rows of attached buildings, more like two-story apartments, but they were all detached homes, tall and narrow with a driveway running between each building. All were of either tan or soft red brick siding, each with an upper balcony and ground-floor porch. Colson nodded in admiration of their simple yet elegant design. He had done his share of yard work over the years and didn't miss it at all, but the front yards of these homes, at ten by ten feet square, were no more than a token of suburbia. Colson calculated the grass could be cut in an hour with a pair of scissors, but he still preferred a back yard composed of sand and surf only. Zero maintenance.

Colson slowed the 'Vette, glancing at numbers on the wrought iron mailboxes as he eased down the quaint street. He pulled into the driveway next to number 104 and stopped behind a white Caprice bearing a Fulton County government tag. He cringed at the sight of the squat car. During his last year with Clay County, Ford had broken the news about ending production of the Crown Victoria for law enforcement and other government use. Colson had spent years driving marked and unmarked Crown Vics for the job and had grown to love them. Now police and other government agencies had little to pick from for maneuverability and performance. It would be either the new Taurus, the Charger, or the thing parked in front of him. It was no different from taking away John Wayne's horse and making him ride a donkey.

He silently shook his head while climbing out of the car. It was the end of an era.

He brushed out the wrinkles in his BDU pants, took a deep breath, and walked up the sidewalk to a tidy porch with two wicker chairs situated on either side of a small wicker table. Two wire baskets with blue and red geraniums hung from hooks above the railing, and a small ceramic Welcome sign hung from the dark-stained wooden door. He reached for the doorbell, but Beverly pulled the door open before he had a chance to push it.

Colson resisted a gasp. She was more stunning than when he had first met her. She wore blue jeans and a white t-shirt with a round black emblem above the left breast. He had noticed the same emblem, except much larger, on the door of the Caprice. "Fulton County Medical Examiner" was written around the top of the emblem; the acronym FCME completed the lower portion of the arc. The scales of justice were pictured in the middle, with the physician's serpent winding around its base. And she wasn't six feet tall, maybe five-ten at best. Maybe she wore platforms at work for effect or so she wouldn't have to stand on a stool to examine the insides of her lifeless customers.

"Grey," Beverly said with a smile. "Right on time." Her smile morphed to a look of concern. "You look as white as a corpse."

Colson realized he was holding his breath and exhaled. "Ah, I'm perfectly fine. I thought it would make you feel more at home."

Beverly laughed and motioned him inside. "You're being silly. Come in."

Colson followed her into the immaculate townhouse and back to the kitchen. The dark hardwood floors shone as if they had just been polished, and the aroma of cinnamon filled the air. The furnishings were small but elegant, and earth tones surrounded him from floor to ceiling. He thought of Ann and how she loved a variation of simple browns, greens, and burnt orange palates when painting and selecting furniture. Colson grinned to himself. Maybe similar tastes reflected similar personalities.

"Grey," Beverly said, "are you okay?"

Colson turned his grin to her. "More than okay, thank you. I was just thinking that you have a very beautiful home."

"Why, thank you, sir," she said. "Do we have time for me to show you something?"

"I'm retired. I always have time."

Colson followed her to the back door off the kitchen. She pushed it open and took a step down onto the concrete garage floor. Her movement triggered a motion sensor, and four ceiling can lights illuminated the area. Before he could step through the door, Colson was frozen in his tracks by the object before him, silently resting in all its glory in the immaculate garage. It was a gorgeous Daytona Blue, which was the literal name of the color assigned by General Motors. He had seen them on television, but never in person or on the road. The 1963 Corvette was the only year it was manufactured with a split rear window—and it was one of the (if not *the*) most desirable collector Corvettes on the planet.

Colson pushed himself to approach the four-wheeled beauty. He held out his hands as if taking possession of the machine. "This is unbelievable," he said. "It's the most beautiful thing I've seen since…" His voice trailed off, and he turned to Beverly, who now stood off to the side with her hands on her hips. She was smiling from ear to ear. "Well, since you opened the door five minutes ago," he finished.

She cocked her head. "You're just being sweet."

"Where—I mean how—did you land such a classic?"

"My dad. It was his since he drove it brand new off the lot. He left it to me."

Colson shook his head and leaned into the cockpit, taking in the ice blue leather seats, spotless carpet, and perfect dashboard and instruments. He peered at the odometer and almost bumped his head on the doorframe from shock. "You've got to be kidding me. Forty-seven hundred miles? Do you know how much this is worth?"

"Sure," Beverly said. "I could probably get over a hundred thousand."

"At least," Colson said. "Why don't we just take this baby with us and—"

"Oh, no, no, you don't," Beverly sputtered, waiving her index finger at Colson. "I never intend to sell it, and I'm certainly not going to let some pedal-happy retired cop ram it into a wall of Goodyear tires."

Colson laughed. "I don't blame you, but it was worth a try."

Colson bobbed his head just a little in time to the music on the 'Vette's radio. "Have you always wanted to live at the beach?" Beverly asked.

She seemed to be enjoying the passing scenery along I-85. The drive from Marietta was predictable—a lot of interstate and growing traffic around the perimeter highway and the exit to I-85 north, or, as the locals had dubbed the dreaded intersection years ago, "spaghetti junction." But once away from the city and metro area, the scenery opened up to pine forests and manicured medians.

They had been on the road for over an hour and talked the entire time in the intimate cockpit of the Corvette. The fifty miles to

Road Atlanta as indicated on their web page could be misleading to some. It was an accurate estimate from downtown, but twenty-five miles had to be added if traveling from the opposite side of town. Beverly didn't seem to mind the extra time with Colson; so far, the drive had been a lot of fun, with small talk about cars, work, and family.

Colson pondered Beverly's question. "Not always. I hadn't even seen the coast until I visited my brother in Fort Walton when I was eighteen. Ann and I vacationed with her parents in Daytona for years and grew to love it then."

Beverly nodded in silence. "So, you and Ann decided to move there when you retired?"

Colson shook his head. "She was gone before I retired. I moved later to start over."

"I'm sorry about your wife, Grey."

"Don't be—I mean, it was very difficult, but you can either give up and die or move on. I moved on because that's what Ann would have wanted. She was a tough girl, but there wasn't a selfish bone in her body."

"So," Beverly said, brightening, "do you like going to the races in Daytona?"

"Not really," Colson said, shaking his head again. "I like them okay, but you don't see as much of the action as you would on TV, and the noise will deafen you. I get bored with it. They just drive around in circles for hours."

Beverly laughed. "What else would they do?"

Colson scratched his chin in thought. "I figure they should build a figure-eight track. You know, with an intersection. Watching them dodging each other at one hundred and eighty miles per hour would be pretty entertaining."

"You're out of control, Colson," she said, laughing louder than before.

Jonathan Raines paced back and forth in his living room, rubbing the back of his neck. Sheila sat cross-legged on the couch, staring at a spot on the wall. They had said all there was to say and could only pray Emily would walk through the door at any second. They had stopped looking out the window days ago. It was as if the act itself prevented her from coming home. There was no word from the police, and the news of Keith's son being most likely murdered made the prospect of Emily's safe return less likely than before.

Jonathan stopped in the middle of the room and dropped his hands to his side, looked at his catatonic wife, and summoned one last plea. "You're her mother. Surely she did or said something we missed, but I wasn't around her like you were. Please try to think. Was there anything at all out of the ordinary we can give the police? If not, they'll stop looking—if they haven't already."

"Nothing," Sheila said, shaking her head. She was exhausted and realized she hadn't been thinking at all. Then something came to her mind, but she wasn't sure what it was. Her eyes met Jonathan's as she tried to summon the memory. Something like a feather, brushing the edges of her thoughts, but from the first day Emily went missing and not since.

"What is it?" Jonathan asked expectantly. He went to the couch and took Sheila's hand.

"I… I suddenly had the feeling I should be remembering something from earlier, but I don't know what it is."

"Let's go back over everything we know." Jonathan reached for his briefcase on the coffee table and retrieved his laptop. I've been keeping notes, phone numbers, friends' names, everything. Maybe if we go back over—"

"Wait," Sheila interrupted, staring at the laptop. She stood and went to the staircase.

"Where are you going?"

She didn't answer but dashed up the stairs. Jonathan stood bewildered for a moment and then followed. He found her standing in Emily's room. He looked around the silent room and said, "Honey, what is it? What's wrong?"

Sheila said nothing but walked to Emily's desk and began opening and closing the drawers.

"Sheila, honey, we've both been through her room dozens of times. What are you looking for?"

She stopped and turned to face him. "Jon, do you remember seeing a black laptop in here on her desk?"

"What? A black laptop? No, her computer is silver. It's right there," he said, pointing.

"I know that," she snapped, but quickly apologized. "I'm sorry, but I remember what it was. Not something that's here, but something that's not here." She pointed to an empty area of the desk. "There was a black laptop right there. I figured she borrowed it from a friend for some reason. But I only saw it once. It's not here now."

ᴄ⁄ᴾᴄHAPTER EIGHTEEN

Emily was tired of the running and hiding. She had been living with fear every day for the past two weeks, and fear was taking its toll. She missed her family, her own bed, and even the stupid family game night she used to dread and dismiss as juvenile. She missed her friends and wanted to call Tori, her best friend forever, but friendship was no longer a luxury she could afford.

Not when she was running for her life.

Frustration, fatigue, and fear became overwhelming, and her nerves were at their end. Every glance from a stranger set her mind racing. The only way to prevent her lower lip from trembling was to clamp it down under her teeth. She had always considered herself a tough young woman. Indestructible and almost impossible to intimidate. But what happened to Josh had changed everything. It changed her.

She shifted uncomfortably in the driver's seat of the Toyota and glanced over at the backpack on the seat beside her. It concealed the laptop she and Joshua had stolen from the car belonging to Derrick's dealer. There was no way either of them could have known who the guy was. She wished she had never seen the damn thing. It had to be the reason Josh was dead and she was on the run.

The real world wasn't what she had envisioned or hoped it would be, but she was smart enough to know the only way to survive was to stay off the grid and remain invisible. So she used cash to buy everything she needed. The Visa card her parents had entrusted her with on her sixteenth birthday was tempting to use for gas and food, but everyone knew it could be tracked. It was like leaving breadcrumbs for the wolf to follow.

She had cut her hair short and dyed it black the first night after she left, but even those drastic changes didn't relieve her paranoia. She was still too terrified to stop and ask anyone for directions. She had spent the majority of the past two weeks sitting in dark movie theatres where she knew everyone would be looking at the screen instead of her, but even the cheap matinee fees had depleted her funds.

The $400 she had saved since the age of fourteen was whittled down to the last $20. It had seemed like a lot of money on day one, and she congratulated herself on being skillful enough to survive on the streets this long, but now both her luck and her money were running out.

Emily closed her eyes and leaned back into the seat of the Toyota, thinking about her room and her comfortable bed. She thought of Josh and resisted the urge to cry again. Could they have been a normal couple if it hadn't been for the drugs? She shook her head violently. "No," she snapped and quickly looked from side to side for anyone who could have heard, but there were no onlookers in the parking lot. The relationship with Josh was no more than drugs on the buddy system. When he could afford a fix, they would use together. When she could afford it, she shared with him. It always felt better to have someone else use with you. It seemed to justify it. And they had trusted and protected each other. If not, he wouldn't have called to warn her that night. Josh was the only person who ever called her "Emmy," like the award, and it made her feel special.

Her mind replayed the call from Josh that night. She'd had the laptop and her purse in hand and was almost to her car when her cell phone rang.

"Don't come over tonight," Josh had said in a desperate tone.

"Josh?"

"Just don't," he pleaded. "Do you still have the laptop?"

"I have it with me. You said you wanted to sell—"

"No," he butted in. "They think it was me—I mean, I think Derrick ratted me out."

184

Emily had leaned against her car in the driveway and cupped her hand over the phone. "What's wrong, Josh? What's going on?"

"Listen, the last time I copped from Derrick he was acting really weird."

Emily had chuckled. "He is really weird."

"No, you don't understand. He mentioned the laptop."

"What?"

"I'm thinking it belongs to his supplier. He asked me if I had seen anyone around the car when we came by the other day and then said whoever took it should return it if they know what's good for them."

"So," Emily had said, offering a dismissive wave of her hand to no one, "you can just take it back—or better yet, tell him you found out who took it and stole it back for them. They might offer a reward."

"It's not going to be that easy, Emmy. I think it's gone too far."

"Why's that? And why won't you let me come over tonight? Is there someone else?"

"No!" Josh had shouted into the phone. "You know me. It's not that."

"Then what is it?"

"There's someone outside, in the next parking lot. He's in a dark car and he's been there ever since I got back to the room. He thinks I didn't notice or can't see him."

"You're just being paranoid."

"No, I'm not. Cops use those types of cars for surveillance. I've seen it before a bunch of times. At least I hope it's the cops and not someone Derrick's supplier sent. I know something's up, and I don't want anything to happen to you."

Emily's breathing had quickened. Josh was telling the truth, and she knew it. "You need to get out of there. Go out the back window. I'll come by and pick you up."

185

"There is no back window. I'm going to get rid of my stuff in case it's the police. I don't think this guy will sit there all night, so I'll call you in the morning, but it might be from jail. I don't know."

Those were the last words she had ever heard Josh say. She had skipped classes the next morning to wait for his call. After driving by the hotel, she had parked a quarter mile down the road, in a Laundromat parking lot where she could see the front of the hotel from a distance. There wasn't a suspicious dark car in the K-Mart parking lot she could see while driving by, but it could have been anywhere among the two or three dozen cars parked at that hour. Emily had taken Josh's advice and waited, deciding to give it another hour before calling the jail to find out if he had been arrested.

The sirens had come from the opposite direction to her left—first the police car with blue lights and siren, and then the red lights and siren of the fire department's rescue vehicle. She had held her breath as the screaming emergency vehicles neared the hotel entrance, but to her dismay, they had slowed and turned into the parking lot. She couldn't imagine any reason for them to go to the motel other than Josh. She had begun to cry even while checking her cell phone to make certain she hadn't missed his call. But no call had ever come.

A few minutes later an ambulance had driven past the Laundromat, going a little over the speed limit but with no siren or red lights. It had disappeared into a part of the hotel parking lot she couldn't see, just as the police and fire units had earlier. That told her all she needed to know. It was another thirty minutes before the ambulance exited the parking lot and moved past her at a normal speed. No lights, no siren, and no urgency. It was pure luck Emily raised her head and saw it. She had cried the entire time.

Then with an effort Emily had cleared her thoughts, wiped her eyes, and checked her reflection in the rear-view mirror. The face that stared back at her looked hideous, but she had decided to return home and tell her parents about the suspicious man in the dark car and Derrick's veiled threats that Josh had told her about. To hell with the drugs and the exhilaration of the next high—someone had to know. The police had to know. She owed that much to Josh. But reality had reared its ugly head just before she turned the key in the ignition.

"I can't," Emily had said to herself that night. She had jerked her head around to gaze at the laptop lying in the rear floorboard. Then she had quickly scanned her surroundings for the man or men who were probably stalking her at that exact moment. Did they know what kind of car she drove? Had she ever driven to Derrick's house? *Try to remember!* she told herself. With a wave of paranoia washing over her, she had stomped on the accelerator, shooting the Toyota out of the parking lot.

Emily jerked awake, startled by the horrid hammering. She must have fallen asleep while going over the previous days' events in her mind. Was it the sound of gunshots? For what seemed to be the hundredth time, she woke to intense fear, not knowing where she was. That would be expected since she slept at a different location every night. Last night she had parked at the rear of a poultry processing plant in the south end of Atlanta.

She looked out the window and saw an old man standing at her driver's window with genuine concern on his face. His knuckles were poised to rap on her window again. She glanced down at the blanket she had burrowed under late last night and realized it had slid down to her shoulders, revealing her head. She was relieved it wasn't a cop—or was she? No one could be trusted, but would a drug dealer recruit a killer from a convalescent home?

She forced a smile and lowered her window two inches. "Yes?"

The old man gave her a friendly smile. "I'm sorry, miss. Are you okay?

"Uh, yes," Emily said, sitting up in the seat and brushing hair from her eyes. Her reply was practiced in anticipation of this type of encounter. "I'm waiting on my boyfriend," she lied. "He works the night shift."

The old man shook his head sympathetically. He was kind enough not to ask for her boyfriend's name. The poor man had probably worked at the stinking plant his entire adult life and knew everyone on the night shift. He simply gave Emily a grandfatherly wave and hobbled away to his faded blue Cutlass parked nearby.

Emily released a sigh, balled up the blanket, and tossed it in the back seat. She drove several miles until she found a city library, and she parked in a spot out of sight of the roadway near the rear of the building. She went inside the minute it opened, finding a row of computer cubicles lining the far wall. They were empty at this early hour. She sat down in an end booth, logged on to the Internet, and searched for Joshua Bartlett. She felt tears coming again as she waited for the results. She closed her eyes and took deep breaths to maintain her composure before looking at the screen.

There were only four entries. The first was a brief article in the hometown paper's online edition. The headline read "Local Youth Dies in Drug Overdose."

Josh wasn't famous or the son of a wealthy man. Few people knew he had even existed outside of his parents and a couple of friends. To the world, his passing away was just another junkie death. The attention to his death was as short and seemingly unremarkable as his life. The story of his demise had been relegated to page six of an online edition of a small-town paper.

The second entry was Joshua's obituary, the third, a story about Joshua's dad speaking at a Chamber of Commerce event. She found a fourth story about—she scrolled down, skimming the article, and then jumped back up to the beginning. She read the text carefully and almost fell off the chair. Her heart swelled with hope. Why had she not heard about this on the news?

Colson topped the gradually inclining hill and the track came into view. The surrounding landscape and infield were as green and manicured as any high-dollar golf course he had ever seen in person or on television. This place was entirely different from any NASCAR track. What lay before him was a winding, rolling track, curving out of sight in the distance. It reminded him of a mountain road without any mountains to dictate its course. The bend of each curve was protected by short retaining walls of stacked tires, decorated with brightly colored racing banners and advertisements for everything from beer and potato chips to shock absorbers.

Colson exaggerated a nod at the sight before him. "Now that's what I call a racetrack," he said to Beverly with admiration.

"It's huge," Beverly replied. "You sure you want to do this?"

Colson shrugged. "Might as well. I've always wanted to see what this baby could really do. You can't get over forty-five around metro Atlanta unless you're on the perimeter. And that's more dangerous than riding a go-cart on a packed NASCAR track."

"What about Daytona?"

"There's less traffic, but the county boys will write you for five over the limit." Colson chuckled. "Believe me, I should know."

They followed the signs and turned right at a two-foot-high placard that read Free Parking. A white banner a tenth of a mile later was stretched over the access road stating North Georgia Corvette Association. A man in a bright orange and yellow traffic vest motioned with an orange flag for them to move past the entrance of the parking lot. Colson veered left accordingly, and they drove through a tunnel and emerged on an infield road.

"Look at that," Colson said, pointing to his left.

"Nice," Beverly said.

"Amazing," Colson agreed. Without bothering to count, there were clearly over one hundred Corvettes of every year, make, model, and color in two long lines, side by side. Their drivers milled about in clumps, all wearing ball caps and brightly colored T-shirts or golf shirts

Colson glanced in his rear-view mirror as the deep-throated roar of sports car engines shot behind them. Two cars were passing overhead, above the infield tunnel. The squeal of tires immediately followed as the two competing drivers made a sharp left and then right for the last two turns of the course and gunned their engines down the final straight to the finish. A man perched on a high seat and dressed in a white shirt jerked a checkered flag in an X pattern with his right hand and punched a stopwatch with his left. The two 'Vettes slowed their pace and fell into the back of the long line of cars waiting their turn in pit row.

Colson saw the two smiling driver's exit their cars and shake hands as he pulled to the rear of line, dropped the gear into neutral, and set the emergency brake. As a stranger, Colson felt somewhat out of place, never being a member of a car enthusiast's club and never really wanting to be. Colson pulled on his Atlanta Braves ball cap and stepped out, quickly moving to the passenger door to open it for Beverly, but she was already leaning her slender frame against the hood when he rounded the front. She was blocking the sun from her eyes with her hand while looking across the expansive track. The 11:00 a.m. temperature was already a balmy 80 degrees, but the humidity made it feel like 95.

"It's beautiful out here," she said, scanning the field.

Colson rested his hands on his hips and sighed. "It is, but I don't know what I'm doing here."

Beverly squinted at him in the bright mid-morning sun. "What do you mean? I thought you wanted to see what the old LT1 was made of."

"Yeah, I guess," Colson murmured, "but showing off isn't my style."

Beverly shrugged, her hands outspread. "Then why did you come?"

"Partly because an old friend invited me, but mostly because you agreed to come with me. I probably would have been a no-show otherwise. I have a lot going on."

"But you're retired."

Colson laughed, shaking his head. "People keep telling me that."

The bark of tires drew their attention to the front of the line, where two more drivers shot off the starting line for their two-and-a-half-mile race. The view of the red and white cars became distorted by heat waves hovering above the hot asphalt down the first straightaway to turn number one. Turns two, three, and four were gentle turns. They watched the two 'Vettes weave through them without braking as the red car took a clear lead.

"Colson!"

He heard Morgan's voice before he saw him walking in his direction, waving both arms above his head. The D.A. marched up to Colson and Beverly wearing blue sweat pants and a Road Atlanta T-shirt and clutching a white form and a pen in his hand.

"Glad you could make it, Grey," Morgan said with a broad smile. "Just sign this real quick. I've saved you a spot about three sets back from the front."

Colson took the form and glanced at it curiously. "What's this?"

"A waiver of liability. It just says the owners of Road Atlanta aren't going to buy you a new Corvette if you booger yours up."

Colson bent to sign the paper against his leg and handed it back to Morgan. "Larry," Colson said proudly, gently placing his right hand on Beverly's shoulder, "this is Dr. Beverly Walls."

"Ah, yes," Morgan said, "the Fulton County medical examiner. I've heard good things about your work," he added, extending his hand.

Beverly beamed a broad smile and shook Morgan's hand. "Thank you."

Colson pulled his hat lower on his sunglasses and exaggerated rubbing his hands together. "So," he said, turning to Beverly, "you ready for the ride of your life?"

"Oh, no, I don't think so," Beverly said, shaking her finger at Colson. "I trust you, Grey, but if I'm going to race, I want to have control of the wheel."

Colson's eyebrows rose as he gestured to the car. "You want to drive?"

"No thanks," Beverly said with a laugh. "I think I'll just watch you two kids."

"You sure?"

"Maybe next time." Beverly turned and walked toward the grandstand.

"Hang on, Beverly," Morgan said, openly admiring her figure as she sauntered away, but maintaining a businesslike tone. "Can you record the race on your phone? I would like to occasionally remind Colson who the best driver is."

Beverly half turned so Morgan could see her sticking out her tongue at him.

CHAPTER NINETEEN

The Butcher parked in a free parking area across highway 53 and rode an open-air shuttle tram to the grandstand seating area adjacent to turn 10B of the Road Atlanta track. He wore blue jeans, a gray T-shirt, a black ball cap, and sunglasses. A new pair of Bushnell binoculars dangled from a strap around his neck.

He stopped briefly at the souvenir shop, grabbed the first Road Atlanta T-shirt he saw in extra large, paid the boy behind the counter, and strolled into the men's room. Three minutes later, he emerged wearing the new shirt and blended into a crowd of people at the entrance of the small shop. The Butcher scowled at the clumps of women and children wearing Road Atlanta and Corvette T-shirts. Little boys held die-cast metal and plastic cars, making *vroom-vroom* sounds as they rolled them up and down their arms. Little girls fondled trinkets on shelves, and small groups of young mothers chatted among themselves and occasionally laughed at God only knows what. All were there for one purpose: to show off their cars or their outfits, but mostly to socialize and have another excuse for not cleaning the house on Saturday.

The Butcher glared through his sunglasses at a small boy who ran straight into his leg from the side, obviously not paying attention to where he was going. He forced a smile and patted the top of the boy's head before stepping around the little imbecile. He walked out into the scorching Georgia sun, unclipping the phone from his belt. Electronic gadgets were the Butcher's best friends. They did as they were told ninety-nine percent of the time and never talked back unless you wanted them to. He had often wondered how society functioned a hundred years ago without them. Today you could almost do anything remotely. Set your home security system, watch your front door camera from the other side of the world on your smart phone, and even turn lights on and off in your house from anywhere you could send and receive a signal. He grinned at the thought as he selected the appropriate phone application. A small box appeared instantly on the notification bar—no signal.

"Damn it," the Butcher snapped without thinking, and then he immediately looked both ways to see if anyone heard. He jerked the phone to his side and marched to the stands. It was something he should have considered, but he was so proud of his ingenuity it hadn't crossed his mind. He turned completely around, surveying the sprawling track and scattered buildings. There had to be a cellular signal around, but it was probably limited to one lone tower in the middle of the hick town of Braselton. His plan was to remain well out of sight, but now the plan required adjustment. He walked quickly to the foot of the grandstand and started climbing.

Beverly stopped at a souvenir booth, plucked a visor from a display, and handed the attendant a $10 bill before making her climb to the top of the bleachers. Since none of the Corvette Club members were famous drivers, those in attendance were a modest group of friends and family—quite modest in contrast, since the stadium seating could accommodate several hundred for larger events. At least there was room to move around, great seat selection, and there would be no one to climb over or a juggernaut of fans to wade through when it was time to go home. She smiled at small family groups on her way up the grandstand and settled on the top row, looking over the finish line just down from the infield tunnel they had driven through earlier.

Beverly pushed the camera icon on her phone and zoomed in on the line of Corvettes in pit row. She found Colson in the screen, standing next to his car and looking in her direction. She waved and could see him smile and wave back. Morgan appeared to be talking non-stop, but Colson didn't appear to be paying attention.

She lowered the phone when a man in jeans and a T-shirt rounded the corner and began climbing the stands. She released an involuntary sigh. "Just my luck," she whispered, and she scooted ten feet down from the end. The man obviously wasn't a participant in the race or he would be on the track. Since he had no wife, girlfriend, boyfriend, or children in tow, Beverly pegged him as a lone wacko looking for female companionship.

Was it so wrong to be instantly judgmental? She shook her head. Maybe so, but it happened to her too many times to count. Weirdos of every shape, size, and age loitered everywhere she went—even the grocery store. Their demeanor was always similar. At first they would appear preoccupied and not notice her, but eventually they would think of some ambiguous question to ask her in an attempt to strike up a conversation. She wished she had rolled the dice and ridden along with Colson. Turning white as a sheet, holding on for dear life, and repeating the Lord's Prayer was far better than having to avoid another self-conscious pervert.

The Butcher ascended the bleachers with his head down, breathing heavily through his nose—not due to the climb, but from total frustration. He cursed under his breath, watching the outline of the empty bar graph on the cell screen. All of his elaborate planning may have been a waste of time and effort. He glanced up to the top rail and picked up the pace. Another twenty or twenty-five feet to go and he would know for certain. The Butcher scolded himself for not keeping things simple as he always had in the past, and then just as quickly congratulated himself when the first signal bar appeared on the screen. Three additional signal bars appeared when he reached the top of the bleachers.

He rested his back against the top rail, pulled up a contact icon, sent a coded text, and pressed send. He grinned when the return text popped up on the screen, indicating the message had been received and the signal was good.

The Butcher steadied his breathing, lifted his binoculars, and found the green and red Corvettes moving to the starting line. They would be held until the current pair crossed the finish line. They were just now entering turn three, so there was plenty of time. He touched the transmitter icon and watched with satisfaction as the application filled the screen. The on-screen keyboard appeared at the bottom of the screen once he touched the empty entry field. He fingered the keyboard, filled the box with a series of numbers, and waited.

Colson had driven fast before, but today he was feeling butterflies for the second time. Maybe because there was an audience and maybe it was just because Beverly was watching. He had never given a thought when chasing a bad guy and running code with blue lights and siren. There were people watching then, but he was only focused on catching the criminal, not entertaining the citizens. It was the adrenalin keeping the butterflies at bay then. Even the somewhat exhilarating ride during the surveillance of Strawn's limo didn't feel odd because it was something he was accustomed to. It was like work.

He eased his car to the starting line, hoping Beverly wouldn't write him off as some show-off, mid-life-crisis case. It was a little too late now. Morgan would never let him hear the end of it if he backed out.

Colson looked to his left at a smiling Morgan, who gave him a smart military salute off the short bill of his crash helmet. Colson felt like an idiot wearing the helmet. One run and he would be quite done and ready to get back to Beverly. He looked over his shoulder, but his view of the bleachers was blocked. He looked left, past Morgan's car, at the round-bellied man holding a green flag to his side. He was getting hot in the helmet; a bead of sweat ran down his back. Running the air would be a drag on the horsepower, and he knew he'd need it all to give Morgan a good run. Both the windows were down, but there wasn't even a slight breeze blowing. The roar of other Corvettes finishing their runs grew closer and louder. Muffled applause and cheering crept through his helmet, suggesting the two current speeders had crossed the finish line.

"Drivers ready?" shouted the man holding the flag. Colson looked into the distance at turn number one, slipped the gear into first, and held the brake and clutch to the floor. He gave Morgan one last glance as the man raised the flag and jerked it sharply downward.

Morgan shot ahead of him by two car lengths, leaving Colson half a second behind. Colson eased the clutch back and floored the accelerator to catch up. He made up lost ground and closed on Morgan, one-half car length behind and one car width to the right as they approached the first right turn. Morgan dropped in front of Colson in the bank as both cars reached 90 miles per hour.

Beverly stood up, watching both cars drop out of the first turn and rocket toward turns two, three, and four, conveniently labeled "the Esses" in the pamphlet she was using to fan the heat from her neck. She had all but forgotten the lone man propped against the top rail. He had not approached her, attempted polite conversation, or even given her a glance from what she could see. He alternated tinkering with his phone and watching the line of cars with binoculars. But he hadn't been watching the two 'Vettes racing in the previous contest; it was as though he was waiting for something else.

Colson and Morgan dropped out of sight after banking left on turn five. Beverly cut her eyes right to the man against the rail. He was holding the cell phone in his left hand and the binoculars up to his eyes with his right, following Colson and Morgan's progress. It reminded her to pull up the video app on her phone to record the finish. They should come into view down the long straightaway before the sharp left and right turns of 10A and 10B.

She smiled and shook her head. It seemed obvious why the last turns were placed close to the finish. Most of these men would drive flat out at 150 mph if there wasn't something to slow them down. The man was obstructing her view, causing her to step down one bleacher seat to bring the track into view as she pressed "Record."

By turn five the butterflies were gone and Colson was thrilled. He caught up to Morgan and passed him on the inside of turn six. Morgan slipped back under him in turn seven, but they were running side-by-side after turn eight, both engines wide open and topping 125 mph. Colson knew he and Morgan could push their sleds faster, but neither was stupid enough to expect that much out of cars they had never required such power of before.

Turn nine was a shallow left, requiring a limited reduction in speed before the straightaway to turn ten. Colson dropped the gear into fourth and took the high bank, allowing Morgan to move ahead half a car length before both floored their machines again. He was confident he could overtake Morgan on the straight, having spent years driving this car and having intimate knowledge of its capabilities. He punched the clutch, dropped the shifter into third, and slammed his foot to the floorboard. Morgan was now two car lengths ahead, but Colson slipped to his left and closed fast.

Both vehicles topped 140 down the straightaway. To a person crazy enough to be standing directly in the path of the two speeding sports cars, they would appear to have flattened out on the pavement due to the aerodynamic design forcing their frames downward; otherwise they would have become airborne like a speedboat.

The Butcher lowered his binoculars and turned his attention to the transmitter app on his phone. The two cars were well within sight now. The several dozen onlookers in the stands were on their feet, cheering, clapping, and shouting encouragements to one car or the other. The Butcher allowed himself a quick glance at the crowd, but no one was paying him any attention—including the tall and lovely brunette several feet to his left.

"I'll give you something to watch," he muttered, and then he turned back to the track. He was no professional racecar driver as the two worthless slugs in the 'Vettes thought they were, but even a third-grader would know to let off the gas before negotiating the last two 90-degree turns. It simply meant they would need to begin slowing approximately 150 feet prior to the turn. He chuckled. Maybe 100 feet if they were insane, like him. He would give the distance his best guess, but 20 feet too early or late wouldn't make that much difference. Probably only enough for the paramedics to select a spatula rather than a sponge to collect the remains.

The Butcher held up his phone to keep Colson and Morgan in view above the transmitter app. The increasing pitch of their engines clearly indicated they were continuing to accelerate down the straightaway. His finger hovered over the send button directly below the frequency he had typed in earlier.

Morgan was ahead of Colson by half a car length. Just when it appeared they would begin easing off the gas, the Butcher touched send.

A number of police agencies across the nation conduct operations known by some as bait car stings. Usually reserved for high crime areas where statistics show a high number of car thefts, the bait car sting can be beneficial in discouraging thefts, at least for a period of time. Agents select a vehicle commonly preyed upon by thieves, install the bait car device, park the car in a high theft area, set up surveillance, and wait. The beauty of the device is two-fold. Not only can it track the stolen vehicle via GPS if the car thief dodges surveillance, it can also remotely kill the engine and lock the thief inside to await arrest. Liability being a concern, the engine is typically extinguished at a stop sign or at slow speeds. Executing a car thief by killing his engine at seventy miles per hour or risking the death of another driver or pedestrian would be seriously frowned upon by the county or city attorney.

Not many things excited the Butcher, but getting his hands on one of the unique devices and watching it in action made him absolutely giddy.

Beverly sighed again when the man shifted left and into her video screen, but she kept the two approaching cars in view. Then it happened. At first she thought a tire had blown on the red Corvette. It wiggled slightly and slowed a fraction. Colson was nose to nose with Morgan now and beginning to pull ahead. She felt a slight grin forming the instant before the signals reaching her brain revealed the reality of what was taking place. Almost as quickly as Colson pulled ahead of Morgan, the green Corvette fell behind as Colson downshifted and slowed for the sharp left turn. Her eyes flashed to the left, ahead of the cars to the retaining wall, now a hundred or so feet away. Morgan was pulling away from Colson and didn't appear to be slowing at all. Beverly gasped. The front-end wiggle of the red car grew to an exaggerated jerking motion. Morgan's car began drifting into a shallow left turn when the rear wheels locked on the hot asphalt, leaving an off-white cloud of smoke in its wake.

Larry Morgan was perplexed for a fraction of a second, then went into full panic mode. Two seconds earlier, his mind had been doing double duty—simultaneously concentrating on his driving and practicing his victory speech. Both thought processes vaporized in an instant, replaced by a single thought: survival.

The engine had shut down as if he had killed it himself. Feelings, emotions, memories, and what limited driving skills he had manifested themselves as one during the next three-and-a-half seconds. Morgan stabbed at the start button on the console. The keyless system had never failed him as long as the key fob was within range. He struggled in an attempt to hold the dead steering wheel steady with one hand, causing the front end to drift left and right, while he pressed on the starter button with the other. Nothing. No power, extremely limited steering—and the brakes felt like a wet sponge under his foot.

Morgan glanced at the retaining wall, growing ever larger in his view by the millisecond. In one last effort to avoid the inevitable, he jerked the emergency brake and pulled down hard on the steering wheel. He heard the scream of the rear tires fighting asphalt and momentum, but the front end barely responded. An image of his wife and children was the final visual in his mind, and a muffled THUMP was the final sound. Then there was nothing.

Colson had already downshifted for the hard left when he saw Morgan's car begin to wiggle. He immediately hit the anti-lock brakes and could feel the discs grab and release with fury. Morgan's actions appeared exaggerated from behind, and Colson couldn't understand what he was trying to accomplish. The car continued on its straight course toward the retaining wall and didn't seem to be slowing, even though its brake lights flickered.

"Come on, Larry," Colson shouted as if his friend could hear. "Slow down!" The red Corvette was pulling away from Colson, and he could no longer see what Morgan was doing through the rear window. The wiggling of the car diminished and developed into a shallow left turn, but it wasn't enough to avoid the retaining wall. Colson estimated the speed of the slowly turning car hadn't fallen below 90 mph when the front passenger side corner made contact with the white tarp covering the columns of old tires beneath. Colson was forced to veer left through the turn, still braking at 45 mph. He jerked his right arm to cover his face while he steered with his left hand.

The explosion was deafening, and the extreme heat from the flash of fire rushed through his open passenger side window.

Colson stood on the brakes, skidded the car to a stop, and threw his door open twenty yards after the turn. A siren began wailing in the background. He ran around the retaining wall and into the grassy infield, dodging large and small chunks of metal and fiberglass debris scattered in a path at least fifty yards long.

The smell of burnt fuel and rubber enveloped Colson as he dived into the gray cloud of smoke billowing from the debris. Before him lay the charred, mangled body of Larry Morgan, the late D.A. of Clay County.

$\mathcal{A}$CHAPTER TWENTY$\sim$

The return drive to Clay County was silent and somber, with neither Colson nor Beverly saying much. Morgan hadn't been Colson's close friend, but he was a friend nonetheless. Colson's mind was on Morgan's wife and children for the majority of the drive back to Beverly's condo. He felt her hand on his arm again.

"I'm so very sorry about your friend," she said.

Colson nodded. "He was a professional friend. This was actually the first time we'd done anything social. I just hate it for his family, and I feel like a foolish child for agreeing to race him."

"You can't think of it like that," Beverly. "If he hadn't raced with you, he would have raced with someone else. You know you shouldn't be blaming yourself for something you had no control over." She looked out her window and sighed. "It's selfish of me to feel this way, but I'm glad it wasn't you."

The first one on the scene, Colson had realized with one glance that Morgan was gone. His charred remains were missing an arm and both legs. The paramedics had rushed to the scene from their stand-by location in the infield, but there was nothing they could do for Morgan, except to help the medical examiner's investigator collect his missing limbs. The remaining two hours of the event were mercifully cancelled. The participants and Road Atlanta employees kept their distance, standing in near silence outside the crime scene tape around a large perimeter of the crash area.

Colson looked down at the business card on his console. Sheriff's investigator S. Latham had given it to him following the interview. He had described to her what he'd witnessed to the best of his recollection—the shuddering and wiggling of Morgan's car; how he appeared to be wrestling the wheel; and the shallow turn, as if he had lost the ability to steer. Colson had promised to call if anything else came to mind, not bothering to ask her first name, but Latham seemed competent and made her own promise. "If I come up with anything out of the ordinary, I'll call you."

"Are you planning to notify his family? Colson asked. "I didn't really know them."

Latham shook her head. "They are close to the president of the car club, and he's a fellow attorney. He wants to take care of it."

Colson heaved a deep sigh at the thought of breaking the news to Morgan's wife. He hoped no one from the Corvette club had jumped the gun and made a call before she could be told in person. He shifted the car into fifth and then took Beverly's hand. "With all of those people gathered around, I wouldn't be surprised if his wife already knows."

Beverly jerked her head to Colson, eyes wide. "Surely no one told her over the phone."

"You know how some people are," he said. "They probably knew better than to call her direct but can't resist the temptation to call all their friends. Not to mention how they will all try to be the first to post photos and videos of the crash to their Facebook and Twitter accounts. Then the dominos start falling. Morgan was well known as a D.A. and even more so for his stance against drug legalization. Chances are it'll be on the news at four, if they haven't already broadcast a news bulletin."

"But wouldn't the Hall County Sheriff's Office tell them to hold off until the family is notified?" she asked.

Colson nodded. "Under most circumstances, yes, but they may not beat that crowd to the punch, and I honestly didn't think to warn Latham at the time. There were at least two hundred people standing around, and I guarantee most of them were on their cell phones."

They rode in silence for several minutes. Colson glanced over at Beverly; she was staring out her window again. "Are you okay?"

he asked. She turned to him with a half smile. "What is it?" Colson said.

Beverly shook her head and turned back to her window. "It's probably nothing."

Colson heard a buzzing sound and flipped open the console. A blue light blinked slowly at the top of his cell phone, indicating missed calls. He ignored it and clicked the lid back down. He was more concerned that he might have done or said something to offend her. "Please, Beverly, what is it?"

She reached out and touched Colson's arm. "It's not you. Really, it's probably nothing at all. I didn't even think about it until you mentioned everyone gathering around the scene of the accident."

"There's nothing too insignificant if it's bothering you," Colson said flatly. "Tell me, and if I think there's nothing to it, I'll tell you so."

"Well," she began, "when something so tragic happens, everyone has to watch or go see what happened like you said, whether it's out of concern or morbid curiosity."

Colson nodded. "Exactly. That's why I suspect someone already called—"

"No," she interrupted him. "Not everyone went to the infield."

"I'm not following you. What are you talking about?"

"There was a man in the stands recording the race on his cell phone. He was alone, and it felt like he was—I don't know—out of place from the rest of the spectators. Maybe it was his body language and I didn't think about it at the time, but now that we're talking about it..." Her voice trailed off.

"Didn't think about what?" Colson asked expectantly.

"At the time I was in a rush to get to you and see if Morgan was hurt. It's human nature."

"So what's bothering you about the man?"

"Now that I remember, he was ahead of me going down the stairs, and I nearly had to shove him out of the way because of his nonchalant manner. He turned at the bottom of the stairs and went the opposite way." Beverly paused a beat. "I find that rather odd, don't you?"

Colson squinted and thought for a moment, possibilities swirling in his head. How could Morgan's death be anything other than a terrible accident? It seemed to be a crazy, paranoid notion, but stranger things had happened. Beverly's seed of doubt was now planted in his head, and he wouldn't be rid of it until the crash investigation was completed.

"The investigation," Colson said.

"What?" Beverly said.

"What did he look like?"

"I didn't get a look at his face. He was wearing a ball cap and sunglasses and—what are you doing?" she asked, watching Colson flip open the console and pull out his phone. He handed it over to her.

"Please dial the cell number on the card," he said, pointing to the business card in the console. "Try to remember anything else unusual about the man. Anything at all."

Beverly punched in the numbers. "I'll do my best, but we can both take a look when we get back to the condo."

Colson gave her another squint. "How's that?"

She handed Colson the phone, and he held it to his ear. "Because he was in my way while I was trying to record the race. I'm sure I have several seconds of him from behind on video."

Colson's eyes widened with approval. "Good—very good," he said while waiting for an answer, but his call went to voice mail. "Investigator Latham," he said, "this is Grey Colson from earlier. Please call me back ASAP. I need a big favor."

"Tell your boy I want my money back," Strawn demanded from behind his desk. He touched an icon on the glass top, muting the news report of Morgan's fiery crash, and then he pointed his fat finger at Haggart. "He's been dragging his feet finding that girl, and fate beat him to the punch with Morgan."

Haggart dropped his frame in the chair across from Strawn and held up his cell phone. "He must have thought you'd say something like that, because he sent a coded text fifteen minutes before the crash saying it would happen within a half hour."

Strawn's eyebrows rose. "How would he know that? I mean, how did he..."

"He's good," Haggart said with a smile.

"Well," Strawn said, examining the cigar he rolled between his fingers, "why didn't he take out Colson when he had the opportunity?"

Haggart shrugged. "That I don't know, and he doesn't go into details with me. If he eliminated both, it might draw too much suspicion, and if he got caught he might—"

"If, if, if," Strawn barked, waving his hand in the air. "If the queen had balls, she'd be king, wouldn't she. We don't deal in ifs, ands and buts, Haggart. You send him a message and tell him to take care of what I paid him to do, and he'd better get his ass in gear—you understand?"

Haggart nodded and walked out of the office.

Emily jerked awake and checked her surroundings. She rubbed the back of her sore neck and turned the ignition without starting the car. The clock on the dash read 6:13, and the little hand on the fuel gauge read less than a quarter of a tank. She felt sticky in the humidity of the car, and her hair felt like a massive lump of clay. She caught a glimpse of her eyes in the rear-view mirror but dared not flip the mirror flap down on the visor, for fear of the creature she might see peering back at her.

The withdrawals had ceased two days ago, now she was famished. Her last $20 wouldn't buy much, but it was time to use it and regain her strength. It was as if she had awakened from a coma. Through the pangs of hunger she now realized that her head was clear and at least some of her paranoia had subsided. Emily didn't dismiss the reality of danger surrounding her, but it was becoming easier to accept and guard against. She had to eat, and then she would decide her next best course of action. She nodded and even smiled, now that her decision was made. Mom and Dad would hear from her today and know she was all right. It should never have gone this far.

She cranked the engine and eased the Toyota to the street, looking down the road in both directions. A huge billboard in the distance caught her attention. It was twice as high as the other billboards in view. Emily tried to remember what a Flying J was. A little light flashed in her head. She turned right and toward the expressway, recalling a time when all she had to worry about was whether or not grandma had her favorite warm banana pudding waiting for her.

"How long will it take to get to grandma's house?" an eight-year-old Emily had asked her father during a long road trip.

Her dad had glanced at her in the rear-view mirror. "About six hours, dear."

She had seen a large sign and asked him what a Flying J was.

"It's a truck stop," he had told her.

"Why do they have truck stops, Dad?"

"Well," he had said with his characteristic chuckle, "so truck drivers can have a place to eat, get gas, and take a shower."

She remembered asking him, "Why don't they take a bath at home, like we do?"

Her comment was answered with laughter from both parents. "Because they stay on the road for a long time and can't go home. You see…"

Emily hit the brakes when the car in front of her stopped abruptly at a red light, thrusting her focus back to the present. She took a deep breath and brushed the tears from her cheeks. She had let everyone she loved down, but maybe she could make it right. Maybe she could be forgiven. She turned into the giant parking lot of the Flying J and drove around a long line of semi-tractor trailers, each truck emitting diesel fumes from its massive idling engine. The low rumblings reminded her of wild, sleeping beasts. Strong exhaust fumes enveloped her until she pulled up to the front entrance and parked in a space near the glass double doors.

There were more trinkets, bobble-head dolls, pine-tree air fresheners, hats, car cleaning stuff, binoculars, and radios stacked on shelves than Emily had ever seen. She walked past a sign that read C.B. Ultra-Boost Antennas, but she couldn't remember if her dad had ever told her what C.B. stood for, or if she had even asked. She dismissed the thought and scanned the rear area of the sales floor. They were on opposite sides of the room. Open doorways with "Men" to the right and "Women" to the left. She walked down the left-hand hallway, which opened into a locker room that was mercifully vacant. Beige lockers lined the wall to her immediate right and down the wall in front of her. To her left was a line of shower stalls hidden behind cheap, vinyl shower curtains. The room smelled a little musty, but the thought of a warm shower overwhelmed her. To her left stood a rough, homemade shelving unit. Two faded and folded bath towels rested on the lower shelf. She got undressed and hung her clammy shirt and jeans on the shelf, grabbed a towel, and stepped into a shower stall.

Jack Strawn rubbed his hands together, contemplating the best strategic approach in light of current events. It took Haggart less than ten minutes to drive him from Strawn Tower to the CNN Center in Midtown. He silently scolded himself for not being more prepared. No amount of money or influence would make his goal a reality without public support. The combination of both was required. With a short nod, Strawn decided on the best course of action.

A make-up artist hovered around the forty-ish, dark-haired news anchor seated across from him. Strawn had refused to allow the flittering, alternate-lifestyle type near him, but he didn't object to the well-endowed female studio manager who clipped a miniature microphone to his suit lapel. Studio lights glared in Strawn's eyes. He turned away and glanced out the floor-to-ceiling plate glass, overlooking the atrium where herds of people milled about the huge complex, entering and leaving shops and restaurants. The low mumbling of cameramen, hidden in the dark background of the studio, suddenly went silent at the voice of the man who stepped just into view of the hot lights, holding his hand up with fingers spread.

"We're live in five, four, three," the man recited sternly, dropping one finger at a time as he counted down. He dropped the last two fingers in a silent countdown and pointed to the anchor. A little red light appeared on top of the camera that was pointed in the anchor's direction, and a beaming smile crossed his face.

"Good morning," the anchor began, replacing his smile with a serious, down-to-business expression. "I'm Stanley York and this is *CNN Politics Today.*"

Strawn could hear the sounds of symphony horns playing some sort of theme in the background to alert the audience to the serious, political nature of the segment. He sat patiently and silently practiced a series of responses in his head. The theme music faded, and York continued.

"The Georgia House of Representatives is expected to consider a bill to legalize possession of marijuana and narcotic substances in the coming weeks. If passed through committee and approved by a majority in the House, it would be the first time in American history that a state adopted the legalization of not only marijuana, but most all narcotic substances. With me today is business mogul Jack Strawn, owner and president of Strawn Industries."

A red light appeared on top of a second camera, directed at Strawn, who offered an expressionless nod. Strawn saw both York and himself in a flat-screen monitor as York began his questioning.

"Mr. Strawn, I'd like to get your reaction to the results of a CNN poll taken just yesterday. Forty-nine-point-eight percent of Americans support the legalization of marijuana for personal use, and over sixty percent are in favor of legalization for medical purposes."

Strawn drew a breath to respond but was held at bay by York's raised hand. "Hang on a second; here's what I'd like you to respond to. The first two poll questions were about marijuana, and those numbers have remained constant for the most part over the last five years. The final poll question was about the legalization of all drugs—marijuana and controlled substances such as heroin, LSD, cocaine, methamphetamines, etcetera. Now, the percentage of those who support such legislation stands at only eighteen per cent. That leaves approximately eighty-two per cent against the legalization of hard drugs."

Strawn pushed his hands together as if in prayer and rested his lips on the tip of his fingers. The red light illuminated on the camera directly facing him, meaning it was a solo shot. He gazed into the camera and lowered his hands. "First, Stan, if I may, I would like to express my condolences to the family of the late Clay County district attorney, Larry Morgan, who died in a tragic car crash yesterday."

"Yes," York said with a nod, "we at CNN are sorry for the loss of D.A. Morgan. His work with the state's Department of Behavioral Health and Developmental Disabilities was honorable, and I'm certain his will be difficult shoes to fill. Now, he was in essence your enemy, I mean, on a professional level. It was Morgan who was leading a campaign against the proposed legislation."

"No." Strawn pointed a fat finger at York, causing the anchor to flinch unexpectedly. "That's where you're wrong. Morgan was no enemy of mine. He was a fine man who fought for his beliefs as we all do. The enemy here is the government, whose goal is the continued expenditure of billions of dollars they steal from taxpayers to fight a war they cannot win, nor have any intention of winning."

York recovered from Strawn's minor outburst and answered with a determined glare of his own. "But getting back to the poll, you don't have the support of a majority of Americans, regardless of the government's war on drugs. Why not follow suit with other states that have successfully passed laws permitting the personal use of marijuana?"

Strawn controlled his tone, lowered his voice, and smiled. "I can answer your question two ways." Strawn held up his index finger. "First and foremost, I'm a libertarian and always will be. Did you look at the internals of those who participated in the poll?"

"As a matter of fact..." York began as he shuffled through papers on the news desk.

"You don't have to check," Strawn said. "I know the numbers, and you'll find over ninety per cent of libertarians agree with me. The title 'Libertarian' means we stand for liberty and the individual rights of all citizens to freely live their lives as long as it brings no harm to anyone else."

"Some may argue differently, Mr. Strawn."

"Some have and will again, but they can't make a logical argument. Second," Strawn said, holding up two fingers, "I didn't become the successful businessman I am by doing things in half measures. History is clear about the prohibition of alcohol, and if people seriously consider it, all other substance use eventually will be legalized. I say let Georgia be an example for the rest of the nation to follow."

York nodded. "Well, we can only wait and see what happens in the coming weeks. Back to Larry Morgan—who do you see as his replacement? Who will take up the torch, so to speak, as leading the public opposition to your agenda?"

Strawn exaggerated a shrug. "I wouldn't know. They don't typically invite me to their strategy sessions."

"But doesn't he have people working with him? A second in command?"

"A second in command," Strawn responded with a chuckle. "That could only be Grey Colson, but I believe second in command is not the proper term. If they were to ask my opinion, which they most certainly will not, I would suggest a successful person in the business community who understands the real economic impact drugs have on society, not some washed-out retired cop turned government flunky."

CHAPTER TWENTY-ONE

fternoon traffic on Whitlock Avenue was a daily nightmare, even if such a term is an oxymoron. The morning rush to work and the afternoon rush would be better named the morning and afternoon crawl. The two-lane main artery into the county seat of Clay County should have been widened to four lanes a decade ago, but the wealthy residents near the Square in Marietta, in their million-dollar-plus colonial homes, wouldn't abide anything of the sort. As a consequence, the road became a parking lot for an average of four hours per day—or five or six hours whenever a finder-bender occurred.

Larry Morgan's graveside service was scheduled for noon based mainly on traffic conditions.

The two-hundred-car procession eased out of the lot of the giant United Methodist Church on the downtown square at 11:30 a.m., led by twenty-four police motor units and six marked sheriff and police units for the somber three-mile journey to Cheatham Hill Cemetery. Fifteen additional police and sheriff units representing every metro Atlanta agency brought up the rear. The procession of family, friends, and politicians, bracketed by the sea of brilliant blue LED police lights, took over fifteen minutes to exit the church parking lot. Before the Clay County sheriff's deputy driving the tail car exited the church parking lot, the first motor unit was turning in to the cemetery. Two city officers stood at parade rest next to their police interceptor units, blocking both lanes of traffic at the entrance as the long line of cars turned slowly into the cemetery. The Fox 5 News van parked in the deceleration lane by the entrance could be seen for miles with its satellite mast raised to its full height.

Colson was third from the last pulling into the lot and parked behind the car ahead of him. By then, the winding cemetery road to the graveside was completely lined with vehicles, nose to tail. It was a five-minute walk to the graveside. Colson and Beverly stood back under the shade of a hundred-year-old oak tree, since the mob of mourners was packed in a knot and growing into a tightly pressed group from underneath the canopy. The casket had apparently been moved under the canopy; all they could hear was the muffled voice of the pastor giving the typical words of comfort to the family.

Colson took Beverly's hand. "Thank you for coming with me," he said.

She squeezed his hand gently. "Of course," she said. "I'm very sorry about your friend." They stood in silence for several minutes until the muffled voice stopped. Sobs replaced the pastor's words, and the outer fringes of the mob began to break up, with people beginning to walk slowly away from the graveside. Colson and Beverly took their time walking back to Colson's car.

"I had planned on driving home on Sunday, but I really need to head back tomorrow," Colson said.

"What's the rush?"

"I have to check in with Taylor and see how he's coming along with the case he's working on." He rolled his eyes. "Well, the case he's supposed to be working on."

"When are you coming back?"

Colson laid a hand on her arm, and they both paused. "I'd like for you to join me. We could spend a day or two at the beach."

"I'm not retired like you," she said with a laugh. "I have to work." She nodded in the direction of Colson's car, and they walked on. Neither noticed the female reporter watching them from the open door of the news fan.

The reporter took another look at the photo of the man on the Internet page. She stepped outside with microphone in hand and scanned the crowd of mourners walking slowly to their cars. She grinned and motioned for the cameraman to follow, trying to walk quickly, but not so fast as to appear disrespectful.

Colson didn't see the reporter at first and wouldn't have expected she would want to question him even if he had. He was reaching to open the car door for Beverly when the reporter stopped, with the cameraman coming to a halt behind her.

"Mr. Colson," the reporter said, "it's being rumored that you will be taking over as director of the state's Drugs Don't Work program since Larry Morgan's tragic accident. Can you confirm if that's accurate?"

"What?" Colson said, surprised by the reporter's sneak attack. His brief look of confusion changed to a snarl. "Why are you talking to me? This is a man's funeral, not a press conference."

"So you are assuming the directorship then?" she said, sticking the microphone closer to Colson's face.

"I don't know where you get your information from, lady, but no, I'm not taking over anything," Colson snapped.

The reporter referred to a paper in her hand. "According to Jack Strawn, you're 'just a washed-out retired cop.' Is it because he's afraid of you taking the job, or do you agree with his assessment?"

"Let's go," Colson said to Beverly, holding his tone in check and turning away from the reporter's sarcasm. Beverly slid silently into the passenger seat while Colson clicked the door closed. He walked around the rear of the Corvette and grabbed the door handle, but the reporter stepped around the nose of the car and met him at the door.

"It's a very important position, Mr. Colson. Either Jack Strawn is correct and you aren't qualified, or he's afraid you'll be as effective or more effective than the late D.A. in defeating his pro-drug legislation."

Colson paused before opening the door and resigned himself to answering the reporter's ridiculous question. "It's not one or the other, lady. You're giving Jack Strawn's words too much credit."

The reporter's eyebrows rose. "Really? Why do you say that?"

"Because Jack Strawn has a serious problem, and I suspect you suffer from the same condition."

"What's that, Mr. Colson?" she said mockingly with a slight tilt of her head.

"He hasn't heard the pop yet."

The reporter squinted. "What's 'the pop'?"

Colson jerked his door open, stuck one leg inside the car, and gave the reporter an even stare. "That's the sound you hear when you finally get around to pulling your head out of your ass."

The Butcher marched to the glass door at the end of the long hallway, mumbling curses under his breath. He stepped from the cool of the building into the intolerable heat and humidity of the asphalt parking lot, clenching his fists as he walked.

"No one tells me when or how to do my work," he snapped while jerking open the car door and plopping into the driver's seat. He snatched the door closed with a thump, started the engine, and flipped open the center console. A little blue light blinked slowly on the cell phone beneath. He snatched it up as he nosed the car toward the parking lot exit and touched the "Missed Call" icon. The call was answered before the first ring ended.

"The blue Toyota was spotted by a taxi driver," the urgent voice said. "I doubt the police will treat it as a priority and may not check it out right away."

"Why didn't you call?" the Butcher snapped.

"I did."

The Butcher spoke through gritted teeth. "Where is it?"

"Just south of the city on I-75, in the parking lot of the Flying J truck stop at exit two-two-two."

The Butcher glanced at the digital clock on the dashboard. "It'll take me over an hour to get there through traffic. Send someone to keep an eye on it until I get there."

The line was silent for a long moment. "You know I can't do that."

"You can and you will," the Butcher shouted into the phone.

Another pause before the even-voiced reply came: "You seem to forget, I'm just a dispatcher who washed out of the academy. I can't tell the damned Henry County police what to do." And then the call was terminated.

The Butcher cursed, threw the phone on the passenger floorboard, and wove his car through the early lunchtime traffic to the interstate.

Emily sat on the musty-smelling couch, chuckling at Colson's retort to the reporter on the old television in the common area. She felt better than she had in days and needed the laugh, momentarily forgetting the fear of her situation. Her clothes had dried somewhat from their clammy state while she showered and didn't feel as filthy as they had earlier.

She had wandered to the rear of the truck stop after getting dressed and found the mock living room where weary long-haul drivers could relax and experience an hour or so of normalcy before hitting the road again. The old couch was probably acquired from a nearby Goodwill, but it felt like new. Anything outside of the cramped space of her car was a welcomed improvement. The television across from her on the cheap entertainment center was not a flat screen but the old boxy projection kind, and the colors were faded to faint suggestions of their original brilliance. The picture was almost impossible to make out if you stood at too wide of an angle. Emily closed her eyes; the shower and feel of the couch were making her drowsy. A hand on her shoulder made her jump.

"I'm sorry, honey," the fifty-ish female said in a rough smoker's voice, "you can't sleep here."

Emily rubbed her eyes. "But I just sat down a few minutes ago."

The woman smiled. "You've been sleeping for almost two hours. I let it go because you were sleeping so soundly, but I don't make the rules, dear. You're going to have to move on now."

"Two hours?" she said, trying to clear her head. "Okay, I'm sorry. Do you have pay phones?"

"Sure," the woman said, pointing to the wall behind her. "Can you call someone to help you?"

Emily nodded.

"Don't go off with any of these truck drivers," the woman said sternly. "Some are okay, but most are trouble and it's hard for a young woman to tell the difference. Ya hear?"

Emily felt a sudden chill and looked down at her arms before the goose bumps subsided. The woman was exactly right, and she had been careless to lounge around a public place and take a nap. She was becoming complacent since nothing had happened over the past week, but now a new surge of paranoia struck her like a tidal wave. The goose bumps made her realize the former paranoia was drug-induced, not genuine. Emily scanned her surroundings. An overweight man with a long gray beard who was wearing overalls and a green John Deere ball cap snoozed in a chair next to the couch she had napped in. Two children chatted and examined a row of bubble gum near the front register, while others milled around the aisles of merchandise. Her eyes fixed on a man standing with his back against the wall by the restrooms with his hands clasped in front. He wore blue jeans with a large silver belt buckle, a plaid shirt, and sunglasses. She froze in place, unable to move until a woman stepped from the restroom and touched the man's arm. She exhaled with relief when the man gave the woman a warm smile, and both walked toward the exit.

Emily followed the couple's path to the exit and peered over a rack of magazines until they climbed into a pickup and backed from the parking space. The shiny blue pickup made its way in front of the long row of idling semi-tractor trailers and left the lot.

She started to turn away, but something caught her eye. Something was out of place. A dark sedan was parked next to the farthest tractor. There were plenty of parking spaces for cars in front of the truck stop. The only cars not in those convenient spaces were getting gas at the pumps. Emily looked at the merchandise around her for something she had seen earlier. The binoculars were one aisle over to her right.

She adjusted the binoculars to bring the car into view. *There's a man in a dark car watching me from the parking lot*—those were

216

the words she remembered Josh saying on the last day of his life. Operating the binoculars was foreign to Emily, and her view would clear, blur, and clear again with every adjustment she made. The car windows were tinted dark. She held the binoculars as steady as possible and concentrated until she saw movement. Just enough sunlight seeped through the rear glass of the car for her to detect movement inside. She waited and watched.

Emily's entire body flinched when a hand touched her shoulder again. For the last ten minutes her world had encompassed nothing but the car she was watching through the binoculars and the form inside. A form that moved slightly every minute or so.

"Honey," came the female smoker's voice, "is your ride coming?"

"Ah," Emily hesitated, formulating her lie, "yes, but I have to call him back because I think I told him the wrong exit."

The woman held out her hand, and Emily gently gave her the binoculars.

"Sorry," she apologized with a smile of embarrassment.

The woman took the binoculars and nodded back to the bank of pay phones on the back wall. "Then I guess you need to call him back."

The special investigative unit of the APD known as F5 was located on the fourth floor of police headquarters in downtown Atlanta. The desk sergeant directed Colson to Special Agent Floyd's office on the fourth floor. When the elevator door whooshed open he was greeted by a sign on the door in front of him that read "F5 Task Force. Restricted Entry." Colson expected nothing less.

He stepped to a stainless steel button situated above a stainless steel speaker and pressed it. The steel magnetic locking mechanism at the top of the door and the dark, half-moon lens covering the camera on the ceiling hadn't escaped his attention.

"May I help you?" came a dry-sounding female voice through the speaker.

He took a step back and waved to the camera. "Grey Colson. I have an appointment with Agent Floyd."

There was no welcoming response or buzzing noise to indicate the door was now unlocked, only the slight sound of the magnet being released above his head and the illumination of a green light the size of a pinpoint on the face of the box granting him access. He stepped through to a small reception room with two wooden chairs facing each other. No table or magazines. The office obviously didn't receive many visitors. The few who did visit were most likely snitches, attorneys, or persons of interest who willingly agreed to submit to an interview—the type of people law enforcement didn't feel obligated or inclined to provide with comfortable accommodations.

The upper torso of a shorthaired, dark-skinned woman was visible behind thick Plexiglas above the half wall across from Colson. A small faux wood plaque stuck to the wall beneath the window read, "J. Prince." She seemed to study him for a moment before she spoke in the same dry speaker voice. "Agent Floyd's office is straight down the hall, through the bullpen to the far right corner."

Colson nodded and passed through a gauntlet of old government desks arranged in a haphazard fashion in the large bullpen area. The refuse of recent fast-food breakfasts littered the surface of the desks. Two men in shirtsleeves, their ties askew, labored over piles of papers in boxes stacked in the middle of the room. The remaining detectives sat at their desks talking on their phones or typing on computers as Colson walked passed. He could have been a ghost by their lack of reaction to his presence, clearly confident in the visitor-screening abilities of the stone-faced J. Prince in the bulletproof reception booth.

Floyd's door was open. He stood and walked around his desk as Colson stepped across the threshold. "Major Grey Colson," Floyd said warmly, extending his hand, "I'm glad to finally meet you."

Colson returned the smile. "It's just Grey. I'm retired."

"Yes, of course." Floyd nodded. "It's a professional courtesy. You earned the rank." He gestured to another wooden chair across from his desk. "Please have a seat."

218

Colson slid into the chair and patted the armrests with the palms of his hands. "I'm proud of you guys."

"Really," Floyd said, settling into his high-back mesh swivel chair. "Why's that?"

"These solid wood chairs. You haven't gone green, and that must really tick off the tree-huggers."

Floyd laughed, then sobered. "Detective Meador said you wanted to talk about the possible murder of a junkie kid."

"He was the son of a friend of mine. Keith Bartlett."

"Sorry. I just thought—"

Colson dismissed Floyd with a wave. "It's not a problem. I've used the same term a million times. The boy OD'd in a seedy motel room on Candler a couple of weeks ago."

"No surprise," Floyd answered. "That area is a melting pot of drug addicts and homeless people. You can't walk through a parking lot over there without stepping on broken wine bottles and used syringes."

Colson nodded. "His dose was laced with a little something extra."

"Yeah?" Floyd said. "That happened to one of my informants once. He got burned and ended up with a hot dose of poison junk cut with strychnine. Hit him so fast he didn't even get the needle out of his vein. That's how they found him—syringe full of clotted blood hanging out of his arm. So how do you believe the death of your friend's son ties in with our division?"

Colson uncrossed his legs and leaned forward in his chair. "Last Tuesday, Keith and I had a little meeting with your number one target. The next day, Keith gets beat like a drum and his home ransacked."

Floyd's eyes locked with Colson's, and for a moment they sat in silence. Colson knew Floyd's respect for a retired cop was genuine. He also knew Floyd's immediate reluctance to reveal information about any case his F5 Task Force was working. Colson completely understood because he had felt the exact same way just a little over two years ago. But he also knew when he needed help from the outside and wasn't too proud to ask for it. Floyd would have to make a decision, and that's apparently what he was doing right now.

"So," Floyd finally said, "with all due respect, who might my number one suspect be?"

"Jack Strawn."

Floyd stood, turned toward the window and immediately back to Colson, rubbing his chin. "Nothing personal, major, but I'm going to beat Meador's eyeballs out for talking to a civilian about our cases. He's a—"

"Hang on a minute." Colson raised his hand to stop Floyd. "Don't take it out on Meador—I threatened him."

Floyd crossed his arms and cocked his head. "Threatened him how?"

"Told him I'd beat his eyeballs out if he didn't tell me."

Floyd rolled his eyes and exhaled loudly while dropping back in his chair. "You sound awfully confident, believing Strawn would be our number one target."

It was Colson's turn to roll his eyes. "How many of your other targets are worth over a hundred billion dollars?"

"Fine. Tell me, how do we know the kid got a hot dose?"

"Lab results of the residue in the spoon. Heroin, cut with quinine as usual, and a little something extra."

"Like what? Strychnine?"

"No. Something super nasty, according to the M.E. A substance called Abrin."

"I'm not familiar with it." Floyd gazed into space. "Exotic?"

"I suppose you could call it that. But one thing's for certain— it's not something your run-of-the-mill dealer would be messing with unless he had a death wish."

Floyd picked up a pen from his desk and studied it. He sat silently in thought, rolling the pen between his fingers. Cases assigned to F5 weren't for public consumption or even public knowledge. They worked cases the local police agencies couldn't dedicate the time or resources to on a long-term basis. Not many even knew the F5 Task Force existed. Floyd knew Colson's reputation, but he was no longer in his official capacity, and sharing information was taboo. But Floyd needed a break. Their suspicions of Strawn's criminal activities were well founded, but you can't prosecute someone based on reasonable suspicion alone.

Attempts to slip a confidential informant into Strawn's organization had failed twice in the first year. For a wholesale furniture company, that caused substantial suspicion on its own. There was simply no reason for such a company to be as watertight as a frog's ass. Twenty-four months into the investigation, Floyd was confident enough that probable cause was present to go up on a wiretap, but that was summarily shot down by a superior court judge. The case was now in limbo, stored in five brown cardboard boxes in the corner of his office, taunting and mocking him every time he walked through the door. Until Colson walked into his office, Floyd had more or less resigned himself that there was never going to be a solid case against Strawn. His supervisors had told him as much from the start when he requested approval to initiate the case.

Floyd shook his head. In reality, maybe there was no case to prosecute. Maybe his cop intuition was skewed by his loathing of Strawn every time he heard the man speak on television. His haughty attitude and cigar-puffing, condescending demeanor made Floyd furious to the point he had to force himself to listen. But he would listen and record every word Strawn said in public. People who loved to hear themselves talk often made mistakes. He knew Strawn would be no exception, and Floyd would be waiting, recording and documenting his case file.

And now Colson showed up and was sitting across from his desk with his arms crossed. Floyd had a decision to make. How much should he trust him? The better question may be—what did he have to lose at this point?

Floyd dropped the pen on his desk blotter and looked at Colson, "What can you tell me about the kid's father, uh, Keith?

Colson handed him a dossier with Keith's name on the front. "Successful small business owner in Atlanta. Owns a security alarm and electronics company. Clean record, upstanding member of the community. Just your typical good citizen."

Floyd flipped through the dossier. "So are Keith Bartlett and Jack Strawn enemies? Would poisoning his kid be payback for something?"

"Strawn didn't know Keith from Adam's housecat until last week."

Floyd closed the dossier and threw Colson a confused look. "Then I don't follow you. How are you tying the boy's death back to Strawn, and if he didn't know Bartlett until a week ago... I'm just not following the logic. What happened last week?"

Colson mirrored Floyd's look of confusion. "I would have thought Meador briefed you on all of this since you have an active case."

"No," Floyd said, shaking his head, "he just called to vouch for you and set up our meeting."

Colson exaggerated a sigh and leaned back in the uncomfortable wooden chair. "Well, strip my gears and call me shiftless." He motioned around Floyd's office with his hands. "All these new computers and smart phones, and you guys still don't communicate information any better than we did in the eighties."

"Well, major, why don't you bring me up to speed?"

Colson paused to gather his thoughts in chronological order. "Keith Bartlett obviously was distraught over his son's death. Prior to that, he hadn't given Jack Strawn's pro-drug crusade a fleeting thought. Well, not until it impacted his family. He set up a meeting with Strawn and asked me to accompany him."

Floyd's eyes widened. "You met with Strawn?"

Colson nodded. "In his office with Keith. Oh, and standing guard was Strawn's testosterone-inflated bodyguard. Anyway, Keith wanted to convince Strawn to change his mind about the legislation he was trying to push through."

"I'm sorry." Floyd chuckled and waved his hand. "I bet that went over well."

"Like a turd in a punch bowl. But the one thing out of character was Strawn's unusual curiosity and feigned regret over the boy's death," Colson said flatly.

"Go on."

"As a favor, I got an old snitch of mine to make a buy from the dead son's dealer. A little justice for Keith and his family, if you will." Colson crossed his arms. "I suspect Meador didn't bother to tell you about that either."

Floyd answered with a headshake.

"So," Colson continued, "days later the dealer was found dead. Shot execution-style in his living room."

"There's more, I hope?" Floyd asked.

Colson held up his hand. "There's more. Just days later Keith was surprised by a home invader who beat him and ransacking his house.

"Bad coincidence," Floyd said, "but hardly remarkable, wouldn't you say?"

"Under normal circumstances, yes, but not this time."

"How so?"

"Keith didn't get a clear look at the intruder, but I'm ninety-nine per cent sure it was Strawn's bodyguard-slash-limo-driver, Clay Haggart."

"But you said he didn't get a good look at him."

Colson shook his head. "It was the warning he gave Keith before he blacked out. He told him to stay away from Strawn."

"I see," Floyd said, picking up the pen from the blotter and pointing it at Colson. "But they haven't come after you?"

"Not yet." Colson stood and stepped to the door. Floyd watched Colson stop at the door, turn, and offer the first smile of their short, professional relationship. "But hope springs eternal."

CHAPTER TWENTY-TWO

Colson's phone rang during his elevator ride down to the first floor of APD headquarters. Keith Bartlett, on the other end of the line, sounded tired. Colson wished there was better news to pass along, but he had no idea if Floyd would run with the information or not. He pushed through the double glass door entrance and stepped into the humidity. Wooden benches sat on either side of the entrance; one of them was currently shaded by a hundred-year-old oak tree. Colson eased himself onto the bench for the conversation.

"How'd the meeting go?" Keith asked, and then, "Do you know this guy, Agent Hugh Floyd?"

"I do now," Colson said.

"Well, is he a good guy?"

"You remember the old saying, 'It takes one to know one'?" Colson wiped his sleeve across his forehead.

"Sure. What did he tell you about Strawn?"

Colson decided it was best to be direct, even though he knew Keith expected him to discover some shocking revelation about Strawn Industries. "Floyd has a case on Strawn. Several boxes worth of case file material are stacked in his office, but I don't know how actively he's working on it right now."

"But you told him everything, right? I mean, that didn't stoke him up? I mean—"

"Hang on," Colson said, halting the series of questions. He flicked a fly from his nose and wished for a breeze to relieve the stifling humidity. "Yes, I told him everything that's happened, and it may very well help him, but it's his case and—"

"And it's my son, Grey."

"I know, but you have to be careful with this stuff. You come on too strong and start asking a detective about his case, and he'll shut you out so fast it'll make your head spin. Let him digest the information for a few days. Then I'll check back in with him."

The line went silent for several seconds, and Colson hoped Keith was overcoming the shock of the case not being solved with just one visit to the F5 Task Force. He wished he could make Keith understand the difficulty of properly conducting a major case investigation, but only years of experience can teach a person that. Colson remembered the early years of his career clearly, being impatient and jumping the gun on several occasions. He had later realized you can't make good, solid cases unless you're determined to work meticulously and deliberately.

Floyd's boxes of documents and recordings were a classic case in point. The world of criminal investigations is totally alien to the average person. Even small cases require pain-staking work at times. It would be easy to write a four-word report when an arrest was made—"Saw drunk, arrested same." But a cop could lose the most basic case if he was lazy and produced sloppy work. Colson understood Keith's frustration, but he was beginning to sound like he was losing control.

"Then we need to help him out, right?" Keith said.

"What do you mean, we?" Colson asked, although he could predict where this conversation was going. He had worked with grieving parents like Keith before.

"I need to help him out," Keith said. "What can I do? Nothing stopped you from saving your daughter, did it?"

"That's true, Keith, but please hear me out. If there was anything you or I could do to save Josh, I would say the cops be damned, you know that. I can't tell you how sorry I am about Josh, but there's nothing we can do to bring him back now. Our focus now should be to assist the police to the best of our ability and allow them to make a solid case against Strawn for whatever he's doing. You

can't let Strawn win because you interfered in the investigation. Try
to look forward to the day when you'll be sitting in the courtroom as
they pass sentence on that piece of garbage. I promise you, justice
will be done for Josh."

"Fine," Keith said. "You've told me what cops can and can't
do. You even said that was one of the reasons you retired. I
understand the restrictions on cops are very frustrating. They have all
these rules to go by, but I remember some other things you told me."

"Like what?"

"Well, your undercover work for example. You said if an
upstanding and reputable member of society just happened to find
himself legally in a position to see illegal drugs in someone's house,
and if that concerned citizen notified police, then they would have
enough for a search warrant."

Colson shook his head. "Let's not go there, Keith. I know
what you're driving at, but Strawn isn't going to welcome you into
one of his warehouses to snoop around. If that were the case, Floyd
would have had someone inside a long time ago."

"I realize that, and I'm not asking for your help in any official
capacity."

"What official capacity?" Colson said with a chuckle.

"Look," Keith said as if he hadn't heard the comment, "in
addition to finding evidence to take Strawn down, there may be
evidence of what happened to Joshua in that big warehouse Strawn
visited. There also could be an answer to where Emily might be. Put
yourself in her parents' place. You have a daughter. I'm asking for
your help, father to father."

"I strongly advise you against doing something stupid,
Keith," Colson said, trying to keep his tone friendly but firm. "As a
former cop, but more so as a friend, I'm asking you: please don't do
anything that may cause your family even more heartache."

"This isn't a black-or-white situation." Keith's tone suggested
his decision had been made. "What is right isn't always what is noble
or honorable or legal. Look, you broke a half dozen traffic laws
chasing Strawn's limo driver. This is one of those times. If we wait
for the wheels of justice to turn, it may be too late. I have to break the

rules. I have to find out what really happened to my son and why. I have to try to find Emily. If I don't, I won't be able to live with myself."

"Listen," Colson said, "I may not work for the sheriff's office anymore, but I'm still a cop, and I'm telling you not to take matters into your own hands." Colson rested his elbows on his knees and his head in his hands, waiting for Keith's response, but the line went dead. "Lord, help me," he sighed, "I've created a monster."

Colson swung the Corvette left on Spring Street and almost made it to 35 mph before stopping behind a line of traffic at the Mitchell Street light. He pondered his conversation with Agent Floyd as well as Keith's question about whether or not he was a good cop. Floyd seemed to be a good cop, but it was becoming increasingly difficult to say for sure these days. He hadn't offered Colson any information, but who could blame him? It was almost impossible to trust anyone, retired cop or not.

Colson decided to leave and save Floyd the trouble of citing policy about not divulging information during an ongoing investigation. He would have said the same thing in his shoes. He just hoped the new information would give new life to his investigation.

It was time to get out of the city and head south to the beach. The sunny Atlanta day was nice enough, but the sun hanging high and hot over Daytona Beach was better. The aroma of the salt air, the sandpipers skipping across the beach, and the sound of the surf beckoned him. Colson grabbed his cell to call Beverly and realized he hadn't returned Jonathan Raines' phone call from the day of Morgan's death. He closed his eyes in a moment of dread. He wanted to give comfort and hope to Emily's parents, but he wasn't a counselor and often thought he made matters worse.

He touched the missed call notification, and the cell dialed automatically. "Grey," Jonathan said expectantly after the second ring. "Have you heard any news about Emily?" His voice morphed to a hesitant tone with the question as if he were afraid he might get an answer, but not the answer he wanted.

"No, and I'm sorry for the delay of returning your call. The operations commander at the sheriff's office did me a favor and sent out a statewide BOLO. There's a lot of good dirt-road deputies with their eyes out for the car. Copies are even in the hands of every cab company and transit service across the state. But over the last couple of days it's been hectic, and I haven't had a chance to follow up."

"Oh, that's right," Jonathan said. "I heard about the accident with your friend. I'm sorry."

"Thanks. I wish I had good news for you about Emily."

Colson heard Jonathan sigh into the phone. "I know you're busy Grey, but when you have a chance..." he said, his voice trailing off. " Could you hold a second? I have another call coming in."

Jonathan clicked over to the waiting call and heard a shaky voice say, "Dad?"

Jonathan jumped to his feet, shoving his office chair against the wall. "Emily! Thank God—where are you, honey?"

"Daddy, I need for you to pick me up." Jonathan could hear noises in the background. Voices, music. She was in a public place.

"Listen, honey," he said, his heart hammering so loud he could hardly hear his own voice, "calm down and tell me where you are."

"It's a Flying J, just off of I-75. I'm scared, Daddy."

"Don't be scared, Emily. Now what exit is it off of? Try to think."

"But you don't understand," she cried, and he winced when he heard the raw fear in her voice. "I think they're watching me from outside."

"What do you mean watching you? Who are they?"

"The same people I think killed Josh. He told me they were watching him the night before he was found dead. Same type of car and everything." She began to sob. Jonathan knew she was in trouble and felt helpless to do anything about it.

"Emily, sweetheart," he said, speaking as slowly and calmly as he was capable, "which exit off I-75?"

"I—I don't know. Something like Jericho Road."

"You mean Jodeco Road, honey? Are you sure?"

"I'm pretty sure." She sniffled, and Jonathan longed to take her in his arms and cuddle her and keep her safe, as he had when she was a toddler. He looked at his watch. It would take him an hour or more to get to Emily; if what she said was true about people watching her, could he get to her in time?

Suddenly a wave of relief washed over him. In his panicked state, he hadn't been thinking clearly. The police would protect her until he got there. "Listen, honey, I'm going to click over and call the police. Don't hang up. I'm going to call them and then be on my way to you, but I want you to stay on the phone with me at least until they arrive. Do you understand?"

All he could hear was a quiet sob and another sniffle.

"Emily. Did you hear me?"

"Yes. I'm sorry. Yes."

Jonathan pressed the call icon on the screen, but before dialing 911, he heard a voice. He had completely forgotten about Colson being on the other line.

"You still there, Jonathan?" Colson said.

"Yes, it was Emily. I need to let you go and call the police."

"Hang on," Colson said, "the police won't be in a rush. She's considered an adult, not a juvenile. Why would she need the police anyway?"

"Emily believes the same people who were following Josh Bartlett the night before his death are watching her. For some reason she thinks they killed him. I have to do something, Grey. I'm over an hour away from where she is."

"Where is she?" Colson said.

"A Flying J truck stop on Jodeco Road at I-75."

"I'm right at I-75 in Midtown and can be there in fifteen minutes. Tell Emily I'm wearing a white golf shirt and black BDUs—and tell her to stay put. I'll find her."

Jay Taylor snarled when he emerged from the drive-through to the beachside parking lot of the Sundowner complex. There were a total of three parking spaces against the building, and he usually didn't have a problem finding one vacant. The residents typically parked in the same spaces every time and should know he used one of them. Well, except the aggravating tourists. There was a three-wheeled motorcycle taking up one space, and someone had parked a squatty pull-behind trailer in another, clearly against condo rules. He had no idea what was sitting in the remaining spot, but it wasn't a vehicle at all. It appeared to be a giant folded blob of bright red, yellow, and purple rubber material that covered the entire space.

He jerked his car around the middle row of cars, parked in a space against the sea wall, climbed out, and slammed the door before marching across the lot to chastise whoever had dropped their junk in the remaining open spot. A man and woman stepped out of the glass sliding door of the ground floor condo behind the heaping pile of rubber and started talking as Taylor approached. In reality, he hadn't put his anger to bed about Strawn, Haggart, and the little blond assistant of the now-retired and partially blind Dr. Cooper. He stopped five feet from the couple and stared at them through his sunglasses, but they didn't pay him any attention. He exhaled heavily and cleared his throat. The woman look vaguely familiar, but that didn't matter. They should know better. The woman finally noticed him standing there.

"Oh, hey," she said and turned back to the man to continue their conversation.

"Taylor," a small voice said. It seemed to come from the ground along with the tug on his shirttail. Taylor glanced down to the source of the voice and saw little Clara, grinning from ear to ear. "Do you like my jump castle?" she said.

Taylor squatted down to her level. "What jump castle, Clara?"

Clara pointed past Taylor to the folded pile of rubbery plastic. "My birthday is this Saturday, and Mommy got me this jump castle."

"Really?" Taylor said, feigning understanding and approval, but he still had no idea what she was talking about. Clara twisted from side to side in her one-piece swimsuit. Her delicate blond hair was pulled back in a ponytail, and she was wearing yellow flip-flops. "I'm going to be eight years old." She stretched her arms wide, as if to hug him. "Mommy said they would blow it up and make it even bigger than my bedroom. Then me and my friends can jump in it all day. It's so cool. You can come, you know," she said, beaming.

"Don't bother Mr. Taylor, Clara," the woman said. "He doesn't care anything about coming to your birthday party."

"No, but I do," Taylor said and turned back to Clara. "I know you'll have fun, sweetie. I'll be sure to get you a present, but I probably shouldn't jump in your castle. I would break it."

"I was going to knock on your door," the woman said apologetically, "but I couldn't remember which condo you lived in. I've been coming out as people drove up to explain. The office manager said I could set it here for a couple of days until the party as long as we allowed all the children in the condo to jump for free on Saturday."

Taylor stood, smiled, and offered the mother a dismissive wave. "Anything for Clara," he said, patting the top of the little girl's head. "You have a very happy birthday and fun party, sweetie."

Taylor stopped at a bank of mailboxes and pulled out a handful of letters, bills, and advertisements before making his way to the suntan-oil-scented elevator. He leafed through the pile of mail on his ride up, but he didn't pay any attention to who they were from or who they were addressed to. He couldn't take his mind off what he had seen on YouTube, and it was eating him alive from the inside. Colson was busy and out of town, already snooping around Strawn for his own reasons. For the past two days he had struggled with the idea of telling Colson what he suspected about Strawn's involvement with Dr. Cooper. Half the time he suspected Colson would crank up his snarky sarcasm and call him a crazy conspiracy theorist or a paranoid Cyclops. The other half of the time he thought Colson might show compassion and interest in his theory and promise to help him solve the mystery. He could never predict the man.

Taylor slapped the mail on the kitchen counter and sat on the bar stool in front of his computer tablet. He was amazed the only damage was a cracked screen. It had taken him less than five minutes to find it next to a shrub in the parking lot island, face down in the mulch. He didn't even bother looking for it until he had cooled off from his own personal hissy fit. It was a miracle some kid hadn't seen it and relieved him of it forever. Colson was due back tomorrow, so he would find the right time to bring him up to speed.

He stepped to the balcony door, slid it open, and looked out over the horizon. The familiar staggered line of seagulls glided with the up-draft at the edge of the sixth-floor roof, and the sounds of the beach floated upward with the warm sea breeze. Maybe he would tell Colson and ask for his help.

On the other hand, maybe he would wait until Colson was finished with Strawn and take care of business on his own.

The Butcher cursed, jerked the door handle, and pushed open the car door. The digital clock on his dashboard told him he had been sitting for over an hour waiting for the girl to emerge from the Flying J, and his patience had run out. Not to mention suffering from a serious case of flat-ass. If she wasn't coming out, he was going in. The chances of her leaving the laptop in the car were good. If it was just a matter of breaking into the car, he would already have it delivered to Strawn and be on his way to terminate his last target. Colson. But that wasn't the order. The girl had to go, so he used the majority of the last hour to formulate a plan. The situation was fluid, leaving him little time for a clean, sophisticated kill.

He quickly dismissed the idea of going inside to find Emily, although the urge to satisfy himself she hadn't hitched a ride or ducked out another exit was compelling. Cameras were everywhere, and some investigators eagerly await reviewing hours of video to crack a case and get their next promotion. He had already spotted five cameras on the exterior of the Flying J and was confident they were mainly for customers to notice and make them think twice before buying gas with a stolen credit card. Two were mounted eight feet high and ten feet to the left and right of the front entrance, and three hung from under the gas pump canopy. It was the half dozen smoke-colored domes fixed high on the street light poles in the parking lot that could pose a problem.

His second idea was to watch the girl leave and follow her until an opportunity presented itself for a tap in the rear at a stop sign on a quiet street, but there was no such thing as a quiet street in, near, or around the metro Atlanta area. His thoughts occasionally diverted to how he would handle Colson. As strange as it may seem, planning a hit on a grown man was easier than on a teenage girl. One thing for certain, he would never again agree to take out a teenager on the run. It was too much like work. Colson went to work and often stayed overnight. Simple enough. He would be either there or at his daughter's house, with the daughter's house being the last resort. Then it occurred to him Colson was a dual resident of Georgia and Florida. He cursed under his breath for forgetting that little piece of information.

"Damn," he snapped while reaching into the gym bag in the passenger floorboard and pulling out a ball cap with blond human hair hanging from the back seam, along with a silenced Walther PPK .380 caliber pistol. Cameras or no cameras, it was beginning to look more and more like the girl ditched the car and caught a ride. It was time to find out one way or the other. "Time to make it happen," he scolded himself while pulling the cap down to his eyes and dropping his feet to the pavement. He untucked his shirt and slid the pistol down the small of his back, securing it inside the waistband of his pants before stepping out of the car.

The air was hot and thick with diesel fumes as he faced away from the building and stretched. He rolled his neck and listened to his bones popping with relief just as the brown Henry County Sheriff's Office marked unit stopped behind his car.

ᴄ⁓CHAPTER TWENTY-THREE⁓ᴄ

"Eight-Eleven to dispatch," the deputy said in his microphone.

A female voice answered in a mechanical tone. "Go ahead."

"I'll be out at the Flying J checking a suspicious vehicle."

"Ten-four,"

"Stand by dispatch. Show me out with the signal 54 vehicle near the main entrance. Alabama drive-out tag on a charcoal Pontiac, dark tinted windows. Appears to be occupied one time."

"Clear."

Colson's attention was naturally drawn to the sheriff's office unit parked on the fringe of the Flying J parking lot. Even two years into retirement he slowed down whenever he saw an officer or deputy on a traffic stop and away from the relative safety of their squad car. Most cops do in case the officer suddenly needs assistance. If the individual they were dealing with appeared agitated or used exaggerated hand gestures, stopping was a no-brainer. It was amazing how strength in numbers seemed to give belligerent people a moment of pause. If the stop was routine and the individual was causing no problems, the officer would typically notice the passing cruiser and hold up four fingers to signify he was okay or code 4. In this case, the deputy had not activated his blue lights and simply appeared to be casually talking with the blond haired man in the ball cap. The deputy was even laughing at something the man said. Colson put the deputy out of his mind and drove around the perimeter road.

As he circled, he caught a glimpse of the blue Toyota nosed in at the front of the truck stop. If Emily was right about being watched, whoever it was should have their eyes on the car. Colson continued around the access road to a rear entrance and slid the Corvette in between two transfer trucks. He flipped up the middle console, plucked out his ASP, and slid it down the deep front pocket of his BDUs as he stepped out into hot diesel fumes. The rear glass entrance of the truck stop appeared distorted through the heat rising from the asphalt, combined with hazy exhaust from the idling trucks.

Colson scanned the parking lot for anything or anyone suspicious as he walked to the door.

Emily had felt the man's eyes on her for the last ten minutes. He had a full beard and wore a cowboy hat, blue jeans several sizes too small, and a red-and-black plaid shirt. He had a beer belly hanging over what may have been a dinner-plate-sized belt buckle, with only the lower portion of the oval visible below the mass of fat. It couldn't be the man from the car. She could have seen the outline of the bushy beard. No, this was some sloppy redneck pervert with his back leaned against the wall at the end of the bank of pay phones. She didn't dare tell her father and make him go into a panicked frenzy, so she continued making small talk about what she had been through over the past week. The crying was over, and all she could think about was sleeping in her own bed tonight.

Sunlight flooded the pseudo-living area where Emily had napped. The rear glass door didn't appear tinted when closed, but it became obvious when someone opened it to the midday sun. Emily squinted at the silhouette of the man walking toward her. He appeared to be just under six feet and broad across the chest. The door eased shut and the moderate dimness of the room returned. It was the man her dad had described and the same man she had seen on television a few hours ago. "He's here," she said into the phone and hung up.

"Hey, darlin,'" a rough voice said to her right. She turned to look at the man. His bushy beard was somewhat deceiving because he sounding like he was no more than twenty-five years old. She looked back toward the door Colson had come through; he saw her and was taking long strides in her direction. "I said hey, baby," the bearded man said again, his irritation evident. "You need a ride, honey?"

Emily shook her head. "I've got one," she said as Colson stepped up behind her.

Colson eyed the bearded kid and slid his hand down inside his pocket. He got a firm grip of the non-slip handle of the ASP.

"Is this—" Colson began.

"No, he's in the parking lot and doesn't have a beard," Emily said quickly.

Beard Boy pushed his fat away from the wall and returned Colson's glare. He spoke to Emily but kept his eyes on Colson. "What, you got your daddy to pick you up?"

Colson cut his eyes left and right, taking in the couch, TV, and cheap chairs in the trucker's lounge area. A soap opera was on, clearly indicating no one was watching. He cut his eyes back to Beard Boy and rested his hands on Emily's shoulders.

"He's not my—"

"We need to go, Emily," Colson interrupted her. He turned her around and guided her with his left hand.

"Hey," Beard Boy said from behind. "I was talking to her. You hear me, boy?"

Colson felt the presence of the redneck moving in behind them as they walked. He knew that the moment the three of them stepped outside and clear of the door, he would feel a grimy hand on his shoulder. Just one more sentence to give him an accurate distance was all Colson needed. It didn't take long.

"I'm talking to you, boy. You think you're gonna run outside and—"

Colson took an extra-long stride and then turned while simultaneously slipping the ASP from his pocket. He shot his arm downward to extend the metal shaft with a sudden clack, and in one fluid move he swung the ASP in an arc as if pitching a bowling ball. Beard Boy's contrived badass expression instantly morphed into mild curiosity about the metal stick Colson had produced from nowhere. And then the ASP separated Beard Boy's testicles with a muffled thud. His groan assured Colson he had hit his target. Colson knew that a searing jolt of pain had hit Beard Boy a millisecond after his brain told his pain sensors what had happened.

Colson looked past the bent-over redneck, but there was no one looking in their direction, just a few oblivious bobbing heads near the front counter. Beard Boy was groaning, spitting, and clutching his groin with both hands, as if his family jewels were attempting to escape his pants.

Colson looked down at Emily and said, "Step inside with me and stay against the wall for a second."

Colson grabbed Beard Boy's shoulders and guided him through the men's restroom entrance and into the open locker area. He quickly scanned the musty-smelling locker room, surprised it was as vacant as the lounge area. A row of shower stalls lined the wall to his left. Directly ahead were a half dozen toilet stalls, urinals, three sinks sitting below one large mirror, and two hand dryers on the wall to the right of the sinks. The only sound other than the scuffling of their feet on the gritty tile and the low groans of Beard Boy was a steady dripping sound coming from one of the shower stalls.

Colson spun Beard Boy around and shoved him against the middle stall door. The door latch clacked loudly in the cavernous tiled room as metal struck metal from the force of the boy's bulk. The impact caused him to stand erect, the momentum propelling his cowboy hat up and over the top of the door and into the toilet behind.

Colson couldn't contain a grin. "Lost your lid, kid," he taunted. He watched Beard Boy's eyes, waiting for the sign. It took about eight seconds. If Colson read his pedigree correctly, the only thing more important to a drugstore cowboy than his signature gut, dinner-plate belt buckle, and cowboy boots was his cowboy hat. Probably a Stetson if he was a diehard shit-kicker—the crown jewel of every cowboy this side of the Mississippi. Beard Boy realized he'd lost his hat and jerked the stall door open. That occurred in the first two seconds. The horseshoe-shaped toilet seat was raised, and the brim of the capsized cowboy hat fit perfectly over the rim of the bowl with a quarter inch of toilet water resting in the soft tan leather like a dinner-sized serving of "pee" soup.

Beard Boy spun back around with a look of disbelief. That took another two seconds, bringing the total to four. Colson couldn't resist his next observation; he scratched his chin and offered Beard Boy a serious face. "You know, it really did make you look taller."

Passing the seven second mark, Colson knew it wouldn't take much longer. Beard Boy's expression of disbelief fled like a wild horse out of the gate, replaced immediately with the unmistakable squint of pure hatred. His anger and the adrenalin required to maintain it were clearly trumping the pain in his testicular region. Colson could have seen Beard Boy's jaw clenching if his heap of facial hair hadn't concealed it. Colson adjusted his grip on the ASP and waited. Beard Boy didn't say a single word in response to Colson's taunts, but simply pushed himself off the stall door and charged. Colson angled his stance and held the ASP in both hands like a baseball bat, but instead of swinging for the fences, he lunged forward and drove it deep into Beard Boy's stomach like a lance. It required little effort on Colson's part. Three hundred pounds of flab moving at four miles per hour and running into an inch-in-diameter steel rod should get the kid's undivided attention.

Beard Boy doubled over for the second time, gagging, spitting, and gasping for air. He staggered around the room, and Colson almost felt sorry for the drugstore cowboy. He guided the kid backward into the stall and plopped him down on the toilet and the soaked brim of his Stetson.

Colson patted Beard Boy's cheek. "Breathe. You'll survive." Beard Boy coughed. "Okay," Colson continued, "just nod if you're listening to me, and this will all be over." Beard Boy finally offered a weak nod. Colson tapped the end of the ASP on the tile floor and bent over, face to face with the kid. "Do you know what a colonoscopy is?"

Beard Boy's breathing began to settle into a normal rhythm. He shook his head and sputtered. "What?"

"You know," Colson said, "a colonoscopy. I bet your daddy's had one if he ever took a break from feeding the chickens."

"Yeah, okay. I know."

"Good. Now listen real close, cowboy," Colson said in a fatherly tone while continuing to tap his ASP on the tile. "If I see that Charlie Daniels gut of yours sticking out of this stall in the next fifteen minutes, I'm going to give you a free one about twenty-five years earlier than normal. Do you understand?"

Beard Boy coughed, nodded again, and tilted his head back against the wall. Colson stepped out of the stall, knelt to one knee, and collapsed the ASP into its seven-inch barrel. He fast-walked into the lounge with Emily in tow.

"We need to move," he told her. "We only have a few minutes before that mad cow comes out of there and tries to take back his man card."

The Butcher ducked into his car and eased away from the sheriff's cruiser. If he hadn't been concentrating on getting away from the scene and dumping the car, he would have exploded with the frustration of missing the girl and the chance to recover Strawn's precious laptop. He threw the ball cap/wig combo in the floorboard and seethed. Strawn would pay him, no matter when he got the job done. That's exactly why he never rushed his work or accepted time limitations. Something always got screwed up.

He wiped a stream of sweat from his face and could feel dampness running down his back. What should have been an easy task of running that snot-nosed deputy off had just turned into another problem. But the boy was a motor mouth and wouldn't shut up. And he had seen the Butcher too closely. Slow-minded people infuriated him; he had no tolerance to listen to their meaningless drivel.

The Butcher pulled out his cell phone and pulled up a map app while he waited for the light to turn so he could take the entrance ramp onto I-75. He quickly took a mental snapshot of the route he would take and merged into the freeway traffic. Two minutes later and two miles to the south, he took the Jonesboro exit to the right, and then took another right on Chambers. Two more right turns and he was driving at the respectful speed of 20 mph on Cypress Lane. He checked the map app again and hoped he could use this location and not have to find another.

The end of Cypress Lane ended abruptly without the typical cul-de-sac turn-around. Just a steel guardrail with white and red reflective triangles to alert drivers they could either stop or destroy the front end of their car. The lake would be east or to his left. He grinned at the vacant, overgrown lot and checked the street behind him in the rear-view mirror. It was too early for school buses to be bringing kids home, too hot for the women-folk to be out planting flowers, and all the working stiffs didn't get off work for another three hours minimum. In short, the neighborhood street was deserted, with the exception of a dead and mostly flat cat fifteen feet behind him.

He eased the car onto the curb and through the overgrowth. Briars scratched at the paint as he moved cautiously, dropping the right front tire in a low spot while easing the left over a rock the size of a basketball. The lot took a slight decline, then a steeper angle downward. The Butcher held his foot on the brake, maintaining a manageable speed until the lake came into view a hundred feet away. He brought the car to a full stop and studied the landscape. Satisfied with the angle of descent, he dropped the gear into neutral and pressed the emergency brake to the floor. A train whistle blew in the distance as he wiped off his pistol and pocketed his cell phone.

He stepped out of the car and looked around for any witnesses before squatting next to the car door and releasing the brake. The car began a slow forward roll, quickly picking up speed, its hood bobbing with the uneven landscape on its voyage to the bottom of the lake. A muffled splash announced the car's contact with the water.

The Butcher had already turned and was walking southeast toward I-75. After thirty-five minutes of walking through scruffy lots and stepping over fallen trees, he was awarded with a view of Jonesboro Road, the sounds of the intersecting freeway, and the sight of the Fairfield Inn and Suites a few hundred yards south. That's where he would head.

The walk didn't take long. He dusted off his pant legs before striding into the hotel and paying cash for two nights in advance. He took the stairs, not the elevator, and let himself in. The coolness of the room enveloped him; the shower a few minutes later was invigorating.

The Butcher walked to the window, pushed aside the thick curtains, and stared out at the interstate. He would operate on his timetable from now on; no one would threaten to cancel his contract again. If Strawn didn't like it, he would give him a personal visit and stick a gun in his mouth until he paid up. He smiled at the thought. Maybe he would give Strawn a visit in either case.

He watched the never-ending stream of trucks and cars of every type speed down the interstate, cutting from one lane to another. The spinning wheels of the vehicles were nothing but a blur, but those in his mind were moving with clarity. He pulled a deep breath of cool air through his nose and blew it out of his mouth.

"It's your turn, Colson."

"Wait." Emily put a hand on Colson's arm and pointed to the rear exit of the Flying J. "Did you park in back?"

"Yeah, but I drove around the access road and didn't see anything suspicious except—hold on," he said, pausing in mid-stride. "Where was this person you think was following you?"

Emily pointed toward the front. Colson kept Emily close to his side, and they moved to the front window. "Over there," she said with a nod, "where that police car is now—but the car I saw is gone."

Colson peered out at the Henry County cruiser and saw the silhouette of a man sitting behind the wheel. "Let's go," he said, walking her back to the rear door. "I saw him talking to a man in that same spot. I'll stop and ask him what it was about and if he got an ID on him."

"Will he tell you?"

"Probably."

"But I need the computer out of my trunk out front."

"We'll drive around and I'll get it for you."

"But what about my car?"

"I'll explain it to the deputy. It'll be better for your dad to have it towed for now."

Colson stuck his head out the door before allowing Emily to step out into the open, but he didn't notice anything unusual. They walked quickly to the Corvette, and he opened the passenger door for Emily. The cruiser was still sitting in the same place when they rounded the corner of the building.

"Give me your keys," Colson said. He kept an eye on the cruiser as he parked directly behind the Toyota, jumped out, and pushed the button on the remote. He grabbed the backpack, slid back in the driver's seat, and laid it on the luggage deck behind him. Colson drove the car through open parking spaces toward the cruiser instead of taking the long way around.

"Emily," Colson said, "why would anyone who may have been following Josh be following you now? Did you both witness something?"

Emily lowered her head and looked at her clenched hands in her lap. "No, we both stole something."

"What?"

Emily pointed her thumb back over her shoulder. "The laptop. Josh took it out of a drug dealer's car."

"Did you two mess with it or see what's on it?"

"No—I mean I don't know," Emily said, shaking her head. "We didn't know the password."

"It's okay." Colson pulled up next to the Henry County cruiser, driver's door to driver's door. Something wasn't right. The deputy's window was down, and he sat with his chin resting on his chest. He couldn't have been far enough into his shift to be that sleepy. Colson rolled down his window and tapped the side of his car door with his ring finger. "You okay, deputy?"

No response. Colson scanned the lot in front and his rear-view mirror. Nothing. He was too close to the cruiser to open the door and, fearing he might not like what he found, he pulled forward so Emily couldn't see. "I'm going to wake up the deputy," he told her, "and ask him about the man. Stay in the car please."

He went to the deputy's cruiser and leaned in. "Deputy, are you okay?" The officer wasn't sleeping. His right hand was turned palm up on his lap, and his left arm hung limp between the seat and the door panel. Colson reached in and pressed the man's carotid artery with two fingers. No pulse. He placed his left hand on the deputy's clammy forehead and eased it back. A small stream of drying blood had oozed from a small hole just above the top of the deputy's Kevlar vest at the neckline. The outer cloth covering of the vest was a dark reddish color where a small amount of blood had soaked in.

Colson lowered the deputy's head and glanced in the back of the patrol car, but then he realized the steel prisoner cage would have stopped the bullet if it had penetrated the driver's seat. He dared not disturb the crime scene further. He knew the deputy was dead, but the call still had to be made. He looked on the hood of the car for the big unit number decals and pulled out his cell phone, searching through his contacts, hoping he had saved a certain one. Colson had worked with dozens of cops from all the metro Atlanta agencies in one capacity or another over the years. Some he had worked closely with on the DEA Task Force in the nineties; one of them worked for Henry County. The contact for Paul Robbins showed both his old cell and office numbers. He touched the office number and hoped his old friend hadn't retired yet. He found out after the third ring.

"Sergeant Robbins," came the familiar voice from the past.

"Paul," Colson said, "this is Grey Colson."

There was a pause while Robbins processed the name through his memory bank, then a bright, "Hey Buddy!"

"Listen, Paul," Colson said in a flat tone, "I'm sorry about this, but I just came up on one of your deputies at the Flying J off of Jodeco Road. He's been shot. He's in unit five-six-nine-zero."

"What?"

"Just listen, Paul. I didn't shoot him, and I can't go into great detail right now, but—"

"Are you jerking me around, Colson? I—"

"Please listen, Paul. I'm not jerking you around. You need to contact Agent Hugh Floyd with the Atlanta F5 task force and tell him about this incident. I got a quick glance at a man the deputy was talking with before he was shot."

Colson heard Robbins barking orders to someone in the office before directing his agitation back to Colson. "You stay right there, Colson. If you saw something—anything—your ass better be there when I get there."

Colson shook his head. "I'm sorry but I can't. That's why you need to call Floyd and tell him what's going on. And tell him I've located Emily Raines."

"The hell you say, I'm not calling—"

Colson clicked his phone off and trotted back to the Corvette and his passenger. Time to get Emily to a safe place.

CHAPTER TWENTY-FOUR

etective Latham walked around the grid laid out on the concrete floor of the warehouse and shook her head. It had taken the most meticulous work of her career to duplicate the scene of D.A. Morgan's accident. It was like working for the NTSB after a plane crash.

She almost didn't pass on Colson's request to her sheriff. It was absurd, but she was glad she had when Sheriff Hogue reacted the way he did. At first she expected to be called an idiot when his eyebrows shot upward, but not after his comment.

"You tell Colson we'll be glad to give it all the attention it needs and all the manpower it takes. Morgan was a good man and a real pro-police prosecutor," he said, drawing out the word *po-lice* as any self-respecting southern sheriff would.

Latham would find out later about Colson making a case and subsequently arresting the neighboring county sheriff when assigned to the DEA Task Force in the early 1990s. Sheriff Hogue had made a complaint to the feds about the dirty sheriff selling seized property from local drug cases and pocketing the money. He then offered the services of a confidential informant who coaxed him into bragging about it and implicating himself in a taped phone conversation. Colson was assigned to the case as the informant's controlling agent, and the dirty sheriff was in federal custody within the month. Detective Latham was still in high school at the time, but she remembered her dad saying what a slug that sheriff was.

As a result of Colson's request, two additional detectives and one arson investigator were assigned with her to sift through the wreckage, looking for anything out of the ordinary. The fifth individual on the team was a little unorthodox in her opinion, but whatever Sheriff Hogue wanted, he got.

The fifth team member wore dark blue coveralls with the name Carl stenciled on his left breast. Latham couldn't help being reminded of the main character in the *Sling Blade* movie her husband had insisted she watch with him. That Carl's hair was cut in a similar fashion—close-cropped on top and almost completely shaved around the sides. This Carl walked slowly and squinted down at the wreckage as if trying to work out a massive puzzle in his mind. He would bend over and occasionally squat to give each block in the grid his full attention. She watched him move methodically from one block to the other for the third time while she finished her water bottle.

"Ma'am," Carl said, making Latham flinch because he sounded almost identical to the character in the movie.

She walked along the perimeter of the grid where he was squatting and turning something over in his hands. He stood and held up what appeared to be a charred piece of electronics with exposed wires dangling from both ends. She looked at the item and shrugged. "What have you got there?"

Carl squinted for a beat with a slightly astonished look, as if Latham should know the answer. "I don't reckon this belongs to this car."

"I don't understand—tell me what it is," Latham said, now surrounded by the other two detectives and arson investigator.

"This here," Carl said, turning the item over in his hands again, "is like those things you see on the TV where the insurance company says it'll save you money if you plug them in so they can keep track of your good driving."

"That's what that is? Why would that be unusual?" Latham motioned around the warehouse. "And how do we even know it was on this particular car and not just picked up with the wreckage?"

Carl pointed at the device. "It was on this car alright because even though the wires are cut, it's still plugged into the Corvette's computer access port."

"So he wanted to save money on insurance," Latham said, growing slightly impatient. "Who wouldn't need that, driving a $70,000 sports car?"

A grin crossed Carl's face. "'Cause it ain't no insurance-saving device."

"I thought you just said it was."

"No." Carl shook his head. "Those have the insurance company name stamped on them, and this one here just has a serial number. I've seen these before. Ya know where?"

"Where?" Latham said, increasingly irritated with Carl's slow cadence and penchant for playing twenty-one questions.

"When I worked for fleet maintenance down there in Atlanta. Those car theft detectives used them on their bait cars. About every third time they'd use them, they'd forget you have to shut down the car before it gets away too fast or the thief will total the car out." Carl looked down and scratched his chin. "I reckon I worked on a dozen of the ones that could be repaired. You know, when the prongs got bent and such."

Latham looked down at the item again and unclipped her cell from her belt. "I'd better tell the sheriff."

"It's important that you tell me everything, Emily," Colson looked over at Emily; she sat stone-faced in the seat beside him.

"I believe what Josh was telling me. He was genuinely scared to death," she said without taking her eyes off the rear-view mirror.

"I'm not saying he wasn't scared of not telling you the truth." Colson drove down the entrance ramp headed north on I-75. "And don't take this the wrong way, but you know how paranoia sets in when you've been using."

"I know," she insisted, "but the dealer threatened him, and I saw the guy watching the truck stop—"

"And," Colson interjected, nodding, "the dead cop in the parking lot. I know there's a lot more to it. I just want to be sure I'm right before I get out the stick and start poking the wrong tiger."

"What?"

"I'll tell you about it some other time." Keeping one eye on the road, he punched a contact icon on his phone.

Emily made herself relax somewhat. She didn't know this man, but she did trust her father. At least she wasn't alone anymore. She couldn't wait to see her parents and sleep in her own bed. If she didn't have the laptop, there would be no reason for anyone to come after her. Unless they didn't know she no longer had it.

Colson seemed to know, or thought he knew, who was behind all of this, but would he tell them? Would he return the laptop and make everything go away? How could he, especially now that they were cop killers? She looked again in the rear-view mirror, not even knowing what she was looking for. Another dark car with tinted windows? She resigned herself to the fact that she would be paranoid about dark cars for the rest of her life. She heard her name being called, but it took a moment for her to realize Colson was talking to her.

"Emily?"

She shivered and turned to face him. "I'm sorry. What?"

Colson laid the phone on his seat between his legs. "I'm going to call your dad when we get to where we're going."

Emily's heart skipped a beat. "But we're going to my house, aren't we?"

"No," Colson said, "not until this is over."

A single tear ran down Emily's cheek at the news. She wouldn't be sleeping in her own bed tonight or seeing her parents after all. She wiped the tear away and said, "It'll never be over."

Colson reached over and patted her shoulder. "It will end, but I need to find out what's on that computer."

"You can't," Emily said, shaking her head. He seemed like a nice guy, but didn't he understand? "It's password protected. Josh said it was probably encrypted."

Colson smiled. "I know somebody who can un-encrypt it."

248

"But I still don't know why I can't go home."

Colson looked straight ahead and hesitated, as if he was reluctant to answer her. Then he glanced over at her again. "Because the bad guy or bad guys have already been there and will come back. It's the first place I would have looked for you."

Emily felt her tears begin anew. She just wanted to go home.

Jonathan Raines' secretary couldn't concentrate on her work. She tried to imagine what her boss had been going through with the disappearance of his daughter, but even after he said she had been found safe, he still seemed disconnected from reality. He still sat at his desk with his head in his hands, apparently murmuring low prayers every time she walked in. He said he was thanking God Emily was safe, but he couldn't stop thinking about her being truly safe until she came home.

But what did he mean? Why wasn't she at home? What was the big secret? It was perplexing to her and her friends in the office, but it made for interesting lunches with her and the other female staff as they bandied about the possibilities.

He had worked himself into a frenzy the other day after calling the police to let them know Emily was safe. His office door was open and she heard a very pleasantly excited Jonathan tell a detective on the phone that Emily had been found. Then his tone and voice inflection began to build as if it was a volcano about to explode.

"What do you mean, okay, we'll clear the case?" he had barked sarcastically into the receiver. "What ever happened to, we're glad she's safe, or we're happy to hear she was found unharmed?"

Directly outside his office, the secretary sat wide-eyed, as he had ended the conversation by shouting, "You cold hearted bastards," before slamming the phone down on his desk.

Today wasn't much better. He wasn't in the same foul mood he had been that day on the phone with the detective, but clearly something was still bothering him. She heard him moving around in his office and mumbling under his breath. Her console blinked an incoming call. She covered the mouthpiece with her hand and just caught him as he was stomping out of his office.

"Keith Bartlett calling for you," she said. "Are you here?"

He pinched the bridge of his nose and seemed to settle down. "Yes." He said and took the receiver. "Hi Keith—any word from Colson?"

The secretary began typing on her keyboard, half listening to Raines' side of the conversation.

"You need what?" Jonathan asked and turned his back to the desk. The secretary became curious and drawn to the conversation by Jonathan's suspicious tone. "I can't do that, Keith. You should know that."

She continued typing but paid no attention to her document. Jonathan listened for over a minute before speaking again.

"Thank you. I'm sure she's in good hands," he finally continued. "I can't thank you and Colson enough, but—"

She watched Jonathan lift his hand and hold his palm to his forehead, listening again.

"When? It will take at least twenty-four hours."

The secretary snapped her attention to the computer when Jonathan turned back to the desk.

"Okay, I'll call you later," he said, ending the call and handing the receiver back to her. She replaced it on the cradle and watched Jonathan walk away, shaking his head.

Keith Bartlett sat at his kitchen table, going over the plan in his mind for the fifth or sixth time. He was too distracted to keep an accurate count. Each move he would make and the methods he would use to get into the building had to be perfectly planned and executed, so he spent the entire morning meticulously ironing out the details. He had no illusions of *Mission Impossible* grandeur, but with twelve years of experience in alarm installation with his own company, he was confident he could get the job done. In fact, bypassing any modern-day security system was as simple as taking advantage of the same basic design flaws inherent in every security system, no matter the manufacturer. They all had pretty much the same guts with different brand names stenciled on the front. Of course, Colson had warned him about taking matters into his own hands and recited a laundry list of felonies he could be charged with, but Keith didn't care. Someone had to see justice done for Josh—and he was that someone.

Bypassing computer password systems was easy enough. If you could install a security system, you could uninstall it just as easily. The most difficult part of his endeavor would be the human factor—the guards. He first considered trying to get past Strawn's security team with a little monetary persuasion, but he seriously doubted that would work. Maybe with some $6 per-hour guard at Wal-Mart, but not with Strawn's team. These guys could be retired FBI for all he knew, being paid sixty grand a year.

Over the past three nights of his surveillance of Strawn Tower, Keith had nailed down the schedule. There were two security guards on duty overnight. One sat in the gatehouse in a swivel chair watching a bank of mounted TV monitors, while the other patrolled the complex. A control console in the gatehouse provided the guard with access to dozens of cameras throughout the property. Every half hour, one of the guards would make a full circle tour around the exterior of the tower, and the guard from the gate would walk around the outside of the fence. It was a lot of ground to cover for only two guards, but the system was designed to rely heavily on the sophisticated technology of the cameras and alarms. The human beings were merely there to add a secondary layer of deterrence and to confirm legitimate alarms for police response, or cancel them in the event of a false alarm.

Keith loaded his equipment into the back of his Audi at 11:20 p.m. and drove to Midtown Atlanta. The heat of the day had surrendered to a still-humid, but cooler temperature. He dropped his windows and allowed the rush of clean, cool night air to clear his mind and work out a few of the details. The Sunday night traffic was extremely light, so he drove carefully, but not so slowly as to attract attention. Driving the posted speed limit in metro Atlanta was unheard of, so he drove at least five miles over limit. Being stopped by a cop as a suspected drunk driver would immediately shoot down his plan. Even though he hadn't had a drop of alcohol, being dressed in all black with a hand gun and a backpack full of what could be considered burglary tools would draw instant suspicion and most likely would result in him being detained on the side of the road for an extended period of time, until the cop couldn't tie him to any recent break-ins.

Strawn Tower stood menacing and mostly dark against the skyline as he slowed near the corner. Exterior-mounted light fixtures were mounted at the corners of the building on every second story, their beams not aimed outward but up and down the sides, giving it the appearance of an older skyscraper of King Kong fame. He parked on the adjacent street in a line of parallel-parked vehicles and waited for a small group of pedestrians to cross behind him and into the nightclub at the end of the block before slipping out and crossing the street.

The first barrier was the rear exterior fence. He removed a small pair of bolt cutters from his backpack and snipped just enough of the chain link to squeeze through. Once inside, he ran low to the ground until he reached cover behind a row of shrubs. Luckily the moon was only a sliver, hidden behind the clouds, giving just enough light for him to see, but not enough to reveal his presence.

Nerves on edge, he crept closer to the edge of the pristine lawn surrounding the rear of the tower, thankful that the guard patrolling the fence line hadn't spotted him and put a bullet in his back. He stopped to catch his breath. He felt as if he had just finished an afternoon run—not as the result of physical exertion, but rather due to the nervous anxiety of committing his first felony. He watched the patrolling perimeter guard climb into his golf cart and drive to the front gate. He would be relieving the gate guard for his first break and assuming his post for the remainder of the night, just as he had the previous two nights.

Keith ducked low, ran to the back of the building, and knelt beside the network interface box. Once he cut the telephone lines, the silent alarm was effectively disabled. He moved quickly to the east wall of the building, took a cautious peek around the corner, and then crawled five feet behind the shrubs to the audible alarm case mounted on the exterior wall. He snipped the hard-wired phone cable and the external siren wire leading into the box. No siren would activate, and no signal would be sent to a monitoring station. He quickly wired a remote looping device in the event the monitoring station sent an automated ping to check the system's status, but he wasn't planning on staying long enough for the system to figure out it was being deceived.

Keith checked the luminous display on his watch for the third time in ten minutes. It was after midnight, but the clouds had cleared enough for the moonlight to expose the large air-conditioning ground units positioned behind the tower. He crouched again and ran across the open courtyard to the four-foot-wide gap between the huge condenser units. With his back braced against one and his feet against the other, he was able to work his way up between the air-conditioning units to the top. He sat on the smaller unit and forced himself to breathe normally. Then he stood, grabbing one of the pipes extending from the condenser. Twisting his body around, he pulled himself up onto the larger of the two units. He had been an athlete in high school and college, and he still ran, lifted weights, and climbed ropes—but at forty-five years old, his body wasn't responding as well as he thought it should. Not to mention the pain still remaining in his ribs from his encounter with Strawn's thug.

Now atop the tallest air-conditioning unit, he grunted as he jumped and grabbed for the bottom rung of the fire ladder, but he missed. He bent over with his hands on his knees and breathed hard before trying again. He succeeded on the third attempt, climbed silently, and pulled the ladder up behind him. A steel fire door greeted him on the landing. He removed a stainless steel lock-pick gun from his belt, slid the business end into the lock, and pulled the trigger three times, until the knob turned freely in his gloved hand.

He paused while holding the knob for a few seconds to prepare himself for what would almost certainly happen if he had made a mistake and the alarm sounded. What if there was a backup alarm system? But no, he had done his homework and would have spotted it. There wasn't enough time to keep second-guessing. Sweat ran down his face and back, and his legs became weak. He held his breath, pulled the door open, and blew the tension from his lungs when no siren sounded.

253

The door opened into a concrete stairwell with steel handrails. Keith knew he'd have to pace himself for the challenge. Thirty-five minutes later, he reached the top floor and opened the door to a concrete corridor. As much as he had prepared for the technical aspect of his first felony, there was no way to plan for logistics. Any effort to obtain a diagram or blueprint of the building would no doubt be a smoking gun pointing right at him when the police investigated the break-in. That thought reminded him to pull his nine-millimeter pistol. He should have had it out earlier, but he wasn't a cop and didn't think like one. He prayed he wouldn't have to use it as he stepped into the corridor.

There were only three unmarked doors, equally spaced. He soft-footed down the length of the corridor, taking his best guess as to which door was the right one. Should he choose the bachelorette behind door number one, two, or three? He slowly opened the door at the farthest end of the hall and peered inside, somewhat surprised he didn't get shot in the face. He stepped inside, into an area with a carpeted hallway, and closed the door behind him.

He walked into a vestibule area and moved quickly down the corridor, stopping at the end of the hallway in front of Strawn's corner office. The Sentex keyed lock on the door required the use of an electronic card and the entry of a sequence of numbers on a keypad. He entered on the keypad, placing the lock in admin mode, and then he entered the factory-default password, bypassing the card and key requirements. Once he heard the lock release, he entered * once again to exit admin mode.

He took another breath and turned the knob. Nothing greeted him but darkness and the soft hiss of air whooshing from the movement of the door. He took a step inside, locked the door behind him, and clicked on a flashlight, shielding the lens with his hand to prevent the guards or any cleaning crews in the adjacent buildings from noticing the light through the floor-to-ceiling windows. He crossed the room to Strawn's massive computer monitor on the wall and unplugged the power supply. Not doing so would result in it flashing on like a lighthouse beacon when he powered up the processor.

He scanned the room while pointing the flashlight beam on the floor. It permitted just enough ambient light for him to recall the observations he and Colson had made while sitting across the desk from Strawn. It was literally a shot in the dark, but the best place to conceal the guts of the computer would be locked inside a safe behind one of the wall panels. He had installed similar systems several years ago and recommended similar set-ups for his higher-profile clients. A portion of the side molding in the proper location would look slightly different—not to a casual observer, but to an installer. Strawn was the type of person who would never permit a lowly computer tech behind his desk, so the access panel would be either on a sidewall or on the monitor wall. He would have suggested the monitor wall for easier access.

He turned and studied the wall beneath the monitor—and there it was, a piece of molding with a clean, hairline crack. He pressed against the left side of the molding, and a panel slid upward noiselessly, revealing the face of a Secrulogic wall vault, about the best unit money could buy. Keith had expected no less.

He removed an electronic sensor from his backpack and placed it over the tumblers. Maybe he wasn't Mr. Phelps, but he was feeling a little like Indiana Jones. He spun the dial slowly until a red light appeared, indicating he had located the first number. He repeated the procedure four more times, until the bolt unlatched with a soft click. He swung the door open.

There were no drugs in the safe, but he didn't really expect to find any. On the top shelf sat several stacks of hundred-dollar bills, a black bag containing five gold bars, and a jewelry box with a fortune in gold and silver jewelry. Boxes of documents sat on the second shelf. A quick scan revealed what appeared to be a record of bribes and hush money paid to government officials and law enforcement officers throughout the United States. He recognized the names of two well-known U.S. congressmen and three attorneys general. Keith wished he had enough time to copy the documents. Hopefully, the computer would contain the same information in electronic format.

The computer's console was on the bottom shelf. He eased the CPU out enough to reach the back ports, took a flash drive from his pocket, and plugged it in. He sat cross-legged and removed the six-inch monitor with the tiny keyboard from his pack and plugged it into a second opening. He started the computer and repeatedly tapped the F8 key before the Windows program had time to load. The Windows Advanced Options menu appeared, and he selected Safe Mode. The Administrator screen appeared with Strawn's username. He selected Go To, then Start, Control Panel, Users, and finally clicked on User Account to the Change Password prompt. He changed the password to JOSHUA and hit Save.

When Strawn realized he could no longer access the computer with his password, he would have an IT tech take a look at it. The tech would simply use the same process he just used to reset Strawn's original password, without ever knowing it had been changed.

He rebooted the computer, and in what seemed a long few minutes, he was inside Strawn's accounting program. He selected All Files and copied them to the flash drive. When finished, he removed the flash drive, keyboard, and monitor and stored them in his pack. He returned the console to its position within the safe, closed the safe door, and had just pressed the molding to close the wall panel when the office door opened. A stream of light ran across the floor three feet to his right.

ᏔᏂᎯCHAPTER TWENTY-FIVEᏔᏂᎯ

C olson crossed the Georgia–Florida state line at 11:35 p.m., fifteen minutes after Keith Bartlett's departure from his home to Strawn Tower. Totally unaware of his friend's felonious plans for the evening, his thoughts were two-fold, split ninety to ten percent—the ten percent being what Taylor could potentially pull from the laptop, and the ninety percent being the safety of Beverly and Emily.

Unless he was being tailed 24/7, none of Strawn's people would know where Beverly lived, and there was nowhere else to safely leave Emily. It required more than a little convincing for Jonathan to agree, but in the end he knew it was the best move. The last thing Colson wanted was to involve Beverly, but she gladly insisted on taking Emily in while he delivered the laptop to Taylor. He briefly thought about sending the laptop via Fed Ex, but he didn't dare risk that it might be lost or appropriated by someone with the shipping company. He was certain Strawn had influence over the owners of many corporations, and it wasn't worth the risk. And Colson could get the laptop to Taylor in seven hours—or six and a half if he put it in the wind.

Colson pushed the Corvette to 90 mph. The highway south of the Florida line to the Lake City exit was nearly deserted. He would keep an eye out and slow down accordingly when approaching overpasses or long curves in the roadway. That's where Florida state troopers would be this time of night, with a chase car at the top of the exit waiting to pounce.

Colson used the time to think. If there was just one hit man, he was a miserable failure. The laptop had been in the hands of a teenager for over two weeks now, and each additional day made it more likely someone would be able to access whatever information was stored in it. He had told Emily the truth: if he were the killer, the first place he would have looked for her and her car was at her parent's house. Haggart had found Keith easily enough, but Haggart was sloppy and most certainly not the longhaired cop killer at the truck stop. Haggart was built like Taylor, and his wide back would have been unmistakable. No, Strawn's hit man would have put a bullet in Bartlett, not beat and threatened him.

Colson almost missed the exit to I-10. A long, lonely stretch of highway lay ahead between Lake City and Jacksonville. With almost no civilization or exits until ten miles this side of Jacksonville, Colson glanced at his gas gauge and congratulated himself for thinking to fill his tank in Valdosta.

He opened the Corvette up to 100 mph, turned off the air-conditioner, and dropped his windows. Cool night air rushed around Colson and cleared his mind, but something chewed at his gut from the inside. He was allowing the situation to drive him instead of being in control of the situation.

The headlights of an oncoming car made him ease off the gas in case it was a bored trooper hungry to write a ticket. The car shot past, and Colson floored the accelerator again. Now he was the lone car for as far as his headlights illuminated the long highway ahead. In a millisecond, the little creature chewing his insides revealed its ugly head. Colson took his foot off the gas, punched the brake, and rolled to a stop in the emergency lane.

He stepped out into the darkness and walked into the familiar wide-bladed grass. The pitch-black woods were filled with a chorus of bug and crawling critter sounds from within. He took a moment to stretch and consider the bold move he was about to make. As far as Strawn or his killer knew, Emily still had the laptop. Colson had told no one else except for Jonathan. That meant Emily's hunter was still out there looking for her. If Morgan had been murdered, the hit man may have seen Beverly with him at Road Atlanta, making her condo another address to visit. He had left Beverly his .38-caliber revolver, telling her to just point and pull the trigger if anything happened, but now he realized how stupid the whole idea was.

Colson slapped his forehead with his palm and scolded himself out loud. "That's what you get for allowing the threat to drive you instead of you driving the threat, you idiot." He had to lead Strawn's bloodhound in a new direction.

He pulled out his phone, accessed the Internet, and found the number to Jack Strawn's office. He called it, leaning against the back of his car in the muggy night air, knowing he would get a recording at this hour. A lone pair of headlights topped the rise in front of him and slowly grew larger. The tractor-trailer rig blew past him with a roar and rush of hot wind just as the recording began. Colson missed the first couple of words spoken and held his free hand over his opposite ear. The roar of the semi subsided, and he heard a woman speaking in a thick English dialect.

"...If you are calling after hours, you may leave a message at the sound of the tone and the appropriate party will contact you the next business day. Thank you for calling Strawn Industries."

Colson pondered his approach while waiting for the beep. "Sorry, lady, I didn't feel like pressing the number one, but I have no doubt you will get this recording to Jackie Strawn when he drags himself into the office tomorrow." Colson paused for effect and then continued. "I have a news update for you, Jack. Your boy missed the girl at the truck stop, but I didn't, and now I have your precious laptop. I just can't wait for my tech guy to show me all your dirty deeds so I can hand the whole package over to the cops. I'm willing to make a deal if you're man enough to come to Daytona yourself and talk about it. Just think, you could launch a new line of swimwear while you're down here. Maybe you could call it the Strawn Thong Line. But if you want to make any money, I'd advise you not to model the first pair yourself." Colson busted a sarcastic laugh just before ending the call.

He pressed another contact on his phone and waited five rings. A groggy-sounding Jay Taylor answered. "Hello?"

"Wake up, Taylor," Colson said.

"Colson? What's going on? It's one o'clock in the morning."

"Listen—I'll be there in two hours, so wake yourself up, grab a shower, make some coffee, and exercise your fingers. We have work to do."

The hair on Keith Bartlett's neck stood at full attention, and fear froze him solid. The beam of light swung from left to right, but the guard didn't step over the threshold of the doorway—yet. There was nowhere for Keith to run or hide. If he tried crawling across the office to slip behind Strawn's massive desk, he may as well stand to his feet and give up.

He silently leaned against the wall and waited for the inevitable. At least there was a chance, since he was against the same wall as the door. There was no explanation for his being there, so he decided not to even try. He closed his eyes until the guard spoke.

"Hey!"

Keith's eyes shot open, expecting to be blinded by the flashlight's beam. There was no blinding light or gun in his face. He jerked his head to the left and saw the beam of light pointed at the floor, just inside the door. He heard the guard chuckle and say, "I know it's late, but I knew you'd still be up. What are you wearing?"

The office door eased closed with a click, and Keith realized the guard was on his cell phone. He blew out the air he had been holding in his lungs for what seemed an eternity and felt his heart beating rapidly in his chest. His entire body jerked when the electronic deadbolt automatically shot into place; for an instant he thought the guard had seen something suspect and was returning to investigate, but the diminishing sound of his voice assured Keith he had dodged the bullet.

Unfortunately the stream of light from the door had revealed what he almost hoped he wouldn't find. His mind had been made up earlier that day, but now he wanted to allow himself an excuse not to act.

A squat end table sat to the right of Strawn's desk. It appeared to be oak and looked similar to Keith's bedside table with the exception of the glass panels on the top, front, and sides. Keith sat with his back to the wall and stared at the small table, now only a dark silhouette across the room. He had the information he needed to turn over to the police, but what would they do with it? What would they do with him? Most likely interrogate him about how he acquired it and charge him with burglary. He closed his eyes and tapped the back of his head against the wall. No, this was about Joshua—and it was now or never.

Five minutes later he was moving as quietly as possible to the end of the hallway. He opened the door to the concrete corridor a fraction of an inch and listened. The back hallway and stairwell were empty and silent. He slipped through the opening, quietly closed the door behind him, and raced as lightly as possible down the concrete stairs. Once on the second floor, he made his way through the fire door and out to the ledge, where the moon was now hidden behind thick clouds. He stepped outside and let his eyes adjust to the dark. He crouched, scanning the grounds and listening to make sure no guards were nearby, and then slowly he began lowering the fire ladder. It was impossible to prevent the sound of metal on metal as he eased it down. He stopped and listened carefully after every creaking noise the ladder made until it was fully extended.

Once on the ground, Keith quickly crossed the complex. With the adrenaline rush slowly draining away, he made his way back across the lawn, through the hole in the fence, and back to his car.

Haggart stood stone-faced across Strawn's desk, with his hands clasped in front of him, knowing somehow he would be at fault for the hit man's failure. He watched Strawn's face flush beet red while he listened to Colson's snarky recording for the third time. Strawn stood behind his desk with his hands on his hips, patting his foot methodically on the floor, heel to toe to heel to toe. He was too furious to sit, stand, or even walk, and that left nothing else to do but swipe his hand across his desk and rake the desk phone to the floor. He pointed to the floor where the phone base came to rest. The cordless receiver had made it all the way to the opposite wall.

"You hear that smart ass?" Strawn shouted.

Haggart responded with a nod, knowing nothing he could say would calm Strawn's fury. He stood with his eyes cast to the floor, waiting for his marching orders. Strawn turned to the window and crossed his arms. "There's no more time for elaborate schemes, taking weeks to plan impressive car crashes, or spiking a junkie's dope with exotic chemicals." He turned back to Haggart and pointed at his chest from across the desk. "You call your boy—"

Haggart knew this would be blamed on him. "Your boy" implied Haggart had found and employed the ghost assassin, when it was Strawn himself who had received the recommendation from some unknown source and directed him to make the initial contact. To point out the obvious or argue the matter was foolishness. If he had to take responsibility, that's what he would do—but he wasn't going to take much more of it.

"You tell him," Strawn continued, "to forget about that damned teenager and go after Colson right now. You understand?"

Haggart nodded again, but added, "Yes, sir," this time.

Strawn slapped the table with his palm. "Not tonight, not tomorrow, and not when he feels like it. You tell him to get his ass on a plane this very instant. You also tell him he's not getting paid for the girl, and if I don't hear that Colson is dead and the laptop has been recovered in the next forty-eight hours, I will ruin his reputation so bad he'll be bagging groceries or cleaning toilets for a living."

Haggart nodded and remained motionless for a moment too long.

"Now!" Strawn barked.

ᒚCHAPTER TWENTY-SIXᒡ

The Butcher made a second pass in front of the Sundowner condos, glancing up at the far right exterior hallway. There was unit 510, no activity at 4:30 a.m. He knew most tourists were sleeping off hangovers, sunburns, or headaches. He gripped the steering wheel of the stolen Ford pickup, despising the feel of it. The black, rubber-coated wheel was loose with age and missing a six-inch section of rubber from years of use, exposing pocked, black metal beneath. He shook his head, turning the remaining old rubber around and around in his hands. The common man's existence nauseated him. How anyone could be satisfied living a life dependent on pensions, token Social Security checks, and dilapidated pickup trucks was beyond his imagination.

He brightened at the memory of the previous morning. He had sat in a rental Taurus, backed into a space at the side of the Waffle House on International Speedway Boulevard, just a quarter mile east of I-95. Although the Butcher had never crossed the threshold of such an establishment, he knew the clientele by casual observation and common sense. His close surveillance proved his accuracy as usual. A standard-size semi-tractor trailer bearing commercial tags from Louisiana was parked on the street side of the parking lot. Other vehicles of various makes and models had come and gone over the past forty-five minutes, also bearing out-of-state tags—a few with couples, weary from a long drive, and others with bouncing children, probably on their way to Disney World.

He continued to wait patiently for another thirty minutes. Any longer and he would risk drawing attention from nosy patrons or a waitress from the other side of the wall-to-wall windows. He was rewarded twelve minutes later when his potential target arrived and nosed into a space directly across from him, driving a late 1970s Ford pickup. The Volusia County tag bolted to the bumper of the Ford was worn with age and slightly bent inward at the bottom. He estimated the driver's age at around sixty-five. He wore blue-jean overalls and a red flannel shirt, and his hair was trimmed in a close flat top.

The Butcher waited for the elderly man to disappear through the first set of glass doors before stepping out of the Taurus and into the Waffle House. The solid weight of the Walther PPKs pistol assured him it was still securely strapped to his ankle. He saw the old man take a seat in a booth and begin studying the menu through reading glasses. The Butcher slid onto a stool at the counter, directly behind the oblivious old man. He gave a short nod when the waitress said "Coffee?" and watched her pour the steaming liquid into a ridiculously small mug. He raised the cup to his lips and immediately winced when the strong, hot beverage hit his tongue. It tasted like tar. He tried to lower the cup inconspicuously and hide his disgust, waiting for the right moment.

The Butcher was momentarily impressed by the speed of the short-order cook, who was flipping eggs and bacon while simultaneously memorizing ridiculously coded phrases for new orders being barked by scurrying waitresses. It was only a matter of a minute or two before the old man's breakfast was unceremoniously plopped in front of him. He immediately set about his task, consuming a lonely breakfast of eggs, bacon, and gravy-smothered hash browns.

Two teenage boys with girlfriends in tow practically ran through the glass doors of the nearly full restaurant, not breaking stride until they swung their skinny frames into the last empty booth, giggling the entire time. The old man glanced back to the Butcher in disgust, noting a similar grimace on his face. Only their facial expressions were similar. The old man's contempt for the young people was due to their lack of respect for other patrons who were trying to enjoy their meal. The Butcher's contempt was based only on the fact that he considered himself too sophisticated to be in such a dive. The old man mumbled disdain under his breath about how the world was going to hell in a hand basket due to the entitlement-minded generation who had seized control of the country. The Butcher seized the opportunity to reinforce the old man's diatribe.

"No father figure in the home is my guess," he said while examining a huge laminated menu he had pulled from a wire stand on the greasy bar.

The old man nodded. "Probably right, young man. And nowadays you can't even punish the little heathens in school without going to jail."

The old man must have grown tired of craning his neck around to speak, or he was simply lonely, because he invited the Butcher to take a seat in his booth. His invitation had the tone of an apology. The small restaurant had begun to fill with people waiting on a seat, and there he was, occupying a booth alone. He probably thought it was practically un-Christian not to offer the man the seat opposite him. The Butcher was casually dressed in tan slacks and blue golf shirt. His hair was a neatly trimmed and bleached dirty blond. His fake wire-rimmed eyeglasses gave the appearance of a teacher or accountant. Maybe even a professor. He gave the old man a grin, picked up his coffee, and slid into opposite side of the booth.

The Butcher examined the old man close up. His thin flat top was nearly invisible against his skull. The old man offered a slight grin and sipped his coffee.

"I never liked eating alone anyway," the old man offered. "You know these kids. You probably have to put up with them a lot. You remind me of a teacher. Is it high school, or college maybe?"

"Sales," the Butcher said evenly, unfolding his napkin and dropping it into his lap. The old man looked genuinely disappointed.

"Oh," he said, "I see."

The Butcher grinned. "Nothing exciting, but it pays the bills."

The old man raised his eyebrows. "Insurance?" he asked, perhaps attempting to redeem his novice psychic ability.

"Firearms, actually. Winchester firearms to be exact," the Butcher said, "but I deal with young store manager clients regularly, and they're pretty much all the same. You know, the 'What can you do for me?' mentality."

"Yep." The old man's eyes brightened. "Winchester, huh? Do you travel for the company?"

"Yes," the Butcher replied. "Do you like our product?"

The old man nodded. "I used to hunt, but that was years ago. Winchester's probably the most respected firearm in the world."

The Butcher smiled, and then feigned disgust. "I should probably be looking for another line of work. When the government confiscates all the guns, I'll be in the unemployment line."

The old man set his coffee cup down on the table with a thud and pointed in the Butcher's face. "No offense to you, young man, but I'll never surrender my guns to anyone. They come after me, they better bring plenty of body bags with them."

The Butcher held up one hand, as if to keep the old man's anger at bay. "I'm right with you, sir. Believe me, I wouldn't be working for them if I didn't support the Second Amendment. So," he continued nonchalantly, "you teach your grandchildren gun safety, I imagine?"

The old man looked down at his hands, then back to the Butcher. "I would if I had any. My boy lives out west and is too busy with his career to give me any grandchildren. I'd probably never see them unless I drove cross-country, which I'm not."

The Butcher concluded the old man wasn't married, sitting all alone for breakfast. He released a sigh and glanced past the old man to the waitress, who was busily cashing out a customer at the bar. "I just flew in and got a taxi here before going to the hotel. I can't eat on a plane. It all tastes like cardboard. I think the waitress is ignoring me." It was important to stay close to the truth, but he was no more a salesman than the old man was a Chippendale's dancer, and he would rather eat cardboard than what the old man was consuming across from him.

The old man scooped a fork-load of hash browns into his mouth and took a sip of coffee. A waitress in a white blouse and yellow apron finally stepped to the booth with pen and pad in hand.

"Ready to order?" she asked impatiently.

"Just the coffee," the Butcher replied. The waitress rolled her eyes and cocked her head in disgust. He raised his hand slightly to prevent her from coming across the short wall separating the booth from the narrow food preparation area behind her and smothering him with her bulk.

"Fine," he said, "how about a piece of that fine pecan pie on the counter?"

The waitress scribbled in shorthand on the pad and shuffled off. The old man peered at the Butcher. "I figured you'd be hungry."

"I was," the Butcher confessed, "but now I'm just tired. My bags should be at the hotel by now, and I just need some sleep." He appeared to be in thought for a moment before continuing. "How long do you think it'll take for me to get another taxi to pick me up here?"

"Hard to say." The old man shook his head and looked around at the growing restaurant crowd. At least a dozen people had arrived, waiting patiently for an open booth in a row of chairs under the wall of windows by the front entrance. "It's almost race week, and these idiot fans are pouring in from all over the country. You're lucky to already have a hotel room, or you'd have to find a homeless shelter. I wish they'd move that ridiculous race out of here. It brings nothing but trouble with all the white trash it draws in."

"Well then," the Butcher said, unclipping his cell phone and pretending to punch in a search, "I should pass on the pie, and get busy finding a ride." He slipped a $10 bill from his pocket and dropped it on the table as he stood. He looked over his phone at the old man. "It was nice talking to you, Mr. ..."

"Just call me Harold," the old man replied, and then he raised his eyebrows in a question. "Which hotel?"

"I'm sorry?" the Butcher said, looking back over his phone.

Harold turned his palms up on the table. "Where are you staying? I'll drive you."

The Butcher smiled and lowered his phone. "I wouldn't ask you to go to the trouble, but thanks."

His objection was dismissed with a wave. "Just sit down, son, and eat."

The Butcher considered Harold for a beat and then feigned surrender to his fatherly command. He slid his frame back across the

267

plastic seat just as the waitress plopped down his slice of pie and a long, yellow receipt with hastily scribbled numbers. She then retreated to wait on a man at the counter. The Butcher threw her a disgusted look and briefly considered returning to the restaurant later to stalk and kill her—but now was not the time for fun. He had a job to do.

Harold raised one side of his mouth in a victorious grin while the Butcher ate the dried-out pie in four bites and set the $10 bill on top of his plate. If the waitress wanted to earn her tip, she would have to waddle her cottage cheese bulk over to the table and get it. Harold gulped down the rest of his coffee, pulled $20 from his front overalls pocket, and dropped it on top of his plate in like fashion.

The Butcher followed Harold to his truck and was greeted with the loud creak from the old metal hinges as he pulled the passenger door open. He slid onto the cracked vinyl and sank two inches into seat springs that had given up their battle against human weight years ago. He pulled the door shut while Harold settled himself behind the tattered steering wheel, cranked the engine, and shifted into first. They sat in silence as the truck moved slowly toward the exit. Harold looked north and south on International Speedway and then to his passenger.

"You never told me your name."

"Butch," came the flat reply.

"Well, Butch," Harold said with a grin, "which way?"

The Butcher relaxed and morphed into his true identity, readying himself for what was to come. "That depends."

Confusion crossed Harold's face. "Depends on what?"

"On where you live."

Harold aimed a quizzical glance at his passenger, and his eyes were immediately drawn to the shiny compact pistol in the Butcher's hand, leveled at his stomach. His eyes met the Butcher's, and the Butcher knew that he saw something far different now from what he had seen earlier in the restaurant.

"I'd like to see that gun collection of yours first," the Butcher said.

Keith Bartlett rolled out of bed at 5:30 a.m. He was too keyed up to sleep, thinking of all the potentially damaging information contained in the flash drive. He dressed, made a pot of coffee, and sat in the living room with his laptop. No matter what he found on the flash drive, there was still more work to do, and he had a few days left to do it. Teresa would be home Sunday afternoon, giving him at least two more days to build up enough confidence for his next and hopefully last felonious act. He needed at least another day to go over his plan and let his nerves recover from coming within a fraction of an inch of being caught last night. But he couldn't pull it off if Teresa were home. No wife would understand her husband leaving late at night wearing a black commando outfit and returning three hours later. Even nosy neighbors might take note of Keith's unusual activities, so he had to consider a different approach with an airtight alibi.

The more he looked at the data, the more his amazement grew. It appeared Strawn Industries was bringing what had to be large shipments of heroin from Afghanistan, India, and Pakistan into Rotterdam. From there, the shipments were transferred to Mexico and Canada, combined with cocaine shipments, and then transferred to warehouses throughout the U.S. Warehouse storage made sense because, other than a rare police patrol after dark, there would be little surveillance of the industrial parks where the warehouses were located. Strawn's furniture business was serving as a convenient cover for the fleet of trucks used to deliver the drugs. A multitude of trucks coming and going with furniture would never draw the suspicion of the casual onlooker. But those same trucks were transporting something far more valuable than furniture—tightly wrapped bundles of cash to the loading dock and hundreds of pound of drugs from the loading dock.

One document detailed a huge indoor plant-growing operation housed in a closed-down peanut factory in Georgia with twenty-two employees listed. That would be a marijuana grow. It was producing five thousand plants per month. Fifty plants to make a pound, one hundred pounds per month. When pot was legalized in more states, it would turn a nice legal profit.

He continued scrolling through the extensive files and suddenly recognized yet another transport method. Strawn Industries operated a decorative plant supply division and was providing live and artificial plants and flowers to thousands of corporate offices throughout the country. There were hundreds of florist shops across the nation listed as receiving daily deliveries of plants and flowers, which were then shipped out to Strawn's customers. Tractor-trailer loads of plants from Mexico and Miami. Huge orders of flowers and decorative plants being moved from the florist shops up into Canada. That's how they were concealing the drugs and their odor. Supposedly no drug dog could detect the smell of drugs through tons of flowers. Smart delivery system. Drugs were passing back and forth across both borders of the U.S. without detection—or, being allowed through by corrupt border officials.

If drugs were legalized, Strawn would instantly become the number one supplier in the nation. Everything had been set up in advance. Millions of dollars were already flowing into Strawn's hands on a monthly basis, carefully counted and recorded by a small army of accountants. From there, the money disappeared down hundreds of paths, both legitimate and criminal. Everything the police needed was right here in Keith's lap. If he could only find a way for them to have legal access to it.

The stress of the previous night and anticipation of what he might find in the files were catching up with him. Keith found his eyes involuntarily closing while scrolling through the list of files, so he decided to examine them later. He finished his coffee and took a shower, thinking about his wife and son. He was torn between regret over the crime of stealing the files and pride in knowing his actions could result in bringing Strawn down and saving another Joshua from dying at the hands of drugs.

He stepped from the shower to towel off and looked in the steam-covered mirror above the sink. He couldn't see himself. He swiped the mirror with his forearm as a sudden realization crossed his mind. What if he was out of the picture after being killed or arrested? What would happen to Teresa and his son? He slipped on his housecoat, walked to the kitchen, and tore a piece of paper from a yellow legal pad on the counter. It had to be large enough to catch Teresa's attention. If all went well, he would just wad it up and throw it in the trash when he returned. He scribbled on the paper and stuck it to the refrigerator door with the exterminator's business card magnet.

An hour later he sat behind the wheel of his car in a preppy yellow golf shirt, tan Dockers and comfortable boat shoes. He slid on his sunglasses, started the ignition, and glanced in the back seat at the black bag he had tossed in there thirty seconds ago. His mental checklist assured him he had everything he needed for the night. He looked up, studied the half-million-dollar home he and Teresa had worked so hard for, and shook his head. Had his relationship with Colson turned him into some undercover wannabe? Was he really going to such lengths to see justice done for Joshua, or was he fulfilling a delusional fantasy fueled by a mid-life crisis?

Breaking into Strawn Tower last night was done; there was no putting that genie back in the bottle. But if he was discovered, life for his family would crumble. He would lose his business, their home, and worst of all, his family. He rested his forehead on the steering wheel and said a short prayer. Would anyone ever view his actions as honorable and justified? Only time would tell.

There comes a time when what other people think no longer matters, Keith reminded himself. As Colson had mentioned to him on multiple occasions, what mattered was doing the right thing. Keith slipped the gear in reverse and let the car roll back into the street. He turned right out of the subdivision and left at the first light, just as Teresa turned her SUV into their neighborhood.

ᴄ͟ᴏ͟CHAPTER TWENTY-SEVENᴄ͟ᴏ͟

The white-over-orange pickup merged into the right lane of I-95 south. Traffic was heavier than normal due to the Coke Zero 400 scheduled for this coming Saturday. The mid-morning sky was a cloudless, brilliant blue, but neither man paid it any attention. Harold's eyes were fixed on the road ahead and the Butcher knew what he was thinking. *What does this man want?* He kept his two-handed grip on the old steering wheel and dared not look or ask a question.

Harold and the Butcher rode in silence during the ten-minute drive to exit 256. Harold coasted his old truck down the ramp to the stop sign and pulled the worn signal arm to indicate a left turn. The Butcher noticed Harold's hands were trembling on the wheel. He tried to feel sorry for the old man, but the feelings just weren't there.

"You all right there, Harold?" the Butcher asked as if he actually cared. Not many opportunities presented themselves for him to toy with his victims. His jobs were typically quick and dirty, but he occasionally made time to enjoy himself.

Harold almost responded at first, but the moment passed without a response. Apparently fear had locked his jaw tight. His jaw clenched and his face appeared ashen while he turned the wheel to make a slow, arcing left turn onto County Road 421, and then a right on Taylor Road. Harold wasn't in a hurry. It gave the Butcher pleasure knowing Harold was terrified. Old movie scenes flashed through his mind—tough men being held at gunpoint and ramming their cars into concrete bridge supports, catapulting their assailants through the windshield. But Harold was no hero. He was just a retired old man with an old truck, an older house, and a measly Social Security check.

The Butcher surveyed his surroundings as Harold turned right onto Spruce Creek Road. They had entered a rural, residential area of Volusia County that most tourists would never see. These were residents who had no interest in souvenir shops, beach blankets, or bikini babes. He shook his head while taking in the scattered palm trees and scrub bushes along both sides of the two-lane road—a miserable existence assigned to the average Joe Schmo.

The Butcher took note of the four-lane road ahead that dead-ended into Spruce Creek. A public transit shelter stood encased on three sides with Plexiglas. A woman stood next to a small blue sign showing the white outline of a bus. He gave a short nod, satisfied his plan was coming together nicely. He glanced at the speedometer: only 25 mph. He began to lose his patience. "Let's pick it up, Harold," the Butcher said through clenched teeth. "I don't have all day. The sooner we get there, the sooner I'll be out of what little hair you have left."

Harold glanced down at the speedometer but didn't accelerate. They were at his driveway. He gently turned the truck in and stopped. The Butcher paused, looking at the house. The unremarkable ranch home was set back about thirty yards off the road, its tan brick siding and shingled roof almost the identical color of the few surrounding trees and dead grass. A two-car garage was attached to the north side of the ranch, while a single detached garage sat ten yards to the right with a white, enclosed pull-behind trailer parked in front.

"Drive between the house and the garage to the back," the Butcher instructed. "You do have a back door, don't you?"

Harold moved the truck slowly forward, driving it onto the grass and around the side of the house. After Harold parked, the Butcher pocketed his pistol, slipped on a pair of black leather gloves, and followed Harold through the rear door and into a small kitchen. A fifties-style laminate table sat in the middle of the room, flanked by two mismatched wooden chairs.

Harold rested his hands on the back of the farthest chair and looked directly at the Butcher for the first time since leaving the restaurant. "Please tell me what this is about," he asked with as much respect as he could muster.

The Butcher cocked his head and raised his eyebrows. "I already told you—I want to see your gun collection."

Harold shook his head, turned, and walked through the kitchen door with the man walking behind him. He glanced at the Butcher's gloves and must have noted the absence of the gun. The Butcher grinned, wondering if old Harold was calculating his chances of calling 911 without getting shot. He wished he had tried.

They continued walking through a hall and into Harold's modest bedroom. The Butcher took note of three photos hanging in the hall as they passed. One photo showed a younger Harold with a woman and a teenage boy, and another showed the same boy, a few years older, grinning broadly and holding a large fish dangling from a line. The last photo showed a much younger Harold in a U.S. Army uniform. Harold stopped in front of a tall wooden gun case with a glass display door and key lock.

"You can have them all," Harold said in a nervous tone.

The Butcher didn't reply as he took silent inventory of the collection. Standing silent and proud behind the glass was a 12 gauge double-barreled shotgun, what appeared to be a .444 caliber lever-action rifle, and two black powder rifles, both probably .50 caliber. On either side wall of the case hung two handguns, supported by wooden pegs. One was clearly an 1840s model, single action Colt .45, and the other was a stainless Smith & Wesson .357 Magnum with a short, two-inch barrel.

Harold broke the silence, stuttering, "And the truck. The guns and the truck are yours, if you'll just leave me alone."

Harold had broken the Butcher's concentration. He loved firearms of all types, sizes, and models—specifically their look and feel as he hefted them in his hand. He admired those who designed and constructed such wonderful instruments of destruction. He had momentarily put Harold out of his mind while examining them. He turned and chuckled when what Harold said registered.

"Take your guns?" he said. "Who do you think I am, some California liberal?"

Harold squinted. "Then I don't understand what this is about."

"Open the case," the Butcher said, ignoring Harold's comment.

Harold hesitated, but only for an instant. He pulled his keys from his pocket, fumbled with a small key, and clicked open the lock. The Butcher reached in and lifted the .357 Magnum from the wooden pegs and turned it over in his hands, giving it a closer examination. He spun the cylinder and thumbed the release, allowing it to drop open. He turned to Harold with slightly raised eyebrows.

"It's loaded?" the Butcher said.

Harold shrugged. "Not much good to me if it ain't."

The Butcher nodded in agreement. "Let's go."

Harold walked slowly past the Butcher, down the hall, and into the living room. "Stop," the Butcher said once Harold reached the foot of a leather recliner. "That's far enough."

Harold's back was to him, arms limp by his sides, hands trembling.

The Butcher eyed Harold with mild amusement and permitted himself another grin. This was the moment of absolute power he craved. It was almost inebriating. How long would Harold stand silent with his back turned before curiosity overwhelmed him? The game was exhilarating, and he savored every moment, but as with the waitress, there was no time for fun and games. The job must be done; time is money. He raised the revolver, thumbed the release to drop the cylinder to the side, and silently pulled one round from the chamber. He closed the chamber with a soft click, leaving a live round behind the hammer and the empty chamber to the immediate right. The game would be fair. Almost. The double-action revolver had a long trigger pull, giving him more than enough time to play his game.

"Do you like old west movies, Harold?" the Butcher asked. "Turn around so we can talk."

Harold spun to face him. "Please, Butch, or whoever you are, just take what you want and—"

"Oh, it's Butch," he interrupted. "I wouldn't lie to you, but you haven't answered my question."

Harold sighed. "Yes, I watch them."

The Butcher smiled. "Very good. You will be able to appreciate our game then."

A surge of adrenalin caused Harold to breathe audibly through his nose. The Butcher walked toward him, holding out the revolver and offering it to Harold butt first. He avoided the Butcher's eyes and stared down at the revolver in silence. The Butcher glanced over Harold's shoulder to the mantle clock. "Perfect," he said in a whisper, "it's two minutes until high noon. Close enough." Harold's body jerked involuntarily when the Butcher shouted, "Take it!"

Harold grasped the revolver in his right hand and lowered it to his side as the Butcher stepped back four paces, holding his hands away from his side in surrender. Harold could only shake his head.

"Concentrate, Harold," the Butcher said. "You have about a minute before your clock chimes on the hour, then you can take all six shots at me. I know you can get off at least three before I can pull the Walther from my pocket."

"I can't do this," Harold said, still moving his head slowly left and right.

The Butcher knew what was going to happen, even before Harold realized what he had to do. He saw it the moment Harold stopped moving his head and met his eyes. It was the survival instinct buried deep in every human being, whether they are a teenage boy, schoolgirl, Catholic priest, or old man, what is commonly known as the "fight or flight" syndrome. There were twenty-five seconds to go before the top of the hour when Harold telegraphed his intention with his eyes. The Butcher had already taken one large stride in Harold's direction by the time he raised the revolver and yet another as he pulled the trigger, dropping the hammer on the empty chamber. In the silence of the room, the result was a loud click.

The old man's eyes widened an instant before the Butcher grasped his wrist with his left hand and slammed a karate chop to the nook of his arm with his right, driving him down into the recliner. He felt the Butcher's hand move over his. He didn't have the strength to pull his finger from the trigger guard as another finger slipped over top. Then he felt the pressure of the cold steel barrel against his temple before everything he was and everything he knew instantly vanished.

Keith parked his car in the long-term parking lot at the Atlanta Hartsfield-Jackson airport and made his way to the main domestic ticketing area holding his small black gym bag. It was known as the world's busiest airport, and endless mobs of people from every continent scurried to make their flights, dragging luggage and carry-on bags. Keith slipped through the crowd to the sliding glass door entrance, where an invisible speaker repeatedly announced the area was restricted to picking up and dropping off passengers only.

To Keith's left sat the luggage carousels, surrounded by dozens of people waiting for their luggage to appear. To his right were the ticketing counters, hanging above were a dozen large monitors with lists of flight arrivals and departures. He watched as the screens periodically blinked, updating the information. There were three outbound flights from Atlanta to Miami, the last one scheduled to depart at 2:35 p.m. He checked his watch: 10:05 a.m. His earlier Internet search had listed another three flights that evening, but the earliest wouldn't depart until 7:05 p.m. Keith had experienced this process for years and knew how it worked. He just hoped it would work when he needed it to.

He walked toward the ticketing desk, but instead of joining the growing line through the roped off amusement-park-type lanes, he stepped to a self-ticketing computer monitor and pulled up the flight information. He touched the screen for the 2:35 flight, slid his credit card in the slot, and waited. A small row of squares appeared on the screen in a wave pattern to let him know the program was searching. Only a few seconds passed before "YOUR FLIGHT IS CONFIRMED" popped up in a green box, followed by a boarding pass being spit from a slot to the tray below. Keith grabbed the boarding pass, suffered through the TSA checkpoint, and rode the subway tram to the gate. He stopped to get a sub sandwich and a bottle of water for the four-hour wait, lounged in a chair near the departure desk, and tried to relax and clear his mind.

The Butcher allowed Harold's hand to drop into his lap. The blood-spattered revolver lay askew in his hand, with his lifeless finger resting in the trigger guard. The Butcher took a step back to review the scene. Convincing enough for the local cops. It wasn't perfect, but it would suffice. There would be enough gunpowder residue on Harold's hands to make a convincing case for suicide. It wasn't as clean as the Butcher would like, but he felt quite proud of himself for today's ad-lib project. Time permitting, he would return the truck to Harold's driveway after the job and casually walk to the public bus stop for a ride back to his car at the Waffle House. If the waitress with the cottage cheese legs got nosy about the rental car, the worst that could happen would be the cops contacting the rental company and having it towed back as abandoned by a phantom with a fictitious name.

Suspecting Harold kept his precious belongings safe from thieving teenagers, the Butcher slipped the keys from the old man's overalls pocket. He slowed on his way out of the living room, flipped the thermostat to sixty degrees, and casually walked out the kitchen door to the rear of the detached garage. The old rear door was held secure by a padlock and hasp. He quickly identified the correct key on the ring, went inside, and immediately found what he was looking for. He hefted the six-foot ladder from its wall brackets, walked it out to the truck, and set it in the bed. He returned to the garage, replaced the padlock, and laid the keys on the kitchen table before locking the back door of the house from the inside and pulling it closed.

Keith stood periodically to stretch, but dared not leave his seat next to the departure desk. Two hoards of passengers had accumulated at the gate, waiting for two earlier flights and jockeying for position when their boarding process began. In all Keith's years of flying, he never understood the rush. The plane wasn't leaving the ground until all passengers were on board anyway. Now passengers were arriving for the 2:35 flight to Miami, and it was just a matter of a few more minutes before he would know if his plan was going to work.

It was 1:40 p.m. when a young man with shoulder-length hair stepped up to the departure desk with his backpack. Keith leaned forward and placed his chin in his hand to listen.

"How may I assist you?" the gate agent asked, addressing the young man.

The boy handed a slip of paper to the agent. "I missed my earlier flight and am on standby for this one. Can you check to see if you have room?"

The agent handed the slip of paper back silently without even taking a look at it. He was no doubt used to such questions from rookie fliers. "Please have a seat. You can watch the computer monitor on the wall for your seat approval. Those on standby will be indicated by the first three letters of your last name. The names in blue remain on standby and those in green have been approved for the flight."

"Thanks," the boy said, and sat down and slouched in a chair, repeatedly looking from the screen to his standby ticket. Keith stood with what remained of his bottled water when a seat opened next to the boy. He casually walked to the empty seat, sat down, and began studying the screen on the far wall. It was now 1:58 p.m., and the boarding process would begin in minutes.

"Thank God," Keith said when the green screen cycled on the monitor.

The boy turned his head. "Were you on standby too?"

Keith chuckled. "Yeah. Now I don't have an excuse to miss my worthless business meeting."

"I don't guess I'm going to make it," the boy said, hanging his head slightly. "My parents are going to be pissed."

The gate agent picked up his microphone. "Ladies and gentlemen, may I have your attention. Flight twenty-three-ten to Miami International will begin boarding in the next few minutes. Those who need assistance or extra time for boarding may move to the gate now with your boarding pass, and then we will begin seating our first class passengers."

An older woman with a walker, an elderly man being pushed in a wheelchair by a flight attendant, and two mothers with baby strollers moved toward the gate. Keith jerked slightly as if the vibration of his cell phone had alerted him to a call. He held the phone to one ear and stuck his finger in the other ear to stifle the sound of chattering passengers.

"I can barely hear you, Kent. What?" Keith said into the phone, and then he sat straight up on the edge of his seat, speaking with urgency and loud enough for the boy to hear clearly. "Dear God, are they all right? Where are they?"

The boy turned his attention away from the standby screen and looked at Keith with mild curiosity for a moment before looking down at his boarding pass for the fiftieth time.

"I'm on my way," Keith said sharply, and he stuck his phone back in his pocket. He put his head in his hands. "God, let them be all right."

"What is it?" the boy said.

Keith looked at the boy for a moment as if he hadn't heard him, although he clearly had and was counting on his comment. "My wife and daughter," he said in disbelief. "They've been in an accident."

"Are they okay?"

"I don't know. I have to get out of here. I have to get to the hospital."

"I'm sorry," the boy said with genuine concern in his voice. "I hope they're okay."

Keith nodded and stood up, and started to shove his boarding pass into his pants pocket. "Did you not make the flight?"

"No," the boy said, looking down at the carpet.

Keith bent over to the boy and extended his hand with the boarding pass. "Here," he said in a low voice. "Take mine. They don't check IDs from this point."

The boy looked up in amazement. "Are you sure?" he said.

"I can't go. Just take it."

The boy took the boarding pass as Keith fast-walked away from the gate. "Thanks, man, uh, sir," he said as Keith disappeared into the thick crowd of travelers.

Keith ducked into the men's room next to the gate and stepped into a stall, where he took a dark blue Atlanta Falcons T-shirt and ball cap from the gym bag. He slipped on the shirt and pulled the ball cap down low on his forehead. He turned the flimsy gym bag inside out to reveal the gray lining, stuffed his yellow shirt inside, and casually walked down the terminal to the subway tram. He had no way of knowing the number or placement of cameras in the airport, but he felt luck was with him. A small rush of adrenalin swept through him. He wondered if it was the same type of rush Colson talked about when he worked undercover. He resisted a grin from under the brim of the cap. The plan for his alibi required hours of investment, but it had worked—for now.

He silently scolded himself for not thinking about it before the Strawn Tower break-in, but *hey,* he reminded himself, *we learn as we go.* Colson would be proud.

CHAPTER TWENTY-EIGHT

The Sunsations souvenir shop was a squat, one-story building at the corner of A1A and Hillside Avenue. Its exterior stucco was painted a beachy tan color, as is the case with most tourist traps on the coastal roadway. A wide band of teal-colored trim relief surrounded the roofline, giving it tropical appeal. Sheets of brown cardboard covered the front windows where brightly colored T-shirts, bikinis, beach towels, and hats used to hang in the late '90s, when the economy and tourist trade were robust. The low-rent customers and knick-knack collectors who frequented the souvenir shop in years past now had to walk a little farther down the strip to browse for trinkets to prove their visit to the once-thriving Daytona Beach area. At 4 a.m., the bright colors of the inventory in the remaining open shops along A1A weren't vivid as they would become when the searing Daytona sun made its appearance above the Atlantic waters directly across the street.

Across the street from Sunsations stood the Sundowner Condos. The five-story white stucco structure sported its own colored accent band around the roofline, painted a deep ocean blue instead of teal. The Butcher backed up Harold's old pickup near the service entrance of Sunsations and sat for a moment in the dark silence of the cab. He couldn't observe traffic on A1A from this side of the building, but he knew it would be nearly nonexistent this early in the morning. He had been studying Colson's condo for hours. Not seeing his car in the rear parking area on his casual stroll down the beach access walkway and talking with the security guard in the underground garage the evening prior told him Colson hadn't arrived yet. The sixty-something security guard ran his mouth like an old woman. The Butcher, wearing his fake moustache and glasses, let him ramble on all he wanted.

"No," the old security guard had said last night, rubbing his chin, "Mr. Colson's been gone for over a week now as I can remember. He usually comes back every weekend or so when he works out of town. Can't help but notice his car in space sixteen when I do my rounds. He keeps it spotless and shining like new money. Most mornings I see him on his balcony watching the sunrise, and then he'll usually leave for an hour or two. I think he said he goes to the gym somewhere down International Speedway Boulevard." The guard had squinted Popeye-style at the Butcher. "You say you're his police buddy from Georgia?"

"Yes, sir." The Butcher had suffered through the guard's drivel, but he needed the information, so he acted cordial and interested. "I have my family with me in town, and I thought I'd drop in on him."

The guard nodded. "Well, then, if you're gonna be in town for the week, I'm sure you'll catch him. You want me to tell him you came by? If you have a business card, I'll—"

"No thanks." The Butcher held up his hand. "It's been years, so I'd like to surprise him. Maybe we'll stop in one afternoon."

"Well, if you do that, you might want to look on the beach. He'll be out there under his canopy if he isn't sitting on the balcony."

The Butcher left the old man standing in the parking garage so he could return to his miserable existence as the sole protector and defender of justice at Sundowner Condos. If his suspicions were correct, Colson would return to this forsaken place to practice his next self-serving speech for the mind-numbed herds of workers being held captive to listen to his pitiful sales pitch. The Butcher didn't have an opinion about drug use one way or the other, but his opinion about Colson was that he was giving lip service for part-time money and full-time glory.

The Butcher knew Colson's history almost as well as he knew his own: twenty-nine years with the Clay County Sheriff's Office; retired a major two years ago; undercover narc, fugitive investigator, and internal affairs commander. Giving up such power and authority on the command staff of such a large agency to survive on a measly pension and sporadic private investigation jobs amazed the Butcher. Accepting his current position as a minion and advocate for a "drug-free workplace" made the Butcher shake his head in disbelief. If anyone needed psychiatric treatment, it was Colson.

But the Butcher didn't discount Colson's abilities. With decades of experience and training, taking him out wouldn't be a walk in the park, his obvious faults notwithstanding. There had been other times when he knew the suicide approach wouldn't work as it had with old Harold. This was one of those times that called for striking from a distance. Colson kept himself in good physical condition and clearly wasn't the type of distraught individual people would suspect of committing suicide. Quite the opposite, actually. As opposed to a lonely old man, however, there were hundreds, maybe even thousands, of suspects with a reason to kill Colson. No doubt he had locked up enough of them over the past three decades to make a detective consider a retribution killing.

And then there was Jay "The Terrible" Taylor. The one-eyed former UFC contender, Colson's current flunky and sole employee. There was no kill order for him, but the Butcher would throw him in for free if Taylor got in his way.

It was a balmy 78 degrees, and there was a decent overcast sky holding the full moon at bay. Only a hazy glow illuminated the clouds, revealing the moon's position in the night sky. With the exception of the occasional hiss of vehicle tires on A1A and a light breeze, the night was as silent as an empty church.

The Butcher stepped to the rear of the pickup and climbed into the bed. He extended the aluminum ladder, set it against building, and climbed silently with one hand on the rungs and the other holding a soft-sided gun case about the size of a briefcase. Once on the asphalt roof, he pulled up the ladder and laid it flat on the roof and out of sight. He leaned his back against the three-foot front wall on Sunsations' flat asphalt roof and assembled his Remington modular sniper rifle by feel alone.

He glanced at the luminous marks on his watch: 5:19 a.m. The Butcher leaned his back and head against the wall, crossed his arms, and relaxed. Colson would stick to his normal schedule or he wouldn't. He would repeat the process the next day if needed, so he closed his eyes and waited.

"We're out of coffee," Taylor said, shaking the ceramic container as if agitating it would replenish the supply. He set the container on the countertop with a loud clack and shoved it against the backsplash. Colson hadn't heard him from the balcony. He walked through the sliding door. "We're out of coffee."

Colson looked up from his tablet with a grin. "So call Juan Valdez. He delivers right to your window. I've seen it on TV."

Taylor pointed at Colson. "You're the one who woke me up at the crack of black last night to work on that laptop."

Colson nodded. "Good job, by the way, with the encryption."

"Amateurs," Taylor said with a wave of his hand. "A college kid could have accessed that computer."

"Did you check the flash drive to make sure everything downloaded?"

"Two separate flash drives," Taylor said, holding up two fingers, "and of course I checked." He cocked his head at Colson. "You're not going to work out this morning?"

Colson shook his head. "I've got a lot on my mind. I think I'll take the day off. Probably the next couple of days. There's something I need to make you aware of, other than the dirt on Strawn."

"That woman again?" Taylor's sarcastic tone made Colson cringe a little. Ever since Colson had returned from Atlanta, he'd been distracted. Taylor understood being upset about his friend Morgan, but there was more to it than that. Colson hadn't stopped talking about the woman he had met. Taylor guessed he shouldn't be too hard on Colson. He had missed an opportunity at love himself more than once during his fighting career. The two things just didn't mix well. There was too much mental and physical preparation involved in his sport for a female distraction to get in the way. He wouldn't have been able to focus on the fight with the familiar voice of a beautiful, bouncing brunette screaming his name from ringside.

But sharing the condo with Colson was working out well for both of them. They didn't bug each other, and each did as he pleased when not working an investigation. What would happen if Colson had a full-time female companion? He knew he would be a third wheel, and staying on at the Sundowner would be out of the question. Taylor shook his head. He was just being selfish.

"Sorry," he said. "I should mind my own business." He held off saying anything about Strawn's involvement with Haggart and Dr. Cooper. Colson was so worked up about the laptop when he arrived, he couldn't get a word in edgewise. "I've had a lot on my mind too."

Colson gave him a dismissive wave. "No problem. I'm acting like a teenager, but that's not the part I was going to warn you about."

"Warn me?"

"Yes, warn you." Colson sat up straight, set his elbows on his knees, and gave Taylor a serious look. "What we already have on Strawn is overwhelming. If we can get the phone records on the numbers you found, I'm pretty certain there will be some communication between Strawn and his hit man about the murders."

"How will you get that? The police can get it, but you haven't turned the laptop over to them yet. I figured you'd be racing back to Atlanta as soon as we—I—broke the encryption."

"I, uh… texted the numbers to Sheriff Langston an hour ago. With a little coaxing, he'll have the information to me by late afternoon."

"Isn't that a little illegal?" Taylor said.

Colson shrugged. "Not when Langston cuts a case number and has his secretary type up a subpoena." A huge grin crept across Colson's face. "If you recall, he owes me one."

"But if you turn all this over to that Atlanta guy—what's his name, Floyd—he can do the same thing."

"Possibly, but I still don't know if I can trust anyone else to get it done, and I want to personally know how involved Strawn is, in case the police can't or won't use the information to prosecute him."

Taylor nodded. "So you can take care of business yourself if they don't?"

286

"You could say that," Colson said under his breath.

"So that's what you wanted to warn me about? You're the one who could get in hot water over this."

Colson shook his head. "No, I wanted to warn you to keep your eye open for whoever Strawn is sending here to kill me."

Two short vibrations of the cell phone in his pocket alerted the Butcher he had received a text message. He grinned to himself, knowing who sent the message as he slid the slim device from his pocket. No matter the content of the message, he was conducting business his way now and would ignore any further orders from that belligerent billionaire. No other client had ever questioned him, ordered him around, or told him how to do his job. They knew better. That's why they hired a professional. If they knew how to do the job better, they would simply do it themselves and save the cash.

The sun had risen and burned off the hazy clouds. The beachfront buildings blocked its early morning glare, yet he still had to shield his phone screen from the emerging blue Florida sky to pull up the message. He cupped his left hand around the screen, swiped his finger across it, and mumbled a curse. The imbecile had sent an uncoded message. He saw letters instead of numbers, but he had to lean over and bring the phone to his face to read it clearly.

COLSON IN DAYTONA WITH COMPUTER
GO NOW!

The Butcher read the seven words again to reassure himself he was reading correctly. "But how did Colson..." he mumbled. He twisted his body around on the warming roof of the souvenir shop to peer over the short wall. His lower back protested against the move, causing him to groan. Still no movement from the exterior hallway of unit 510, and no traffic coming or going from the beachside parking lot or underground garage. He dropped back onto his butt and tried to reason in his head how Colson could have possibly come into possession of the laptop. And then a feeling of accomplishment washed over him, making him smile. His intuition had been proven perfect yet again. Colson and the laptop in one place? You couldn't ask for anything better.

His intention of ignoring the text message was immediately replaced by a thrilling anticipation to respond. He entered his five-word response slowly and carefully, still cupping the screen with one hand to see the tiny keyboard.

GOT HERE YESTERDAY

STOP TEXTING!

The Butcher pulled a magazine of ammunition from the bag, tapped it against the palm of his hand to seat the rounds solidly in the clip, and slipped it into the magazine port. From a second zip compartment he slipped out a brown beanbag filled with silicon beads, the approximate size of a legal envelope. He scooted his butt around on the rough asphalt to face Colson's condo, gently laid the beanbag on the top of the short wall, and checked his watch: 7:40 a.m. If Colson held to the routine eagerly offered by the dimwitted security guard, he would know soon enough.

The sky continued to brighten, but the five-story Sundowner mercifully blocked the sun rising from the waters of the Atlantic. The Butcher took a deep breath and blew it out while adjusting his position from one butt cheek to the other. The asphalt roof was tolerable now, but it would become unbearable when the scorching sun began working on it. He focused his thoughts away from being on the ridiculous roof for hours and concentrated on the task at hand. He didn't even permit himself to think about the money or his planned vanishing act from the continent. Strawn had paid him more for this project than all the others combined.

He grinned, thinking of how much Strawn yet owed him, and he completely forgot about the literal pain in his ass at the moment. But at 8:23 a.m., Colson was behind the security guard's schedule. He would call it off for the day if nothing—

The Butcher's eyes widened at the sight of the green Corvette's nose coming into view beneath the drive-under breezeway, but he was prepared. There was nothing left to do but find Colson in his sight picture, take a breath, and pull the trigger. He lifted the silenced rifle and laid the end of the barrel on the beanbag just short of the ledge where pedestrians below or anyone in a passing car could see.

The Corvette came into full view as it eased over the first yellow speed bump, then the next and into the side parking lot. The Butcher worked to control his breathing. His heart raced somewhat more than he expected, but this was Colson. He was different from the others. He put his eye close to the Leopold scope, found the windshield of the Corvette in the cross hairs, and pulled the trigger twice.

Instantly, two spider-webbed holes appeared just above the 'Vette's steering wheel.

CHAPTER TWENTY-NINE

Three minutes and forty-one seconds prior to the Butcher's well-placed shots, Taylor stood with a perplexed expression, processing Colson's words for a long moment.

"Now who's paranoid?" Taylor finally said sarcastically, "and why wouldn't they have tried to take you out while you were in Atlanta, the same way they did Morgan? You know, with that device that lady detective called you about."

"He couldn't have done the same thing with my car." Colson put his feet up on the low table on the patio and leaned back in his chair, his hands behind his head. "It's twenty years old and doesn't have the same type of computer interface. And it would have been too obvious anyway if both cars just shut down at the same time."

Taylor held up his hands. "I still don't understand. Strawn doesn't know you have the computer. For all he knows, the girl is still on the loose with it."

"He knows now."

"What makes you so sure of that?"

Colson grinned at Taylor. "Because I called his office and told him." Taylor's eyebrows rose over his new sunglasses. He stood speechless, absorbing what Colson just said. Colson stood up and placed his hand on Taylor's shoulder as if he hadn't revealed a hit man was on his way to their condo as they spoke. "Now," Colson continued, "you want to run out and get us some coffee before we go into caffeine meltdown and tear each other's throats out?"

Taylor feigned a cough. "Huh? Tear my throat out? You've been drinking something stronger than coffee this morning."

"Just go," Colson said.

"Fine, but it'll take me a while. I have to gas up my car."

"Just take the 'Vette."

Taylor's good eye shot open wide, and he grasped his chest as if having a heart attack. "Now I know you haven't been drinking. You're doing hard drugs."

"Just go, you shot-out Cyclops," Colson commanded.

Taylor made a fist and shook it at Colson before disappearing into the condo, where he grabbed Colson's keys. He stuck his head out the sliding door. "I need to show you a video when I get back. If I'm right, Strawn has more to worry about than the police, or even you."

Colson looked up from his tablet. "After coffee, okay?"

"Sure," Taylor said, ducking back inside. Colson grinned from his seat and touched the gallery icon to pull up a photo of Beverly, smiling from ear to ear in her white T-shirt and blue jeans.

"Taylor," Colson half shouted.

Taylor answered from inside, "Yeah?"

"Go down to the pier and pick us up an omelet from Crabby Joe's on your way back."

Bullets can be… unpredictable. Once they leave the barrel, all bets are off. For years cops carried magnum rounds that could sail through almost anything short of heavily armored vehicles. However, wounded and dead civilians and subsequent wrongful death lawsuits in recent years convinced most agency heads of the wisdom of issuing hollow-point rounds that would hit, penetrate, and disintegrate inside the bad guys without hurting a bystander or someone in an adjacent apartment. But even if you intended to penetrate a barrier, there were still factors such as wind speed, density of air, and angles of the shot to be considered. Most military and police snipers took all of these factors into account and adjusted accordingly, but no one got it right every single time. Just as water bends light, any barrier can deflect a projectile—even one traveling over 3,000 feet per second.

The two rounds fired at the steeply sloped Corvette windshield were on the ride of their short lives in the thousandths of a second it took them to travel from the roofline of Sunsations across South Atlantic Avenue.

Taylor briefly thought Colson's car had been invaded by a swarm of yellow jackets in the first second after the .223 rounds struck the windshield, exploding the safety glass into tiny cubes, and hurtling them like miniature bullets into his face and chest. Striking the glass at such a steep angle, the rounds were deflected to Taylor's left and right. The first traveled through the passenger side headrest and buried itself in the luggage area behind the seat. The second was deflected upward and lodged in the steel frame of the targa top just above his head, warping it just enough to crack the glass cleanly in half.

Taylor stomped the brake and flung open the driver's door to escape the swarm of attackers before the two nickel-size holes in the windshield caught his attention. He jerked off his sunglasses and glared at what was left of the spider-webbed windshield, seeking the shooter, but he saw nothing but cars parked along both sides of the lot and minimal traffic on A1A in front of him. He instinctively swiped sweat from his forehead, flinging his new sunglasses to the floorboard, but realized it wasn't sweat at all when he saw the smear of blood on his palm. He glanced at his muscle shirt and stared with his good eye at bloody splotches growing larger by the second. He patted his chest and stomach for a bullet wound, but found none. It had to have been the safety glass.

A third clink of glass breaking and a new hole appearing in the windshield made Taylor jerk and suddenly realize the assault wasn't some drive-by incident. The shooter was still out there, and Taylor was a sitting duck.

Taylor jerked the door closed with a thud, slammed the gear into reverse, and stomped on the gas. He was now blinded and disoriented by blood flowing freely into his good eye. The rear tires squealed and boiled smoke. Taylor's attempt to steer with one hand and swipe blood away from his good eye with the other caused the car to back at an angle. The driver's side rear tire jumped the curb where the concrete support pillars stood between the entry and exit lanes of the breezeway. A fraction of a second later, the rear glass hatch pulverized with the impact of the rear fiberglass bumper against the concrete pillar.

"Damn," the Butcher said sharply, dropping down to his butt while simultaneously breaking down the rifle and stuffing it in its case. Stooping over, he jogged to the edge of the roof, ignored the ladder, swung his legs over the top, and dropped the rifle bag into the truck bed. He paused for a fraction of a second to prepare himself and then pushed off, dropping eleven feet to the bed of the truck next to the bag. The half-century-old bed springs squealed in protest against the impact of the Butcher's weight. He quickly looked left and right across the vacant rear parking lot, checked his belt to ensure his pistol hadn't dislodged from the jump, and swung over the side of the truck bed to the ground. He winced at the sharp pain in his knee from landing at a slight angle while his body leaned in the opposite direction.

Glare from the deepening blue sky above reflecting off the steep slope of the windshield had prevented him from seeing Colson's reaction, but at least one of the three shots had to have hit Colson. No doubt about it. He had watched each round strike the windshield at the precise spot of his aim. The subsequent spider webbing of the glass reduced his chances of watching Colson die to absolute zero. The sudden backing of the car into the support pillar told him Colson must not have been killed instantly.

The Butcher raced to the side of the vacant souvenir shop and stopped short at the corner when he heard the faint wail of a siren from several miles north on A1A. He tucked his semi-automatic pistol in the small of his back, pulled his shirttail over it, and casually walked to the front of the building. He had to be certain Colson was dead before looking for the computer.

Taylor jumped from the driver's seat, pulled his shirt off over his head, wiped blood from his good eye and face, and ran to the relative safety of the stairwell several feet to his left. The bleeding from the deep cut on his forehead was relentless. He swiped the shirt across his face again as he slammed his frame into the steel door. He cursed, bouncing off the door, before remembering it had to be pulled open. He jerked on the handle, barged into the stairwell, and pushed off the concrete wall to boost himself up the first flight of stairs. The bright, aqua blue child-like painting of a smiling octopus on the cream concrete blocks now sported a bloody smear across its face. He held the shirt against his forehead with one hand while pulling his weight up the stairs with the other. Five flights and ten sets of stairs.

Taylor knew the bullets were meant for the sarcastic retired cop upstairs, but that sarcastic cop was his only friend—his best friend. He had to get to him before the shooter could. There was little chance the man just packed up and went home unless he was certain the bullets had found their mark. On the other hand, this would be the second time Taylor had taken a bullet for Colson, and he would never let him forget it.

Taylor counted as he climbed the rough concrete stairs. He was blinded again by the time he reached the third set, between the second and third floor. His blood-soaked shirt became worthless, only smearing the warm muck across his forehead. He threw the shirt against the wall, kept his hand on the banister, and continued counting the flights as he climbed. He stopped to catch his breath for a second time on the fourth floor landing. That's when he heard the scuffing of rubber-soled shoes below.

Colson looked up from his computer tablet at the faint sound of squealing tires, partially muffled by the strong sea wind buffeting against the exterior walls of his balcony. Most times, there was nothing unusual about teenagers burning their expensive tires down to worthless donuts of slick rubber on A1A, but this time it was different. The squealing sound rising five stories to Colson's ear sounded much closer, and the following crunching impact clearly announced a collision.

Colson stood and peered over the balcony railing. Nothing but foot traffic was passing through the breezeway beneath. He concluded one of the tourists had also failed to hear the pop and had pulled out into traffic on A1A and got nailed. The nearing sound of a siren indicated he was right.

He sat back down and plugged Taylor's flash drive into the tablet. He would give the information from Strawn's computer a fresh look before... Taylor? He stood to his feet again and looked over the railing. More people were walking into the breezeway and pointing at something through the opening. Surely Taylor would have called his cell if he had been involved in an accident. That is, if he were physically able to call.

Colson stepped into the condo and slid the heavy glass door closed behind him. He laid the tablet on the counter next to his ASP and went to the front door.

The Butcher slipped on his sunglasses and pulled a ball cap down on his head while walking to the front corner of Sunsations. A small crowd was assembling around the demolished Corvette, chattering and pointing in various directions. He still couldn't see Colson's form behind the broken windshield, so he casually walked across the street to the sidewalk in front of the Sundowner. Cars and SUVs lined both sides of the front parking lot. Those to his right were nosed in at an angle against an eight-foot block wall, separating them from the public beach access walkway and the vacant lot he had surveyed early this morning from the roof. Normally he had no reason to walk into the middle of a crime scene, but there really wasn't any way around it this time. His view of the car would be blocked by the high wall if he took the beach access walkway. No, he had to verify Colson was dead and see if the laptop was in the car before the paramedics and police arrived.

He crossed the parking lot and pushed his way through the small crowd to the driver's side of the Corvette. The car wasn't steaming or hissing since the front end hadn't been damaged. The engine idled at a low rumble, and a greasy crimson stream of transmission fluid ran from under the car, winding its way through chunks of shattered safety glass. The steering wheel, tan leather seats, console, and gearshift were smeared with blood, and a pair of broken sunglasses lay on the floorboard—but no Colson.

The small interior of the car was easy to search at a glance. There was no computer either. The Butcher snapped his head from one side to the other, looking through the breezeway and across the small crowd, scanning for the retired cop.

Something caught his eye beneath the alcove to his left: a blood-smeared door handle below a sign that read Stairs. The Butcher checked the crowd before moving to the door. No one paid attention to anything but the bloody abandoned car. He heard a female voice from within the crowd say, "Colson's car," as he reached the stairwell door. There was no time to waste. Some nosy neighbor or the police would be at Colson's door within minutes.

He used the tail of his shirt to open the door and immediately took note of the bloody octopus on the wall to his right and the blood-smeared hand railing. The ponderous footsteps he heard were coming from several floors above, so he took the stairs two at a time.

Taylor pulled himself upward with new urgency. The person behind him wasn't a teenage girl headed to the roof deck to sunbathe. This individual had big feet and was moving fast. He briefly lost count and stopped at the next landing, frantically feeling around the door casing for the raised number on the door placard. But it may as well have been written in Braille. His bloody hands gave him no clue as to what number he was feeling. He took an instant to remember his count. He couldn't be at the top already, so he would have to resume his climb.

Taylor reached to his left, found the handrail, and started to pull when he felt a fat hand come in from behind and grab his neck. He instinctively shot his left elbow backward and clawed at the hand with his right hand, now sticky with coagulating blood. A sharp sting followed by instant numbness ran up his left arm after his funny bone struck a corner of the metal railing, and then a searing hot pain sliced into his right kidney as a large fist buried itself deep into his flesh.

Taylor didn't know if he was on a step or the landing. The punch to his side immediately doubled him over, and his head spun out of control. Disoriented, he flailed his arms, swiping the air around him. He made contact with something, but it felt like cloth before he realized he was airborne. He flailed his arms again, not knowing if he was falling face first or back first.

The four-foot plunge may as well have been fifty feet with Taylor's bulk. The impact of his back on the concrete floor drove the air from his lungs, and his backward momentum slid his frame back against the wall, driving the back of his head into the concrete blocks. It was as though Taylor was living in a YouTube video and someone pressed the "escape" key as reality winked out.

The Butcher gave Taylor a fleeting glance as he rounded the fourth floor landing. "Damn it, Colson," he muttered, slamming his feet on every other step. He reached the fifth floor landing, pulled the pistol from under his shirt, and pushed the bar release on the door. He stepped onto the exterior hallway directly in front of unit 510 and took a step back to kick the door when he heard the deadbolt click and saw the door begin to open. Amazed with his timing, he adjusted his stance and rushed the door.

Colson was stunned by the force of the metal door, knocking him backward five feet. He stumbled but regained his footing by grabbing the inside of the bedroom doorframe. The silhouette standing before him wasn't large enough to be Taylor, and his eyes required several seconds to adjust to the sunlight spilling in behind the intruder. The door was stuck open, held by a flimsy rubber welcome mat, bunched up and wedged under the bottom door seal. The first object he clearly recognized was the gun being held at arm's length by none other than—

"Butch Sutton?" Colson's eyes widened with disbelief.

"Step back, Colson," the Butcher ordered. He motioned with his pistol. "Stay away from the counter. You're at least smart enough not to go for a stick in a gun fight."

"I have to admit, you really threw me with this one, Butch," Colson said, stepping backward into the living room. "I always knew you were a worthless slug, but in reality you turned out to be a full-blown piece of shit."

"Just sit on the floor and shut up. It's ironic you feel that way, Grey. Maybe if you had spoken as sternly with your subordinates, you wouldn't be retired right now. Hell, you would probably be chief deputy of Clay County. But not you. You took the soft and mushy approach with your boys." The Butcher stopped in the middle of the room with his gun aimed at Colson.

Colson sat on the floor in front of the sliding glass door, poised for action, watching his enemy carefully. "That's why we never got along, Butch. Unlike you, I earned respect by giving respect, not demanding feigned loyalty out of fear and intimidation, Hitler-style. Exactly how long have you been working for that slime Strawn?"

Butch, "The Butcher" Sutton narrowed his disgusted gaze at Colson. "I don't work for anyone. That's what you do."

"Well," Colson said with a smirk. "You can count on not working for the sheriff's office anymore."

"Oh, it breaks my heart," Sutton scoffed. "You aren't gonna be around to run your smart mouth anyway, but don't worry about your precious sheriff's office. It was just a means to an end. I don't want anything more to do with it now than you do."

Colson shook his head. "Of all the thugs and felons I expected to kill me over the years, it's a damn shame to be wasted by one of you Alabama boys."

Sutton adjusted his grip on the pistol and sneered. "You have a problem with people from Alabama?"

"Of course not. Did you know the man who invented the toothbrush was from Alabama?"

"What?"

"Damn right," Colson said, as if imparting some little-known historical fact. "If it had been anywhere else, they would have called it a teethbrush."

Sutton took a step closer to Colson and trained his pistol to a point between his eyes. "Shut up, smart ass."

The wailing in the background grew to a fevered pitch and just as quickly went silent. Both Sutton and Colson knew EMS and sheriff's units had turned into the complex and killed their sirens, leaving their strobes to bounce blue flashes against the building's exterior. Even in broad daylight, Colson caught a glimpse of the strobe lights reflecting off the metal frame around the open doorway. The beautiful sight made Colson smile.

"Volusia County's finest," Colson said, nodding to the open doorway. Sutton glanced over his shoulder for an instant, giving Colson just enough time to slip his hands behind his back and inch backward and a bit closer to the glass door.

"They're here for a wreck, not for a murder. I wouldn't count on those half-assed sand dune cowboys." The Butcher gave a short laugh. "Anyone who would settle for a job in this depressing excuse for a town won't be causing me any heartburn. Oh, I almost forgot. Too bad about your little green toy."

Colson felt blood rush to his head. Being consumed by conversation with the armed psycho standing in the middle of his living room had made Taylor slip from his mind. How in heaven's name could Sutton have gotten the best of Jay "The Terrible" Taylor? Colson would never forgive himself if Taylor was dead because of him. He felt a moment of selfishness knowing if he hadn't made the call to Strawn, it would be Beverly and Emily dead instead of Taylor.

Sutton must have noticed by Colson's facial expression that he had put two and two together. "Oh, and too bad about your one-eyed sidekick."

Colson sent the Butcher a glare of pure hatred. "Where is he?"

"In the stairwell, but there's no rush to check. You could have heard his back break all the way across the street."

Colson shook his head and looked down to his lap. He took three deep breaths through his nose and concentrated while he stuck his fingers into the balcony doorframe and prayed he hadn't locked it when he came in. He couldn't remember, but he would know soon enough.

"Look, Colson," the Butcher said, "as much as I'd like to stay and talk about old times, I have more important things to attend to, so—"

It was open only a fraction of an inch, just enough to get four fingers of both hands between the metal casing and doorframe. It would be difficult to get much leverage from a seated position behind his back, but adrenalin and hatred combined to give him a boost. Colson shoved to the left with a snap of his arms, sliding the glass door open fully. With the front door standing open wide, the dead airspace on the street side of the complex created an instantaneous vacuum and rush of air seeking an outlet. It was the same 50 mph wind constantly blasting through the breezeway on the ground floor.

Colson watched as the front door dragged itself away from the wall and slammed with the deafening sound of a shotgun being fired. It slammed with such force that the outer doorknob dislodged and flew like a knuckle ball, colliding with the aluminum railing of the exterior hallway with a sharp CLANG! Sutton spun in a crouch, leveling his pistol at the door. Colson had hoped for more than one second of confusion and he got it. Although Sutton was no better than any other cold-blooded killer currently rotting in prison, his police survival training would remind him not to turn his back on the door too quickly in the event someone had slipped in and ducked into the half-bath to the immediate right of the doorway.

Colson launched himself to his feet. In two long strides he was at the counter, wrapping his hand around the hard rubber handle of his ASP. In the next two strides, Colson raised and fully extended the ASP with a flick of his wrist and swung it straight down to Sutton's right collarbone as if chopping firewood. He felt the metal shaft impact the bone and drive through it, breaking it cleanly in half. Sutton's intense shriek almost surprised Colson. It dwarfed the sound of the door slamming and the knob impacting the railing, but the result was exactly what Colson planned. The pain could be best compared to being stuck with a red-hot poker. Searing pain would be shooting around Sutton's neck and down his right arm, causing his fingers to spring outward.

The pistol fell with a clack on the floor, chipping the tile. Colson kicked the pistol across the floor, and it hit the threshold of the sliding door, briefly took flight, and tumbled perfectly through an opening between the railing and out of sight over the balcony ledge. He gave Sutton a hard shove in the opposite direction, over the recliner and against the wall. Then he darted toward the bedroom and reached for his go-bag, which contained his sole retirement gift—a Glock model 21, .45 caliber semi-automatic. Before he could get his hands on it, a loud POP and a bullet impact to his right diverted him back to the kitchen, where he dropped behind the breakfast bar. A second POP penetrated the breakfast bar and lodged in a crock-pot, obliterating the thick ceramic bowl inside.

Sutton backed against the wall, attempting to steady the Walther PPK in his left hand. He rolled to his knees, stood, and walked around the recliner. His face was contorted as he spoke. "Enough, Major Colson. You think I'm not smart enough to carry my back-up, or did you not pay attention in officer survival training?"

Colson glanced out to the balcony, with his back pressed against the bottom cabinets. There was no other place to go.

"You hand over the laptop and we'll call it a day," Sutton said with a tone of negotiation. Colson didn't gratify his lie with a response. But what was Sutton waiting for? Then he realized Sutton was in too much pain to have seen Colson kick his pistol off the balcony. The police survival training kicked in for Colson this time.

You have to use every tool in the box if you want to survive, he reminded himself.

"Think about it, Sutton," Colson said. "Those deputies will be up here any second since you fired those shots. You don't have any time, and there's no guarantee you'll get away, but there's one thing I can guarantee: you get close enough where I can see that pumpkin head of yours and I'll put a bullet in it. Unlike you, my right hand still works."

Colson waited for Sutton's response, but before Sutton had time to process Colson's words, a second loud THUNK came from the hallway, and a blast of air rushed into Colson's face through the glass doors. Sutton looked down the hallway, aimed his Walther with his left hand at the dark figure running toward him, and fired. The increasing pain in his neck and arm caused his aim to be low. The bullet buried itself in the ceramic tile three feet in front of a charging Jay Taylor, who emerged from the dark hallway in a full sprint.

Sutton's eyes widened at the one-eyed mixed martial arts fighter, wearing a ball cap soaked to the brim with blood. The blood smears across his face and nose made him appear to be a deranged warrior. The hair on Sutton's neck stood as the charging lunatic screamed like a banshee and closed the distance between them before he could adjust his aim. Taylor altered his angle of approach and raised both hands, palms outward, and shoved Sutton with the strength of an NFL defensive lineman.

Colson got to his feet, both amazed and relieved at the sight of Taylor. His friend was almost unrecognizable. For an instant, Colson believed it was Satan himself coming to escort Sutton to his well-deserved, after-life retirement home.

Taylor struck Sutton with the force of a transfer truck, propelling him backward with his arms flailing. Sutton continued his stumbling dance over the sliding door threshold, but he regained enough of his footing to spin and catch himself against the railing with his one functioning arm. But his maneuver failed to slow his momentum. The left side of the railing gave way and buckled under his weight as if Sutton were pushing open a flimsy saloon door. He didn't lose a fraction of speed while somersaulting over the edge of the balcony and disappearing from sight, head first.

Colson's mouth dropped open. He turned to Taylor, who stood bent over with his hands on his knees, taking deep breaths. Colson finally spoke. "You didn't fix the railing like I told you?"

Taylor stood erect, peered at Colson with his good eye, and shrugged.

☙CHAPTER THIRTY❧

Keith took a cab from the airport to the Marietta Diner and found a booth next to the bar. He spent the next hour scribbling on a napkin, thinking of the security measures he would have to overcome, and hoped the equipment he invested in was sufficient for the task. First, there was the fence around the perimeter of the warehouse complex topped with razor wire. He couldn't cut through the fence because it was welded razor mesh constructed of high-tensile steel.

Then there were the closed-circuit cameras recording everything within fifty feet of the buildings and the silent and audible alarms on the warehouse doors protected by the tamper switches. Finally, there was the padlock itself. Getting past all that security would be difficult for the average burglar, but Keith was pretty sure the same alarm company who installed the system at Strawn Towers had set up the same or a similar system at the warehouse, and he had been able to get into Strawn's office without much difficulty.

He watched the low-volume flat screen above the bar when the weather forecast popped up. Still clear and warm with no rain predicted. A thunderstorm was drifting south but was expected to miss the Atlanta area. *Good,* he though. *Rain would hurt more than it will help.*

The news resumed, and Strawn's hideous face blinked on the screen. Keith asked the bartender to turn up the volume. A reporter was talking about Strawn Industries' philanthropic efforts. Strawn went on and on about how the company had saved many future lives with its large donations to fight global warming. Keith shook his head in disgust. The apocalyptic attention given to global warming was a little much, and he knew the truth. The top management at Strawn was actually just a bunch of shallow, greedy opportunists. He also knew the reporter was getting his facts about global warming wrong, but the sheeple—as Colson would say—wouldn't know that, would they? *Typical media hype,* Keith thought. *They always go for sensationalism over the truth every time. It's about selling airtime, not reporting the truth.*

He turned his attention to the medium-rare steak and baked potato on his plate. He still had several hours to burn, and a solid meal of protein would fuel him for the night.

"Who are you calling?" Taylor said, stepping around Colson and onto the balcony.

"Sheriff Langston." Colson punched a contact icon and held his phone to his ear. "His deputies are going to be up here, and—"

"Colson!" Taylor shouted over his shoulder.

Colson held one finger over his ear, trying to listen while the phone rang on the other end. "What?"

"He just shoved Mr. Hammond down at the access gate, and now he's running down the stairs to the beach."

"What are you talking about?" Colson squinted at Taylor's back. He was standing back from the ledge with one hand propped against the sidewall and the other holding onto the doorframe.

"There!" Taylor shouted again, pointing downward.

Colson stepped to the right of Taylor and saw a crippled Sutton plodding through the thick sand near the sea wall, staggering like a drunk with his limp right arm swinging like a pendulum with every step. In his left hand, a stainless steel pistol reflected the early afternoon sun. Sutton stumbled around the tailgate of an SUV backed into the sand, where two young ladies in bikinis lay to the side on beach towels, totally oblivious.

"But how—" Colson looked over the ledge and saw a brightly colored object in the parking space below. "What the hell is that?" Colson completely forgot about his call to Langston. He didn't hear the voice mail answer while holding the phone to his side.

"Some jump castle thing," Taylor replied.

Colson spun and shot through the glass door, dropping his cell phone on the kitchen counter. He collapsed his ASP on the floor, cracking another tile, turned to Taylor, and barked orders in a military tone, as if he were still wearing the oak leaves of a major. "You go down and get those deputies. I'm going after Sutton." He sprinted to the front door.

Two hundred yards south of the Sundowner complex, Crabby Joe's Restaurant and Bar sat midway down the Sunglow fishing pier. The modest one-story structure hovered over the shore of the Atlantic, built of weathered planking painted a creamy yellow. The individual piers supporting Crabby Joe's were barnacle-laden above the waterline in low tide from years of standing in the ever-pounding waves of the Atlantic. A metal placard affixed to a post jutted from the water to warn barefoot swimmers of the razor-sharp growths beneath and sternly cautioned them not to venture further.

A beach scene mural of blues and greens greeted patrons walking the length of the pier toward the entrance. Inside, photographs of celebrities who had visited the infamous location throughout the years decorated both walls of the foyer. At mid-morning, customers occupied a majority of the tables that overlooked Daytona Beach through the open sidewalls, eating omelets made to order and drinking steaming coffee from Styrofoam cups. The rear exit of Crabby Joe's opened to the remaining half of the Sunglow pier, where dozens of early morning fisherman dropped their lines to the surf below.

Sutton had no interest in omelets, coffee, and certainly not fishing as he limped onto the entrance to the pier. His neck and arm felt like an enormous toothache, and his knee was sprained from the fall. He considered himself unbelievably fortunate for landing on whatever that lump of vinyl was in the parking lot. The fall happened so quickly, he hadn't even had a moment for his life to pass before his eyes. There was no police activity in the parking area on the ocean side of the building, but plenty on the other side. The beach was his only escape. Sutton was not accustomed to running away. For a fleeting moment, he experienced the same fight or flight response Harold must have felt before raising his gun in the ranch house the day before.

Sutton knew he would recover and would have his way with Colson—and Strawn—before it was all over. He began to psych himself up for the challenge. It was exhilarating. Until today, everything had been planned, set up, and easy. Now he seemed to be starring in a super-hero action movie, complete with car accidents, chases, and shoot-em-up scenes. A typical person would have been dead by now, but Sutton knew he was exceptional, not typical. He concentrated on walking without limping while dropping the Walther in his pocket and stepping into Crabby Joe's.

Sutton ignored the smiling photographs on the wall, ducked left into the men's room, and shut a stall door behind him. He sat on the toilet seat and allowed the air-conditioning vent overhead to spill cool air on his throbbing head and down his shirt. Within three minutes of sitting beneath the cooling flow, he was ready. He stepped from the stall and washed his face in the sink before slipping around the tables of the main restaurant and out to the fishing end of the pier, paying no attention to the couples dressed in bathing suits and shorts and stuffing their faces. He stopped under an umbrella stuck in the middle of a steel-mesh table and sat where he had a view through the restaurant to the pier entrance.

Sutton saw a black Silverado pickup pull into a parking space. A man stepped out of the driver's side and walked to the tailgate, where he met a young boy. The man reached into the bed of the pickup and removed two fishing poles, handing one to the boy. They walked down the pier and briefly disappeared on the side of the building where those who just wanted to fish could detour around the restaurant. They reappeared and walked past Sutton to a spot on the rail.

Sutton walked up behind the boy just as they were preparing to lower their filament lines, with their backs to the few others concentrating on their own lines. Sutton pulled the Walther from his pocket and set the barrel at the base of the boy's head, where only the man would be able to see. The man jerked his head to the left when he caught Sutton in his peripheral vision and gave him a stunned look.

"Take it easy," Sutton began in a low but normal tone of voice. "All I need is your truck."

"Please," the man pleaded.

"Calm down. We're just going to walk to the truck, you'll give me the keys, and you'll watch me drive away—or I'll be at your house tonight and this boy, you, and anyone else I find there won't live to talk about it. Now slowly hand me your keys."

The man gulped, nodded, and reached in his pocket.

"You walk first, then the boy. Around the side like you came in. Don't turn around or speak to anyone."

The man looked down at the boy and mouthed, "It's okay," then turned to lead the trio over the worn timbers to his left.

"Stop!" The voice came from the far end of the walkway. Sutton looked past the man in front and saw a deputy holding a semi-automatic pistol at low-ready, pointed at an angle to the decking below. The man stopped short, causing the young boy to bump into his back. The deputy began giving the standard commands Sutton himself had given hundreds of times. "You two and the boy, on the ground with your hands to your sides away from your body, palms up."

The man looked over his shoulder at his captor, who nodded approval, but Sutton had no intention of complying with the deputy's demands. The man placed his hand on the boy's shoulder, and they began to ease down to their hands and knees as Sutton raised his Walther and fired two shots at the deputy, striking the corner of the building and the old planking at the deputy's feet. The deputy took aim but didn't return fire in fear of striking the man and boy, who weren't fully out of his sights. Sutton ducked back around the corner amid the screams and footfalls of dozens of people running to the exit of Crabby Joe's, but not everyone was running from the action. As he rounded the corner, Sutton caught a glimpse of Colson running full speed through the center of the restaurant. Sutton stopped and emptied the last three rounds from the magazine of his Walther, but Colson continued his charge. The gun was worthless, and both avenues of escape were blocked.

He quickly limped to the edge of the pier and glanced over, gauging the water's depth. Whitecaps rolled over each other directly beneath his position; there wouldn't be enough depth to safely break his fall. He ignored the pain, ran another thirty feet down the pier, and dragged his frame up onto the railing. More shouting came from behind him.

"Get down off the railing," the deputy yelled, "or I'll shoot!"

Sutton glanced over his shoulder. The deputy stood in a classic Weaver stance with his gun trained at his mid-section. Colson stood with his hands on his hips slightly behind and to the left of the deputy. There were only seconds available to make a decision. Sutton looked down at the surf and estimated the depth of the water at between eight and ten feet. With his good fortune today, he could survive, make it to shore, snatch an unsuspecting teenage driver out of his car, and be at the beach access exit before Colson and the deputy could catch up to him. And no matter what the deputy said, he wasn't going to shoot. That he knew for certain.

"You've used up all your luck, Major," Colson said, exaggerating the title.

Sutton smiled, turned has gaze back to the surf, and slipped off the railing.

Colson had only seen in photos what happened next from a similar incident in 1999. The odds of the same thing happening again were astronomical. He could hardly believe it then and it was almost unbelievable now. He ran to the pier railing. He heard the deputy say something into his radio as he stopped beside him and leaned forward to find Sutton. It took the deputy and Colson a few moments to realize what they were seeing. The deputy was holding his gun to his side when he took two steps back. Colson turned and looked at the ashen-faced deputy, his gaze blank as if in a trance while he tried to holster his gun by feel, missing with both attempts. The deputy collapsed to one knee, bent over on both hands, and spewed vomit across the weathered boards of the old pier. Colson shrugged and laid a hand on the deputy's back while the man spit the remaining remnants of his breakfast on the pier.

Sutton's decision to jump was not completely outrageous—there was probably a good eight to ten feet of water to break his fall. But he never experienced the impact.

The fall itself was uneventful. Sutton' body was positioned as if he were seated in a recliner. He had felt himself dropping and psychologically prepared himself for the hard splash. For a long moment, he had watched the blue horizon in the distance. It seemed to be rising as he fell. But what he couldn't see was the area directly beneath or the sheet metal warning sign affixed to a galvanized post jutting from the water.

If the average Joe were asked to identify the foramen magnum, he might guess that it was the name of the latest action movie, or a semi-automatic pistol manufactured in Prague. The average Jane might say it was the name of a men's cologne—but in fact it is none of the above. The foramen magnum is the opening in the skull through which the spinal cord passes to become the medulla oblongata, turning pesky tasks like maintaining blood pressure, breathing, and heartbeat into involuntary functions. That's a real time-saver, since having to consciously conduct such functions on one's own would require a person's full, undivided attention twenty-four hours a day.

At three feet above the water level, Sutton's body had maintained the recliner position but gained momentum as he fell. As perfect as threading a needle, the six inches of post above the top of the steel sign punched through the skin at the base of his neck and drove its way through the foramen magnum, turning Sutton's medulla oblongata and the better portion of his brain into slush. Once the post reached the top inside of his skull, the weight, and speed of Sutton' bulk ripped his body cleanly away from his head. His body plunged nine feet through the waves to the sandy bottom.

CHAPTER THIRTY-ONE

Sheriff Stuart Langton stood with his hands on his hips and shook his head at the water's edge, watching a paramedic slip a plastic Kwik Mart bag he had found in the fire rescue truck over Sutton's severed head. The scorching noon sun beat down on Langston, roasting him inside his thick polyester uniform. Parallel streams of sweat ran down both sides of his face.

Echoing with the macabre screams of dozens of sunbathers, swimmers, and volleyball players, the beach area around Crabby Joe's was now deserted, with the exception of a handful of CSI investigators, two paramedics, and uniform officers manning the perimeter. After the initial shock, a mob of vacationers had returned to rubberneck from behind the yellow crime scene tape.

Colson stood next to Langston with his hands in his pockets. "What? They're not going to try CPR?" he said.

Langston threw Colson a disgusted look. "You really know how to clear out a crowd, Colson, and you've just turned our day into a total cluster. I don't have enough staff to begin with, and you've given me four crime scenes to work simultaneously." Langston held up his hand and began to count, extending one finger at a time. "One here, one at the souvenir shop, one in the parking lot of the Sundowner, and one in your condo. I won't even have time to scratch my ass until next week. Oh, I almost forgot." Langston held out a legal-sized envelope. "Here are the records you asked for. I think this makes us even."

"Agreed," Colson said, taking the envelope. "Thanks."

Langston sighed and looked back to the paramedic now wading his way back to shore. "Oh, well. This is the first time in my career I've cut a case number before the crime was even committed."

"See, it's all on the up and up," Colson said with a chuckle, patting Langston on the back. "You already had a legit case and didn't even know it."

Colson saw Taylor plodding through the thick sand at the sea wall. He stopped near Colson and Langston, holding a cell phone in each hand. "Colson," he said. "Can I talk to you for a second?

Colson took a few steps away from Langston. "What is it?"

Taylor held up one of the phones. "The shooter dropped this in the condo, so I hooked it up to the computer and jail-broke it."

Colson cocked his head. "Jail-broke it?"

"Never mind," Taylor said with a wave of his hand. "Anyway, they were using a ridiculous keypad encryption, just like if you were typing in the last name of a person to get their extension."

"So it should be easy enough to pin down Strawn as his contact," Colson said, holding up the envelope from Langston.

"Right," Taylor agreed. "I picked it up before the CSI people came in. I haven't had time to go through all the messages yet, but I did play around with it some. Should we give it to Langston?"

Colson thought for a moment. "Later. We'll need it for the time being. What do you mean; you played around with it some?"

Taylor shrugged. "Nothing, really."

"Yeah, right." Colson poked Taylor in the chest with his finger. "Stop tampering with the evidence."

"You're a fine one to be telling me that." Taylor handed him the other phone.

"What?"

"A Teresa Bartlett just called and wants you to call her back ASAP. Says it's urgent."

At 11:40 p.m. Keith Bartlett was dressed in black and crept to the rear of the industrial complex on foot. Tractor-trailers roared past on the interstate behind the property. Night vision equipment enabled him to see the uniformed officer who would be making the next perimeter patrol seated in the security truck near the front gate drinking a cup of coffee. He knew he had less than thirty minutes to get over the fence, inside the building, and then back out again.

It took him less than a minute to climb the fence in back of the warehouse. After placing a folded Kevlar blanket over the sharp wire at the top, he eased over and down the other side, taking the blanket with him. He moved quietly from shadow to shadow until he reached the back door of warehouse number 11. The electronic jamming device in the side pocket of his black camo pants prevented all the video cameras within ninety feet from recording his movements. He realized the cameras were flanked by spotlights, but he was familiar with this system and knew the lights were wired into the cameras and would only come on if the cameras were activated.

He knelt down next to the building and disabled the tamper switches on the audible alarm, and then he cut the phone line and power to the silent alarm. Finally, he pulled the lock gun from his backpack and inserted the tension bar and picking needle into the door's padlock. After two clicks of the gun's trigger, the lock released.

He opened the door slowly and looked inside. The night vision equipment wouldn't work without ambient light, so he clicked on a small pocket flashlight. The narrow beam illuminated more than a dozen rows of large propane tanks, stacked up like a pyramid of cannon balls he had seen at the Kennesaw battlefield, each group of tanks held together with metal straps. He shrugged, let his backpack slide off his shoulder to the concrete floor, and removed a SABRE 4000 contraband detector from a zipper pocket. The $8,000 portable unit weighed only seven pounds and had a battery life of four hours. It was more than Keith was willing to spend, so he felt lucky the retailer had agreed to rent it for a day.

The man told him the unit required a ten-minute cold start time, so he had made a mental note to switch the power on before climbing the fence. He pointed the instrument at the nearest stack of tanks and waited for the three-inch color screen to respond. Within ten seconds, the display read

Presence of Heroin Detected.

He moved to the next row of tanks and knelt, pointing the device at the bottom tank.

Presence of Cocaine Detected.

One more stack. He waited a couple of minutes for the screen to clear and then pointed the SABRE at the third stack:

Presence of Methamphetamine Detected.

Keith released a low whistle and remembered something Colson had said. Heroin, coke, and meth—the unholy trio of drug abuse. All three could be injected, snorted, or smoked. Heroin could be heated and the vapors inhaled, or as Colson called it, "Chasing the dragon." And heroin could be mixed with coke or meth to create a speedball.

Shaking his head in disbelief, Keith returned the detection device to his backpack. He had to get this information to the police as quickly as possible. He could not allow one gram of this deadly powder to hit the streets, knowing how many lives it would ruin.

He walked to the stairs leading to a mesh steel catwalk circling the warehouse and climbed fast. When he reached the catwalk, he sprinted to the side opposite the stairs. From there, in the glow of his flashlight, he saw the interior warehouse space was about three hundred by one hundred feet—larger than he first thought—and filled with row after row of stacked propane tanks.

He took out his phone, disabled the flash, and snapped photos of individual stacks, illuminating each with the small flashlight. The broad shots of the entire interior might be too dark to make out, but he would send all of them to Colson and Agent Floyd regardless.

In the southwest corner of the catwalk, overlooking the storage area was a framed wood-and-sheetrock partition of enclosed offices with windows cut in the sides. He removed his lock pick gun, slipped into one of the offices, and went directly to the computer on the corner desk. He booted up the CPU and set the monitor on the floor facing the wall to hide the screen's glow from the main area below. He removed a flash drive from his backpack, stuck it into a

USB slot on the front side of the hard drive tower, and repeated the process of downloading the data as he had in Strawn's office. He sat on the floor and waited, checking his watch: 12:22 a.m. Depending on the amount of information, he should be on his way out the door in three to five minutes.

Keith stiffened at the vibration of his cell phone. No one should be calling him at this hour. He bent over low, cupped the screen with his hand, and looked at the display. Grey Colson's name hovered over his number on the home screen. He almost answered it, but hesitated. As a former cop, it would have been pretty easy for Colson to guess what Keith had planned for tonight, but he was back in Florida, and nothing he could say would stop Keith. He let the call go to voice mail.

"Well, it's about damned time," Strawn said, taking a long draw on his cigar.

Haggart grinned, dropped down into the chair across from Strawn, and crossed his legs. Strawn may even give him a bonus for his effective and quick handling of the assassin. It was just this morning when Strawn ordered him to send the hired killer to Florida after Colson's smart-ass phone call last night. He would never admit the assassin was two steps ahead of the game and already in Daytona on Colson's trail.

Strawn laid his cigar in the ashtray and gave Haggart a serious stare. "When?"

"Ah," Haggart said, "around noon today."

"You're expecting me to believe that you called your guy late yesterday afternoon and told him to find and kill Colson, and he does it in, what, less than twenty-four hours, plus he recovered the laptop?"

Haggart hesitated, squirming a bit. Maybe he should have told Strawn that the assassin was already in place when he called, but it was too late to admit lying. Actually, there was never a good time to admit lying to Strawn. Before he could formulate an explanation, Strawn held his hands out in a questioning manner and continued.

"After three weeks of jacking me around, he couldn't even find a teenage girl, but I'm supposed to believe he flew out of state and took care of Colson that quickly. What kind of independent verification do you have?"

Haggart shifted in his seat. "Well, he texted me that—"

"I don't give a damn about a text." Strawn pounded his fat fist on the table. "You and this—this assassin of yours—think I'm that stupid?"

Haggart could only shake his head and let the belligerent man continue. If given time, Strawn would see his independent verification, but Strawn never allowed anyone to finish a full sentence without one of his explosive eruptions. He would be fine once Strawn permitted him to speak again. Until then, there was nothing Haggart could do but entertain his boss's furious diatribe.

Strawn picked up his cigar with one hand and pointed across the desk at Haggart with the other. "He's not getting one dime transferred until I have irrefutable verification of Colson's death."

Now it was Haggart's turn to prove his thoroughness and worth to Strawn. "If I may," he began, clearing his throat, "I did obtain independent verification, sir. First, I received his coded text around eleven-thirty this morning, telling me the job was done and the computer was retrieved. Then I spoke with an ex-trainer of mine who operates an MMA gym right off of A1A near the main pier. He was in the area of the Sundowner Condos and was stuck in traffic where the police blocked off the street and appeared to be conducting an investigation."

"So? They do that all the time," Strawn said.

"Yes, sir. But there's more. He told me he saw a totaled out green Corvette in the parking lot with crime scene tape around it. And then there's this." Haggart leaned across Strawn's desk and set his tablet in front of the boss.

"What's this?" Strawn asked, slipping on his reading glasses and focusing in on the *Daytona Beach News Journal's* web page. The title caught his eye first.

Man Decapitated After Falling from Pier

315

Terrified tourists fled a gruesome accident scene today when an unidentified man fell from Crabby Joe's pier and was decapitated as a result.

Sheriff Stuart Langston told reporters he could not comment due to the extensive investigation being conducted at multiple locations in the South Daytona Beach area and would not reveal the identity of the victim until family notification was made. The sheriff added the incident was being considered a homicide until the investigation revealed otherwise.

One source close to the scene describe the victim as a white male in his late forties or early fifties and a second confidential source within the department told a reporter the man had identification on his person, indicating he was employed as a major with a sheriff's office in Georgia.

Out of respect for the family, the source refused to reveal the name of the victim or which department he was employed with. More to come in tomorrow's print and online edition of the Daytona Beach News Journal.

Strawn peered at Haggart over his reading glasses and smiled his approval.

The security guard stepped out of the restroom in the front office, stretched, and checked his watch. It was 12:30 a.m., but it felt like it should already be 6:00 a.m. and time to clock out. He adjusted his gun belt, giving the old, worn leather a disgusted look. Strawn made billions, but they claimed their security budget limited them to issue this shoddy hand-me-down equipment from the city police department. They must have spent the bulk of the budget on his issued Sig Sauer P229 nine millimeter with night sights. But what army was going to break into a furniture warehouse? The retired twenty-year army veteran shrugged. At least the salary was better than he had expected, and the shift differential was a nice added benefit.

The guard stepped into the vast warehouse and looked for the hundredth time at the freestanding rows of giant industrial shelving packed with enough plastic-wrapped furniture to fill a skyscraper. It was similar to walking through one of those popular warehouse clubs, but the merchandise was difficult to see and impossible to reach without a forklift. His routine for the interior (after lunch and a restroom break of course) was to walk each row twice before relieving his buddy in the gatehouse for the remainder of the shift.

The rear of the warehouse was a bit of a mystery. He was told never to venture there unless there was an emergency. The warehouse manager had made those orders quite clear the day the guard was hired.

"Unless you have a very good reason to enter the back warehouse, just leave it alone." He had motioned to the two-story storage racks. "This is where the valuable merchandise is. We use the back to store the propane tanks for our transport trucks. You check the locks on the double doors leading to the back, the outside entrance, and the loading dock rolling doors."

"Yes, sir." The guard had nodded. "If I find a door has been breached, I call the police?"

"No," the manager had snapped. "You'll have my cell number. I have it with me at all times. You'll call me and only me."

"Yes, sir."

"It's not that we don't trust you or the rest of the security team," the manager had said, "but there have been too many problems in the past with security employees sneaking back there to sleep through their shifts or to have a little play time with their girlfriends. One was caught on camera smoking back there around all that propane. Can you imagine our liability if we permitted that?"

"Certainly, sir." And he still understood the manager's words to this day and had never violated his directive. He was a military man and always followed orders without question, but the only thing bugging him was the lack of trust. He would never sleep or have sex on the job, and he hadn't smoked in a decade. You should always trust your troops, even with your life. He shook off his minor frustration and began walking among the towering furniture. It was on his second round that he heard a noise from the forbidden area of the warehouse.

Keith nodded with satisfaction when he read Download Complete on the monitor. He removed the flash drive from the computer and peeked over the sill of the window. Nothing had changed. No lights, no movement, no sound. He put the flash drive away and clicked the small flashlight back on before the monitor lapsed into power saver mode, leaving him in total darkness. He would have to hurry; he had forgotten to put a new lithium battery in the flashlight, and it was going dim.

Keith slipped out of the office, locked the door, and trotted around the catwalk to the stairs. Half way down he heard something, but he couldn't make out if it was the scuffing of feet or the scurrying of a rat. The sound made him freeze. He swung the dimming flashlight right and left but saw nothing. He felt in his pocket for the old Smith & Wesson .38 special revolver his dad had left him in his will and wished he had asked Colson to teach him how to shoot it. Colson probably would have tried to talk him out of it, considering the recent circumstances and his emotional state. He never intended to use it unless his life was in danger, but this could be that moment.

By the time he reached the bottom step, the flashlight provided very little ambient light for the night vision to amplify. He aimed the light toward the exit and turned his body at the same angle to make a straight walk for it if the light went out. And it did—an instant after the thought passed through his mind.

Keith pushed his goggles up his forehead and stood on the concrete floor in total darkness, his body angled in the direction he set for the exit. He held the gun low and was pointing it directly ahead when he felt it being ripped from his hand. An instant later, he was jerked violently backward. The back of his heels struck something solid. He waved his arms in the pitch darkness and fell against a pyramid of propane tanks, with his backpack taking the brunt of the impact. The night vision goggles jumped from his head and bounced down the stack of tanks to the floor, clacking loudly in the relative silence of the cavernous warehouse.

Keith slid down the propane tanks and dropped to his butt, disoriented. He quickly got up into a crouch and moved to his left, feeling for the back wall. A sliver of light flooded the darkness of the room, revealing a man standing five feet in front of him—pointing his dad's old revolver at his head.

CHAPTER THIRTY-TWO

A gent Floyd looked at his bedside clock for the third time in the last half hour. It read 1:10 a.m. He eased the sheet down, swung his legs over the bed, and rested his head in his hands. He had always heard it wasn't healthy to take your work home with you. Some people could get away with that, but he'd never had the luxury of leaving work at work. Not in police work.

There was an old saying his buddies used to recite years ago and laugh about—"Little cases, little problems. Big cases, big problems. No cases—no problems." Floyd found himself laughing along with them, but that's when they were working the street and a big case was considered a three-page report.

Floyd's head swirled with information, details, and deadlines. The F-5 Task Force was currently working a dozen high-priority cases with more than one hundred lower-priority complaints floating in the background. And he was being held responsible for coordinating, prioritizing, and assigning them, as well as reporting updates of their progress to his superiors. A city councilmen and a county manager misappropriating funds, nineteen local firefighters suspected of steroid use, and of course, his "pet" case: the elusive Jack Strawn.

The two-year-old case was set aside half a dozen times to work on time-critical cases, and it was about to be set aside for good. Floyd was sick of beating his head against the wall and losing sleep over the billionaire. His supervisor was tired of hearing about it and was probably right when he said too much time and valuable resources were being expended on, as he called it, Floyd's "career case."

He had put the matter to bed and actually felt liberated of the headache until Sergeant Robbins called him yesterday demanding to know what the hell Colson was doing and where he was. Robbins insisted Colson was off the chain and had either witnessed the murder of his deputy or committed the murder himself.

Floyd resigned himself to another sleepless night. He walked to the kitchen to make coffee, then sank into his black leather recliner in his townhouse living room, clicked the remote on the stereo, and waited for the beep to announce the caffeine was ready for consumption. He closed his eyes and tried to think of something—anything—but work, when he heard the sound. But it wasn't the coffee maker.

"What now?" Floyd said aloud, grabbing his cell phone off the glass-top coffee table. "Who the hell would be calling at this...?" His voice trailed off, and his expression of mild frustration turned to puzzlement when he saw the caller's name on the screen.

Keith's mouth dropped open at the sight of the man in the black watch cap who was pointing his own revolver at him. A wave of relief swept over him when the man shifted his stance, pointing the gun toward the source of the light behind him.

"Leave the door open, step inside, hold your hands out where I can see them, and don't touch your radio," Colson said—but he wasn't talking to Keith.

Keith stuck his head around the stack of propane tanks and saw an older man in a security guard uniform. He snapped a look back at Colson. "It's you?"

Colson didn't acknowledge Keith, keeping his focus on the guard. "Please step over here and join us."

The guard reluctantly complied. "Look, mister," he said, "you won't get any trouble from me—I'm retired."

"That's a coincidence—so am I," Colson said with a slight smile. "Just sit over there with your back against the wall, and you'll be fine." Colson nodded to Keith while keeping his gun trained on the guard. "Take his gun and radio."

The guard raised his arms and rested the backs of his hands against the cold cinder block wall as Keith unclipped his lapel mic and slid the radio from his belt and set it on the floor. Keith started for the gun but hesitated, looking back at Colson.

"Level three?" Colson said to the guard, who acknowledged with an affirmative nod. "Okay, press down on the top strap and rock it forward," Colson said, instructing Keith through each step. "Depress the button you'll find at the back of the trigger guard and simultaneously rock the gun back to pull it out."

"What are you going to do?" the guard asked.

Colson ignored the guard's query and switched guns with Keith. "Nice hand gun. It's an expensive one for a guard in a furniture warehouse. Now open the case on the back of his belt and cuff him."

Keith hesitated a moment, lowering his voice. "How did you know? I mean, who…?"

"Your wife was worried," Colson said, cutting him off. "She said you left home without a kitchen pass, so I caught the next flight."

"She's home. She wasn't supposed to come back until tomorrow." Keith handcuffed the guard and returned to stand by Colson.

Colson sighed. "Well, you know what they say about the best laid plans. She read me your note. What do you expect a wife to do when you tell her if you aren't back in twenty-four hours to call me?"

Keith smiled. "But it worked out," he said, gesturing to the rows of propane tanks. "Strawn has a warehouse full of heroin, cocaine, and meth."

"Wait—what?" the security guard said, sounding shocked.

Keith eagerly pointed to three different areas of the warehouse. "There, that's cocaine over there. That stack is heroin and," he turned to the stack Colson had pushed him into, "this one is full of meth."

The guard shook his head in disgust and said, "Ridiculous."

"Oh?" Colson pulled a small crowbar from a loop in his BDU pants, shoved the guard's gun in his large side pocket, and walked past Keith to the stack of tanks. He seated the end of the crowbar in the seam of one of the tanks and leaned his weight forward, pushing hard on the opposite end for leverage. It didn't move for a moment, but then the top end popped opened half an inch. He repeated the move two more times, once at the five o'clock and once at the nine o'clock position on the round face of the tank. Keith looked over Colson's shoulder as he removed the end of the tank and laid it on the concrete floor. The guard leaned forward and craned his head to look.

"Is that how they pack it?" Keith asked, looking at the tightly wrapped, off-white-and-tan-colored blocks filling the cavity of the tank. "It looks completely full of them."

"I'm sure it is," Colson said.

"I don't believe it," the guard said. "We confiscated those types of packages once from a cargo plane that flew into Warner Robins. I still can't believe that all this time—"

"I believe you," Colson said to the guard. "When will the other guard be looking for you?"

"He won't," the guard said. "It's my turn on foot patrol until six, but he'll radio me from time to time."

Keith turned in a circle, surveying the massive warehouse. "I can't believe there's just the two of you guarding this stuff."

"I can," Colson said. "An army of guards would draw a lot of suspicion. Strawn obviously has been accumulating these drugs for years, and there's never been a hitch in his operation until now. He's become too comfortable."

The guard looked at Colson. "Are you guys the police? You said you believed me. You aren't gonna arrest me for this, are you? I had nothing to do with—"

"No," Colson said. "No, we're not the police and no, we're not going to arrest you or hurt you."

"What now?" Keith asked.

Colson stood silent for a long moment. "That's the problem."

Keith crossed his arms. "What problem? You said if a concerned, upstanding citizen..."

"I know what I said, and although you are a concerned citizen, you're not upstanding right now because neither of us are where we are legally supposed to be. And having that gun," Colson said, pointing to the revolver in Keith's hand, "during the commission of burglary is yet another felony. And all this?" Colson extended his arms to make the point. "Well, the police will gladly seize all of it, regardless of our crimes here tonight, but you—we—will go to jail right along with Strawn. Are you willing to make that sacrifice?"

Keith lowered his head for a moment in thought and then looked back to Colson with a determined stare. "Yes, I am."

Colson nodded and raised his cell phone.

"You calling Meador?" Keith asked.

With his back to the security guard, Colson held his index finger to his lips and shook his head in the negative.

"What will my wife do now?" Keith muttered.

Colson held his finger over Floyd's contact icon on the screen. "That's why I asked you the question. Look, I can't imagine losing a child, but I can almost predict how I would react. But you still have a wife, a home, a job, and more importantly, another son. You can't forget that."

Keith turned away and slammed both fists down on top of a methamphetamine-stuffed tank. "This shit killed my son!" he bellowed and began to sob, repeatedly pounding the tank.

Colson walked over to Keith and rested his hand on his back. "I'm sorry, but what's done is done." He stood behind Keith, trying to think of any alternative, but there was none.

"I'll tell them," the guard said from his seated position on the cold floor.

With his concentration on Keith, Colson didn't make out what the man had said at first. "What?"

The guard glared at Colson, "I said I'll tell the police I found it."

Colson walked toward the guard and stopped two feet away, looking down at him. "You'll lose your job, mister—"

"Walker," the guard said, finishing Colson's sentence. "Ralph Walker, retired master sergeant, United States Army. I don't have a job. I won't work for drug dealers."

Colson gave Walker a grin and bent over to help him to his feet. He unclipped the keys from the guard's duty belt and released him from his handcuffs. "You're a good man, Master Sergeant Walker." Colson reached in his pocket, handed over the Sig Sauer, and touched Floyd's contact icon.

"You're bullshitting me, Colson," Floyd barked into the phone. "You're crazy. I can almost understand the kid's dad, but you know better." Floyd paced the room with the cell phone to his ear. "You've put me in a no-win scenario here. I have a good mind to come down there and put the cuffs on you myself and—"

Floyd was interrupted, so he listened. He walked to the kitchen counter, ignoring the beeping coffee pot, and grabbed a pen and note pad from a cabinet drawer. He stared at the darkness beyond the window above the sink as he considered Colson's proposal. He closed his eyes and made the decision. "What's his name?" he asked, scribbling furiously on the pad. "Fine. I'm going to wake up the entire task force. In the meantime," he said, glancing at the wall clock, "I'm sending a squadron of uniform cars there. You have no more than ten minutes to get your ass off the property."

The vast sea of blue strobe lights surrounding the perimeter fence and inner building of Strawn's massive warehouse could have been seen from space at 2:00 a.m. The stunned gate guard stood talking with the warehouse manager, scratching his head. Both had been identified and had already given their statements to an investigator assigned by Floyd. Both were also instructed to remain on scene for further questioning, but the second guard was more curious than concerned, asking the manager what in the world was going on.

On the other hand, the manager stood stone-faced, knowing very well what was going on but having no intention of admitting it. He received the call from the gate guard when the convoy of police units and unmarked cars screeched to a halt at the gate. The ten-minute drive allowed him sufficient time to alert Strawn before he arrived to play the role of ignorant warehouse manager.

"That's ridiculous," the manager said when questioned by the detective.

The detective scribbled a note in his pad. "You expect me to believe you've worked here for over five years and never, even once, inspected the rear of the warehouse?" he said without looking up.

The manager nodded vigorously. "That's exactly right." He gestured to the gate guard. "He can verify that. None of the workers were permitted in the back. I was told to pass those instructions on to every employee."

The detective held up his hand to stop the manager. "Don't worry about the guard. I'll talk to him in a minute. So you were told to never enter the rear of the warehouse?"

"Yes, it's the truth."

The detective scribbled again and looked into the manager's eyes. "Fine. Who gave you those instructions?"

"Mr. Strawn's executive assistant, Clay Haggart," he answered without hesitation.

The detective took both the manager and gate guard's I.D.s and told them to stay put until he returned. Three dark blue sedans drove slowly toward the entrance and stopped at the gate. The man in the lead car rolled down his window and motioned for the detective with his credentials in hand.

"Agent Hadaway, DEA," the driver said to the detective. "I need to speak with your incident commander."

"That would be Agent Floyd," the detective said. "Did he call you guys?"

Agent Hadaway shrugged. "All I know is my supervisor woke us up and told us to get our asses down here."

"I'll have to radio him and let him know," the detective said and pointed to the warehouse. "Take the right access road to the rear."

"Thanks," Hadaway said, and led the two rear cars through the gate as his cell phone rang.

"Yes," he said into the phone. "Yes, sir, we just arrived."

Hadaway paused and listened to his instructions and acknowledged. "I'll pass it on, sir. We've got it from here."

Floyd stood amidst the stacks of propane tanks with his ear to his cell phone. He still had difficulty believing the amount of drugs contained in the hundreds of tanks. Strawn had to have been accumulating them for years. He tried to concentrate on what his detective was saying while pondering where to store the huge number of tanks.

"The manager and gate guard are saying they were instructed to never enter the rear of the warehouse," the detective explained.

"The guard inside said the same, and I'm inclined to believe him for now, but you have to listen fast—get down to the magistrate's office and secure a search warrant for this and the other warehouses ASAP. APD and the Fulton County Police are already on their way to secure the other locations, so don't waste any time."

"Yes, sir," the detective answered. "There's an Agent Hadaway with DEA driving back to see you."

"DEA?" Floyd said.

"Yes," Hadaway said, walking up behind Floyd and extending his hand.

"Who called you in?" Floyd asked without returning the gesture. "This is APD's case."

Hadaway held up his hands in surrender. "Don't kill the messenger," he said. "I didn't just wake myself up and decide to go on a drive through a warehouse complex. My group supervisor, Donny Augustine, called after the SAC called him at home."

Floyd tilted his head. "Someone had to call your Special Agent-in-Charge—unless he has ESP."

"Look," Hadaway continued, "I'd just as soon still be in bed, but we do what we're told to do right? Augustine called again a minute ago. He said Strawn had called the SAC."

Floyd's eyebrows rose. "Strawn?"

"Yep," Hadaway nodded. "Augustine said Strawn wanted to let whoever was in charge know, and I quote, that he doesn't trust the 'locals' and 'wants to know what debauchery is going on at his warehouse.' Unquote."

ᑕᔑᗩCHAPTER THIRTY-THREEᑭᔕᑐ

Taylor pulled the rental car next to Keith's rental and stopped. Colson glanced in the rear-view mirror from the passenger side and saw Keith bent over in the back seat, with his head in his hands. The sirens were still distant, but their wails would no doubt grow in intensity as the police units began to arrive in less than a minute.

"You okay?" Colson said to the rear-view mirror. "You need to get that car out of here before APD swoops down on us."

Keith raised his head a fraction of an inch. "I feel sick."

Colson craned his head around and reached back to pat Keith's shoulder. "You'll be okay when the adrenalin subsides, but you need to move."

Keith nodded, brushed his hair back, and pushed the rear door open. "How do you do this stuff, Colson?"

Colson grinned. "I don't. Remember, I'm retired. Now go home to your wife and son."

Taylor pulled away once Keith got behind the wheel and drove off. "What happened in there?" he asked.

"Long story."

Taylor nodded. "There are several more coded messages on Sutton's phone I de-coded on the flight. If I can get Haggart's phone, I bet they'll match."

Colson sat in silence, staring out the window. "I could have easily been locked up tonight," he finally said and turned to Taylor. "Still could be if the wheels fall off this plan."

"So, you think this will do it? Be enough to put Strawn away?" he asked.

Colson sighed. "Under normal circumstances, yes. It seems like a slam dunk, but I learned a long time ago not to count my bad guys until they were convicted."

The news of the three warehouse seizures and tons of cocaine, heroin, and methamphetamine with an estimated value of well over a half-billion dollars made national news for over two weeks. A fourth warehouse was located under a fake company name containing the most sophisticated, clean, and well-organized meth lab the DEA had ever seized. A team of specially trained meth lab agents wearing hazmat suits swarmed the location to make it safe and break it down before allowing the case agents to inventory and test the hundreds of pounds of the highly addictive substance.

With the vast amounts of evidence involved, moving such a quantity was not only costly, but too risky to even comprehend. Tractor-trailer loads would require a convoy of armed agents to protect them from hijacking attempts. Finding a location to securely store the tanks was almost impossible, and accusations of dirty agents liberating a few kilos during transport would never cease, so the U.S. attorney quickly decided to have the drugs inventoried, weighed, and tested on site. A team of laboratory agents, flown in from Miami, spent the next ten days testing the contents of each package, one by one. Eight U.S. marshals were detailed to each warehouse to arrest the property as evidence and stand guard twenty-four hours per day, with a relief shift of another eight marshals every twelve hours. The outer perimeter of each property was also monitored twenty-four hours a day by a brigade of local uniformed officers on their off days, their salaries subsidized by DEA funds.

Strawn's team of attorneys pleaded with him not to speak with the media, but he insisted and, as usual, got his way. The four attorneys flanked Strawn, two on each side, as he staunchly denied any knowledge of the drugs.

"I understand how this appears," Strawn explained, waving his cigar in a small circle, "but just because I propose drugs be legalized doesn't mean I don't abide by the rule of law. Quite the opposite." Strawn placed his hand on his chest as he continued. "I'm the one who was trying to pursue every legal avenue to provide every citizen the right to possess and use their substance of choice. Any reasonable person would know I wouldn't donate so much of my personal time and considerable expense had it been my intention to break the laws of our great county."

Strawn's attorneys sat silent as they had been instructed, each resisting the urge to stand and collectively place their hands over Strawn's mouth as he continued. "Hell, I was the one who called the DEA and insisted they take over the investigation. If guilty of any wrongdoing, I could have just as easily been on my jet and off to a country without an extradition treaty with the U.S."

Strawn patted his hand lightly on the long table and looked directly into the bank of television cameras. "If I were involved in any crime, I would be in federal custody this very minute. I have cooperated fully with the federal authorities and have turned over all my facilities for them to complete their investigation. I have every confidence their investigation will reveal the individual or individuals who have taken advantage of my reputable business in an effort to halt the ongoing legislative efforts to provide Americans the freedom of choice our founders fought and died for."

In reality, if Strawn had been a mid- or even upper-level drug dealer, he would be sitting in federal detention. But people like Strawn, who are mercifully rare, tend to give law enforcement and prosecutors a moment of pause. Not necessarily because of their pseudo celebrity status, but rather their power, influence and significant campaign contributions. Agent Floyd knew there was more than enough probable cause to shove Strawn in the back of a caged police unit and cart him off to jail, given the abundance of evidence collected; however, recent history has clearly demonstrated that juries have been coerced into believing the term "proof beyond a reasonable doubt" literally means, "proof beyond all doubt," leaving prosecutors and police with a dilemma. They had to have all their ducks in a perfect row and quacking in harmony before they locked up an influential person such as Strawn, or they might soon be applying for Master Sergeant Ralph Walker's recently vacated security guard position.

Sweat beaded and ran down the side of former security guard Ralph Walker's face before he could swipe it with his hand. He sat on his screen porch in deep thought, his bottle of beer resting on a napkin drenched to the point of saturation. He hadn't taken a sip in an hour. An ear-piercing screech broke his concentration. His granddaughters were playing with the water hose in the back yard, and one had just sprayed a cold blast of water on the other.

He wiped his brow with his forearm, reconsidering his actions from that night just two weeks ago. He still considered what he had done as noble and good, but now he wished it had been someone else in the back of the warehouse. *Damn,* he thought to himself. *Why wasn't I in the gatehouse, leaving the other guard to surprise the intruders?* He watched the news coverage every day, and he had caught Strawn's press conference. There was plenty of time to watch TV, since he was no longer employed. He shook his head. Was there a chance Strawn wasn't aware of the drugs? But the most important question was, what would now happen to his family if it ever came out that he didn't tell the whole story to the police? How could he cope in jail at his age for making false statements, and what might the great and powerful Strawn do to his family? Sue him for every penny he had? Or possibly sever him from his military pension while he spent the last few years of his life in prison, never to see or hold his granddaughters again.

"Daddy," Ralph's daughter said, sticking her head through the porch door, "there's a man at the front door. He has a U.S. Marshal's badge and says he needs to speak with you."

Ralph sprang to his feet and gave his daughter an empty stare. "Did he say what he wanted?"

"No," she replied. "Are you okay?"

Ralph only nodded, stepped around her, and walked to the front door of his modest ranch home of thirty-five years. He opened the door to a clean-cut young man in a smartly pressed gray suit.

"Mr. Ralph Walker?" the young man said.

"Yes,"

The marshal held out a piece of paper. "I have a subpoena for you. It's for a deposition."

The U.S. attorney for the northern district of Georgia, Reid Kennedy, was well aware of the consequences of jumping the gun in such a high-profile case. The media attention was overwhelming, with each network and cable outlet conducting public polls as to whether Strawn was guilty of drug trafficking or if they believed the government had set him up to squelch his efforts to legalize drugs. The numbers were unexpected. Polling in the first week was strongly in favor of the government, with seventy-eight percent support, eighteen percent in favor of the conspiracy theory, and four percent undecided. But since Strawn's public national address and endless support of the liberal press, the numbers had flip-flopped: fifty-six percent in Strawn's favor, thirty-nine percent in support of the government, and five percent undecided.

The answer was not to arrest Strawn with a warrant, based on the affidavit of a single DEA agent, but to present the case directly to a federal grand jury and arrest him pursuant to a true bill of indictment. It wouldn't silence all the conspiracy theorists, but should tone down the rhetoric. The case was scheduled for grand jury presentation in less than ten days. The U.S. attorney wasn't the least bit surprised that Strawn's high-dollar attorneys were ready for it.

The Richard Russell Federal Building is located on Spring Street in Midtown Atlanta. Built in 1978, the twenty-six-floor structure, named in honor of a former Georgia governor and U.S. senator, is unremarkable for its off-white exterior and rectangular shape. Strawn occasionally scoffed at its squat appearance from his penthouse office whenever he bothered to take notice.

In anticipation of the grand jury's decision, Strawn's lead counsel petitioned the court for a hearing immediately following the issuance of the indictment. But considering the overwhelming evidence, U.S. Attorney Kennedy could only suspect the hearing was nothing more than a delay tactic by Strawn's counsel.

Kennedy and the assistant U.S. attorney were fully prepared and arrived thirty minutes early with Agent Hadaway's case summary, a copy of the indictment, and a cardboard box stuffed with neatly labeled supporting documents at their feet. At 8:55 a.m., Strawn marched through the twelve-foot-high mahogany doors, followed by his lead counsel. Both silently slid into their respective seats at the defense table. Strawn's attorney carried only a slim briefcase, which he set on the table and clicked open.

Kennedy narrowed his gaze and turned to his assistant. "Only one attorney? What do you think they're up to?"

The assistant could only shrug his shoulders, while a uniformed guard swung open the courtroom doors for the press and general public to enter. A handful of metro police chiefs and sheriffs were permitted entry first and took seats in the pews directly behind the prosecution table. Two uniformed guards stood back to allow the remaining mob of curious citizens to funnel into the courtroom, cramming themselves into benches and standing along the back wall. Since no cameras were permitted, members of the press held small notepads and pens at the ready, not wanting to miss one syllable of testimony. With the exception of the scuffling of shoes as onlookers squeezed past others seated in the wooden benches and the occasional clearing of throats, the courtroom sat silent until a bailiff wearing a dark blue blazer stepped through a door to the side.

"All rise. The United States Federal Court for the northern district of Georgia is now in session, the Honorable Quinton Carter presiding," the bailiff announced in a strong, even voice.

Judge Carter lumbered through a door directly behind the bench in his official black robe. He slipped on a pair of reading glasses while taking his seat. "You may be seated," he said, looking across the room at Strawn and quickly cutting his eyes to the prosecution table. He sighed and adjusted the microphone down an inch. "Mr. Kennedy, you may begin."

"Your Honor," Kennedy said, rising to his feet with the indictment in one hand and pressing his dark blue tie down against his crisp white shirt with the other, "This is case number CR-14072 in the matter of the United States verses Jack Wellington Strawn. As the court is aware, the grand jury handed down this true bill of indictment

334

yesterday morning. Sufficient probable cause has been established for trial, and I find it unorthodox at best to hold a pre-arrest hearing to determine what the members of the grand jury have already affirmed."

Judge Carter nodded and shuffled through papers on the stand. Kennedy could see only the top of the page Carter was reading above the raised mahogany portion of the bench. The judge spoke, keeping his eyes on the document. "This, Mr. Kennedy, is a motion to suppress hearing, not a pre-arrest hearing."

Kennedy glanced briefly back to his assistant and Agent Hadaway seated in the first row behind the half wall. His assistant sat bewildered; Agent Hadaway was looking down at his hands. "One moment, Your Honor," Kennedy said, stepping back to the prosecution table and lifting a document. "It's on the calendar for pre-arrest, your honor; my office was not notified of—"

"Consider yourself notified," the judge said, cutting off the prosecutor. "Now, if you are not prepared to continue, I can reset the motion hearing for later this afternoon."

Kennedy couldn't imagine why Strawn's attorney would even dream of making a motion to suppress such a massive amount of evidence. At least not until trial as a desperate first move. He had no idea where this was going, but was confident Strawn would only be leaving the courtroom under the escort of United States marshals.

"Your Honor, if it please the court, the government is ready."

"Mr. Darby, you may proceed," the judge said to the lead defense attorney, who now stood with both hands resting on the defense table.

"Thank you, Your Honor." Darby pulled two copies of stapled documents from his brief case, stepped to the prosecution table, and handed one copy to Kennedy before readdressing the court. "This was filed an hour ago for the court, and I apologize for not providing a copy to Mr. Kennedy earlier, but this was my first opportunity." Darby turned to the judge, holding the packet a little higher. "I move to suppress all the evidence in this case and request the indictment be dismissed immediately."

Kennedy shot to his feet. "If it please the court, on what does the defense base this ridiculous motion?"

"On evidence obtained illegally," Darby said, turning to face Kennedy.

"Order," the judge snapped, slapping his desk with his gavel. "You'll have your say, Mr. Kennedy. Now, continue, Mr. Darby."

"Your Honor," Darby began, "the document submitted is a sworn deposition of former Strawn Industries Security Officer Ralph Walker. He admits in the deposition that he walked in on two unidentified intruders in the warehouse who held him at gunpoint and contacted an agent with the police department."

Kennedy looked over his shoulder, giving Agent Hadaway a piercing stare. Hadaway leaned forward and whispered to Kennedy, "I don't know anything about any so-called intruders. That's bullshit."

Kennedy stood. "I object, Your Honor. The guard plainly stated he heard a suspicious noise from the rear of the warehouse and located the drugs himself." He held out his arms, palms upward, as he continued. "And how can the court lend credence to this testimony if the government can't cross-examine the witness?"

The judge nodded. "Mr. Darby, can you produce your witness to testify in open court?"

Darby nodded, "Yes, Your Honor, if necessary. But I believe the court can settle the matter with a very credible witness who is present at this time."

"Very well. Call your witness."

Darby walked back to the defense table. "The defense calls Detective Mike Meador."

CHAPTER THIRTY-FOUR

Colson considered himself well hidden in the back row, wearing an English style duckbill hat pulled down to the top of a pair of fake eyeglasses. The large head of the heavy man seated in the row directly in front of him added yet another layer of camouflage. The mention of Master Sergeant Walker's name made him stiffen initially and then almost bolt from the courtroom. He had to control his reaction and think. Did either he or Keith use each other's name in the warehouse? No, he was sure they hadn't. Colson recalled consciously not making that mistake.

An image of the former Army sergeant and security guard formed in Colson's mind. He could clearly see him seated at a long table across from a quartet of Strawn's high-dollar attorneys, who were throwing questions and accusations at him faster than he could answer. Walker was retired military and a man of integrity. Colson could only imagine himself in the same position when confronted with either telling the truth or repeating a lie. He wasn't mad at Walker or even disappointed, only upset at himself for allowing the retired soldier to be involved in the deception.

But the name Darby just announced as his next witness completely threw Colson. At first he thought he misheard what the man said. Did he just call Det. Mike Meador? But why? Meador wasn't called to the scene and had nothing to do with the case. Colson's mind raced, trying to summon images from that night in the warehouse. It was apparent almost everyone else in the courtroom was as mystified as Colson, based on the rumbling of low conversations.

"Quiet, please," the bailiff said to the gallery in a stern but polite tone.

Colson's eyes shot open wide. That had to be it—one name was mentioned while the guard was present, but he still wasn't sure what Darby hoped to accomplish. He wouldn't have to guess for long, since Meador had just walked through the door and approached the witness stand.

Meador ascended the two steps to the witness stand and turned with a sullen expression on his face. He remained standing while taking his oath and took his seat as Darby approached with Walker's deposition in hand.

"Detective Meador," Darby said, "I understand you've been with Atlanta PD for twenty-three years, correct?"

Meador nodded. "Yes."

"And of those twenty-three years, ten of them have been in the detective division where you are currently assigned?"

"That's correct. CIU, or Criminal Investigation Unit."

"And you've been the case agent on how many cases?"

"I would estimate hundreds."

Darby nodded. "And of those hundreds of cases, how many times would you estimate you've given testimony in court?"

Kennedy shook his head and stood to his feet. "Your Honor, I object," he said, gesturing to the defense attorney. "Mr. Darby is wasting the court's time with these meaningless preliminary questions. Detective Meador has nothing to do with this case."

Darby held up his hand. "Your Honor, I'm prepared to demonstrate that he has everything to do with this case. I was simply establishing for the court that Detective Meador should be aware of his oath since he has no doubt provided sworn testimony before the court on numerous occasions."

"All right, Mr. Darby." The judge turned to Meador. "Detective, do you fully understand the oath administered to you and the potential consequences of not being truthful in these proceedings?"

"Yes, sir."

"There," Judge Carter said, "and now that the matter is settled, please go forward with your questioning, counselor."

Darby walked toward the defense table as he spoke. "In the security guard's deposition, he could not provide the identity of the two intruders in the warehouse on the night of the incident other than a description." Darby pulled at a yellow tab in the small stack of papers, flipped to the page, and read aloud. "They were white males of medium build and height, both wearing black military-style clothing." Darby flipped the deposition closed. "The guard testified he only heard one name mentioned when the men were talking. Are you familiar with that name?"

Meador leaned a couple of inches closer to the microphone. "I'm sorry, but I'm not familiar with the security guard, and I haven't read the deposition."

"I can help you with that," Darby said, handing Meador the deposition. "What name did Mr. Walker indicate he heard one of the intruders say? You'll find it on line one-thirty-one."

Meador scanned down the numbered lines of the statement to line 131. "Meador," he said, handing the document back to Darby, "but as I mentioned, I don't know the man."

"That's fine, that's fine," Darby repeated with a wave of his hand, "but you do know who the intruders were, don't you, detective?"

Kennedy didn't wait to stand before speaking this time. "I object, Your Honor. The defense is putting words in—"

"The intruders who committed burglary," Darby cried with a dramatic flair, cutting Kennedy off. "The intruders who were in possession of weapons during the commission of a felony, holding a Strawn Industries security officer against his will and intimidating him to provide a false statement to the DEA about the events that night in the warehouse."

339

Kennedy matched Darby's volume. "Your Honor, the defense isn't questioning—he is testifying and badgering the witness. I object to this ridiculous sideshow."

Meador sat, staring straight ahead, as the attorneys battled. He flinched with the sharp smacks of the judge's gavel. The whispering from the gallery had grown to a low roar.

"Order!" Carter rapped his gavel three more times, until the courtroom fell relatively quiet. "Mr. Darby, do you have a direct question for the witness?"

Darby took a deep breath and settled down. "Yes, Your Honor, and I apologize." He walked directly in front of the witness stand and glared at Meador. "Detective Meador," he said in an even tone, "do you know the identity of the two intruders who entered the warehouse of Strawn Industries on the night of the incident?"

Meador looked past Darby and the prosecution table to the crowded courtroom and the front two rows of chiefs, sheriffs, and command officers who were hanging on every word.

"Please answer the question, detective. Yes or no."

"Yes," Meador said, and the room instantly erupted once again.

The judge rapped his desk with his gavel three times with greater intensity and scolded the audience. "This is not the British parliament. These outbursts will stop right now."

Darby crossed his arms and smiled. "Thank you, detective. Now tell the court the identity of those two men."

Meador lowered his head for a long moment and then turned to Judge Carter. "Your Honor, with respect I decline to reveal the identity of my confidential informants."

Kennedy sat with his head in his hands, his expression reflecting the shock of Meador's testimony. He knew that the case against Strawn was falling apart in front of his eyes, even before the drug kingpin saw the inside of a jail cell. It didn't make sense why Meador refused to give up the names—there was no reason to not reveal the names of the men—unless...

Kennedy jumped to his feet and addressed the judge. "Your Honor, I feel it's extremely pertinent to remind the witness that it is not necessary or even lawful for an officer to conceal the name of a confidential informant who has committed a crime, especially when said crime was not sanctioned by the officer."

As Kennedy spoke, Darby walked to his briefcase and removed a document. "May I approach?" Darby asked. The judge nodded and Darby walked to the stand. "I have prepared a motion to disclose for the court's consideration. What Mr. Kennedy stated is correct." He turned to Meador after handing over the document. "The officer must disclose the identity of his confidential informants unless he himself ordered the warrantless break-in. The informants are material witnesses who could potentially provide evidence that my client is innocent. I would also respectfully remind the court that without probable cause, exigent circumstances, or a search warrant, all of the evidence in the government's case is fruit of the poisonous tree and is inadmissible at trial."

The judge looked up from the document. "I believe I fully understand the rules of evidence, Mr. Darby."

Kennedy stood. "I concur with the defense, Your Honor."

Judge Carter studied the motion Darby had handed him and nodded. "I will grant the motion to disclose," he said. He turned to Meador. "Detective, I have granted the motion to disclose. Are you willing to reveal the names of your confidential informants at this time?"

"Your Honor," Kennedy said, "may I address the court before the detective answers your question?"

"Go ahead, Mr. Kennedy."

"Thank you, Your Honor. May I request that the court advise the detective not only of his obligation to disclose the names, but that failing to do so would suggest to the court he was complicit in the alleged crimes committed? Although he is a police officer, he still has the rights of any citizen against self-incrimination."

The judge thought for a long moment and nodded. "Agreed," he said. "Detective Meador, do you fully understand the potential implications of your response?

"Yes, I understand," Meador said with a sigh. It seemed there was no way out. He was caught.

"How do you respond to my question?" the judge said. "Will you now disclose the names of your informants?"

Meador looked over the crowd in the gallery once again and focused on the officers in the first two rows. How could he ever face them again? His eyes moved to Strawn's lead counsel, Darby, who returned a blank stare. He then turned his attention back to Judge Carter.

"Your Honor, I respectfully decline to answer under the protection afforded to me by the Fifth Amendment."

A collective gasp flowed from the gallery. The two rows of officers sat stoic, respecting the judge's order of no further eruptions, but each sighed a quiet groan of disappointment and disgust. Kennedy collapsed into his chair at the prosecution table as if he had been stabbed in the back and his life was instantly snuffed out.

Judge Carter rocked back in his high-backed leather chair, glanced at the ceiling, and took a deep breath. He didn't bother to lift his gavel to silence the gallery for the third time; instead he leaned forward once the commotion subsided. "Mr. Darby, do you have any further questions for the detective?"

"No, Your Honor."

"Mr. Kennedy?"

Kennedy didn't appear to be paying attention. He began wondering how much longer he would be working for the U.S. attorney's office following the ruling that was certain to come.

"Mr. Kennedy," the judge repeated. "Do you have any questions for the witness?"

"No, Your Honor."

"You may be excused, detective."

Meador stood, stepped off the stand, and quickly made his way down the center aisle and past the row of officers, keeping his eyes on nothing but the floor. The Atlanta police chief rose from the front row and followed ten paces behind Meador as he pushed open the mahogany doors and disappeared down the hallway. Colson was ten paces behind the chief.

Judge Carter put his hands together, rested his arms on the bench, and looked left and right across the gallery as he spoke. "In light of the clear and convincing testimony in this hearing, it is clear to the court that the evidence in the government's case was discovered illegally by unidentified individuals acting under the direction of the police, without a warrant, probable cause, or exigent circumstances. I hereby grant the motion of the defense to suppress all evidence in the case of the United States versus Jack Wellington Strawn."

A single slap of the gavel made Kennedy flinch, followed by Carter's proclamation, "The indictment is dismissed. Mr. Darby, your client is free to go."

Colson looked both directions down the broad hallway and saw the APD chief walking briskly around a corner toward the bank of elevators. Colson sprinted after him and saw the elevator door closing as he rounded the corner. He punched the down button and impatiently waited for another car to arrive. It seemed to take an eternity for the door to open. He punched the B1 button for the parking garage, stuck the worthless eyeglasses in his pocket, and snatched the ridiculous hat off his head. He heard a raised voice echoing in the parking deck even before the elevator door opened. Halfway down the line of cars to his left stood the police chief, nose to nose with Meador. It was the police chief's voice he had heard, and it wasn't pleasant, regardless of what was being said.

Colson slipped off to the side and stood next to a minivan, keeping the police chief's back between him and Meador. The man's shoulders appeared tense under his dress uniform, and his gestures were quite animated. Colson could only imagine what an embarrassment Meador had been to him and the entire agency.

The chief fumbled with something in the pocket of his jacket and then stomped away. As the chief headed back to the elevator, Colson got a good look at his expression. He had seen it before from his own supervisor when he was royally pissed off. It made Colson momentarily happy he was retired, before he turned his attention back to Meador.

Colson intended to sprint to Meador's car before he had a chance to climb in and drive off, but he didn't have to bother. Meador's back was to him. He was propping himself with both hands on the top of the doorframe, and his head hung so low it reminded Colson of the headless horseman. He casually stepped behind Meador.

"Why, Mike?" Colson said in a fatherly tone.

Meador quickly spun on his heel and sighed at the sight of Colson. "I really can't deal with this right now, Grey."

"What do you mean you can't deal with it? You lied in federal court, and that slime is going free. You know what you said isn't true." Colson gritted his teeth in anger. "Don't tell me you can't deal with it."

Meador shook his head, threw Colson a sarcastic grin, and laughed. "Oh, but it's just fine for you to commit multiple felonies. Look, Colson, if I had testified about what really happened, I would have had to reveal your identity—and the dead kid's dad. Both of you would have been indicted. Either way it went, Strawn's case would have been dismissed, so don't give me your holier-than-thou speech."

"This isn't about me," Colson said. "Keith and I were prepared—hell, we expected to go to jail if it meant seeing Strawn and his drug empire go down. First offense, a little jail time, a little probation, and we'd be no worse for wear. It was everything I could do to keep from jumping up in the courtroom and shouting, 'It's me'."

Meador slapped the sides of his pant legs. "Well, maybe you should have."

"I probably should have, but by that time, the old buddy I'm looking at right now had already pleaded the fifth and implicated himself in the crime."

"Look, Colson," Meador said, shaking his head, "I'm serious. I really can't trust anyone right now." He climbed into the old Crown Vic and gazed over his steering wheel. "Not even you, Grey. Maybe we'll talk later."

Colson tapped on the driver's window as Meador started the ignition. Meador lowered it after shifting into reverse. "Answer one thing for me. How did you even know Keith and I were involved?"

"I had a couple of my guys shadowing you since you came back to town."

Colson's eyebrows shot up. "You had me under surveillance? But why?"

"I heard about what happened in Daytona. I thought someone would still try to kill you."

Colson nodded. "Okay. What did the police chief say?"

Meador took a deep breath and blew it out. "You mean other than calling me a lying disgrace and sack of shit?"

"Yeah, other than the normal pleasantries you expect from the top brass."

"He told me to give him my gun and badge and to take this car back to headquarters and that I would, quote, ride my ass back home on the city bus. Now I really need to go." He rolled his window up and eased the car out of the space.

Colson watched the car pull away; the tires of the old Crown Vic squealed on the smooth concrete around the first turn. "Why are you in such a big hurry, old buddy?" Colson said aloud.

CHAPTER THIRTY-FIVE

All eyes were on Strawn as he walked down the center aisle of the courtroom like a man on a mission. The reporters crammed their pens and pads into briefcases and backpacks, pulled out their voice recorders, and crowded in behind Strawn, jockeying for position and shouting questions. Strawn drew a cigar from his suit pocket, shoved it in his mouth, and lit it as he stepped through the courtroom doors to the lobby.

An old bailiff in a dark blue blazer walked straight up to Strawn, shaking a bony finger in his face. "You can't smoke in here. It's against the law," he scolded.

Strawn took a long draw on his cigar and blew smoke in the man's face. "Get out of my way, you old bastard."

Three U.S. marshals stood near the bank of elevators and held back the throng of reporters while another two marshals accompanied Strawn and Darby to the elevator and down to street level, where Strawn's limo idled curbside.

Haggart stepped from the driver's side and stood at attention near the rear door. He knew the drill, and he knew Strawn. His boss didn't talk to reporters unless there were cameras present. He enjoyed seeing himself on television too much. And the cameras were there, on the steps of the Richard Russell Federal Building, not in the courtroom.

Darby stepped up to the bouquet of microphones to address the reporters and the thousands of viewers across the nation. Strawn stood at Darby's shoulder as the attorney removed a folded piece of paper with his prepared comments from his suit jacket.

"Let me just say that we are pleased with Judge Carter's ruling today. Although it has been an expensive setback and inconvenience for Mr. Strawn and his company, he is pleased with the work of the DEA's Atlanta Field Office and their diligence in seizing the drugs located in his storage facilities. Even though they jumped the gun, so to speak, with the indictment, it is somewhat understandable they would suspect Mr. Strawn due to his political position, but I want to make it clear that there is no animosity between Strawn Industries and the Department of Justice."

"Can we just ask—" a female reporter shouted from the crowd, but Darby raised his hand to stifle the question.

"Please let me finish. Now, Mr. Strawn insists the DEA continue their investigation and bring to justice the guilty parties who are responsible for manufacturing and storing narcotics in his facilities and tarnishing Strawn Industries' good name. That will be all for now."

Darby was pleasantly surprised that his client had done as instructed and not opened his mouth during the press briefing. Haggart was shocked for the same reasons and moved to open the door as Darby followed Strawn to the limousine. But Darby and Haggart's moment of surprise was fleeting. Just as Strawn was about to climb in the rear seat, a male reporter shouted a question that drowned out the others, catching Strawn's attention.

"Do you really expect anyone to believe that tons of drugs were being manufactured and stored in your warehouses, right under your nose, and you knew nothing about it?"

Strawn stopped at the door, took a long drag on his cigar, and blew out the smoke. He was away from the microphones, so he shouted his reply to the mob. "Works for the president, doesn't it?"

Strawn climbed in the back, followed by Darby, who rolled his eyes but kept them halfway closed so no one would notice.

Colson sat at his desk with fingers steepled, waiting for Keith to speak. They were across from each other in Colson's office at the small conference table where they first met. The day following the dismissal of Strawn's indictment was a continuation of the media circus from the day before, with commentary and analysis of every move made by Strawn's attorney. It didn't matter which media outlet you turned to, Strawn's attorney was touted as being brilliant, and the U.S. attorney was labeled as totally incompetent. And those were some of the more conservative comments.

Keith shook his head, "I can't accept this."

Colson leaned forward in his chair. "We have to accept it, Keith. It is what it is."

"How could Meador ruin the case like that?" Keith stood and walked to the window.

"Now, that," Colson said, "I still don't quite understand. He claimed it was to keep us out of jail, but he ruined his career in the process."

Keith shook his head, staring down to the street below, where cars and trucks jerked from lane to lane in an attempt to move one vehicle length closer to their destination. He turned and held up his hands in resignation. "All the drugs and even more damning, the computer records that clearly lay out everything Strawn was doing."

Colson leaned back in his chair and closed his eyes. The process of making a solid case on anyone depended on the integrity of the evidence. The last thing he wanted to do was scold Keith, but he had to make him understand. "We talked about this, Keith, and I warned you about taking independent action."

Keith spun and met Colson's eyes. "But the evidence is—was—overwhelming, Grey. How could any judge in good conscience—"

Colson raised his hand to stop Keith mid-sentence. "Yes, the evidence is there, but the way it was collected taints it. I'm no attorney, but even I could effectively argue that you were motivated by the death of your son to manufacture all of the data you collected. That's exactly why the police have to collect the evidence and maintain an irrefutable chain of custody for it to be used in court."

"And what about the laptop you took from Emily? Why is that different?"

"It's not," Colson said with a sigh. "I have to admit I was somewhat distracted by being stalked by an assassin."

Keith walked back to the desk and dropped in his chair. "So we're done? We lose and Strawn wins?" Colson's face was blank, and Keith continued, "I'm not finished with Strawn. Either directly or indirectly, he caused Josh's death. We know for certain now that his assassin is linked to it."

Colson leaned forward and pointed his finger at Keith. "Listen to me: you've done enough. I'm telling you, we are both fortunate not to be in a two-man cell in a federal lockup, and I can't emphasize to you enough not to take any further action against Strawn."

"You sound like Haggart when he threatened me," Keith said, instantly regretting it. "I'm sorry, Grey. I know you're just thinking about my family. It's just eating my soul and it won't stop."

"I can understand. You need to leave this to me and stay out of it for now."

Keith gave Colson a hopeful look. "Are you planning something?"

"Maybe, but don't get your hopes up, and by all means, don't do anything else to help—okay?" Colson waited for a response but got none; Keith simply looked down at his hands in silence. "Okay?" Colson demanded.

Keith finally raised his head. "From this point forward, I'll do nothing more."

Strawn shifted in his chair and adjusted the ear monitor as it worked its way out for the second time. He hated remote interviews, especially at the cramped studios of the Fox News affiliate in Midtown, and particularly this early in the morning. Half the time he couldn't hear the questions clearly or know for certain the lapel microphone was picking up his answers. He kept his eyes on the camera, but he could see the reporter on the monitor to the side. She gave him the look of a mother who had just caught her teenage son looking at porn.

"But surely you can understand," the female reporter said, "how suspicious this appears. It would take years to accumulate such a vast cache of drugs, and you still insist you had no knowledge of it?"

He had answered the question numerous times, but the woman simply would not let it go. It was everything Strawn could do to control his temper, knowing he had a talent for storing up his anger and releasing it on the first person of convenience later.

"As I have stated numerous times, Strawn Industries is an international concern. I don't tour every office and certainly not every warehouse, any more than Sam Walton toured every Wal-Mart across the globe. What seems to be left out of your interview is the fact that I contacted the DEA the instant I was made aware, and I am fully cooperating with their ongoing investigation to this very day."

Strawn stormed into the elevator following the interview and glared at Haggart when the doors slid closed. "Damn reporters," he scoffed. Haggart stood silently with his hands clasped at his waist. Strawn stuck a fat finger in his chest. "You call Williams over at CNN from the car and have him set up an interview as soon as possible. I'm tired of these so-called conservative pundits trying to make me look like a fool."

"Yes, sir," was Haggart's short reply.

Haggart walked behind Strawn wherever he went. Strawn was aware he had learned the proper techniques in the six weeks of executive protection training to always keep the client in front of you and to maintain a six-foot distance for a wider view of potential threats. But with his years in the UFC, Strawn didn't care about techniques as much as he counted on Haggart's bulk and ominous appearance to encourage most threatening individuals to give him a wide berth. No one had ever attempted to assault him yet, but Haggart had politely shoved away the occasional aggressive reporter and slugs who claimed to be down on their luck.

They rode the elevator to the parking garage without another word. Strawn stepped out ahead of Haggart, plucked a cigar from his suit pocket, and shoved it into his mouth, waiting. Haggart was already prepared with the engraved platinum-plated Zippo. Haggart flicked the top and spun the tiny wheel to spark the flame in one fluid move. With his eyes focused ahead of Strawn, he held the flame to the tip of the stogy until it was lit to Strawn's satisfaction. He pocketed the lighter and reassumed his strategic position behind the billionaire for the last twenty-five feet of his employment with Strawn Industries.

Taylor held the utility room door open a quarter inch, waiting for Strawn and Haggart to walk past. He couldn't see Colson standing in the shadows behind a large support post across from the utility room, but he knew he was there. He worked to control his breathing, but with his adrenalin flowing there wasn't much he could do about it. The temperature in underground parking garage was cool, especially this early in the morning, but a bead of sweat ran down his face nevertheless.

This opportunity couldn't have come soon enough. Colson had seemed caught off guard by Taylor's account of the YouTube video but was genuinely sympathetic and supportive of Taylor's plan to make both men pay for the career they had stolen from him. He wished Colson had agreed to let him deal with both Haggart and Strawn right now, but he respected Colson and knew he would keep his word. Strawn's time would come.

The garage was silent. He flipped the light on and off for a quick second to survey the room. The ten-by-twelve utility room was a little cramped for what he needed to do, but he would improvise as he had so frequently in the octagon. There was a larger plan in play than getting even with Haggart. In retrospect, Haggart was merely a puppet in the hands of Strawn the entire time.

The wall to his right was lined with metal breaker boxes attached to the cinder block wall. A variety of tools were hanging on a pegboard behind him, and to his left were metal shelves with cardboard supply boxes. The middle of the room was open, clean and free of clutter. The last thing Taylor needed was to be tripping all over the room and making unnecessary noise. Taylor was mildly impressed at the speed with which Colson had picked the door lock, but he wouldn't have dared compliment him. No reason to inflate Colson's ego beyond what it already was.

351

Taylor held the door open and listened. Colson had told him that Strawn kept a tight schedule but enjoyed nothing more than hearing himself talk, so he might run overtime. A hiss of the elevator door sliding open, followed by a loud ding of the bell, quickly got Taylor's attention. He pulled the door closed to half an inch and waited, keeping his good eye near the opening. There was the scuffing sound of dress shoes on concrete for a moment, and then it stopped. Taylor heard the unmistakable sound of a Zippo lighter flipping open and a gruff voice, but he couldn't make out what was being said. The scuffing sound resumed, and Taylor caught the aroma of cigar smoke. Taylor pulled the door closed to a quarter inch as the footsteps grew louder.

The timing had to be right. He would have to move fast and quiet for plan A to work. The sounds grew louder; he could hear both men walking now, individual footfalls instead of the muffled noise from moments ago. The separate and distinct footfalls would be those of Haggart; the scuffing ones, those of the lazy, overweight Strawn. Taylor estimated their distance closing from fifteen feet, although they hadn't yet come into view through the small opening, which now was barely over an eighth of an inch wide. It was simple luck the two men were walking near the wall on the right side instead of the left.

Taylor pushed the toe of his shoe at the foot of the door and applied pressure. He held the door handle with his left hand to prevent it from swinging open and ruining everything. He was ready. Strawn cleared his throat, doing Taylor a favor by giving away his distance from the door. In a flash, Strawn's form passed the opening. Taylor paused for the count of two and then pushed the door open, blocking Haggart's path. It took another count of two for Haggart's brain to register the door materializing in his path and recognize the man holding it open.

Haggart froze and his eyes went wide. Before he could utter a sound, Taylor had him in a chokehold, dragging him backward into the dark room. The door eased closed with a click. Haggart spun in the pitch darkness of the room and lunged toward the sliver of light at the base of the door. Taylor shot forward and caught Haggart around the neck before he could reach the door, diverting his momentum to the cinder block wall just left of the door. The impact of the wall in front of him and Taylor's considerable bulk from behind caused the air to rush from Haggart's lungs. The only sound in the room, with the exception of the muffled slap of flesh against the cinder block wall, was the clack of metal on the concrete floor.

Taylor brushed his hand on the wall next to the door, found the light switch, and flicked it on. The snub-nose .357 caliber Smith & Wesson revolver Haggart had carried in his waistband had been dislodged by the impact and now lay at Taylor's feet, while Haggart was doubled over with his back against the wall, gasping. Taylor hefted the stainless steel revolver and clenched his fist around it. Haggart stared into Taylor's eyes with pure hate and lunged forward, but Taylor was ready. He grasped the revolver tighter in his fist, swung his arm back, and then shot it forward in an uppercut to Haggart's abdomen. Haggart grunted out the remaining air from his lungs and draped over Taylor's fist like a table napkin on a waiter's arm.

Colson slipped in behind Strawn, marching through a cloud of cigar smoke. He waved the haze away from his face with one hand and silently pulled the ASP from his jacket pocket with the other. Taylor's move had been cat-like. Swift and silent. Strawn hadn't even turned at the click of the metal door after Taylor and Haggart disappeared behind it. Colson smiled. Strawn's confidence in Haggart's talent as a bodyguard must be unwavering. What would he think of him now?

Taylor would have to hurry if this was going to work. Strawn was only a few feet from the rear of the limo and closing fast. There was no doubt Strawn was still boiling about his arrest and the seizure of his products. It reminded Colson of the old cop saying: "You may beat the rap, but you can't beat the ride." Strawn had to know the feds had suffered a black eye from the embarrassment over the indictment dismissal, but his satisfaction would be dwarfed by a half-billion-dollar loss in inventory he had accumulated, waiting for one stroke of the pen to instantly make him the single most wealthy and powerful person in history.

Strawn's performance today was simply damage control. Unlike beloved athletes and movie stars, the American public had little sympathy for a corporate type summarily excused of wrongdoing. The only silver lining for Strawn was the fact that the public trusted the government even less than they trusted big business.

Colson took a quick peek over his shoulder at the steel door. It was still closed, and there was no sound whatsoever. He turned his attention back to Strawn and considered plan B. There were about two seconds left before he had to decide. Strawn obviously was waiting for the same sound Colson was hoping for. His pace slowed when he passed the trunk of the limo, and he began to pivot to his right, probably to ask Haggart what he was waiting for. Colson took a long stride forward and raised his left hand to grab Strawn by the shoulder. In the same instant, the door locks clicked open.

Taylor lowered Haggart to the opposite wall as the bodyguard heaved and gasped for air. Haggart's expression of hatred was replaced with an agonizing need for oxygen. Tears rolled down his cheeks when he met Taylor's eyes—partly due to his struggle to breathe, but mostly due to not knowing what his one-eyed former UFC opponent had in store for him.

Taylor shook his head. "Haven't been working out much, have you, Mad Man?" Taylor jerked Haggart to his feet by the collar of his suit jacket and applied a textbook strangle hold. "You know," Taylor whispered, "I used to have to dress like you for a psycho rich boss." He applied gradual pressure to both sides of Haggart's neck, cutting the flow of blood from his carotid artery to his brain. "It never works out very well," were the last words Haggart heard before blacking out.

Taylor eased Haggart to the floor on his back and quickly patted his pockets. He pulled the Zippo from his right pocket and found the limo fob in his left. He took two long strides to the door, pushed it open with a whoosh, and stuck his head around the edge to find Colson. He and Strawn were almost to the limo. He depressed the limo fob's unlock button before letting the door ease closed. Colson had instructed him to leave him alone with Strawn. "There's no good reason for you to be identified as being involved in this yet,"

Colson had warned him. Taylor pocketed the snub-nosed revolver and Zippo and stepped back to Haggart, who lay on the cool concrete floor, lightly snoring.

In an open parking lot with vehicle traffic, people chattering, horns blowing, and the sounds of the city, such a noise would be muffled to nothing. But at 5:45 a.m., in a deserted parking garage, the click of the door lock mechanism sounded like someone racking a round into a shotgun. With plan A now firmly in play, Colson stopped Strawn with a firm grip to his shoulder blade and pressed the tip of the collapsed ASP firmly in his back. He then pushed Strawn's barrel chest against the rear window post of the limo and glanced to the steel door. Taylor's arm protruded through the door, his hand making a thumbs-up gesture and the limo fob dangling from his pinky. The hand slipped back inside just as quickly and the door softly clicked closed again. He would be keeping Haggart company while Colson held a prayer meeting with Strawn.

"What the hell's going on?" Strawn loudly protested.

Colson released Strawn's shoulder but held the ASP firmly in the middle of his back. He reached to open the rear door and shoved Strawn's thick frame sideways. "Get in, Strawn."

Strawn snapped his head around. "Colson?" he gasped, as if seeing a ghost.

Colson grinned and cocked his head. "Yep. Back from the dead."

"Haggart!" Strawn yelled.

"Shut up and get your fat ass in there," Colson ordered.

Strawn slid across the long back seat of the limo with ease. Colson could smell the strong aroma of new leather combined with liquor and cigar smoke as he slid in alongside Strawn. There was enough room to lay a queen-sized bed between the long rear bench seat and the two middle seats facing him. Between the two seats sat a bar with a dozen liquor bottles, held safely by a small brass railing against the middle bulkhead and a tall crystal container with a brass lid containing a half-dozen cigars.

Colson shifted the ASP in his hand, stuck it in Strawn's left cheek, and shoved his face against the bulletproof door window. The cold steel tip of the ASP would convince Strawn there was the muzzle of a handgun a millimeter from the hinge of his jawbone. The pressure Colson applied flattened Strawn's face against the glass, causing his words to be somewhat muffled and falling short of the commanding tone he typically enjoyed.

"I'll have you killed, Colson."

"You already tried that, Jack," Colson mocked. "You better start working out because you'll have to try it yourself next time. Your attack dog is dead."

Strawn squirmed in his seat. "You don't know what you're talking about."

"Sure I do," Colson said. "Butch Sutton came to visit me just the other day. He changed his mind about killing me and decided to take flying lessons without an airplane. He's logged more time in the air than the Blue Angles."

"I don't know any Butch Sutton, you idiot. What I do know is that you have attacked and assaulted me. Some cop you are. We'll see how long you survive on the other side of prison bars when I'm finished with you."

Colson pushed the ASP deeper into Strawn's cheek, causing his upper and lower jaw to part. "Why don't you let that wound beneath your nose heal, Strawn? Just shut up and listen. You'll never see me wearing a jailhouse uniform. Would you like to know why, fat boy?"

Strawn gurgled but was otherwise silent. Colson sighed and continued. "You've been so busy manipulating the feds' case, you forgot about the local cops."

Strawn chuckled through his gurgling. "You don't have anything on me. They dismissed all the charges against me. I'm a free man, and they won't dare charge me again and risk even more humiliation."

"There you go again," Colson said. "Your thinking is too narrow. Haven't you ever heard that the devil's in the details? I'm talking about your business relationship with Butch Sutton."

Strawn tried to shake his head. "I told you I don't know anyone named—"

"Shut up," Colson shouted in the confines of the limo. "The Hall County police have the device used to kill Larry Morgan, I have a car full of .223 caliber rounds, and until the meat wagon left the beach, I literally had the head of your assassin on a stick."

"None of what you're saying has anything to do with me," Strawn insisted.

"Let me finish." Colson slapped the window next to Strawn's nose with his free hand. "I'm an easygoing guy, but that only makes me more pissed off than most when you push me over the line. You understand me?"

Strawn gave Colson a quick nod.

"Now," Colson continued, "your anonymous employee, Sutton, changed cell phones like I change socks, but all of his messages can be and are being backtracked to Haggart. Volusia County detectives are going over your financials with a microscope and finding the payments made to your assassin through Haggart's ghost account, and they're coming up with some interesting information. Such as how each payment to Sutton coincides with the murders of Josh Bartlett and Larry Morgan. The boys in brown in Henry County are matching the round that killed one of their deputies with your assassin's Walther PPK, making you an accessory to a cop killing, and Agent Floyd tells me there was even a street dealer thrown in as a bonus."

Strawn continued to shake his head. Colson responded by driving the ASP deeper into his face. "Your first screw-up was a payment transferred to Sutton immediately after Keith Bartlett's son shot up a hot load of poison-laced heroin. You might remember how distraught he was with me that day in your office. You should know he's still pretty pissed about that."

"Stop it! Get that gun out of my face, Colson," Strawn shouted.

Colson eased back on the pressure but kept the ASP against Strawn's face. "Got something profound to add, Strawn?"

"Yeah," Strawn scoffed. "You undoubtedly got your information without a search warrant as usual. After your last fiasco, you'll be run out of the state. You're a pariah to the police. I'm not surprised you were Meador's informant."

"Really? Which state is going to run me out, Jack?" Colson said. "Georgia or Florida? The police in Hall County, Fulton County, and Volusia County are putting the finishing touches on their cases right now, and this time everything will be official and by the book. How do three counts of felony murder and one count of attempted murder sound to you?"

"Go to hell," Strawn growled.

"And speaking of Detective Meador, I've been meaning to ask you about him."

Strawn barked a laugh. "Funny how you went from a major with one of the largest metro Atlanta counties to some flunky informant for a lousy city cop."

"I hate to break it to you, but I didn't need permission or direction from Meador to do anything. I'm sure you already know that since it seems he's on your payroll. But don't be down on yourself, Jack. There is one thing you did right, but purely by mistake. You created a computer guru out of the man you stole the UFC Championship from." Colson shook his head. "Oops."

"Well," Strawn sputtered, "no matter what you do with your supposed information, I'm still going to file a complaint against you for assaulting me with a gun."

Colson twisted the ASP and pushed it deeper than before. "And who is your witness?"

"Ha!" Strawn laughed. "Haggart saw it happen. Whether he did or not, he'll swear to it, by God,"

Colson gritted his teeth. "If," he hissed in a whisper. "If Haggart can still speak, he won't be doing anything for you from now on."

"What makes you so sure of that?"

Colson rubbed his chin. "I knew there was something else I was meaning to tell you. In whatever condition Haggart is currently, when he wakes up he'll find a printout of his and Sutton's decoded messages stuffed in his shirt. The entry being of the most interest to him will also interest you, Jackie boy. I'm referring to the fifty thousand he offered Butch Sutton to take you out when this was all finished. Granted, it's a mere pittance compared to his usual fee, but even Sutton knew his days working for you were over once he took me out, so why leave town with a banana split when you can have the cherry on top?

"Then there's a little tidbit of information we're giving to Haggart about you secretly fingering him as being the mastermind behind the drug operation."

"That's insane," Strawn snapped.

"Not according to my source at the DEA. I worked with them for years. They'll do anything to save face, and Haggart will be an easy target. If he knows what's good for him, he'll disappear like a fart in the wind, and you should seriously consider doing the same— unless you think you can squeeze your fat ass into a six-by-eight jail cell."

Strawn shook his head violently. "I don't believe that. And I'm still having you arrested."

"We'll see about that. The good news, whether both of us end up in jail or not, is that your dream of selling your nightmares to our kids is over." Colson moved the ASP away from Strawn's face and jerked it open with a loud click. "Be sure to tell them I did this with my gun." Colson swung the ASP wide and raked it across the bar like he was swinging at a low fastball. The liquor bottles and crystal cigar case exploded like hand grenades. Strawn instinctively threw his hands in front of his face to prevent the flying shards from shredding his eyes. By the time he dropped his hands and jerked his head from one side to the other, Colson was gone.

Taylor looked down at the bulky fighter and wondered if he knew Strawn had paid off the optometrist to blind him. Maybe that's why Haggart left the UFC after winning the belt. What real fighter could live with himself, knowing he had to cheat to become champion? But he had to have known. Colson told him this wasn't the time or place for retribution, and he would respect his wishes—for now.

He pulled a folded piece of computer paper from his back pocket and gently laid the decoded messages on Haggart's chest. He grinned, looking at the helpless face of his one-time UFC championship opponent, and said, "Catch you later."

ᴄ◈ᴄʜᴀᴘᴛᴇʀ Tʜɪʀᴛʏ-Sɪx◈

A gent Hadaway sat at his desk, reading over the new indictment two floors below the courtroom where he had been made a laughing stock exactly ten days prior. Of course Haggart couldn't be prosecuted based on the same evidence thrown out in Strawn's hearing, but the seventy kilos of meth found in Haggart's townhouse was a different story.

Hadaway leafed through the case file and the various profiles of Haggart's South Florida associates. Substance abuse in the sports culture was nothing new, but recent media attention had been more prevalent in the better-known and nationally televised sports such as professional football and baseball. Nevertheless, it existed in all physically demanding sports to some extent. The UFC was no exception.

The tip from Strawn wasn't enough probable cause for the search warrant, but an extensive background investigation of Haggart's activities and interviews with former contenders regarding steroid use supported the affidavit. Not to mention the ounce of meth found in his abandoned car on the curbside at Hartsfield-Jackson Airport.

Hadaway rubbed his forehead. Was there even a glimmer of truth to Strawn's adamant denial that he knew nothing about the drugs in his warehouses? No way. But the DEA wasn't going to be made the fool, according to the special agent-in-charge. The stash from Strawn's warehouses dwarfed any weight a South American drug cartel could produce in years, and someone was going to federal prison for it. And that was that.

Now the SAC could go before the press and announce the indictment of the real mastermind behind the largest documented drug seizure in US history: former UFC champion Clay "The Mad Man" Haggart.

Hadaway closed the file and pushed it across his desk, thinking he might be retired before the FBI located the former UFC champion. Haggart apparently had fallen off the face of the earth. Hadaway silently hoped they would never find him so he could forget the whole fiasco.

For over two days, one tractor trailer after another filed into the parking lot of the Fulton County Humane Society. Pallets stacked four feet high were unloaded one by one from the trailers by forklifts under the heavy guard of federal and state authorities. Each pallet was wheeled to a large incinerator normally used to dispose of dead and stray animals. The tightly bound blocks of cocaine, heroin, and methamphetamine were tossed inside by a small team of deputies, supervised by a sheriff's office captain and the DEA's evidence agent. Officers and agents worked twelve-hour rotating shifts until the entire inventory seized from the warehouses went up in smoke, while local and national news cameras recorded file footage for their respective broadcasts.

Jack Strawn silently puffed on a cigar and glared at the huge monitor on the opposite wall. His new executive assistant, recently cut from the Atlanta Falcons roster, stood silently to the side and watched the monitor without comment. It was the new assistant's fourth attempt to win a position as a walk-on in training camp and his fourth failure. After being told he was simply getting too old to be considered, he had decided to move on to bigger and better things. Although his title was officially that of executive assistant, he wasn't stupid. He was nothing more than a bodyguard and fetch-boy for the recently embattled Strawn.

The camera zoomed in on billows of gray smoke streaming skyward from the roof of the Humane Society building and rising out of view into the atmosphere. The camera panned down to the reporter standing in the foreground of the building as a single tractor-trailer turned onto the road.

"As you can see," the reporter said, pointing back over his shoulder, "that was the last of the convoy of trucks delivering thousands of pounds of drugs for destruction. All in all, over thirty tons have been destroyed over the past forty-eight hours."

Strawn rested his elbows on the desk and dropped his head in his hands. The glowing tip of his cigar was so close to his thinning hairline that the new executive assistant almost lunged forward to prevent his boss from catching on fire. Strawn jerked his head up before he could move and met his eyes.

"Has the money been transferred to the offshore accounts?" Strawn asked.

The assistant nodded. "This morning, sir." He set the computer tablet in front of Strawn for review. Strawn nodded and crushed his stubby cigar in the crystal ashtray. On the TV monitor, the reporter continued blabbing while Strawn spun his cigar until the smoldering tip was extinguished.

"Because the Georgia legislature officially tabled the drug legalization bill indefinitely, Jack Strawn's problems with the law may not be over quite yet. We are still waiting on official word from the FBI director, but unconfirmed leaks within the agency say yet a second indictment is forthcoming. This time it is not related to the tons of drugs you see being incinerated here today, but rather interstate conspiracy to commit murder. It is being alleged that Strawn and another—"

The monitor went to black, cutting the reporter short, when Strawn touched an icon on his desk panel.

"The plane and pilot?" he said to the assistant.

"They're standing by at Peachtree-DeKalb. The pilot wants a destination so he can file his flight plan."

Strawn dropped the cigar into the tray, stood up slowly, and reached for his jacket. "Well, people in hell want ice water but they're not getting it, are they?" he snapped and jabbed his finger in the assistant's face. "If he calls back, you can tell him he'll know where we're going when I get there."

The assistant was caught off guard by his new employer's first outburst. He briefly wondered if he shouldn't have accepted the water boy job offer from the head coach. At least he could have hung out with the cheerleaders.

"Am I not going with you, Mr. Strawn?" he asked.

Strawn reached into his coat pocket and pulled out an envelope. "I don't know how long I'll be gone, so there's a bonus in here for you. I may be calling on you to take care of a few things while I'm away."

"Yes, sir," the assistant said, folding the envelope and sticking it in his pocket. He and Strawn stepped into the private elevator, and he punched the button for the garage. The two men rode in silence for a moment. Strawn cleared his throat and adjusted his tie.

"Any problems with our guest in the penthouse?" Strawn asked while watching the backward count of the floors on the small screen above the down button.

"No, sir," the bodyguard said. "All quiet. How do you want me to handle the situation once you're gone?"

Strawn glanced down at his shoes in thought and back to his assistant. "Just make it go away."

The would-be NFL linebacker nodded as they exited the elevator and stepped into the garage. A young Hispanic man with a white rag draped over his shoulder stepped from the rear of the waiting limousine and closed the door with a click. The limo's black paint shimmered under the fluorescent lights as if the ride had just arrived from the factory. Strawn would occasionally pause to admire his prized transportation before climbing inside, but current events would not permit him such a luxury today. The young man turned, and his eyes widened at the sight of the huge bodyguard. He backed away as Strawn stepped to the rear door.

"Mr. Strawn," the young man said in a thick Latino accent, "I cleaned out the broken glass, and placed a new, err, crystal container inside for your Cubans."

In an unusual twist of personality, Strawn placed his hand on the young man's shoulder. "It looks good, son," he said, placing a $100 bill in the young man's shirt pocket and climbing into the limo.

"Thank you, Mr. Strawn," the young man said. He watched as the bodyguard clicked the rear door closed and walked to the front of the limo, slid into the driver's seat, and pressed the control to raise the rolling garage door.

A man leaned against the driver's door of a sedan with his arms crossed in a parking space just outside the rolling door. He wore sunglasses and a dark blue suit. The limo cleared the garage, and the driver pressed the control to lower the door before stopping. He climbed out of the driver's seat to open the rear door for the waiting man, but he was waved off. The man opened it for himself and ducked quickly into the back with Strawn.

Strawn glanced at his Rolex and gazed at the man seated across from him in the cavernous limo. "You wanted to talk? You have until we get to the airport, so make it worth your while."

The driver turned right out of the parking gate and headed east toward the freeway. "There he goes," said one of the three men sitting in a dark gray rental sedan thirty yards from the gate. The driver of the sedan pushed the gear into drive and fell in behind the limo.

The man sitting across from Strawn removed his sunglasses and slid them inside his jacket pocket. He intertwined his fingers in his lap and took a deep breath. "I need some assurances."

"Assurances?" Strawn scoffed. "I should be the one demanding assurances from you. For example, that you keep your mouth shut about our business deal."

"You know better than that. If I said anything, I'd go to prison."

Strawn pointed to the man and then back at himself. "You don't know the feds like I do. They don't like to lose. I handed them Haggart, but that might not be quite enough to satisfy their egos."

The man looked down and shook his head. "I can't believe I let myself get involved with you. If I had known what would happen, I would have never—"

"Never what?" Strawn snapped while reaching for the crystal humidor. He jerked out a fat Cuban cigar and lit it. The man sat silently while a thin haze of smoke gathered and spread across the headliner of the cabin. Strawn took a deep puff and continued, emphasizing each word. "I—saved—your—ass, Jonathan."

Jonathan Raines raised his eyes to meet Strawn's. "You told me the ephedrine was being used for a new weight loss supplement that would make us both millions—Athletics Rx," he scoffed. "I should have known better and allowed the DEA inspectors to see the huge quantities you were ordering."

Strawn held up his hand. "Look, Jonathan, I saved your company from going under. You have plausible deniability, but it's not going to come to that. The case is closed."

Jonathan was breathing rapidly and his face was turning a deep red. He shook his head in quick motions, slapped the soft leather seat with his hand, and gritted his teeth as he spoke. "You sent a killer after my daughter, you son of a bitch."

Strawn smiled, said nothing, and took a deep draw on the cigar, allowing the smoke to crawl up his face like a smoldering demon.

Jonathan narrowed his gaze. "I wanted to kill you when I finally put two and two together."

"Take a number and get in line," Strawn said, "but if it's your daughter's safety you want assurances about, you don't have to worry. She knows nothing, and no one's coming after her now."

Jonathan breathed hard and nodded. He knew Strawn would say anything to get him off his back and stay quiet, but he couldn't be trusted. How could you count on assurances from a pathological liar? But for Emily's sake, he had to try.

The limo was picking up speed after weaving through the heavy downtown traffic to the highway on-ramp. Raines reached over to the window next to him and lowered it an inch. It was becoming difficult to breathe in spite of the size of the luxurious cabin. He felt a trickle from his nose and pulled a hankie from his jacket pocket. Strawn's cigar smoke began to dissipate, being drawn through the window.

Raines wiped his nose and glanced over his shoulder at the silhouette of the driver through the darkened divider. A sudden shiver ran down his spine. The driver was supposed to take him back to his car, but what might really be his mission? He pictured being locked in and driven to an abandoned industrial complex to be executed. Strawn had been silent for over a minute, and that wasn't like him. Jonathan jerked his head forward and gazed through the haze. Strawn appeared pale. Sweat ran down both sides of his face, even with a dozen vents blowing cool air throughout the cabin. Jonathan wiped his nose again and watched Strawn's eyes. They were looking straight ahead as if he was in a daze.

"Ah!" Strawn blurted in the relative silence of the cabin, and then he grabbed his chest. His body jolted as if he had been electrocuted, and his eyes slammed shut. Jonathan saw a thin stream of blood running from Strawn's nose as he leaned slightly forward and vomited on the plush carpeted floorboard, still clutching his chest. The limo began picking up more speed as it climbed the on-ramp.

"Strawn?" Jonathan said in a curious tone. His mind was searching for something he should remember, but it just wasn't there. In a moment of clarity, he snatched the hankie from his pocket and looked at it in horror. Blood. His memory screamed at him, rewinding and fast forwarding his unusual telephone conversation with Keith Bartlett.

"God help me!" Jonathan cried. He wrestled with the door handle, fighting against the 60 mph wind to widen the opening, and then he launched his body out the door.

ᏕᏧCHAPTER THIRTY-SEVENᏧᎧ

"**O**ne thing that doesn't make sense," Colson said into the rear-view mirror at Taylor as Meador turned right at the on-ramp, "is why Haggart would pay to have Strawn killed. I know Strawn's an ass, but he was also Haggart's meal ticket."

Taylor looked at the reflection of Colson's eyes in the mirror. "Maybe he didn't."

Colson squinted. "What are you talking about? He sent the text to Sutton you found in the phone's log."

Taylor shrugged from the back seat and repeated himself. "Maybe he didn't."

Colson raised his eyebrows. "You mean, you...?"

"Look!" Meador shouted from the driver seat, pointing at the limo ahead. A man leaped from the limo ahead of them, hitting hard and immediately rolling and tumbling into the emergency lane of the on-ramp like a rag doll. He just as quickly stopped, belly down, as still as road kill.

"Meador, stop!" Colson cried. "Jump out and get him, Taylor."

Meador shouted back, "We have to get to Strawn!"

"We'll catch up," Colson said as the sedan slowed to a stop.

Taylor pushed open the back door and sprinted to the man lying on the roadside. He rolled him over, snatched him from the pavement, trotted back to the car, and slid him across the back seat.

"Hurry up," Meador scolded.

Without a word, Taylor shifted the bleeding man to a semi-seated position and slammed the door. Meador stood on the accelerator and shot back onto the highway. The car wove through four lanes of traffic for twenty seconds before the long limo came back into view.

"Is he alive?" Colson said, turning in the seat.

Taylor held two fingers to the man's bloody neck while checking his wrist for a pulse. He nodded. "Yeah, but he's out cold, and his breathing is shallow. He needs paramedics, not us."

"Soon enough." Colson strained to see the man's face, but Taylor still hovered over him. "Let me see him," he said, and when Taylor leaned to his left, Colson glanced at the bloody face of their new passenger. He began to turn around, but a sudden wave of recognition jerked his head around in a double take. "Jonathan?"

Strawn's driver never heard or saw the man leap from the rear of the ridiculously long limousine. His attention was to his left, trying to find a large enough break in the heavy traffic to merge the land yacht. He jerked the limo into a space between two slower-moving school buses and sped around the one in front to pass. At first he thought the flashing red indicator on the dash was the check engine light, until he remembered it was the distress signal from the rear of the limo.

The driver searched for the control to lower the window behind his head and finally found it on the console. "Mr. Strawn?" he said to the rear-view mirror as the darkened partition slipped downward. He strained to see through the cloud of cigar smoke now crawling across the headliner above his head. He pushed a second button on the console to lower all the rear windows and open both rear sunroofs. It reminded the new bodyguard of a science fiction movie where the spaceship's hull was breached and the vacuum of space sucked out the atmosphere. The rear cabin cleared within two seconds, revealing a pale Jack Strawn lying on the rear bench seat with blood covering his nose and lower portion of his face. He was holding out his hand for help, as if he were sinking in quicksand.

"Get help," Strawn shouted over the 70 mph wind rushing through the limo.

The driver jerked his head from side to side but couldn't see the other passenger. "I'm taking the exit to Peachtree-DeKalb right now. You want me to divert to the hospital? Where is the other guy? I can't—"

"Forget him," Strawn shouted, giving the driver a dismissive wave. "Get me there. Get my doctor on the way."

The driver fumbled with his phone and turned down the Buford Highway exit ramp, punching 911 on the screen.

Keith had all but totally dismissed the most sinister part of his plan that night in Strawn's office, but the guard almost walking in on him and illuminating the small table next to the desk had felt like divine intervention. It was one of the many sleepless nights after Joshua's death as he replayed memories of him as a child, working with him around the yard. How he beamed with excitement to be helping his dad rake up the dead leaves and weeds they pulled from the pine islands. Keith smiled at the memories of Josh's infectious grin and childish chatter while working his little-man's rake in random patterns around the back yard.

Memories of that day were highlighted not so much by happiness, but by a painful lesson.

Keith had made sure Josh kept his distance from the pile of burning leaves and weeds as he continued to rake more and more onto the fire. Josh had sat on the porch swing and admired their hard afternoon's work until his dad extinguished the last smoldering twigs and leaves.

It wasn't until the next morning that his wife had rushed Keith to the emergency room after he awoke in agony with a red and swollen face, neck, and arms. The doctor had walked into the examination room, scribbled a prescription, and handed it to Teresa. "I'm prescribing antihistamine for the poison oak exposure," he had said.

That statement had puzzled Keith. "Poison oak? I didn't go out in the woods. I just raked leaves and weeds into a pile and burned them."

"Yes, that's what I figured," the doctor had said with raised eyebrows. "You're lucky you didn't inhale the smoke. It's even more painful and could be very serious if it had made its way to your lungs."

Keith had recalled the memory again upon squatting down in front of the humidor by Strawn's desk. He had clicked open the front glass panel, slid off the top cigar box, and laid it on the floor at his feet. He knew nothing about cigars, but they sounded Cuban and expensive as he read the name silently in his head. *Habanos Diplimaticos.*

With the seal already broken, Keith had raised the lid to find an almost-full box with three empty spaces. He had snatched one out, stuck it in his left side pocket, and pulled a pair of latex gloves and surgical mask from his right. With gloves and mask in place, he had removed a miniature pump spray bottle from a zip-lock bag in his backpack. He had paused and listened for any movement from outside the office door and then pulled the cap off the bottle.

He had caught himself holding his breath. His hand began to quiver as the reality of what he was about to do settled in. There was no more time, and it seemed he was forgetting something. He sat the bottle down and removed a pair of clear plastic shooter's glasses from his bag and slid them over his eyes. He silently was thankful for hesitating or he may not have remembered to take the extra precaution. The airborne particles in the mist would be deadly if they drifted into his eyes. He picked up the small bottle Jonathan had provided him and held it at arm's length, as if he had a serpent by the neck, and coated the top row of cigars with a fine mist.

Just as the poison oak could have attacked his lungs that fall afternoon years ago, the deadly Abrin would be carried to its final destination within the smoke of Strawn's expensive Habanos Diplimaticos.

The Peachtree-DeKalb airport is a 745-acre complex in Chamblee and is second only to Hartsfield-Jackson as the busiest airport in Georgia. Most affluent residents in the metro area prefer the convenient and less hectic PDK, as it is commonly referred to, over the constant chaos of Hartsfield-Jackson.

A frustrated pilot wearing a white shirt, tan slacks, and sunglasses walked around the perimeter of the Gulfstream G150, conducting a second pre-flight check. He had been Strawn's personal pilot for five years and had never before been kept in the dark about their destination. He climbed the stairs to the luxurious cabin, reminding himself that, as long as Strawn didn't bark at him for the delay, it was no skin off his nose.

A PDK security officer stood ready at the VIP gate adjacent to a row of hangars on the west side of the airport. His lapel microphone chirped in his ear.

"Five-oh-one in position?"

The officer squeezed his microphone. "Ten-four. Standing by at the VIP gate."

"Okay. They're one minute away from you. His doctor is en route also, so stand by after the limo clears the gate."

It was closer to ten seconds than one minute. He began to swing the large chain-link gate open and heard the squealing of tires before he caught a glimpse of the limo rounding the corner. The rear tires of the limo squealed in protest once again when the long vehicle swung in an arc to clear the gate entrance. The hefty V8 engine roared when the driver floored the accelerator and shot toward the parked Gulfstream.

The PDK security officer had the gate almost closed when he heard another set of squealing tires at the access road intersection. The scream of the sedan's engine rivaled that of the bulky limo's. He swung open the gate enough to step out and held up his hand to stop the car.

Meador hit the brakes and dug in his pocket for his credentials, before remembering they were most likely in the APD chief's trashcan.

The officer walked to the driver's side and bent slightly, squinting against the sun's reflection in the window. Meador lowered the window, preparing to ram the gate with the sedan if the officer balked about letting them in. He would first give him a chance to do it the easy way and take his word he was an APD detective. But the officer spoke first.

"You the doctor?" he said, still shielding his eyes from the sun.

Meador looked at the officer and then turned to Colson with a confused gaze. Colson leaned to his left and lowered his head to see the officer.

"Ah, yes. I'm Doctor Colson."

The officer nodded. "And who's this?" he said, gesturing to Meador.

Colson smiled. "He's my assistant. Nurse Meador."

The officer nodded, stepped back, and swung the gate open. Meador glared at Colson and gunned the sedan forward. "Nurse Meador," he mocked. "You'd better not turn your back on me, Colson, or you're likely to feel the warmth of own my personal urine sample running down your back."

The rear window allowed the officer to get a glimpse of the two figures in the back seat he hadn't noticed from the glare of the side windows. "Hey!" he yelled to the sedan, which was now pulling away from the gate.

"Straight ahead," Colson said, ignoring Meador's remark and pointing to the limo now dwarfed by the towering Gulfstream. A large man had stepped from the driver's side of the limo and moved to the rear door. Meador kept the accelerator to the floor, closing the distance to the limo, but something seemed odd. After opening the rear door for Strawn, the driver eased himself down and sat on the scalding pavement with his back against the rear tire. There was no movement from inside.

"What the hell?" Meador hit the brake hard and threw the driver's door open fifteen feet from the limo. Taylor had already leaped out of the back seat.

Colson glanced back to the unconscious Jonathan Raines, who now lay across the back seat since Taylor had jumped out. Both Colson and Meador got out, looking and waiting for Strawn to exit the limo. Colson looked over the sedan's hood at Strawn's driver, slumped over on the ground, and then back to Jonathan. The only thing stranger than Raines being with Strawn was that he had jumped from a speeding limousine.

"Hold on," Colson barked at Meador and Taylor. "We need to approach carefully. Something isn't right."

Colson stepped away from the passenger side, cocking his head to the distant sound of sirens. They were growing closer. No matter the potential danger surrounding the limo, time was at a premium. Meador clearly had ignored Colson's warning and sprinted toward the limo, followed by Taylor. Colson sighed and dropped in behind them as the figure of Strawn appeared, crawling head first from the back seat and dropping to the pavement next to his driver.

Colson caught up to Meador and grabbed his arm, twisting him around so they were face to face. "You're too emotional, Mike. Let me try first, okay?"

Meador nodded, too shaken and annoyed to speak. Colson bent down and rolled Strawn onto his back. He appeared delirious, and his nose and face were smeared with blood. The front of his white shirt was ruined with blood and stuck flat to his belly beneath. Strawn's head rocked back and forth; his eyes squinted against the bright afternoon sun. Colson supported the back of Strawn's head with one hand, feeling his thin, sticky hair at the neckline. Colson positioned his head to block the sun from the billionaire's eyes as he locked gazes with the drug kingpin.

"Colson," Strawn said through a cough. "I need a doctor."

Colson considered a sarcastic comeback, but now was not the time. The chorus of sirens grew to a fever pitch. They would be on the access road now. He bounced the back of Strawn's head slightly to keep his attention. "They're at the gate," Colson said.

"Hurry," Strawn pleaded.

"I'm not letting them in until you answer a very important question. I'm literally holding your life in my hands."

"Please, Colson—what—what do you want? Anything."

Colson leaned closer to Strawn's face, the mixture of blood and cigar breath making him nauseated. The presence of this man was already sufficient to make him sick, the blood, and stale breath notwithstanding.

"Tell me right now where you're holding Meador's wife, or this scorching pavement will seem cold compared to where you'll wake up."

CHAPTER THIRTY-EIGHT

"You gotta love these wireless tablets," Colson said from his personal oceanfront balcony perch with his bare feet resting on the new aluminum railing. He wore comfortable jogging shorts and a Crabby Joe's tank top. The morning was perfect, and the sun had crept high enough in the sky to provide shade on the ocean side of the complex. Summer business had improved for Daytona Beach this year. A line of cars, trucks, and motorcycles stretched as far as the eye could see, moving at a leisurely pace north and south on the beach roadway. There was hardly a vacant space along the sea wall, where hundreds of vehicles were nosed in with their windows down and radios cranked, playing a variety of tunes for those lounging on beach towels, folding chairs, and truck tailgates.

Colson looked over his tablet at the white-capped surf. The ocean was as perfect as the sky today. The light green color of the shallow water morphed into medium blue a hundred feet from the sand, and then to a dark navy blue a hundred yards farther out. A lone pelican skimmed along the top of the water a hundred feet from shore and then flapped its wings to gain altitude. At about fifteen feet above the water it appeared to stop in midflight as it tucked its wings and nosedived below the surface. Within a second it surfaced and tilted its head back to swallow its prey.

"It's so beautiful here," Beverly said, stepping onto the balcony with two glasses in hand. She bent over to set one on the table next to Colson and gave him a long kiss. Colson's eyes widened at the sight of her in a white bikini and sheer white cover-up. She slipped on her sunglasses and sat in the chair next to him.

"What are you reading?" she asked.

"News," he said with a grin. "It's amazing that you can read almost any newspaper in the world on this thing." He skimmed over the various stories and ran his finger across the pad to go to a certain one. "Jack Strawn dead at sixty-seven. Autopsy reveals heart attack." He turned to Beverly. "Wow! Those medical examiners must be pretty smart—and beautiful."

"Thank you," she said with a smile and made a kissy motion with her lips.

Colson patted her hand and swiped to the next screen. "Here's another interesting one. Former UFC champion hoisted to the FBI's top ten most wanted list for drug trafficking."

Beverly nodded approval and took a sip of her cocktail while Colson continued with a laugh, "Federal judge arrested for possession of child pornography after FBI receives digital file from anonymous source."

"You're such a naughty boy," Beverly said with a chuckle. She leaned to her side and craned her neck to look at the tablet. "Isn't there another one?"

"I believe so." Colson touched a link at the bottom of the screen. "This one's my favorite. ' APD detective's wife rescued after ten days of captivity in Jack Strawn's penthouse. Detective receives commendation and reinstated to full duty with back pay.'"

Beverly shook her head. "Too much drama for me. Meador was a veteran cop. Why didn't he go to the FBI about Strawn kidnapping his wife and blackmailing him into lying in federal court?"

"This wasn't your run-of-the-mill kidnapping," Colson said, shrugging. "I knew there was something Meador wanted to tell me in the parking garage, but he couldn't even trust me. Nobody knew how many cops and federal agents Strawn had on his payroll. I only wish I hadn't doubted him."

Beverly looked down at the straw in her drink as she twirled it between her fingers. "Would you have lied in federal court for me?"

Colson pushed the power button on the side of the tablet, laid it on the table between them, and looked over his sunglasses at

Beverly. Her huge round sunglasses reminded him of a go-go dancer from the sixties. It made him feel young again, and that was just one of the reasons he was falling in love with her. "Is a frog's ass watertight?"

"Speaking of the news," Beverly said, "you didn't mention anything about Sutton."

Colson nodded. "Fortunately for the Clay County Sheriff's Office, he met his demise down here, and the Atlanta press never got wind of it. He had no grieving family and certainly no children in Atlanta. The media here moved on to bigger and better things and never pressed Langston for more information. I wanted the satisfaction of Strawn thinking I was dead. His reaction was priceless and confirmed what I already knew."

"Did your sheriff's office find the device you say caused Morgan's death?"

"Actually, it's what they didn't find. I suggested internal affairs do an inventory of their bait car remote devices, and guess what they found?"

Beverly shook her head, waiting.

"An empty box where one should have been in the property room. The serial number of the missing unit matched the partial serial number of the one recovered by Hall County detectives. They also checked the computer logs for entries and exits. It showed Sutton using his proximity card entering the building where all the gear is stored and leaving ten minutes later in the middle of the night, just five days before Morgan's death."

Beverly leaned back in her chair and crossed her long, shapely legs. "How is your old sheriff taking the news that his biggest campaign contributor turned out to be a psychopathic hired killer?"

"I don't know and I don't really care," Colson said, mesmerized by her legs. He was a lucky man. "History has repeated itself over and over again, although not necessarily at this level. They should have known better."

"What do you mean?"

"Anytime you give a person a lofty position they haven't earned because of money or the good-old-boy system, it always turns around and bites you in the ass."

"It doesn't make sense that Sutton would even bother to work for the sheriff's office to begin with," Beverly said.

"That's because you didn't know him. There's a practical reason, such as the resources available to him to track and locate his targets and have access to equipment—like the bait car device, for example. The selfish reason was for the power to lord over his subordinates like a tyrant. No doubt the killings empowered him, but he obviously couldn't claim responsibility for them and bask in their glory. Playing both sides of the fence must have exhilarated him more than sex." Colson turned to Beverly, raised his sunglasses, and gave her a sly wink. "That alone confirms he was a psycho." Then he stood and stretched, admiring the beach five stories below. "But enough of this. You look like you're ready for a relaxing afternoon under the canopy."

Beverly stood up and wrapped her arms around Colson, resting her head on his chest. "It's about time, Major Colson. I'm only here for the weekend, and time's a-wasting. Unlike you, I'm not retired."

Colson returned her grin and kissed the top of her head. "Shame, you know."

"Maybe soon," she whispered. "I'll make us a picnic, and then maybe we can take a drive down the beach."

Sheila and Emily Raines walked side by side down the long corridor. They had become immune to the sterile aroma of the hospital over the past five days. Still the fearful mother, Sheila walked close to Emily, regardless of the assurances she was given that the danger was gone. She hadn't slept any better the past several days than she had while Emily was missing. She knew in her heart Emily was relatively safe with Beverly, but Emily still wasn't home with her.

The doctors ran their tests but had yet to identify the specific cause of Jonathan's illness. To add insult to injury, three of his ribs and his nose were broken, one knee was dislocated, and he required a skin graft to replace a thick layer of flesh sheared off by his high-speed skid across the pavement. Today would be the first day he could speak, since his first four days in the hospital were spent on a ventilator. His color was returning, thanks to the intravenous fluids and medications administered to prevent seizures.

Sheila was seriously concerned about the circumstances surrounding Jonathan's accident and more than a little annoyed. The only silver lining around the cloud was the fact that Emily was safe and Jonathan was still alive. She would rather be worried and angry over a live spouse than grieving over a dead one.

Two men stepped from room 401 and passed Sheila and Emily in the corridor. Both wore dark suits and carried leather-bound legal pads. One of the men made eye contact with Sheila and gave her a slight grin and a nod as he passed.

Jonathan's eyes were closed when Sheila and Emily walked in and stood on opposite sides of his hospital bed. When Sheila spoke his name, he opened his eyes with a smile and took each of them by the hand. He gave Emily's hand a firm squeeze as a tear ran down his cheek. "Emily, honey," he said in a raspy voice.

She bent over to kiss his forehead. "I love you, Daddy," she whispered.

He looked up at Sheila. "I know there's a lot to explain—"

"Don't worry about it now, Jon," she said gently. "You need to concentrate on getting better, and then we'll talk." She looked over her shoulder and back at Jonathan. "Who were those men?"

"The one name I remember is Hadaway. They just asked me to make an appointment with them in their office after I recover—to clear a few things up, they said." He turned his head slightly to the doorway. "Keith?" he said as Keith and Teresa Bartlett stepped into the room.

Keith and Teresa hugged both Sheila and Emily and went to stand together at the foot of the bed. "How are you, Jonathan?" Keith said.

"Getting better," he replied. "Thank you for coming by. I honestly didn't expect to see you, and I certainly couldn't blame you."

Keith nodded. "I have to admit this is awkward for both of us, and we probably wouldn't be here if it weren't for Emily's phone call."

Jonathan glanced over at Emily. "You shouldn't have, honey, especially under the circumstance."

"I wanted everyone together. What I have to say will be important to all of you."

Sheila walked around the bed to Emily and put her hand on her arm. "What is it, honey?"

Emily looked from Jonathan to Sheila and then finally to Teresa and Keith. She couldn't resist giving them each a smile.

"I'm pregnant."

Teresa couldn't hold back her tears as Keith drove down the two-lane road, through a shady natural tunnel of century-old hardwood and pine trees. They had made the drive to the Rosewood Cemetery a dozen times since they laid Joshua to rest, and the trips weren't getting any easier. But today was different; maybe the healing could begin. Teresa dabbed at her cheek with a handkerchief and touched Keith's knee.

"She said if it's a boy, she'll name him Joshua."

Keith nodded. "It's like God has given us—I mean me—a second chance to do the right thing."

"I know," she said. "Me too. Are you going to be able to maintain the business if you take on Colson's job?"

Keith nodded. "I'm going to make it work. It'll only be a few days a month. Colson went over everything with me, and he said I'll have an even greater impact, given what we've been through. I'm very passionate about this, Teresa."

Teresa nodded as Keith slowed and turned into the cemetery entrance. The entire grounds were shaded by huge trees, like those lining the quiet entrance road. He drove slowly around the gentle curves, past a sea of old headstones, flower vases, and small American flags, to the rear of the cemetery.

He parked next to a concrete bench where he had sat in thought and remorse many times over the past month. Turning to Teresa as he slid the gear into park, he said, "Give me a minute before you get out. I'd like to talk to my son, man-to-man."

Teresa nodded as Keith stepped out and walked away with his hands in his pockets. He followed the familiar row to the grave. He stood at the foot of the grave and stared at Joshua's headstone.

"I came to tell you something important, son, but just today I learned some things aren't as important as they first seem." He paused to wipe a tear from his eye. "I've learned it's not money, cars, houses, jobs, your status in society, or even… revenge." He reached into his pocket, pulled out a bent Habanos Diplimaticos, and rolled the cigar between his fingers. He held it at face level, snapped it half, and dropped the two pieces at the foot of Joshua's grave. Then he crushed the broken pieces in the grass with his heel. "The most important thing in life is your family, and the only goal we should strive for is to love and care for each other above all things. I'm sorry I wasn't there for you, son. I promise to do better."

Keith glanced over his shoulder and saw Teresa walking down the row of headstones. He turned back to the grave as she stepped to his side and wrapped her arm around his waist. "I love you, son," Keith said, returning Teresa's hug. "Your mother and I have good news for you about Emily."

ᐸᕫCHAPTER THIRTY-NINEᕬᐳ

Colson plodded through the thick sand at the sea wall carrying a cooler and a canopy bag over his shoulder. The tide had risen to its highest level, so he selected a spot near the water's edge. The sand was a glittery gold and shimmered in the afternoon sun. A man and woman in swimwear rolled past Colson on rented bicycles and waved. He couldn't recall their names, but he recognized them from a previous pleasant encounter. The tracks left by their bicycle tires vanished with the incoming wave, leaving the sand as slick and new as it was on the day of creation.

Colson looked north and panned across the vast Atlantic until he was looking down the south coastline. He thought of his dear wife Ann and their daughter Nichole. Memories of being in this very spot with them for so many years washed over him, and he felt a lump in his throat. Above him a lone, puffy cloud drifted across the sky.

"Thank you, God, for those times," he said. "The Lord giveth and the Lord taketh away. Blessed be the name of the Lord." He pulled the zipper of the canopy bag to the bottom, peeled the cover back, and lifted out the collapsed canopy frame.

"Let me help you with that, Grey," came a familiar voice from behind him. It was Roger Hammond, wobbling in his direction. Colson smiled and waved to Roger's wife lounging 20 feet away under a round umbrella. Roger appeared to have lost a few pounds over the last year. Mrs. Hammond had no doubt been hounding him about his weight and walking him regularly.

"Thanks, Roger," Colson said with a smile.

"Nice to see you back, Grey. The job keeping you in Atlanta more lately?"

"It was, but not anymore. I was able to visit little Jack more often, but I'll still make the trek once every month or so."

"So you're retired again?" Hammond said.

"For the most part. I'll still piddle with my part-time business, but this," Colson said, gesturing to the beach with a nod, "is top priority now."

"I haven't seen Taylor lately either. We figured you might have donated him to the Atlanta Zoo or something."

Colson laughed while folding the canopy bag and setting it to the side. "Oh, he's still around, but he's on a working vacation at the time."

The line of slow-moving vehicles passed behind Colson and Hammond. A purple ice cream truck eased by and slowed to allow eager children enough time to beg for three bucks from their parents and run with bills in hand to wave down the driver. Colson thought the tinny sound of Christmas music from the truck was both annoying and amusing. They waited for the truck to pass before Colson grabbed two legs of the canopy and waited for Hammond to grab the other. But Hammond was distracted by something and looking over Colson's shoulder.

"Now that's a classic," Hammond said.

Colson turned to see the 1963 Daytona Blue Corvette rolling slowly and gleaming in the bright sunlight. Similar statements were obviously being made among other beachgoers because heads were snapping and fingers were pointing, and potbellied men stood in long bathing trunks nodding approval all around him.

Hammond shook his head and spoke without taking his eyes off the antique classic. "I'm sorry about your car, Grey. It must make you sick."

"Eh…" Colson said with a shrug. "Not so much."

The Corvette rolled to a stop in front of Colson and Hammond and the driver's window shot downward. Hammond took in the bright Daytona Blue paint. If there was a scratch, blemish, or speck of dust, it couldn't be seen. Only the tires were lightly dusted with the dry tan sand of the beach roadway clinging to the treads. Hammond's jaw dropped slightly when his attention was drawn to the beautiful woman smiling and looking in their direction through large round sunglasses.

"You need some help, handsome?" Beverly said.

"Well, I..." Hammond began until Colson held up his hand to interrupt.

"I believe she's talking to me," Colson said.

Beverly turned the Corvette into the thick sand by the sea wall and stepped out in her white bikini, holding a picnic basket. As her slender frame moved across the sand, the ocean breeze blew her brunette hair back over her shoulder and her tan skin was stunning against her white swimwear as her hips jostled up and down with each step.

"Who's that?" Hammond asked.

Colson gave him a wide grin. "That, my fine man is Dr. Beverly Walls. She's my new pal."

"Doctor, huh," Hammond said in a low, swanky whisper. "I'd let her examine me every day and twice on Sunday."

Colson leaned over to return Hammond's whisper. "If you ever have an appointment with her, it'll be your last."

"Really? She must be good."

"Roger," Hammond's wife called from under her umbrella, looking over her sunglasses.

Colson patted Hammond on the back as he turned and began waddling away. "You have no idea, my man."

ᴇᴘɪʟᴏɢᴜᴇ

Clay Haggart woke with a headache. He lay in bed, staring at the cracked ceiling but didn't dare try to remember events from the previous night until he could clear his thoughts. The images began to appear once he threw back the sheet, allowing the slowly rotating ceiling fan to cool his sweating torso. He slid his clammy boxers below his knees and sighed as the gentle breeze began cooling down his entire frame. With air conditioning being the exception rather than the rule in Ecuador, the humidity felt twice as thick as it did in Atlanta. At least you could escape it in the States, but escaping humidity was secondary to escaping the authorities.

Haggart considered calling Strawn or even going back to his office to explain how Colson and Taylor had set him up with the text messages to the Butcher. He still had no idea how they did it, but never thought Strawn would believe him. Sure, there were days when he had considered having Strawn killed, but he never followed through. Then Strawn set him up with the drugs and money in his townhouse. If he hadn't noticed the misplaced items in his closet, he wouldn't have found the heavy suitcases in the back stuffed with bricks of meth and a hundred thousand in cash before the police arrived. It was enough cash to get him far from the United States and the long arm of the law.

He recalled shaking his head at the open suitcase and shoebox of cash on his bed when his new cell phone rang. It startled him at first, but the incoming number startled him even more. He punched the answer icon.

"Strawn? How did you get my new…?"

Jack Strawn's voice was gruff and urgent. "There's no time. Take the money and get out."

"Why the hell did you set me up, Strawn? I never had any intention of hiring the Butcher to come after you."

"Look, Haggart. I believe you. This is a diversion. You have to get out now if you don't want to go to prison. I can't have you talking to the police. There's a ticket at the airport in your name. Take the cash as a bonus, and we'll talk later. APD and DEA are on their way."

Most DEA agents wouldn't believe such an elaborate setup, but it was nothing but pocket change to Strawn. Haggart had no use for the meth, but the hundred grand would come in very handy under the circumstances. Haggart had run to the window, looking in both directions down the street. When he caught a glimpse of Strawn's limo turning at the stop sign and disappearing down the street, he snapped his head in the opposite direction and saw a marked APD unit at the neighborhood entrance.

He had wasted no time gathering clothing, and then he had bolted down the stairs and around back to his car. He recalled adjusting his rear-view mirror when he had turned his car in the direction Strawn's limo went and catching a glimpse of the marked APD units and unmarked DEA sedans trying to make a discreet approach toward the townhouse.

A clean getaway followed. In less than twelve hours he was in paradise, where the liquor was strong and the women were plentiful— and beautiful. A full day of admiring topless young ladies on the beach at Montanita had led to an evening of drinking, laughing, and dancing at an open-air bar overlooking the pounding waves of the Pacific Ocean.

That much he did recall, the rest, not so much. There was a vivacious brunette, maybe twenty-two or twenty-three years old, at the bar with a sandy blonde of similar age and build. Haggart was accustomed to the stares and smiles of beautiful women. He didn't have the cut and build he used to flaunt, but he still maintained quite the manly physique.

He pressed his right palm to his temple when the throbbing returned. He remembered flirting with the two young women and then dancing between them and feeling their ample breasts brushing against his chest as they twisted their delicate bodies to salsa music being played by the live band. He had no idea how many rounds he bought, but he was certain the $10,000 in his wallet must have suffered a pretty good hit. At least the rest was in his—

"Money belt!" he cried. He jerked his head to see his naked form in the bed and began to sit up, but another series of pounding pains shot through his head, this time in his left temple.

"Señor Smith," came a voice from across the room, "you should remain dressed in case the nurse comes to take your vitals."

Haggart jerked his head toward the voice, making him wince through another series of shooting pains. A short man who looked to be no more than twenty years old was walking toward his bed. His dark hair was matted to his head, and red splotches of acne covered his face. Haggart squeezed his eyes shut in an attempt to make the pain subside with the pressure. He pressed his left temple with his hand, feeling a bandage. He felt the sheet being pulled up to cover his midsection.

"I apologize for not knowing your name, but since you had no identification, we have been referring to you as Smith."

"My belt," Haggart said, straining his words through the monster headache.

"You must rest," the man said, easing him back down by his shoulders. "Your money and personal effects are in the hospital safe. I must warn you how dangerous it can be to carry *mucho dinero*—er, money with you."

"Hospital?" Haggart said. It wasn't until he heard the word that his mind registered the rubbing alcohol aroma in the room, barely covering up the faint scents of feces and mold.

"Yes," the young man said with pride. "The Hospital de Manglaralto. The best in all of Ecuador."

"What happened?"

"Señor Smith, I am not the police, but you are fortunate the assailant did not notice your money belt."

"Assailant?"

The moment he said the word, his final memory from the previous night flooded his thoughts. After the dancing, drinking, and flirting, the two women had agreed to accompany him to the resort. Even stumbling drunk, he knew it could turn into one of the best nights of his life, even if he had to pay each a thousand dollars to participate. Was it a pimp who assaulted him? But then, why leave him with his money? With his arms around both women, he had staggered along the dark shore, down a path brilliantly illuminated by a billion stars and the full moon reflecting off the white sand. They had laughed and stumbled along the surf toward the light of the resort ahead when a beefy arm had locked around his neck from behind. Then nothing—until now.

The young doctor touched Haggart's shoulder. "I regret we could not save the eye."

"What?" Haggart cried. He felt thick gauze covering his left eye. "What are you talking about?" he said, pulling at the tape.

The young man grabbed Haggart's wrist and pulled it away. "Please, you must listen. I took every measure I could, but fragments of your broken orbital bone cut too deep. I assure you there was nothing that could be done. Even in America."

"No, no!" Haggart repeated, shaking his head on the pillow.

"Fortunately," the doctor continued, "you did have enough money for the best optical surgeon. We called him in all the way from Salinas." The doctor turned at the three short raps on the doorframe and addressed an old, bearded man standing in overalls with a worn and scratched briefcase dangling at his side.

"Ah, yes, *por favor,*" the doctor said, beckoning him inside. The old man stood at the foot of Haggart's bed and peered down at him.

"What's going on?" Haggart asked, feeling suddenly fearful and quite helpless.

The doctor nodded to the newcomer. *"Por favor."* The old man set the worn case between Haggart's feet, clicked the cheap front locks, and raised the lid. Haggart tried to focus on the case, but all he could make out were small, colorful orbs stuck into small slits on the interior of the lid.

The young doctor moved to the end of the bed and placed his hand on the old man's shoulder. "Pedro is the best crafter of glass eyes in Ecuador. For just $2,000 more of your American dollars," he said, gesturing to the shapes in the case in the same way a model on *The Price Is Right* gestures toward a new car, "you may have your pick."

The General Ulpiano Paez Airport sets on a strip of land jutting out into the Pacific in southern Ecuador near San Lorenzo Beach. Vacationers not accustomed to the proximity of the main runway to the beach occasionally gasp as large passenger jets descend on final approach, skimming over the sand at a mere one hundred feet in altitude.

A large man wearing a white tank top, black parachute pants, and sunglasses carried no luggage with him to the Delta terminal. He stood silently in line with his boarding pass. A nine-year-old boy standing in line behind the man tugged on his mother's skirt and pointed to the tattoo of what appeared to be three connecting T's showing above the neckline of the man's tank top. The mother looked at the back of the man's neck and quickly pressed a finger to her lips, shaking her head sharply to silence her child before he spoke.

At the gate, the man took his place at the opening to the jet way and held his boarding pass out to the gate attendant, who gave it only a brief glance. It was just yesterday afternoon when the bulky man had disembarked at this gate, wearing the same clothes and glasses.

She frowned a little and said, "You didn't enjoy your stay?"

The large man gave her a sly grin. "Quite the contrary," he said, before sliding into a first class seat next to the window.

In a week the bandages were to be removed, and Haggart thought he would lose his mind waiting for the young doctor to make his rounds. He nervously sat on the edge of the bed while the acne-covered physician wound the bandage off the top of his head and plucked the gauze from his eye socket, all the while making ridiculous small talk about something Haggart didn't bother listening to.

Haggart rose, shoved the doctor to the side, and marched to the small bathroom. He stood motionless before the pedestal sink where the faucet dripped into a drain surrounded by a ring of rust. He took a deep breath, lifted his left palm, and covered his left eye. The same view as before. He lowered his arm, took deep breath, and slowly raised his right hand to his face, covering his right eye. Nothing. No matter how much he willed himself to see the image from moments ago, there was still—nothing. Only the slight pink glow of light that seeped through the imperfect seal his hand made over his good eye.

THE END

AFTERWORD

DR. KAREN RUSKIN

PSYCHOTHERAPIST - MARRIAGE & FAMILY THERAPIST
MEDIA GUEST EXPERT

Why would a Psychotherapist who provides counseling services, often appearing on national television as a mental health and wellness guest expert, write the afterword for a crime novel?

My appearance as a Psychotherapist Guest Expert on FOX News Channel's television show, 'Your World with Neil Cavuto' LIVE in the NYC studio on January 20th, 2014 sparked much debate and response. During this interview, I shared my reaction to President Obama's assertion that marijuana is no more dangerous than alcohol "in terms of its impact on the individual consumer."

Woooo, did I feel steam coming out of my ears when I heard those words come out of President Obama's mouth. I was already completely concerned about and fully disturbed by the fact that marijuana has become so accepted in our culture that legalization is no longer just a far off thought to reality. Then, to have a man in such power of influencing others, and who makes decisions for our country, to so foolishly compare alcohol to marijuana was just downright outrageous as a "sales-pitch" for why legalization is acceptable. Is he blind to the destruction of individuals, marriages, and families that drug use causes? Various studies show the connection between chronic marijuana use and increased rates of mental illness (e.g., depression, anxiety, schizophrenia).

Some may think I am an extremist. I shared during my interview on FOX News that I would have stuck with prohibition. Why do I feel this way? The reason is simple. As a Psychotherapist for 20+ years counseling individuals, couples, and families, I have been witness to what happens to people and their families when they do not live a life of sobriety. Whether ingesting a liquid drug (e.g., alcohol) or a drug via inhalation (e.g., marijuana) or another form of choosing to put drugs into one's body is indeed the destruction of the lives of far too many!

Whether on the air, in my office speaking with clients, written in my blog, print media interviews, or in my much-talked-about and cutting-edge marriage book: Dr. Karen's Marriage Manual, I address the importance of living a sober life. Drugs put you and those you love in harm's way. Post this particular guest appearance on FOX News, the email response was abundant ranging from one person telling me that I am "no fun," to those angry with my stance, to many who were thankful and appreciative that I am speaking "the truth." Doctors, grandparents, parents, pharmacists, educators . . . the varied contacted me stating that they too are concerned about where America is going in our culture of drug use and abuse stating their agreement with me that legalization is not the answer.

As I read the various emails sent to me post my News appearance, emails from strangers from all over America, I evaluated one after another as to whom to email back, and for what projects to consider donating my time. Emails from parents asking if I had links to articles I have written, or advice I could offer as they have a child addicted to drugs. Emails from grandparents emotionally in pain, hurting due to their children's addiction asking for guidance, was also among the mix. I emailed back every hurting mother, father, and grandparent. On Thursday, January 23rd, 2014 early in the evening I received an email from a man sharing with me he wrote a crime novel (his second novel within a series) that he would like me to write the afterword for. This particular email I am referencing was from the man who is the author of this very book. His name: Chris Griffith. The book—The Nightmare Merchant: Code of Misconduct II. At first glance, I wondered if it was a joke from a buddy of mine who knows I love to read crime novels. Upon reading the email fully, it became quickly evident that my appearance on FOX News touched Chris, as it was my assertions that he believed to be in sync with messages within and throughout the book he had written that was soon going to be released to the public.

After reading The Nightmare Merchant pre-publication, I knew I had to make the time to write the afterword. I value what Chris has accomplished in this novel including such an important message, an anti-drug message. The anti-drug message is smoothly blended throughout the novel. The argument 'for' vs. 'against' the legalization of drugs was not underplayed, nor overplayed. In The Nightmare Merchant the dialogue between characters, the communicational interaction, and the specifics of what is stated with regard to the topic of drugs was powerful and will be enlightening to many readers. To provide an educational message and insightful information about drugs, it's destruction of self, family, and community while not appearing to be preaching is not an easy task. Yet this book cleanly does as such.

Specifically, the characters in The Nightmare Merchant portray and address the notion that drugs are destructive. The Nightmare Merchant displays that drugs hurt not only the user, it hurts those who love and care about the user. I am a strong believer, from what I have seen in my Psychotherapy practice, that drugs alter family relationship dynamics. Like a knife into the heart, drugs kill families. Once a family member is addicted to drugs, the addiction is out of the rest of the families' control, they cannot cure it. Real families understand this all too well. This message is articulated in The Nightmare Merchant.

I receive an abundance of emails each day, with significant increase post a controversial TV appearance. Some people share their appreciation of my assertions, while others express their disagreement with my stance. As a Psychotherapist who has seen the destruction of individuals, marriages, and families due to the choice to use drugs, I see this issue as clear. It is interesting that something so destructive is controversial; one would think it would be a clear issue for all, but alas it is not. Thus, I must admit, I found Chris's request for me to write the afterword for his book exciting. Based on what I have already shared thus far in this afterword, if you still are wondering why I would write an afterword for an absolute stranger, I shall share with you that Chris's request touched me not only professionally, and as a fan of the crime novel genre, his request also touched me on a personal level.

I was raised in a home where my father was a NYC police detective. For many years, he worked undercover narcotics and organized crime, prior to entering the homicide division. Although he is long-since retired, being raised in that environment, of course, has played a part in my perspective and mental connection to those in the 'serve and protect' industry. Although I was born in 1970, thus many years has passed since childhood indeed, I am all too aware that it is our childhood that plays a role in our adult connections. Thus, receiving an email from a man, a stranger, who was days away from retirement holding the rank of Deputy Sheriff Major in the Operations and Investigations Division, held an interest in my mind to at least consider his request. Then, once I read Chris's novel that solidified it for me right then and there that I was interested in proceeding from considering his request to taking the next step and writing the afterword.

On that note, let us take a moment for me to share a little bit about myself. Then, I shall proceed to further discuss my philosophy and insights regarding drug use in terms of how it is relevant in reaction to The Nightmare Merchant. So, here we go.

Hello. My name is Dr. Karen Ruskin. Since 1993, I have been providing solution focused counseling and cognitive behavioral therapy. I am a business owner, founder, and director of a private mental health and wellness counseling practice based in Sharon Massachusetts, Dr. Karen Ruskin & Associates, Inc. In my office, I, and my skilled and caring team of therapists, each provide talk therapy for a wide range of mental health issues, counseling individuals, couples, and families. In addition, I regularly share my insights and therapeutic tips in response to varied timely topics often appearing as a guest expert on FOX News and other television networks.

I am also a speaker and a go-to source for various radio shows and print media with national coverage (i.e., magazines, newspapers). I feel it is a privilege to touch the lives of the many through the use of the media forum, for it allows me to share my perspective so as to help the masses by opening dialogue on important topics. My style is that I tell-it-like-it-is, and am direct. I am passionate about my beliefs with strong opinions, and am infinitely thankful to have a venue of which to assert my therapeutic perspective in an effort to help people to help themselves get to a better place by providing on air education. Helping the many with real solutions for real life problems in a positive way, providing do-able tips and strategies along with forward thinking insights is my passion. Also, I am the author of three books. One of the books I wrote provides parenting tips, insights, and techniques entitled; 9 Key Techniques for Raising Respectful Children Who Make Responsible Choices. The other book shares with the reader the top marital do's and don'ts, techniques, do-able strategies for marital success, and the answer to the most commonly asked marital questions entitled; Dr. Karen's Marriage Manual. My most recent publication is, '10 Seconds to Mental Health'. Now that you have learned a bit about my professional side, I shall also share my personal side, which is that I am an every-day gal who is a wife, a mother, a daughter, a sister, and a friend.

Ok, let's get back to The Nightmare Merchant. Among the varied mental health and wellness topics of which I share my insights whether in the office, on air, or in print, my concern regarding the legalization of marijuana is one of the many topics I feel strongly about. The destructive nature of drugs in its impact on individuals, couples, and the family unit is also a subject matter I feel strongly about. It is these beliefs that are the focus of my articulations in this afterword. It is these very beliefs that prompted Chris to contact me.

Currently in our cultural climate here in America, too many are acting like it is no big deal to legalize marijuana. It is a big deal, I say! The legalization of marijuana leads youth to view marijuana as safe. It also places doubt in their mind as to the seriousness about other drugs. In essence, if we as a culture accept marijuana and the initiative to legalize marijuana, the closer we become to acceptance of other drugs into our lives. Further accessibility and tolerance leads to increased consumption and acceptance of what is not healthy. As I stated on air on FOX News, and as I have documented on my blog, Changes in beliefs and attitudes drives changes in drug use!

From an overall perspective, we are a society with a problem. Far too many are accepting and promoting what the actual problem is and disguising it as acceptable—thereby furthering our problem. The actual problem is that we are accepting and promoting unhealthy choices. The actual problem is one of addictive dependency which is destructive to the individual personal self, one's professional self, and one's relationships (e.g., spouse, partner, family, children). It is the very denial of this addictive dependency that furthers the acceptance and promotion of it. How often do we hear that there are many who regularly smoke marijuana as a part of their lives? Too often. How often do we hear people report marijuana helps them relax and to be creative and therefore it is a good thing? Too often. Is it really a good thing to input something into our body that alters our mind and thus our actions, our choices, our life? No! Let us not fool ourselves into thinking marijuana is not a bad thing nor a big deal. It is both problematic and a big deal.

Let us look at just but a few facts about marijuana. Marijuana is reported to interfere with the cognitive processes of a young person's developing brain. Marijuana interferes with cannabinoid receptors in areas of the brain crucial to several of one's cognitive functioning. The areas most especially affected include: a) amygdala (emotional control), b) hippocampus (memory), and c) cerebellum (movement).

Research shows there's an increase in heart rate by 20-100% soon after smoking marijuana that can last up to three hours. Marijuana affects heart rhythms causing palpitations. (Yet this physical response the individual consumer experiences is ignored emotionally and intellectually by far too many). Marijuana contains 50-70% more carcinogenic hydrocarbons than tobacco smoke. (A fact many people ignore, interesting considering all of the anti-cigarette smoking campaigns). Research shows us that long-term use of marijuana does affect fertility in both men and women. (E.g., for men, marijuana causes a lower sperm count and a smaller volume of seminal fluid). Research shows that marijuana use can cause chromosomal abnormalities in the sperm. Therefore, a parent's marijuana use could cause harmful genetic effects in the fetus. Research suggests an increased risk of motor, social, and cognitive disturbances in infants who were exposed to cannabis prenatally. Research shows marijuana use can lead to erectile dysfunction due to its ability to suppress hormones that are important to the male reproductive system. I mention just a few of these medical dangers of marijuana, as it is far too often that our youth culture, as well as adults (including the President of the U.S.) suggest that marijuana is not a danger, and thus should be legalized.

President Obama's statement about marijuana, which prompted FOX News to contact me, ultimately leading the author of The Nightmare Merchant to seek me out—I will share with you as I did on air, it is subjective not objective! Let's be mindful of this.

President Obama's subjectivity is based on his own experience stating that he smoked pot as a kid. His inference is that his experience is what the reality is for all, which certainly, is not the case. Painfully, far too many do not stop smoking marijuana once they start. Do know this—for far too many, marijuana is an addiction, a dependency, as it is their lifestyle. Those who live a lifestyle of smoking marijuana as being a regular part of their life do not view it as an addiction, and rather, just normal. But…that is addiction. If you need to use a drug with consistency to feel normal, then you are addicted, you are dependent on that drug to feel normal. Too many begin their journey of marijuana as the drug they use, and enter into a lifestyle of additional harder drugs. It is so sad that there are people who are not meeting their fullest potential as they are drugged down.

President Obama's statement when he compared alcohol to marijuana, even lumping marijuana use in with smoking cigarettes— waving them both off as trivial, in my humble opinion, is like comparing apples to oranges. Alcohol = bad (e.g., driving drunk injures or kills, addiction, affects mood and behavior and family relationships…). Cigarettes = bad (e.g., causes lung cancer, addictive…). Cocaine, heroin, molly, painkillers = bad, bad, bad. Yet, there is this yearning desire where far too many say, "but... marijuana is okay." "Marijuana is not as bad as _____," "Marijuana is just as bad as _____," Marijuana is no worse than _____," ... Any and all forms of a statement of which marijuana is being compared to any other dangerous, hurtful, brain altering, negative affecting, cognitive affecting drug, or even for it to stand on its own not being compared, either way you slice it, all of it is outrageous. Drugs are bad for the user, the user's family, and for our society! Exclamation point! I have seen such wonderful shifts in the lives of those who stop using marijuana. The dramatic change in the person as an individual, how they are feeling emotionally and mentally, along with the wonderful effect sobriety has on the health and wellness of the couple relationship dynamic is phenomenal.

Alcohol is dangerous for many, destructive, and addictive. Marijuana is dangerous for many, destructive and addictive. Alcohol affects many negatively. Marijuana affects many negatively. One in comparison to the other suggesting the legalization of marijuana is acceptable since alcohol is legal, is an absurd argument to try to promote the legalization of marijuana. Yet, too many people are buying into this philosophy. One wrong does not make for another wrong to be right. Too many are following this line of thinking and agreeing with the initiative to legalize marijuana. From the words of the lead character in The Nightmare Merchant, Grey Colson, with regards to people who are followers of a philosophy that is not healthy and unwise, is that some people are "sheeple."

Each type of drug, each chemical substance affects each user differently. For an example, some people are able to have one glass of wine, or one can of beer with their meal and feel satisfied without proceeding to drink more. Whereas others, just the simple sip of an alcoholic beverage takes them from 0-10 in no time at all. For some people, they smoke marijuana as a teenager on a few occasions and that's it. Whereas others, they start smoking and never stop. One may wonder why can some people have one drink and stop whereas others cannot? One may wonder, why can't a simple request by a spouse or a parent to stop smoking marijuana or using any other drug on the menu list of drugs lead to the outcome of no longer using? A significant piece of the puzzle in the answer to this question is that the vulnerability to develop a drug addiction is affected by the combination of environmental factors, a biological basis, and genetics.

Many researchers agree that there is a biological basis as to why people suffer from addiction. Specifically, researchers suggest that the brains of people addicted to drugs differ from those of others. Therefore, some brains predispose people to become addicted. Drug addiction is often referred to as a disease, specifically, a psychiatric disorder that has a basis in the brain that they were either born with or formed during early life that makes them susceptible to using substances in excess. People's life experiences, environment, as well as their brain structures and genes affect their choices. Therefore, genetics, biology, and environmental factors play a role in the progression from intermittent to consistent drug use. The transition from regular drug use to abuse to addiction is influenced by this very combination. Even the propensity for repeated relapse after being drug free for a period of time is influenced by this combination of environmental factors, biology, and genetics. The predisposition of addiction due to one's biology and genetic influences and how this pre-disposition plays a significant role in one's vulnerability to develop a drug addiction cannot be ignored. The notion that genetics, biology, and environmental experiences influence the vulnerability of being susceptible to addictive diseases is a serious issue and was discussed in The Nightmare Merchant. Yet again, another fine example of why I agreed to write this afterword and how proud I am of Chris that he creatively wove such an important topic within an interesting crime novel. We must all be mindful of the choices we make for ourselves, our family, and our country—addiction is real.

In my office with my clients, I discuss that it is very important to understand that a pre-disposition to addiction is not an excuse for use, abuse, nor addiction. Nor is it an inference that one cannot choose to control one's self. This significant point is also addressed in The Nightmare Merchant. Taking ownership of one's own actions, choosing to live a sober lifestyle is a message within this novel that is absolutely imperative. Having a pre-disposition for addiction likely means one would find it more difficult to use a drug in moderation than in comparison to someone who does not have this pre-disposition. Thus, our philosophy must be one of not using drugs. Prevention through role modeling as adults and educating our children not to use is the message we as parents should be sending and must send. Rather than sending the message of use in moderation.

What is interesting about the theory of predisposition I will share with you is that one's lifestyle can either exacerbate one's predisposition or keep it at bay. Think about it. Researchers explain that the genetics of addiction includes heritable factors that affect and influence the different phases and stages not only in the trajectory of initiation, but also in the progression to drug addiction as well as the level of the risk of relapse, dependency, and withdrawal. If you have the pre-disposition for addiction, and the message in your environment (i.e., friends, family, community, country) states that the use of drugs (e.g., marijuana) is legal, is not so bad, then you are more likely to use, leading to over-usage. This ultimately leads you down the path of addiction and the potential of using other drugs as well. Whereas if you have the pre-disposition for addiction, and the message in your environment is anti-drug use, that the use of drugs is not an acceptable option, then you will less likely use therefore less likely place yourself in the position of addiction. Early intervention through knowledge, before drugs are used, can aide in prevention. In The Nightmare Merchant the main character, Grey, explains to one of the other characters in the book that addiction is a disease and genetics plays a role. Grey stands strong during a debate with a character in the book who is a wealthy man who is trying to get all drugs legalized. Grey asserts that addiction costs us as a society. This is oh-so-true, as research shows us; addiction has some of the highest overall medical health costs. A fine example of how the book matches the reality of a hot topic we are currently dealing with in America.

There are people who smoke marijuana, and the more they smoke, the more they smoke...for they need more to feel the high they desire, thus their quantity increases. For some, the more they smoke marijuana the more they crave, leading them to yearn for a more intense and different high that marijuana is unable to provide. Thereby leading them to use cocaine, and/or heroin—hence, the term often used is, "gateway." Some say marijuana is a gateway drug, others disagree. Why the disagreement? Who is right and who is wrong?

As I shared on FOX News, as I have written about on my blog, as I discuss with my clients in my office, and as I will document now: marijuana is a gateway drug for far too many. For others, that is not the case. The genetics of addiction encompasses heritable factors that influence this since the variation in personality dimensions (e.g., novelty seeking, impulsivity, risk taking) is suggested by researchers may have in part, its own genetic basis. To take this a step further, researchers explain that our life experiences can change the structure of our brain. Wow. Dangerous? Indeed! I cannot say it enough how important it is to make healthy choices.

In The Nightmare Merchant the gateway drug message is masterfully shown in the heartache of parents whose child progressed in his drug use from marijuana to even harder drugs. Research shows that long-term marijuana abuse can lead to compulsive drug seeking, despite the harmful effects it has on functioning in all contexts of one's life (e.g., family, recreation, school, work). Research explains that people exposed to marijuana as young teens are more likely to become dependent on other drugs (e.g., cocaine, heroin, painkillers). This is indeed an example of marijuana being a gateway drug for far too many. I appreciate how The Nightmare Merchant offers the reader the experience of the pain the mother and father feel over the loss of their son. The description of how this young man started out using marijuana and then progressed to stronger drugs was discussed with a very realistic feel, I must say, after hearing real-life stories through the years in my work as a mental health and wellness professional and Family Therapist.

Back in the '80's when I was a teenager, there was a commercial on TV, and it sticks in my mind after all these years. The commercial went something like this: "This is your brain (visually we the viewers see an egg in a shell), this is your brain on drugs (visually we the viewer then see the egg is cracked and splattered in a frying pan cooking)." That's it, bottom line! This commercial aired back when I had a black and white TV, no remote, and bunny ears on the top to help with the static. Technology has changed, times have changed, but the anti-drug use message should remain the same.

What some view as a vice and/or a part of socializing (e.g., alcohol), others self-destruct when they use that very same drug and destroy lives around them. Marijuana, alcohol, heroin, cocaine, pain killers, the over-medication of our youth culture, the over-medication of adults, the addiction to the games some people play on their cell phone instead of interacting with others (e.g., spouse, friend), texting while driving due to the "need" to respond right away—these are additional examples of our reaction for immediate fixes and the impulsive addictive dependent culture we are becoming. What about having a sexual extra-marital affair to escape emotionally from our current relationship instead of confronting the problem and working hard on the relationship? Researchers show the statistical increase in marital affairs. This is yet another example of addiction through escapism (just like drugs are escapism and addictive), and another example of how we as a culture have become more and more accepting of behaviors that are unhealthy and addictive. There are adults who are quite capable of working both from an intellectual capacity and physical ability, yet they are not working, they are not providing for themselves or for their family as they have grown dependent on what is being given to them (whether it is living off of one's parents, the government, or relying on a friend's good graces). Dependency and addiction are intertwined and as a culture too many among us are accepting and promoting this lifestyle.

If marijuana use wasn't such a serious problem, and if we were watching the story of 'the life of marijuana' in the lives of people unfold via a science fiction movie with a comedic twist— perhaps we as the audience would be laughing at the insanity of our current culture. Perhaps we would be laughing at the lunacy, the ridiculousness of the notion of legalizing marijuana. The human mind is fascinating as I share with my clients, we all have within us our emotional mind and our logical mind. Sometimes our emotional mind and our logical mind are in battle with one another, as they are in disagreement. Consider this—we as human beings understand logically and intellectually that chemical substances are bad for us. Even if we don't know all the details of how it is bad. Even if we don't know all of the specifics, we do comprehend as our logical mind does understand that drugs are destructive. Right? Right! It appears to me that the emotional mind (the part of the brain that wants what it wants when it wants it) is winning the fight, the battle in the minds of many. Yes, there is a battle going on between 'logical mind vs. emotional mind'. Each time the emotional mind wins within a human being, the emotional mind's muscle grows stronger eventually taking over the logical mind. Thereby eventually leaving the logical intellectual mind to think that the emotional mind is right.

Alcohol, marijuana, cocaine, heroin, molly...where does it end? No drug use is a good thing. So why have we as a culture brought it into our lives? And why do far too many try to push the message that it's acceptable? Parents who drink alcohol while at a family dinner in a restaurant, and then drive home stating; "I just had two," is not a helpful anti-drug message for their children. What message does that send to their kids? Answer: that substance use is acceptable and to be managed, rather than substance use is not acceptable. Parents who smoke cigarettes, what seed does that plant to blossom in their children? The main character in The Nightmare Merchant, Grey Colson, discusses the topic of alcohol as well as cigarettes with the character in the book whose son passed away. For an example, Grey discussed that parents who smoke cigarettes make smoking a more acceptable option for children, than children whose parents do not smoke. When children see smoke inhalation as acceptable, as commonplace, rather than as unacceptable, that message sticks. This indeed is something for parents to keep in mind when they are making choices about smoking cigarettes. This is just but one of the many fine examples woven throughout the book of smart real messages for real people, delicately placed within a crime novel that is entertaining to read. The message of do not use drugs and drug prevention is communicated in Chris's novel between the characters' in their dialogue masterfully.

We, as people in general, have a difficult time using substances in moderation. Far too many drink alcohol in excess leading to personal mental, physical, and family relational issues. Far too many become addicted to drugs (prescription and non-prescription). There is an overabundance of the overuse of and addiction to prescription medications (e.g., Xanax, Oxycodone, Klonopin, Adderall). There is an overabundance of people self-medicating with non-prescription drugs (e.g., marijuana, cocaine, heroin). The more accepting as a culture that we become of drugs, the more users and addicts we will have. The more users and addicts we have, the more money will be spent on treatment that could have been avoided. It is already difficult to prevent a large number of our population from using marijuana and other chemical substances. To legalize marijuana makes it all the more difficult for parents to teach the message to their children not to use. Legalization infers it is okay. Some may say this book has taken it to the extreme by having a character in power who wants to legalize all drugs. I say this is the reality of the direction of where our culture here in America is headed. I am gravely concerned.

Research shows that there are medicinal qualities to marijuana. Thus, a major argument in favor of the legalization of marijuana is to have the opportunity to use it for those who are suffering (e.g., cancer patients going through chemotherapy). The cannabis plant contains ingredients with medicinal potential (e.g., stimulates appetite, controls nausea, relieves pain). Certainly this is advantageous for some people then, right? Absolutely. I'd be interested in considering the potential for marijuana to be sold in the pharmacy for very specific limited medical cases. That is not the direction our society is headed. If the intent is truly for medicinal purposes for those cases that marijuana is the recommended medicine, then why not consider selling it in a pharmacy only then?

I recognize that we as a culture have a problem with the addiction to prescription medication, as well. Hence, as I have asserted, our problem is not simply marijuana. Our problem is one of an addictive dependency. If we are just simply discussing marijuana for the moment, I will state that I absolutely do not believe in selling marijuana in a gingerbread house for all the world to come and partake, asserting it's for medical reasons, when far too often it is for recreational use. We are becoming a culture of mini bakeshops. This is not wise, and certainly not structured just for the real medical consumer. We are fooling ourselves if we really believe that having medical marijuana businesses is purely for medical marijuana use. If we are thinking beyond marijuana, then we are kidding ourselves if we think marijuana bake shops does not put us one step further toward the direction of legalizing all drugs.

Legalization promotes and sends the message of usage, acceptance and approval. The 'Drugs Don't Work' program discussed in The Nightmare Merchant is a real program which many people do not know about. I am a strong believer that prevention of usage is the key to preventing addiction. Educating parents about what action steps they can take to prevent their children from ever using drugs is the key to prevention. My stance is in line with the 'Drugs Don't Work' philosophy. Although I may not agree with all of the steps the 'Drugs Don't Work' program suggests as far as realistically incorporating as therapeutic and making sense for all families to implement (e.g., regularly testing your children for drugs), I do agree that each and every step in the 'Drugs Don't Work' program makes full sense for some families. I do agree with its theme and philosophical concept. The philosophy of educating parents, helping them to be in the know, and providing them with options for how to help prevent their children from ever using drugs in the first place is the theme, philosophy, and concept I promote, advocate, and fully agree with. What is awesome about the 'Drugs Don't Work' program is that it opens up dialogue for those who attend and thus promotes discussions within their family. It helps adults to think about their own philosophy about drugs and what steps they have or have not taken, and what steps they can consider taking in terms of drug prevention messaging in their home.

When it comes to parenting education, whether in the office, on air, in my parent education workshop, or in my parenting guidebook, I stand by my parenting communication philosophy, which is that parents must value the voice of their children and have open communication by talking with their children not at their children. This is a healthy method of communication so that your kids will listen. Whether the topic is drugs or anything else. Role modeling whatever message you wish to send is imperative. Parents must not live with their head in the sand, must stay involved, and believe in the no usage of drugs mentality, not the "kids will be kids" and thus they will use drugs mentality. Do not turn a blind eye and accept marijuana use in your children, simply because other kids are using. Make the choice not to allow the growing acceptance in our culture of marijuana use, as legalization continues to be on the forefront excuse you from an anti-drug message in your home. The more accepting we are of drug use, the more accepting we become as a culture. Thus, in turn, the more accepting our children will become. Thus, the more accepting our children's children will become and their children. Marijuana addiction for the youth population is a growing risk as society becomes more tolerant. Research shows that more teenagers are smoking marijuana than cigarettes since the 1970's and marijuana is stronger than it was back then. Prime example of the growing acceptance among our youth culture as the years move onward, which is disturbing.

The reality of issues presented in The Nightmare Merchant with regard to the main theme and messages regarding drugs, as well as the detailed specifics within the chapters as it relates to drugs, in comparison to what is going on in our America currently, is; dead on. The Nightmare Merchant is born with twists and turns of which keeps you on your toes. In skilled writing fashion, author Chris Griffith brings the reader into an immediate dive into his pool of words where you do not want to miss a moment. The political and social messaging about drugs is so hot right now, such a timely topic here in America. It is no easy task to blend a crime novel with intrigue while tastefully addressing current social and political issues. This author does it with ease, weaves and blends gracefully.

It's a story of crime, passion for what you believe in, and standing up for those very beliefs, drug addiction, friendship, what you will do for your children, family, life, death, love, grudges, and the need for closure regarding pain of the past and present, how all it takes is but just one person and/or experience to change your life path, business, trust, the criminal justice system, politics, power, money, connections, identity, the courage to do the right thing even in the face of overwhelming odds, and good vs evil. In addition, The Nightmare Merchant includes several characters who are on a life journey of processing the memories of what was, the dreams of what could have been, the acceptance of what shall never be, the strength to create new memories, and relishing in the joy of what is and cherishing what you have.

The interplay between topics of such a serious nature (e.g., drugs, death) is juxtaposition to the humorous interactional dynamics of the characters was masterful. The character development was fluid leading the reader to feel vested in the success of the "good" characters, and the desire for the "evil" characters to be destroyed. As a crime novel enthusiast and a big fan of the superhero genre, I fully enjoyed the superhero-type theme where the main character, Grey Colson, kicks butt physically and mentally. I enjoyed the scene descriptors and the author's smooth reference of visual comparisons throughout the book, which offers the opportunity for the reader to enter into the reality of the characters' experience. For it is the full environment that affects our understanding of any given moment. Senses such as taste, smell, visual, touch, and sound—each of which we create our own interpretation of what we are reading, along with where the author invites us to go is solid through and through.

Along with the various relationships Grey develops, including his relationship dynamic with his main sidekick Taylor and the lives that Grey touches along the course of his journey, the reader learns about Grey in terms of the man he was and is. Woven throughout the book is information about Grey's past and present primary relationships in the way in which only a naturally talented writer can do, which brings us the reader to feel for Grey. His joys and pains, hopes and interests, we as the reader are right there with him. Grey is a character whom you not only would want on your side, but he is also someone you like as a person. Additionally, one of the things I adore about the novel from a crime novel fan perspective is when and what surprises occur one would not expect (good and bad), that happen all along the way. The Nightmare Merchant is a page-turner leaving you wanting to know what is going to happen next. At the book's end I was left feeling satiated, in conjunction with yearning for the next book in the Grey Colson series. I am patiently waiting and ready for Grey's next crime to solve.

Warmly,

Dr. Karen Ruskin

I invite you to follow me on twitter or Facebook for Dr. Karen's weekly mental health tips, keep up to date with my upcoming media appearances, and read my cutting edge widely read blog.

Facebook: Dr. Karen Ruskin- The Relationship Expert

www.facebook.com/drkarenruskin

Twitter: @DrKarenRuskin www.twitter.com/drkarenruskin

Website: www.drkarenruskin.com

✑ABOUT THE AUTHOR✎

Chris is now employed as a Police Officer with the Cobb County School District and currently lives in Dallas, Georgia with his wife, Beverly. His daughter, Brittany Roper, lives in Newport News, Virginia with her new husband, Christopher, who proudly serves his nation in the United States Navy.

Chris and Beverly look forward to lounging on Daytona Beach each summer and plotting the next Grey Colson Crime Thriller. The third novel in the series, "Mosquito Lagoon – Code of Misconduct III," will release in 2016.

CPSIA information can be obtained at www.ICGtesting.com
Printed in the USA
LVOW10s2356181015

458789LV00001B/28/P